George Henry Sumner

Life of Charles Richard Sumner

Bishop of Winchester and Prelate of the Most Noble Order of the...

George Henry Sumner

Life of Charles Richard Sumner
Bishop of Winchester and Prelate of the Most Noble Order of the...

ISBN/EAN: 9783337054823

Printed in Europe, USA, Canada, Australia, Japan

Cover: Foto ©Raphael Reischuk / pixelio.de

More available books at **www.hansebooks.com**

LIFE

OF

CHARLES RICHARD SUMNER, D.D.

BISHOP OF WINCHESTER,

AND PRELATE OF THE MOST NOBLE ORDER OF THE GARTER,

DURING

A FORTY YEARS' EPISCOPATE.

BY THE REV. GEORGE HENRY SUMNER, M.A.,

HON. CANON OF WINCHESTER, AND RECTOR OF OLD ALRESFORD, HANTS.

WITH A PORTRAIT.

LONDON :

JOHN MURRAY, ALBEMARLE STREET.

1876.

[The Right of Translation is Reserved.]

PREFACE.

I DESIRE that the following pages may speak for themselves. A Son is popularly supposed to be a bad judge of his Father's character, and I therefore have not attempted in any set phrases to particularize Bishop Sumner's excellencies. My aim has been so to record some of the principal events of his life, that his actions in the diocese and his bearing in his own home might show what manner of man he was. My earnest hope is, that some in reading this Memoir may have their estimate of Bishop Sumner's wisdom, zeal, power, and Christian love strengthened, as my own has undoubtedly been in writing it. Allusions will be found in it to Sir John Coleridge, which speak of him as though he were still living. He was the last remaining survivor of the Bishop's old Eton friends, and it was after this volume was printed that, in the fulness of years and honours, he

was taken to his Rest. The proof of his Latin verses
(which will be found on page 424) was sent to him for
correction, in accordance with his request, on the very
day of his death.

G. H. S.

OLD ALRESFORD RECTORY, HANTS.
March, 1876.

CONTENTS.

CHAPTER I.

EARLY LIFE. 1790—1815.

CHAPTER II.

EARLY LIFE—*continued.* 1815—1816.

CHAPTER III.

LIFE AT HIGHCLERE. 1816—1820.

CHAPTER IV.

OFFERS OF PREFERMENT. 1820—1821.

CHAPTER V.

LIFE AT WINDSOR. 1821—1823.

CHAPTER VI.

LIFE AT WINDSOR—continued. 1824—1825.

CHAPTER XI.

LIFE AT FARNHAM—*continued.* 1829.

CHAPTER XII.

LIFE AT FARNHAM—*continued.* 1830—1831.

CHAPTER XIII.

LIFE AT FARNHAM—*continued.* 1832.

CHAPTER XIV.

LIFE AT FARNHAM—*continued.* 1833—1834.

CHAPTER XV.

LIFE AT FARNHAM—*continued.* 1835—1837.

CHAPTER XVI.

LIFE AT FARNHAM—*continued.* 1838—1840.

CHAPTER XVII.

LIFE AT FARNHAM—*continued.* 1841—1845.

CHAPTER XVIII.

LIFE AT FARNHAM—*continued.* 1846—1849.

CHAPTER XIX.

LIFE AT FARNHAM—*continued.* 1850.

CHAPTER XX.

LIFE AT FARNHAM—*continued.* 1851—1854.

CHAPTER XXI.

LIFE AT FARNHAM—*continued.* 1855—1858.

CHAPTER XXII.

LIFE AT FARNHAM—*continued.* 1859—1862.

CHAPTER XXIII.

LIFE AT FARNHAM—*continued.* 1863—1865.

CHAPTER XXIV.

LIFE AT FARNHAM—*continued.* 1866—1867.

CHAPTER XXV.

THE BISHOP'S ILLNESS, RESIGNATION, AND DEATH.
1868—1874.

LIFE OF

CHARLES RICHARD SUMNER, D.D.

BISHOP OF WINCHESTER.

CHAPTER I.

EARLY LIFE. 1790—1815.

Birth and parentage of Charles Richard Sumner.—Stories of his infancy.—Is sent
to Eton.—His sister's description of him and his elder brother John.—Eton
friendships.—Obtains the Davis scholarship.—Goes to Sedbergh to read
mathematics.—Enters at Trinity College, Cambridge.—Obtains a scholarship
at Trinity.—Prophecy of a Cambridge Don respecting his future career.—
Takes his B.A. degree.—Is ordained deacon.—Appointed tutor to Lord
Mount Charles and Lord Francis Conyngham.—Travels abroad with them.
—At Geneva is introduced to the Maunoir family.—Is engaged to Mademoiselle Maunoir.—Acts as chaplain at Geneva.—Returns to England.

CHARLES RICHARD, the subject of the present memoir, was
the third son of the Rev. Robert Sumner, Vicar of Kenilworth
and Stoneleigh in Warwickshire. Hannah, his mother, was
the daughter of John Bird, Alderman of London, who married
Judith, daughter of William Wilberforce, Esq. He was born at
Kenilworth on the 22nd of November, 1790, his elder brother,
John Bird, afterwards Archbishop of Canterbury, having been
born ten years previously. The family consisted, in addition to
these two, of Robert, who was born in July, 1781, and after
taking his degree at Cambridge, died in 1804 ; Henry born in
July, 1792, who entered the service of the mercantile navy of
the East India Company, and died in January, 1826 ; and Maria,

B

born in 1794, who married the Rev. W. Wilson, D.D., and died in April, 1834.*

The Vicar of Kenilworth was a quiet, earnest, country clergyman of small means, "not ashamed to give only removes to those who gave two courses," † who died four months after his son Charles had been sent to Eton, in 1802.

Of Charles Sumner's earliest years not much is known. His father writes of him when four years old, as being "as lively as a bird;" and again he writes, "my mother was exceedingly good-natured in amusing Charles all she could, and I assure you he has been much taken notice of wherever he went, for behaviour and sharpness. I am not one of the parents who always puff, but I may to you, for it will give you real pleasure, and he is very anxious that nothing in the directions should be omitted, but, if at all at a loss, refers to what Mamma says should be done."

The Vicar of Kenilworth appears to have superintended his children's studies; for, in 1799, he writes to his wife, "I had the

---

* The following is a Genealogical Table of the immediate predecessors of Bishop Sumner :—

John, Lower and Head Master of Eton, Canon of Windsor, and Provost of King's, died 1772.

Mary. Ann. Eliza. Humphrey, Master at Eton, and Provost of King's, died 1814. John. *Robert*, Vicar of Kenilworth. Richard.

John Bird. Robert. *Charles Richard.* Henry Humphrey. Maria.

The following Table shows the connection between the Sumner, Wilberforce, and Bird families :—

William Wilberfoss, died 1655.

William Wilberfoss, died 1703.

Thomas. Samuel. Ralph.

William Wilberforce, married daughter of John Thornton, Esq.

William. Robert, died 1768. Judith, m. Alderman John Bird.

William. Sarah. Anne. William Wilberforce. *Hannah,* m. Rev. Robt. Sumner. Lucy. Maria.

William. Robert. *Samuel.* Henry. Barbara. Elizabeth. John Bird. Robert. *Charles Richard.* Henry. Maria.

It will be seen from the above genealogy that Bishop Sumner's mother was first cousin to the celebrated William Wilberforce, and that he was therefore second cousin to the late Bishop Wilberforce.

† Extract from Mrs. Sumner's Diary, which stops at the year 1810.

pleasure of seeing the children quite well, and as glad to have me return as if I had not been their master, contrary to the opinion of Dr. Browning, with whom I was discussing the point on Thursday of the possibility of teaching one's own children without incurring their dislike—thinking otherwise." Charles seems, however, to have been a sickly lad, for, in 1799, his father writes: "Charles has had some little of the feverish complaints he is subject to, but I have nursed him up. That is the only time Charles has been ailing, which is more than one could look for in so tender a plant. As to Henry, he never looked better, and, indeed, they are both as little troublesome as one can expect, and go on without many—indeed any —flagellations; a scold now and then does them good." A month later he writes from King's College, Cambridge: "As to Charles, he never looked better than at present; so does Henry, who are both as merry as grigs, and great favourites at the Lodge."

An interesting story is told of the child at this time. He had, in common with all lads, a great desire to possess a knife with many blades. His mother, wishing to combine two objects, told her son that if he would cure himself of some childish trick, to which he was addicted, he should have the much-coveted knife. The boy made up his mind that he would conquer the trick, and he did so, though not till after some weeks had elapsed. The reward had been fairly earned; but when it was given to him by his mother, he declined to have it, saying, " I am so glad I have conquered, but I know that I ought to have done it to please you, and not for the sake of the knife."

Not many stories, however, have been preserved respecting his earliest years.* Nor do I think this a subject of regret. The characteristics of young children are, for the most part,

---

* When, as Bishop of Winchester, he in after years visited Kenilworth, the old clerk who had taught him writing and arithmetic, and who was still alive, said that "Master Charles was the most ink-spillingest boy he had ever taught."

somewhat similar, and those which in fond parents' eyes seem
to be remarkable are generally to the outer world of but little
interest. Be that as it may, in the present instance few records
remain of Bishop Sumner's early years.

In June, 1802, he entered Eton as an Oppidan (his brother,
afterwards Bishop of Chester, and subsequently Archbishop of
Canterbury, being one of the assistant-masters), and two years
afterwards was successful in obtaining a place on the foundation. Until within a year before he left, Goodall was head-
master, succeeded in 1809 by Keate.

The family of the Sumners had long been closely connected
with Eton. The Vicar of Kenilworth had been in his day
Fellow of King's College, Cambridge, and his father, Dr. John
Sumner, after having been successively Lower-Master and
Head-Master of Eton, and Canon of Windsor, was appointed
Provost of King's in 1756. The Reverend Humphrey Sumner,
brother to the Vicar of Kenilworth, was moreover in succession
Master at Eton and Provost of King's, and the Rev. Robert
Cary Sumner also, a cousin, before being Head-Master of Har-
row, had been one of the Assistant Masters at Eton. It was,
therefore, in keeping with the tradition of the family, that the
eldest brother John Bird, Robert the second son, who died
June 11, 1804, and Charles also should be educated at Eton
College.

There is no doubt that at this time he was an unusually
attractive lad. All family letters of this date speak of him in
the highest terms; handsome, with winning manners, making
himself a general favourite wherever he went; his character
open and ingenuous, but tinged with a slight touch of reserve;
very sensitive, and withdrawing into his shell in a moment at
the mere suspicion of any coldness on the part of his friends.
In a diary kept by his sister she thus refers to her recollections
of him in 1804 :—" Charles was my delight and my admiration.
Every holidays that he returned he appeared handsomer, improved in manners and in talents. He was very affectionate,

especially to me, and always brought home some little present
for me. To Mamma his behaviour was exemplary. He was
domestic, studious—in short, in all respects, the most lovely
boy I ever saw."

Of his elder brother John the sister writes :—

" The striking feature in John is his strict conscientiousness.
He orders every particular of his actions by method and rule,
his sleep, his exercise, his eating, his reading, his expenses, and
every moment of his time have specific laws, and his habits of
self-restraint and exertion are so strong that he scarce ever
breaks his resolution. He has taken the measure of his own
powers accurately, and never has to complain of want of time,
of intentions unexecuted, of unsuccessful attempts. His activity
of mind is incessant, and he communicates his stimulus to all
about him. He puts, as Cowper says, so much of his heart
into his act that his example has a magnet's force, 'and all are
prompt to follow whom all love.' I know no one so destitute
of enemies and so abounding in friends. He has just the proportion of feeling which is sufficient for all practical purposes ;
sufficient to make him kind and affectionate to his family,
and a general philanthropist, to make his taste discrimina-
ting, and to enable him to taste all the pleasures of friendship,
but not sufficient to enable him to soar in the highest regions
of sentiment and enthusiasm, not sufficient ever to make him
dependent on others for his happiness, nor sufficient to make
him so interesting to all others as to be first and foremost in
their affection. He has bestowed on his natural talents the
most assiduous culture, and he has had all appliances and
means to boot, so that he is now a man of superior abilities.
He has a very large portion of valuable information very well
arranged, and ready for use, in his mind ; his opinions are all
the result of reflection, and the bent of his studies has been
chiefly on useful and practical subjects. Yet I think his habits
are too philosophical for him ever to be distinguished for usefulness. He is not of a sufficiently sanguine and ardent temper

to be a projector or reformer, and even his aversion to party-spirit would be against his success."

It was no doubt a great advantage to Charles that, during his time at Eton, he was more or less under the eye of an elder brother of the character depicted in the foregoing extract. He was so devotedly attached to his brother that some of his contemporaries at Eton were rather jealous of the close friend-ship existing between them.

One incident, as showing the nature of his literary tastes at that time, may be here mentioned. It had been the habit of his father on the birth of a child to set apart a lamb from his flock, which was considered the child's property. No charge was made for the keep of the lamb, but its produce from first to last was placed to the credit of the child. The first book which Sumner bought at Eton was the "Spectator," and was paid for by him out of what was called by the various members of the family "the lamb's box."

Eight years were spent at Eton most happily. He was several times "sent up for good," and, just before he left in 1809, to his great joy and surprise, was "sent up for play." *

At Eton too were formed friendships which lasted through life. Amongst the friends thus made may be mentioned Lonsdale, afterwards Bishop of Lichfield, who spent a portion of his Christmas holidays, in 1807, at Milford, and charmed the Sumner family with his simplicity and heartiness of character; Edward Craven Hawtrey, himself head-master of Eton, 1834—1853; John Patteson, the distinguished Judge; Edward James, afterwards made examining chaplain, and preferred to a canonry at Winchester by his old friend when Bishop of that see; Henry Hart Milman, afterwards Dean of St. Paul's; Charles Scott Luxmore, Dean of St. Asaph,—and above all, John Taylor Coleridge, late Judge of the Court of Queen's Bench, now of

* To the uninitiated it may be as well to explain, that " sent up for play " cor-responds, in the upper form of the school, to " sent up for good " in the lower forms. One exercise of peculiar excellence is selected to be read out publicly.

Her Majesty's most Honourable Privy Council, who alone sur-
vives of all this band of Eton companions. Throughout life
he was one of the Bishop's firmest friends and most constant
correspondents.

Sir John Coleridge writes thus to me with reference to Patteson, James, Sumner, and himself:—

"We were no set, nor had any rules, but we were what in
our days at Eton was called a 'Con.' Each of us kept a book
in which we entered favourite passages from books we read—
favourite exercises of any boys we had got hold of—compositions in English verse or prose of our own—analyses of books
we were privately reading. All this was done without inter-
fering with school work."—Two of these books which they
called "Sylvas" now lie before me. The contents are of a most
miscellaneous character, answering to the motto in the first
page—

"Sunt bona, sunt quædam mediocria, sunt mala plura."

Amongst the former are many copies of verses by Patteson,
Milman, Coleridge, and Sumner himself.

For some time Sumner shared a study with Patteson, where
they "messed" and read together, but when Patteson left
Eton, in 1808, for King's, Sumner's economical aspirations
(which are most minutely described in letters written to Patteson
at that time) led him to give up a private study altogether, and
to content himself with a "bookcase in chamber where Hawtrey's
bed used to stand," whilst he took all his meals, except dinner
and supper, at the house of his elder brother, the assistant
master. Writing to Patteson, he thus refers to Coleridge's
leaving Eton in 1809 :—

"You may imagine how much I feel the loss of Coleridge ;
as we were most intimate during the last three or four months,
and I regret amazingly that, having just found out his value,
I am obliged to lose him, certainly without any immediate
chance, probably without any, of being with him again for any
length of time."

His letters at this date are full of conjectures with reference to the various University prizes being tried for by his many friends—criticisms on their performances, &c., and all showing a keen interest in classical studies, apart from the mere drudgery of school-work.* Occasionally glimpses are given of his thoughts for the future :—

"—— has ambition, and he would not settle in life till he could make his wife Lord Chancellor's Lady or Archbishop's ditto, for fear it should hinder his prospects. I have ambition, and would marry as soon as I could with any degree of prudence, and then if I *could* would gradually mount afterwards. At all events I would willingly sacrifice many steps in grandeur to domestic happiness."

He seems to have been of very social habits, for he writes to Patteson, at King's, November 13, 1809 :—

"Seriously, what can induce you to give up all you have been doing at Eton ? Is it totally impossible to study, at least in a moderate degree, and at the same time to enter into society ? If so, King's won't do for me, for I must have both ; one in the morning, and the other in the evening, I should like very much. However, I have not the least chance of coming to King's, as it is now more evident than it was before that I must lose it."

Sumner was right in his conjectures with reference to King's, for he was superannuated in 1810, having previously been elected Davis' scholar.† He was undoubtedly very popular

---

* He found opportunity too, whilst at Eton, to indulge his literary tastes by writing a tale of a very sensational character, with the startling title, "The White Nun, or the Black Bog of Dromore." This tale he offered to Mr. Ingalton, the Eton bookseller, who gave him £5 for the copyright. There was some discussion between them as to whether it should be published absolutely anonymously, or as by a young gentleman of Eton, Ingalton wanting the latter course to be adopted. A compromise, however, was at length effected, and the tale was published as "by a young gentleman of note," which, as the publisher remarked, everybody would see was only Eton spelt backwards.

† The Davis' Scholarship was founded by Provost Davis, to be given to any meritorious superannuated King's scholar at Eton as a pecuniary aid towards his

at Eton. Coleridge, writing under date July 11, 1809, to his
friend Patteson, says :—

"I envy you much your journey to Eton. You found
Sumner prince of the school, just as amiable and respectable as
ever, but not so happy, for he is miserably left alone by our
departure."

Writing to his sister, Sumner says that every one of the
sixth form had given him a leaving book. This is the more
remarkable, as his greatest friends were senior to himself, and
left Eton before him.

In the spring of 1810 he went to read for a few months at
Sedbergh, with a tutor who had made a considerable name for
himself, for coaching men in mathematics. In a letter to his
sister, he thus humorously describes the family :—

"Mr. and Mrs. Dawson and their daughter, a young lady of
50, are the most primitive family I have ever seen. They
live in the plainest way possible, and are looked upon with
something more than respect by every one. Take a picture of
the man himself. Imagine a snuff-coloured coat, with silver
buttons, rather the better for age; underneath this a black
waistcoat ; his *smalls* (may I proceed to them ?), brown corduroy,
warm and durable, thus happily blending two useful qualities.
To finish, a pair of blueish hose. His face no powers of description can trace. It is exactly such a one as I have always
fancied Archimedes had; high cheek bones, deep furrows,
sunken eyes, and a double chin, with the most beautiful white
hair, of which he is very proud, and cherishes with great care.
He certainly is a delightful old man."

Before leaving Sedbergh for good, he made a short tour in

University education. It is now thrown open to the public competition of
Oppidans as well as Collegers. Superannuations did not result from any deficiency
of merit, but depended simply upon seniority. It so happened that there were
only two vacancies at King's from Election 1809 to Election 1810. Amongst
those who were superannuated at the same time as Sumner were Milman and
Coleridge. The income arising from the Davis' Scholarship was £42 per annum
for six years.

the Lake district, in anticipation of which he thus writes to Patteson, June 10, 1810 :—

"Notwithstanding these reading resolutions, I intend to set out for the Lakes on Wednesday next in the most interesting manner possible, on foot, straw hat, light-coloured waistcoat and trousers (which make the people here take me for a mountebank), umbrella in my hand, and fish-basket containing clothes at my back. It will take me about nine days according to the tour I have chalked out, which embraces every one of the lakes, and with a tolerably good division as to distance."

Letters written by him to his sister shew that he thoroughly enjoyed the tour. Before he started, he had some dread "of occasional ennui at being sent à pied sans secours;" but he never seemed dull for the want of a companion, and he appreciated to the full the beautiful lake scenery. Near Penrith, he writes that, "There is a walk, called the Terrace, which exceeds anything of the kind I ever saw. Imagine a green platform about 30 feet wide, extending for a mile on a hill between 300 and 400 feet high; bounded on one side by a natural fence of the most beautiful trees, which are now of course in their best colors, and on the other commanding a view, with an horizon of 20 miles distance, taking in as the principal objects, Penrith beacon, the hills above Ullswater, including Helvellyn, and in the distance Wrynose and Hardknot, two bold peaks rising irregularly up above Windermere,—immediately below the feet Lowther's river and village. The scene was complete, and, seen with the evening shades at 9 o'clock, a few hours after a refreshing shower, was irresistible."

But walking in such scenery is hungry work, as the following extract shows :—

"Supped most voraciously on Ullswater trout, chickens, asparagus, and cucumber; with a good fire, which, after the heat of the last five miles had evaporated, was by no means unpleasant. This was a day's work of thirty-one miles, rather long at any time, but especially to one setting out at 9 o'clock, four hours after the proper time; however, I neither felt too much fatigued last night, or at all this morning. Draw an inference hence of my proper condition for walking."

Tourists could not have been so plentiful in the Lake district then as they are now, for

"At Grasmere Church could I have written on my back 'last night dropped from the moon,' the people could not have stared more. I intruded myself into a seat, into which afterwards introduced themselves two dogs, out of fourteen which were in the church. They had as much right as I, so I made no objections, though dreading their probable accompaniments. After church, I walked resolutely up to Mr. Wordsworth's house;—at home, but just going out into the country to dinner—introduced myself, and found him and Mr. Coleridge very civil; stayed half-an-hour with them, admired the situation of his house, and went away disappointed that his engagement had frustrated a plan I had projected for dining there. However, I saw a great deal of them in the time I stayed. Wordsworth is a talkative, and Coleridge a polished man."

In spite of the enjoyments of his tour, Sumner is not forgetful of old friends, for he writes:—"On taking up the newspapers, the first thing I happened to see was the Oxford prizes; and you may conceive my pleasure on finding Coleridge had got the Latin verses. You will recollect I mentioned his chance before."

On his return from Sedbergh his sister writes of him:

"Charles had started at once from a school-boy into an elegant, manly, accomplished gentleman. He possessed every personal grace and every charm of feature and expression. He appeared to me like another Sir Philip Sidney, made to delight all eyes and win all hearts."

The latter expression was unfortunately too true, for this attractive lad of nineteen years of age, who had only just left Eton, without any consultation with his friends or relations, engaged himself, after a very slight acquaintance, to a young

and charming lady of the same age. Mrs. Sumner, when she
was informed of the step he had taken, permitted the engagement, thinking that such a tie would be an additional safeguard
to her son amidst the many temptations of a college life. The
event proved that it would have been wiser in her if she had
counselled greater deliberation in so important a matter, for
before a year had passed over his head it was clear to his family
that his affections were not so entirely given to the young lady
as to warrant the continuance of the engagement, and in the
spring of 1812 it was finally broken off.

In July 1810, immediately after his rambles amongst the
Lakes, he entered as a pensioner at Trinity College, Cambridge, and ten months afterwards was elected scholar of the
same College.

Hardly any records remain of his undergraduate days, but
one story in connection with his Cambridge life was often told
by him in later years. It appears that in those days the
undergraduates wore knee-breeches and white stockings, in
summer the knee-breeches occasionally giving place, in the
case of those who paid the greatest attention to dress, to
nankeen trousers. Sumner, accordingly, was on one occasion
met on the staircase leading from his college rooms by one of
the Dons, who, seeing his nankeen trousers, and, indignant at the
innovation, and knowing that as a further enormity he had a
pet-dog, called out to him " young man, young man, you'll never
come to any good. You wear nankeen trousers and keep a
dog."

His time at Cambridge passed very pleasantly. He was a
thoroughly popular man, and his rooms were the favourite
resort of many friends. Shortly before his degree a fall from
the library steps of King's College injured his arm and shook
him a good deal, but he was able to go in for his examination,
and put on his B.A. gown in 1814, and on the 5th of June of
the same year was ordained deacon by Bishop Bathurst of
Norwich. He had not what is technically called "a title" for holy

orders—that is to say, he was not ordained to any particular cure, but the Bishop of Norwich, who was a friend of the Sumner family, did not consider this an insuperable objection, and accordingly admitted him to deacons' orders.

Shortly after his ordination he accompanied Lord Mount Charles (whose acquaintance he had made as a brother undergraduate at Trinity) and Lord Francis Conyngham to the Continent in the capacity of tutor. A tour abroad at such a time must, indeed, have been full of interest, and he seems to have keenly entered into the varying scenes around him.

Writing to his sister he thus gives his views respecting the politics of the day. The letter is dated from Ghent, August 7, 1814.

" I have been rather curious to find out what is thought of the Emperor, and perceive that throughout Flanders the people are glad of his removal—solely, however, on one account, the return of peace ; for all agree in preferring the Bonaparte to the Bourbon dynasty, could they have had any hope under the former of being left at home to reap the harvest they had sown . . . . . In all the smaller towns the people are in good spirits from the return of their relations from the army, but the larger places, and Brussels in particular, are not well affected to the present order of things, and wait for the Congress at Vienna with considerable restlessness. The Prince of Orange has made Brussels his place of residence at present, but more as a political measure than for the convenience of himself, and he would not have been received within the gates had it not been for the English garrison . . . . . Lord Wellington is expected next week for a few days on his way to Paris. His appointment as ambassador is by no means popular in this country, and there appears too much jealousy of the English in general, and of the military in particular, for it to answer very well. They make no scruple of telling an Englishman that they treat him as a stranger with civility, but had rather commence and end their acquaintance in the field."

They travelled on by Liege and Aix-la-Chapelle to the Rhine at Coblentz, and thence, *via* Basle and Lausanne, to Geneva, which they reached in the middle of October. Here their intention was to remain for about six months, and it was during their residence in that town that a circumstance occurred which affected the whole of the young tutor's after-life.

It has before been mentioned that Coleridge and Sumner were very intimate and close friends. It so happened that Coleridge had left England for the Continent at about the same time as Sumner. He was accompanied by three College friends, Charles Dyson and Nathaniel and Noel Ellison. They travelled in an old family coach, with the same pair of horses, through the heart of France to Lyons, and thence up the Rhone to Geneva.* Here the two old schoolfellows, Sumner and Coleridge, most unexpectedly met. We all know how pleasant it is, even in these days of facile travel, to meet with familiar faces abroad. How much more so must it have been in those days, when a tour on the Continent was at all times an expensive luxury of somewhat difficult attainment, and when, as was the case at that particular time, the whole of Europe was in a state of turmoil from one end to the other. We can therefore well fancy that they would cordially rejoice thus to meet on foreign ground. Coleridge introduced his old friend to the family of the Maunoirs, whose acquaintance he had made at Geneva, little, perhaps, thinking what the effect of his introduction would be. Monsieur Maunoir was at that time a distinguished Professor of Surgery in the College of Geneva. He afterwards attained the highest eminence in his profession, having an European reputation as an oculist. His mind was singularly elegant, his classical stores unfailing, his conversation brilliant. He had married an English lady of the name of Campbell, and, at the time referred to, had three daughters. All who remember the Mesdemoiselles Maunoir will acknowledge that their charms were of no common character—two of them at

* "Keble's Life," p. 41.

least of acknowledged beauty, simple and unaffected, excellent musicians—the one with very exceptional power as a singer, the other (who afterwards married Charles McNiven, Esq., of Perrysfield, near Godstone, Surrey,) brilliant in conversation, a first-rate player on the harp, and exceedingly clever with her pencil. On Coleridge's introduction Mr. Sumner was admitted into their society, and the natural result followed, that he completely lost his heart to the eldest daughter, Jennie Fanny Barnabine. The feeling was mutual, and in the beginning of the year 1815 the decisive word was spoken, and their troth mutually pledged. Mademoiselle Maunoir was one of the most loveable and loving women that ever lived, and her letters to Mr. Sumner, written shortly after that date, show how entirely she had given her heart to the young English clergyman, who on his part cordially reciprocated her affection.

During all this time, however, Mr. Sumner was not wholly idle ministerially. Geneva was a popular place of resort during the winter months for the purposes of education, and there were a sufficient number of English there to warrant him in making exertions to obtain for them a place where the English service could be held. He was successful in his endeavours. The Government of Geneva kindly placed at his disposal the Chapel of the Hospital, and in this building, aided by the Rev. Mr. Crossman, he ministered to an English congregation during the winter months of 1814—1815.

Towards the end of April, 1815, his steps were again turned towards England. His tutorial duties rendered this necessary, but he was very unwilling to leave Geneva. His whole heart was given to Mdlle. Maunoir, and he would fain have lingered at her side. Of this fact clear evidence is given by his letters of that date, which are full of the most tender and devoted affection for her.

His journey homewards must have been very interesting. Napoleon had only a month before been reinstated in power at Paris, and the whole Continent seemed undermined with

suppressed fires which so shortly after broke forth in fury.   No
greater obstacle, however, had to be encountered than those
which usually befell the traveller of that day, and he arrived
in England safely and reached Milford, in Hampshire, where
his mother lived, on the 5th of May.   Much indeed had the son
to tell to his mother and sister, of his hopes for the future in
connection with one whom, as yet, they had not seen.   Immediately on his engagement he had written home both to his
mother and brother, informing them of the step he had taken.
These letters, unfortunately, were entrusted to a private hand,
and whilst Mr. Sumner and Mdlle. Maunoir, in consequence of
receiving no response to these letters, were troubling themselves
at Geneva with all sorts of imaginary fears as to the light in
which the engagement was viewed in England, the fact was
that, from some cause or another, neither Mrs. Sumner nor
his brother had ever received the letters at all.*   All this
however was soon explained, and nothing could exceed the
warmth and cordiality with which, on his representation, Mdlle.
Maunoir was welcomed as a future daughter and sister in the
Sumner family.

* Mrs. Sumner was most anxious with regard to her son's welfare, for no
letter from him reached her from the end of 1814 to May, 1815, owing to the
irregularity and uncertainty of the postal service during the war.

CHAPTER II.

Life at Ramsgate.—Mr. Sumner's relations with Lord Conyngham changed in
consequence of his engagement.—Letter to Mademoiselle Maunoir on the
subject.—Again accompanies his pupils to the Continent.—Remarks on the
state of Europe at the time.—Extracts from his diary.—Letter to Mademoiselle Maunoir as to a woman's domestic duties.—Arrives at Geneva.—
Again acts as chaplain.—His marriage.—Return to England.—Is appointed
curate of Highclere.

At the end of May, 1815, Mr. Sumner left Milford for Ramsgate, in order again to take charge of his two pupils. Lord
Conyngham was still on the Continent. He had been anxious
that Mr. Sumner should in the previous spring have remained
longer at Geneva, and ultimately have joined him with his two
sons, and that the united family should remain on the Continent
all the summer. He had sent a courier express to Geneva with
these instructions. But the courier arrived there after Mr.
Sumner had left for England. And now Lord Conyngham was
anxious to rejoin his sons, and appointed Ramsgate as the
rendezvous, where the tutor and the two young men were to
await his arrival from Ostend.

Thither accordingly they repaired, and waited for some time
in daily expectation of Lord Conyngham's arrival. It appears
from a letter written subsequently from his mother's house at
Milford that he found the life at Ramsgate very trying.

" Il est un si long temps depuis que j'ai vu mes parens, que
je suis vraiment transporté de nous trouver encore une fois ré-
unis. Au reste nous nous occupons d'après la manière qui

c

m'est la plus agréable, c'est-à-dire nous nous promenons, nous lisons ensemble les soirs, comme à Genève. Ce n'est pas la harpe ni le salon à neuf heures (rappelez-vous l'esquisse de Louise que je conserve soigneusement parmi mes trésors ?), mais c'est une manière de vivre moins ennuyeuse que celle-ci que je viens de passer à Ramsgate. Là toujours la société, toujours les cartes, toujours un cercle d'êtres vivans il faut dire, mais plutôt d'êtres végetans que d'êtres animés, sans âme, sans tête, sans cœur."

Still there was some interest connected with the place. He writes to his sister on June 2nd, 1815:

"Ramsgate is an entertaining place of its nature, especially at this moment when it is the port from whence all the embarkations take place—the astonishing draughts which are daily made of men, horses, artillery, and stores of every description, give a grand idea of the resources and activity of a nation which has been for more than twenty years at war with all Europe. From all I have seen and heard it will not require much *external* impulse to drive Bonaparte from Paris. It begins already to be tolerably evident that all that part of the nation which is not military do not prefer his dynasty. The misfortune is that his opponents are necessarily the least effective though the most numerous portion of the nation—merchants, landholders, and private individuals, though a very respectable class of the subjects of any monarch, are his least important supporters when opposed to the soldiery.—Having everything to dread from a state of war, and everything to gain from peace, they would gladly enough sit quietly, if allowed, under any government which would afford them protection. However the question now seems likely to be, not whether the Imperial Government will be willing, but whether it will be capable of supporting itself and them. Anyone who has seen as much of the preparations against it as myself, from the extremity of Switzerland, along the Rhine, and the whole extent of the frontiers as far as Ostend, cannot but be of opinion that a real avalanche would be much less overwhelming than that·which is now ready to be discharged."

At length, however, Lord Conyngham arrived from the Continent, and then arranged that Mr. Sumner should once more accompany his two sons abroad. Their destination was not quite fixed; but the tutor at any rate much hoped, as was natural, that they might be enabled to winter at Geneva. His correspondence with Mademoiselle Maunoir at this time was carried on with considerable difficulty, owing to the unsettled state of the Continent, as all the letters were sent round by Rotterdam.

Before quitting England it was necessary that a distinct understanding should be entered into with Lord Conyngham as to Mr. Sumner's relation with his two pupils. Not long before, he had written to Lord Conyngham to say that the terms of his engagement with him must be somewhat altered. Mr. Sumner had originally agreed to tutorise Lord Conyngham's two sons, and to remain with them till the end of their Cambridge course. Lord Conyngham promised either to give him a benefice at the conclusion of that term, or, if he was unable to do that, to give him an annuity. But Mr. Sumner's engagement with Mademoiselle Maunoir altered the whole aspect of his life. He was desperately in love, and for every reason was most anxious to settle down to ordinary clerical life. It is evident that he sorely chafed under the restraints incidental to the life of a private tutor, and longed to be the free master of his own movements. He accordingly wrote to Lord Conyngham to say that as matters had so changed since the agreement was made between them, he felt that it was impossible for him for so long a time to do his duty by his pupils, and that therefore he must beg Lord Conyngham to release him from his engagement, whilst he on his part, of course, resigned all claim, either to the promised living or the annuity in its stead. Lord Conyngham was willing to meet his views, and it was arranged that the engagement between them should continue only until Lord

Mount Charles had finished his Cambridge career.   He entered warmly into Mr. Sumner's plans for the future.   Writing from Brussels on June 14, 1815, Lord Conyngham says :—

"Mount Charles is certainly improved more than we could have expected during his residence at Geneva, and I only lament the uncertainty of the attack on the French prevents our starting immediately for Switzerland, so much we approve of Mount Charles and Francis' conduct during their residence in Geneva—for which I shall ever feel grateful to you.   I am persuaded they also feel it.   I got a hint of your intended change.*   All I can say is that I sincerely hope you may experience every happiness, and meet in the person of your choice a mind congenial to your own.   I think you have every chance of happiness.   If our good wishes would do, no man would be more so.   Wellington is still here with very fine troops in high spirits.   The time of his marching is not yet determined on.   I believe it depends on Bonaparte's advance, and the joining of the Prussians.   This town, you may well imagine, is a complete English-looking garrison town."

Writing to Mademoiselle Maunoir, with reference to his fresh arrangements with Lord Conyngham, by which he resigned the promised reversion of an incumbency in consequence of his engagement, Mr. Sumner says :—

"It is hard to be obliged to give up what would now be more than ever valuable to me, and to know that I shall have nothing but a temporary remuneration for two entire years of my life, but I saw no other way of asserting my own independence honourably."

And then, lest Mdlle. Maunoir should have any fears with reference to their future income, he enters into the following close calculations :—

---

* The engagement had taken place in January, but it was not until May that Lord Conyngham, just before Mr. Sumner's formal announcement of it to him, accidentally heard of it from an uncle of Mdlle. Maunoir, whom he happened to meet at Brussels.

"With respect to our future income—this is the very vague and random sketch which I have drawn out—many articles being necessarily reckoned from guess rather than experience. I consider our family as twelve in number, including six pupils and three servants, and allow the expenses of *house-keeping* at £8 per week, which of course includes groceries, butcher and baker, being for the year a sum of £416. Servants' wages £40. I do not conceive that at least at first we shall have occasion for more than one man-servant, who must be a good one, a cook, likewise good, and a housemaid. More servants than are absolutely necessary are so many additional plagues, and neither of us have been used to, or are in want of much attendance. Breakage of crockery, &c., I put at £12 per annum. Rent of house and taxes at £150. Then, considering that I have not perhaps made a quite sufficient allowance in the expenses of house-keeping for washing, in which point I am not very economical, I put down an additional sum of £12 for that article. Clothes for both of us, I calculate at £80, of which I take about £30 for my own share, but in this as in every other article, I beg to be considered as forming only a guess, and *by no means* a guide for what you may require. Then, lastly, as estimates are always more or less erroneous, and many little expenses may and must occur, I put down a sum of £100 for *extraordinaries*, making in the whole an annual expenditure of £810. To meet which, and to lay by for the future, I calculate my income as follows. Six pupils at £200 per annum each,* £1200. Curacy at least £120 per annum. I will not put it at more, but it can scarcely be less. Total, £1321. So that the surplus of receipts will be more than £500 per annum, or, calculating that I have never more than five pupils at any one time, which from unexpected removals, or other causes, may happen, £300. Should I have less than five, the expenses of house-keeping, house, &c. will lessen in proportion, but the most confident expectations are held out to

---

* Mr. Sumner did, in fact, afterwards receive £250 for each pupil.

me by prudent people, that I need be under very little anxiety as to this point. *Some* anxiety it always will be to me, but I trust by my own exertions and those of my friends, it will never become a serious subject of alarm to me. I have entered into rather a long detail with you, my own dearest love, but I thought it but fair that you should have some definite idea of the means of the man with whom you connect yourself. I have only one more remark to make upon the subject. You will see nothing charged under the head of books, which, from my habits, will probably be a yearly expense, (though not a necessary one, and which, in case of expediency, might be retrenched) of £20 or £30. But this I shall supply by writing *reviews*, a source which will procure me at least the sum requisite.* If all this has appeared tedious forgive it, and I promise it shall not come before you again, but though uninteresting in itself, it has acquired an interest in my thoughts by being connected with the time from which I shall date all my happiness."

It was on the 6th of July that Mr. Sumner once more left England for the Continent with Lord Mount Charles and Lord Francis Conyngham. The travellers had a very rough passage indeed of twelve hours from Ramsgate to Ostend, and travelled thence by canal boat to Bruges and Ghent, and so on to Spa, where for a time they took up their quarters. Some jottings in a diary of that date, a few of which are subjoined, are full of interest.

" Bonaparte permitted English prisoners at Verdun wounded to go every summer to take the baths, and, on a memorial, to be sent home without exchange. Ten days allowed for passing through Paris, and every *désagrément* on the road avoided. On the death of one of the commandants at Verdun, the English

---

* Mr. Sumner commenced, I believe, at Cambridge to write reviews, and continued to do so during the time he was curate at Highclere, and only discontinued the practice when unable, through pressure of other work, to spare sufficient time for it.

raised £1000 for a monument to his honour, out of respect for the civilities he had shewn them. Parole of three leagues in circuit granted, and absence of several days allowed without difficulty."

"Blucher said of the English, after the battle of Waterloo, that he never had before seen ground so well kept by statues."

"Arrived at Brussels at half-past six. The Prince of Orange made his second appearance at the theatre, since his wound, on the evening preceding, to see the Vestale. Great applause at his entry, and the actress, instead of crowning the altar during the representation, presented to him a crown of laurel—immense applause, God save the King, and Vive Guillaume Roi called for."

"Spa, July 20. Lace-woman at Brussels who dressed the wounds of more than 600 after the battle, and paid two surgeons who were employed solely in her house.

"Sir W. Ponsonby's aide-de-camp killed in the act of taking from the general's neck the picture of his wife set in diamonds, which he always wore about him."

"21. During the time that Bonaparte was absent with the army in the campaign of 1814, it was the fashion at Paris to make scarfs. When the Bourbons were recalled, one of the royalist ladies tore her gown in the streets to give the *cocarde blanche* to every one she met: on being asked 'Que faites-vous là, madame; est-ce que vous faites des écharpes ? ' ' Non, c'est pour vous empêcher de faire de la charpie.' "

Under July 22 it is curious to find the following:

"Finished 'Apostolical Preaching Considered,' and first Ep. to Timothy in Greek and English.

"1 Tim., iii. 7, (in the qualifications of a bishop) 'Moreover he must have a good report of them which are without, lest he fall into reproach and the snare of the devil.'"

"July 26. Finished Epistles to Titus and Philemon in Greek and English, and selections from Silius Italicus. 'En amitié ainsi qu'en amour, rien n'altère la confiance comme une délicatesse excessive, et des reproches déplacés.'   Alphonsine 3, 95.

"Love has the reputation of being very romantic. I should say on the contrary that real love is very prudential; when circumstances make a man scrutinize the grounds of his future hopes, he makes the most scrupulous calculations of his prospects, and no longer sees everything through a bright and indistinct medium. Yet it is a great mistake to fancy busy people unhappy, because they are waiting for some desired object. It is not only a part of the business, but a part of the happiness of life, to be going on towards a port. Horace could never have really intended to say that men labour 'Senes ut in otia,' &c. We labour for labour's sake."

"28. English fondness for travelling attributable to a freedom and custom, as well as a power to think, and independent disposition, careless of trifling embarrassments, and feeling certain of everywhere commanding respect, a constant and complete circulation of intelligence, an active temper, and lastly, a general command not only of comforts but of superfluities."

"August 1. Finished Lord Byron's 'Bride of Abydos.'

"Bonaparte is said to have gained a large sum by the gilding of the dome of the Hôtel des Invalides, by deducting from the army so many days' pay to defray the expense of the work. . . . . Little guillotines at one time sold in the shops as toys for children to teach them the duties of civism."

"Denon superintended the building of the column in the Place Vendôme, 140 feet high. Le jeune Dubois, the crystal flute-player, represented on it as playing at the head of his corps in every engagement—an example of a system which gave room for the hopes of every individual as to personal distinction."

"Dictionary of Boiste; in the first edition the word *spoliateur* was explained by the single word, Bonaparte. On the morning of its appearance, the minister of the police sent for Boiste and demanded an explanation. He said that it was a simple reference, that the word in question was not good French, but

had been used by Bonaparte in one of his speeches, referring
at the same time to the ' Moniteur.'   He was ordered to cancel
the sheet, which was done immediately, and ' second edition '
prefixed to all the copies, but not before some of the first had
been sold."

In one of Mr. Sumner's letters of this date to Mademoiselle
Maunoir he says, " the papers published which were found in
Bonaparte's porte-feuille in the retreat have amused me, espe-
cially the list of his travelling books, a Bible—Homer—English
Civil Wars—Amusements des Eaux de Spâ—Révolution de la
Corse—Ossian ! "

The following extract too is interesting : " I am delighted to
hear of your employment for the wounded soldiers,* though I
trust your services have now ceased to be necessary.   If the
misery which you have seen has been anything like what
reigned at Brussels, it must indeed have been wretched.   I
was greatly shocked at my cousin's death.   He was a fine
young man and in the flower of his age ; passionately fond of
his profession, and likely to rise in it ; how many are there of
the same kind cut off in that one destructive day !   And after
that, if the author of it all is to be suffered to live !   It is an
idea which one cannot suffer, and yet on the other hand it is
quite as revolting to think of putting to death a man who has
played such a part on the first throne of the Continent for so
many years."

In answer to some questions which Mademoiselle Maunoir
had asked him with reference to a woman's domestic duties he
writes :

"SPA, *July* 16, 1815.

"I should despise any woman who did not overlook and
manage the domestic arrangements of the family, provided her
fortune did not set her above the necessity of it, by enabling

---

* The tidal wave of war which was then sweeping over the Continent had so
far affected Geneva, that in June the family of the Maunoirs had serious thoughts
of leaving Geneva and taking refuge in the valley of Chamounix.

her to pay some one else to perform the office, or by making economy a matter of no importance to her. Even in the latter case in my opinion it is the duty of every woman to watch over the comfort of her household, an office which can be delegated to no one. If she can escape by her situation from the mere details of butchers' and bakers' bills, so much the better ; it is all time gained from an occupation which must be irksome to a cultivated mind, and which cannot enlarge, and very often narrows it. This, however, is the privilege only of a certain rank ; all below it are necessitated not only to make the household arrangements themselves, but to see that they are executed properly and without abuse, but there are two ways of performing their duty. The following appears to me to be the right, and you will easily conceive the other by its contraries. A woman may appoint a certain time of every morning, more or less as may be necessary, to settle and put in train everything that belongs to her own department, the dinner, for instance, family concerns, servants' occupations, &c., &c., but all this may be carried on alone, and she need never bring the kitchen back with her into the parlour. She need not talk of the price of meat and butter, how one is dearer this week and the other cheaper; she need not carry a large bunch of keys in her pocket, which the housekeeper is obliged to come for every hour, to get half a pound of sugar or a candle. All this may be regulated behind the scenes. She will give out whatever is necessary, and there is an end of it. Above all, she will never talk of what has been done or what is to do, or that too much bread has been eaten such a day, or that the servants had eaten the meat on such another, or that the butcher had not killed a calf for above a week, &c. There are a thousand other things which can scarcely be described, but which a woman of any tact will perceive at once, and by avoiding them she may be the pleasantest and the dearest of all companions, at the same time that she is the most useful ; for it is a very mistaken idea to fancy that all those who are eternally occupied about their *ménage*, are the best housekeepers. It appears to me that those are the best who succeed in keeping it most out of sight, *provided* that they do really attend to it, and these are not incompatible. I will only add one word about the works which are peculiar to the sex. It is very clear that a woman, especially if she has a family, must be much taken up with them, but here again a little management may be used. I would reserve all those works which are *genteel* (let me use for once a word which I dislike, because there is no other which can explain my meaning) for those times when a woman is in the society of her domestic circle, the evening, for instance. We all know very well that a pair of stockings must be mended, or that a shirt button must be sewed on, but there is no occasion to do it before all the world. A little delicacy on these points may be exercised often with greater advantage than in smaller things. Such are my opinions, my own dearest, at least such are a part of the ideas which occur to me on the subject, for though it is one on which I have a very clear *mental* idea of what I like, yet it is one on which it is difficult to put them on paper. Numberless things of the same kind will doubtless come into your mind, but tell me honestly and openly how far you agree with what I have written, and in what you differ, giving me at the same time your notion of an agreeable as well as a useful housekeeper. It would be miserable indeed for all but the very highest ranks if these two qualities could not be united. Nor can I conceive anything greater than the disappointment of that man who admires a woman for her mental resources and cultivation of mind, but finds on marriage that she degenerates into a mere intendante de la maison."

At the end of August the whole party, which then included Lord and Lady Conyngham, left Spa, and travelling *viâ* Cologne and Basle, arrived at Geneva on September the 11th. Here Mr. Sumner, with his pupils, lodged with a Swiss family *en pension*, and it is hardly necessary to add, that he was most warmly received by the whole family of the Maunoirs, and their

many friends, and the time passed very pleasantly. He at
once endeavoured to arrange that a regular English service
should, as before, be held, and having obtained the requisite
permission, once more made use of the chapel of the hospital
for this purpose. He was thus enabled during the six months
of his stay at Geneva to act as chaplain, and on his leaving the
town in the spring of 1816, the English congregation presented
him with a very handsome gold watch in testimony of his services, with an inscription recording the circumstances under
which it was presented to him. It was a source of great gratification to him that, by making representations in the proper
quarter at home, he was enabled to place the English service
on a permanent footing.

Meanwhile, he was urgent in his desire not again to return to
England without taking his bride with him. But there seems,
even to the last, to have been some uncertainty as to the exact
date at which he would be married. Mademoiselle Maunoir's
parents not unnaturally were most loath to part with their
daughter. His mother, however, wrote from England, strongly
urging that there should be no delay. Writing to Mademoiselle
Maunoir, Dec. 28, 1815, she says :—

"Although I can command no better paper to-night than this
shabby sheet, I will not deny myself the indulgence of expressing to my now beloved daughter elect the warm gratitude I
feel for the affectionate solicitude she already feels for my
health ; could anything be wanting to evince to me Charles'
dutiful love to his absent mother, the favourable impression he
has given you of my character would do it. Charles' temper is
warm, and naturally open, never closing itself to the advances of
an affectionate heart by a cold reserve : it may be constitutional,
there may be no merit in it, but I do confess that temper to me
is irresistible. My wishes now are most ardent, that some
plan should be devised to prevent his third return to
Geneva. My heart sickens at the thought of parting with
him again so far. Surely if my plan is not feasible, it would

be better your parents should consent to part with you at once, when he convoys Lord Mount Charles to take his degree; happy, most happy, shall I be for my house to be your head-quarters till you are fixed in one of your own. It does indeed make me very happy that Charles should now be in the exercise of a part of his professional duty as a clergyman, and I cannot regret that the whole service falls upon him. It will by habit and by accustoming him to the composition of sermons, greatly lessen his labour when he has domestic cares and scholastic duties, added to the care of souls in a parish. With your obligingness of temper, I myself have not the least apprehension of your falling in happily with our English customs. I speak experimentally, when I assure you that it is my decided opinion no life can be happier than that of a private clergyman's wife, when the parties are tenderly united by the bond of rational affection, not expecting un-checkered felicity (which in no station here below is attainable), but meekly resigning to the unavoidable ills of life. *I found it so,* altho' I had more to struggle with in some respects than according to human probability you will have to encounter. It is one comfortable effect of peace that we get our letters so regularly and rapidly. Let us avail ourselves of it, although it is a ruinous expense; we will economise in something else. Assure your domicile, in which I include Charles, of my kind regard, and believe me, ma très chère fille,

"Yours truly affectionate,

"H. SUMNER."

At length, however, all difficulties were removed, and the marriage was solemnized in January 1816. The following is a copy of the certificate :—

" Je certifie qu'aujourd'hui vingt-quatrième Janvier mil huit cent seize dans la Chapelle angloise à Genève, et d'après le rit anglican, j'ai célébré le mariage de Monsieur Charles Richard Sumner, Ecclésiastique anglois et B.A. du Collége de la

Trinité à Cambridge, avec Mademoiselle Jennie Fanny Barnabine Maunoir, du Canton de Genève, en Suisse.

Charles Sumner.

Jennie Fanny Barnabine Maunoir.

Temoins.
> Maunoir Aîné, Prof.
> Sophia Milward.
> Mountcharles.
> F. Conyngham.
> Henry Maunoir.
> Jn. Chs. Maunoir.
> Aug. Berthoud.
> Ls. Ferriere, Diacre de l'Eglise Anglican."

Soon afterwards, the newly married couple went to England, and after a short stay at Cambridge, in order for Mr. Sumner to be there with Lord Mount Charles, he took his bride to his mother's house at Milford, where she was most warmly welcomed. Here they remained until the autumn, inquiries being diligently made on all sides for a suitable curacy. That of Highclere, Hants, was at last selected, and in this secluded country village, the future Bishop's ministerial career commenced. His life, hitherto, since he had taken his degree, had been somewhat of a nomadic character, but he had been during his comparative leisure laying up stores of knowledge for future use. It is clear from his note books, that his range of reading was very wide, and embraced works of the most varied character.

Amongst them I find Lucian's "Dialogues of the Dead;" "Le Siége de la Rochelle," by Madame de Genlis; "Apostolical Preaching Considered;" 1st Epistle to Timothy in Greek and English; 2nd ditto; "La Duchesse de la Vallière," by Madame de Genlis; Scott's "Lord of the Isles;" Byron's "Giaour" and "Bride of Abydos;" "The Epistle to the Hebrews," in Greek and English; 5 first books of the "Iliad;" Park's "Second Voyage in Africa;" "Epistle to the Romans," in Greek and English; "Corinne," by Madame de Staël; "Mémoires de

Grammont," by Hamilton; and "Lettres sur l'Italie," by Dupaty. I have mentioned the above, merely to show over what a wide field of literature Mr. Sumner ranged. It was so throughout his life. He was a cosmopolitan in his selection of books, and in all his writings you could trace the hand of one who was familiar with the works of the best classical authors, both in English and foreign literature.

CHAPTER III.

IT was at the beginning of September, 1816, that Mr. and Mrs. Sumner took up their abode at Highclere. They were able to live in the Rectory House—a parsonage of very moderate pretensions—for the Incumbent, the Rev. W. B. Barter, was also Rector of Burghclere, a neighbouring parish, and therefore practically Highclere was a sole-charge.

The first entry of the newly married couple into the Rectory was rather amusing. In their inexperience as housekeepers they had made no commissariat arrangements before their arrival, and found themselves rather late in the day at the parsonage, with no provisions in the house. A benevolent lady who lived near heard that the young couple had arrived, and just as Mr. Sumner was preparing to sally forth to the village shop to see what he could get, this good Samaritan appeared with a basket containing eggs, butter, milk and bread—all, in fact, that they wanted for their evening meal. This kindness was never forgotten, and Mrs. Davis (then Miss Bull), the provider of their first meal at Highclere, was, in after years, a frequent visitor at Farnham Castle, and up to the day of her death, which only took place a few years ago, the Bishop of Winchester regularly sent her a county newspaper in remembrance of old days.

It was in this little village of Highclere, about five miles from Newbury, that the future Bishop's pastoral experience was gained. Highclere itself is as lovely a spot as you could wish to see. Highclere Castle,* with its beautiful park, fifteen miles in circumference, looks down from wooded heights upon the cottages scattered along the grass lands below. The church, at the time referred to, was close to the Castle, and the parsonage-house just at the edge of the park, which now, like the church, has given place to a newly erected building on a different site. Specially lovely in the early summer is the whole of the neighbourhood of the Castle, for rhododendrons flourish on all sides in the utmost profusion. The Bishop was through life a great lover of the beauties of nature, fond not only of horticulture, but of botany also, and it must have been a great pleasure to him, that the first home to which he brought his Swiss bride should be placed in the midst of English scenery, which, for exquisite colouring and pastoral beauty, almost vied with the loveliness of her native country. The peasants were disposed to receive the new curate with the utmost cordiality, and he, on his part, seems to have laid himself out for the welfare of his parishioners. His first sermon, which now lies before me, preached from Ezekiel iii. 17—19, shewed his people what were his ideas of ministerial responsibility; that he was not placed there merely to live an ordinarily respectable life, but that his one object amongst them, God helping him, would be the salvation of immortal souls. They too had corresponding duties, to listen to the truth without taking personal offence, to open out their hearts to him in religious difficulties, and to seek earnestly that the Holy Spirit would cause the seed sown to

---

* Highclere Castle at one time belonged to the Bishops of Winchester, but was resigned by Bishop Poynet to Edward the Sixth. It came into the possession of the Carnarvon family, through a marriage with the daughter of Sir R. Sawyer, Attorney-General in the reign of James the Second.

D

take root in their hearts. His preaching must have been of no ordinary character, for before the beginning of his ministry, the meeting-house was full, and the church (in which there had been but one service on a Sunday) empty, and ere long the case was exactly reversed, the neighbouring villages contributing a quota to the Highclere congregation.

There was at that time no great educational fervour throughout the country. It cannot therefore be a matter of surprise to find that Highclere, a little remote country village, could not boast of any school. Mr. Sumner at once took the matter up, and after a very few months had passed, was able to establish a very efficient school. Opposition of course was met with, some of the farmers thinking that it was better to keep the poor in a state of ignorance, and that education, however advantageous to the rich, was wholly unsuitable for the labouring classes. Notwithstanding this, however, the school was soon started and flourished. It is interesting to find that long before the days of Government surveillance, conscience clauses, and inspectors, the little Highclere school was periodically inspected by a clergyman—a Mr. Iremonger*—and well reported of. It is evident that Mr. Sumner took the greatest possible interest in the school, for in 1817 he printed and circulated throughout the parish an address to the parents and friends of the scholars ; showing the great influence of home example in the education of children ; and on another occasion I find that he went to Winchester for the sole purpose of seeing the internal working of a school which was well spoken of.

Parochial work, however, did not wholly occupy his time. During the five years which he spent at Highclere his house was always full of pupils. He was very successful as a tutor, and thoroughly succeeded in gaining the love and esteem of those who were placed under his charge. The narrative kindly supplied

* Mr. Iremonger was a clergyman who took great interest in the spread of Dr. Bell's system of instruction, and did a great deal to promote its general acceptance.

to me by (I believe) the only surviving Highclere pupil sufficiently shows this.*

Any tutor would indeed be thankful to get such a letter
as the following from an old pupil. It is from Mr. Matheson,
afterwards Deputy Master of the Mint:

"To REV. C. R. SUMNER,

     "It is my particular hope and wish that I shall be
able, when the weather and state of the roads make a journey
over Highclere Down less disagreeable than at present, to
pay another visit to Highclere, and I feel sure that few
things could give me more real pleasure. In the mean time,
allow me again to express the most heartfelt thanks for the
many kindnesses which I have received whilst under your roof.
Next to the pleasure of conferring an obligation, may be ranked
that of showing one's gratitude for it, and as I have now no
other means of doing so (nor, indeed, could I ever make an
adequate return) I trust you will take my professions, badly
expressed as they are, and at least believe me sincere. The
best return I can make, you will no doubt say, is to prove
that I have not received your communications in vain, and
this is at present my *most anxious* desire. If at last, which
I greatly fear, and as most probably will be the case, I am
not successful, my wish is to be able to console myself by
thinking that I have done my utmost. I shall always look
back with affectionate interest to the days which I passed at
Highclere, and though I cannot go so far as Morgell, in
saying I do not expect ever to be happy again, yet I can say
that they are amongst the happiest which I ever have or
shall spend.

     "Hoping that yourself and family, and also Mrs. Sumner (for
whose great civility and attention I shall always feel very very
sensibly obliged, and for which I beg she will accept my very
best thanks) are well, I am, &c."

* See pages 41—48.

D 2

As a further testimony to Mr. Sumner's success as a tutor, let me add the following extract from a letter from the then Bishop of London (Howley), to whom he had been introduced during one of his visits to London :

"The Earl of —— is desirous of placing his son, Lord ——, now sixteen years of age, under the care of a clergyman for two years previous to his going to Christ Church, after the approaching Easter holidays. I feel the education of a nobleman of his rank and fortune to be of so much importance, that I could not in conscience mention any one's name whom I did not think eminently qualified for such a task. On the present occasion the report of many persons in whose judgment I confide, directs me to you as the best qualified, of all others, to do justice to a pupil of this description."

Mr. Sumner, however, not having a vacancy at the time, was unable to take this pupil.

The following, too, from Coleridge, in connection with this subject, will be read with interest :

"2, Pump Court, *October* 15, 1817.

"My dear Charles,

"I have time for little more than the business I write on. The following is an extract of a letter from my friend John Keble, whom for both your sakes I wish you knew : 'Can you tell whether your friend, C. S., has room for a pupil at present. A clergyman in this neighbourhood, of the name of ——, has applied to me to get an introduction to him for his nephew, who has just been sent away from the Charterhouse— no recommendation you will say, but as I understand the circumstances, it is a case rather of ἀκρασία than ἀκολασία; and as he is said to be a good scholar and (notwithstanding his being warned off) a sort of favourite with Russell, I heartily hope Sumner will be able and willing to receive him.'

"Ever thine truly,

"J. T. C."

Mrs. Sumner was not able to help her husband as much as

she wished in this particular department—for domestic and family arrangements necessarily occupied her time a good deal —but her influence seems to have been very great with the pupils. While retaining the charm and vivacity of a foreigner she became thoroughly English in other ways; and the evenings at Highclere Parsonage, when Mrs. Sumner, whose musical talents were of the highest order, played and sang—the pupils occasionally joining—or when Mr. Sumner read aloud, must have been very enjoyable. The Sundays were passed in a very different manner from that to which she had been accustomed ; but her journal says :

"Je goûte tellement la tranquillité et la sainteté d'un Dimanche Anglois que je ne saurois comment prendre mon parti de les passer autrement. Je suis persuadée que ce n'est pas obéir le commandement de Dieu ' de sanctifier' le jour du repos, que de les passer à danser, chanter et se promener d'une manière bruyante et mondaine, en un mot que nous ne devions rien faire qui nous empêchât de revenir à des sujets religieux."

Mr. Sumner, in consequence of the bodily infirmities of Bishop North, was admitted to Priest's orders by the Bishop of Salisbury, on March 2, 1817, and in June he went up to Cambridge to take his M.A. degree; but otherwise the year 1817 appears to have been spent entirely at Highclere, until the Christmas vacation allowed him to go to his sister-in-law, Mrs. McNiven, in London, and to Milford.

The details of parochial and tutorial life were much the same then as they would be now, but I must mention two matters of pastoral experience. Like most country clergymen, the curate of Highclere dabbled a little in medicine. It happened to him one day, that on visiting a parishioner, he found that one of the children was suffering from a cutaneous disorder in the head. Mr. Sumner thought that a slight alterative was required, and accordingly, said that he would let the mother have a mixture, which he trusted would benefit the child.   A preparation of rhubarb was accordingly mixed at the parsonage, and duly sent.   On calling the next day to inquire after the health of his patient, Mr. Sumner was pleased to find the child much better, and congratulated himself on the success of his prescription; but in course of conversation with the mother, it turned out that she had supposed the mixture in question to be a lotion for external application, and had rubbed it well into the unfortunate victim's head.   Mr. Sumner kept his countenance, and I am afraid took the credit of the cure effected.

On another occasion he was sent for to visit a dying man, under very peculiar circumstances.   It appears that three men had attempted to break into a house in the neighbourhood. The inhabitants of the house, however, resisted the burglars, one of whom was mortally wounded.   Mr. Sumner went to his dying bed, and the man confessed to him that he was one of a band of robbers who lived in a cave in the New Forest.   Mr. Sumner as a parish priest naturally tried to turn the wretched man's death to the spiritual good of his parishioners, and on the Sunday after, when he made it the subject of his sermon, the church was so crammed, that the staircase up to the gallery was thronged, and chairs brought in and placed all down the aisle.

The inmates of Highclere parsonage were greatly pleased in the course of this year by the election of the Rev. J. B. Sumner to a Fellowship at Eton.   Coleridge thus writes about it:

"I congratulate you *ab imo* on your brother's election—it is not half of what he deserves.   The leisure which he has now for professional studies will, I trust, be beneficial to the Church. If he could devise some conciliatory mode of bringing good people together, who are squabbling about words, what a blessing would it be."

A few months after his election as Fellow, his brother went for a holiday to Edinburgh, from which place he wrote the following letter:

"TO REV. C. R. SUMNER.

"EDINBURGH, *December* 31, 1817.

"MY DEAR CHARLES,

"You desired to hear something of me; and as I have been now exactly a week safely landed in this great town, this seems a proper opportunity for gratifying your requisition, though I am not aware that I have anything to communicate worth so long a postage. My journey was tiresome, as it must always be to roll over 400 miles in stage coaches: in no other respect was there any evil attending it, and I felt no fatigue after I had once reached the place of my destination. Here I was so happy as to find all well, and the time passes so agreeably and quickly, that I can scarcely believe a week has already elapsed. . . . . . Rob Roy was born yesterday evening at 6 o'clock, and 1500 copies subscribed by the booksellers of this town alone. The edition is 10,000, supposed to be a larger number than was ever known. No doubt exists *here* as to Scott's parental interest in these works. His best friends are the most convinced: though he keeps the secret religiously even from his children. His eldest son had been primed to ask him. 'No,' he said, 'not I, but Miss Baillie!' They only observe that he is seen reading everything else, but not these. It is already whispered that Rob Roy has less interest than its predecessors; and indeed it would be almost miraculous if it should prove otherwise. I have not yet seen the book, which is much to say of what has been published sixteen hours! The new Edinburgh Review has only one article of any merit or interest, the first on Lalla Rookh—of course by Jeffrey; and, as I think, most just and impartial.

"After all, this is a wonderful city. I was *surprised* to find that I could be so much *surprised* at renewing my acquaintance with the 'romantic town.' Such indeed it is—houses, castle, spires, towers, hills, rocks, all rising one above another, and presenting an infinite variety of charms. Though it is winter, the outlines are grand and impressive, so much so as to lose little of their beauty. I must bring back some memoranda to make your curiosity eager, and I do not believe that the world, take it all in all, has such another city.

" Your most affectionate brother,

" J. B. Sumner."

And so the time passed quietly and evenly along. Occasional visits were made to his brother-in-law, Mr. McNiven, in London, to his mother at Milford, and to his brother at Eton College.

It is evident, from the following letter from his friend Coleridge, dated July 15, 1818, that Mr. Sumner worked very hard and probably enjoyed his holidays as much as his pupils :

" I find you are in the enjoyment of your summer vacation at Milford, with your family all around you, and therefore to increase your happiness by comparison, I send you news of your poor friend gasping in the dusty and calorified air of London. I think of old Falstaff daily—there seems to be really a perpetual thaw of human flesh going on ; and if it lasts, we metropolitans shall be like the tall disproportioned figures that you see in some of Claude's pictures. The accounts I hear of *yours* are better than those I hear of *yourself ;* you are represented as a good deal worn out by overworking yourself; that is not right, my good fellow, for you may depend upon it, strength is like a man's money, capital, and income; a prudent man spends his income only, and he lives longest ; a man engaged in schemes may trench a little on his capital now and hen, but he saves it by economy the next year ; but it is downright ruinous extravagance to live habitually on your capital, which any man does who habitually overworks himself. You may not feel it now, because the stock is large, and you don't calculate, but you will by-and-by. But I will hope for your amendment." *

---

* Mr. Sumner profited by his friend's lecture, for in after life he thus pithily writes to a clergyman who had over-worked himself, " Do less that you may do more."

It is interesting to read in Mrs. Sumner's journal, after a visit to the Rev. J. B. Sumner at Eton, "En verité plus je le vois le plus je l'aime. Il est si bon. On devient sage en l'écoutant."

Before I pass away from this quiet and uneventful history of ministerial life, I wish to place on record the reminiscences of one who was always a very favourite pupil at Highclere—the Rev. F. Oakeley—who seceded, at a comparatively early stage of the Tractarian movement, to the Church of Rome, and has kindly drawn up, at my request, the following sketch of his Highclere days:

"MY DEAR MR. SUMNER,

"You have asked me to tell you what I remember about your dear father, and especially during the three years which I spent in his house and under his care, as one of his private pupils. It is very pleasant to me to recall the memory of a period which I have always regarded as one of the happiest in my early life. I saw your father for the first time on the 19th of September, 1817, when I entered his family at Highclere. . . . Your father was recommended to my parents by Bishop Coleridge as well fitted to train me for the university, and as a clergyman, whose kind and amiable disposition and manners would render him the tutor, of all others, to deal with a youth like myself, who had been used from infancy to the care and indulgences of home. Your mother was confined to her room when I arrived, so that in the first days of my stay at Highclere, I had not the relief and consolation which I ever afterwards derived from her kind and genial influence. One of my greatest pleasures was to steal a march on my companions, and get half-an-hour's conversation with her in the drawing-room, before Mr. Sumner and the other pupils came into the room. I need not say that I found a bond of most agreeable intercourse with her in the subject of music, in which, as you know, she was a proficient, and of which I was from my earliest childhood a passionate lover. I was also able to improve my knowledge of French by occasional conversation with her in that language. Our days at Highclere were ordered as follows : We went into your father's study at eight in the morning, to construe a portion of the Greek Testament, and of some Greek play. We breakfasted at nine after family prayers, and, after breakfast, had half-an-hour's recreation. We then went to our rooms till twelve, when we met again in the study. We had a good portion of the afternoon to ourselves, dined at four, and at seven in the evening carried up verses or other compositions to be corrected. When the evening exercise was finished, we met for tea in the drawing-room, after which your father used to read aloud one of Shakespeare's plays, portions of 'Childe Harold,' an article in the 'Quarterly,' or some other standard work or publication of the day. At ten o'clock we retired to our rooms. On Sundays we either wrote an exercise on some religious subject, or an analysis of one of the sermons. The first sermon I ever heard your father preach made a great impression on me. It was on the text, 'What shall I do to be saved?' and I had never before heard one which appeared to me so striking in matter, or was so impressively delivered. We used to read out our Sunday exercises after tea in the evening, and receive your father's comments on them. On one occasion I remember his telling me, that I had inadvertently slipped into the Socinian heresy. But I venture to think that at another time I had my revenge for this severe criticism ; and, considering all that has since passed, the anecdote is worth recording. During a Greek Testament lesson, I once contended, with somewhat unbecoming vehemence, that our Lord gave the keys of His kingdom in an especial manner to St. Peter. My tutor, whose thoughts were at the moment on another text, and who might have instinctively feared that my argument had a dangerous tendency, maintained that the promise was given to all the Apostles alike. But he was far too honest to shrink from acknowledging the mistake from the fear of compromising his tutorial dignity, and when we met the next morning, he said to me, 'I find, Oakeley, that you were right about St. Peter.' I have often thought of this little incident as if there were something prophetic about it, though as far as I myself was concerned, I can truly say that I was most profoundly ignorant of any theological import in the remark.*

"You may naturally wish to know whether your father employed any direct means of influencing his pupils on the subject of religion. I can confidently say that he did not. We all learned, or might have learned, a great deal in that way from his sermons, occasional remarks, and personal example. But as to anything beyond, he was singularly reserved and even reticent. He not only abstained, as a general rule, from introducing the subject of doctrinal religion, but evaded it when we tried to draw him out upon it. It was chiefly from his sermons, or from some incidental remark, that we were able to infer the tendency of his religious opinions towards a more earnest appreciation of the realities of the unseen world, than most of us had been familiar with in our previous experiences.

"My impressions of your father's character, as exhibited in his daily life at Highclere, must be received with due allowance for the restraint which is apt to affect the intercourse of tutor and pupil, even when, as in our case, the difference of age between them is not considerable. Your father's demeanour was always sedate, yet cheerful; dignified, yet kind and courteous. Whatever was wanting in the way of more genial qualities, was amply supplied by your generous and warm-hearted mother, and thus we had in one and the other a combination and balance of those qualities of the Christian character which constitute the attractions of a religious household. Your father made a point of never dining out, and once when he was compelled to leave home for a few days on business, found reason on his return to appreciate the value of the control

* Probably Mr. Sumner had in his mind St. Matt. xviii. 18, where the same power (whatever that may be) which was granted to St. Peter in St. Matt. xvi. 19, is granted to all the Apostles.

exercised by his presence, from the advantage taken of his absence by one or two of his pupils. With this single exception, I think I may say that a more contented and less troublesome body of youths than was collected during the three years of my residence, never met together under the roof of a private tutor. Our prosperity was never ruffled for a single day by illness or accident, and I, who, up to the time of going to Highclere, was constantly unwell, recovered my health so completely in the fine Hampshire air, that I used to walk several miles a day without difficulty, and laid in a stock of physical strength, which has lasted me almost up to the present time. Your father was a great walker, and we used to fancy that in earlier days he must have been addicted to field sports. He used to carry in his rambles a long hoe, with which ever and anon he would root up the weeds in his path, and whenever a covey of partridges got up, he would take aim at them with the hoe as naturally as if he were carrying a more murderous weapon.*

"As a classical scholar I suppose that your father was elegant and accomplished rather than profound. But he was fully competent to the work he undertook, and none of us, his pupils, were at all events sufficiently advanced to have either the inclination or the ability to criticise his attainments. His *forte*, I should say, was in composition, whether Latin or English, and especially in the criticism of Latin verse. I remember once showing some exercises of mine which he had corrected to my brother, who was an Oxford first-class man, and who expressed a warm approval of the scholar-like manner in which the corrections were made.†

"My little memoir would scarcely be complete, did I not add something about the place which for several years formed the scene of your father's ministerial labours in the diocese over which he afterwards presided, and the natural attractions of

---

* Mr. Oakeley is right in his conjecture. Both Mr. Sumner and his elder brother were, as boys, very fond of shooting.

† Mr. Oakeley, who was never at a public school, or received instruction in com-

which so materially contributed to the enjoyment of those who
were gathered under his roof. I used to fancy that Highclere,
with its magnificent park, its gently sloping hills, its densely
shaded pine-woods, its glassy lakes, and its hedges of rhododendrons, must be the most beautiful spot in creation. But as this
was at an age when imagination is vivid, and experience
limited, I am willing that my opinion on the subject should be
received with the necessary deductions. However, after
revisiting it only a few years ago, I still maintain that it is
almost without a rival in England. Fancy what a treat and
advantage it must have been for us boys to have the run of
that splendid domain, without let or hindrance. It was a rare
act of generosity on the part of the noble proprietor to allow us
this privilege, and I am happy to think that it was in no
instance abused. We had the use of the boats on Milford
Lake, could climb bare Beacon, or woody Siddon without
molestation, while those who, like myself, happened to possess
a taste for floriculture, had access, on stated occasions, to the
gardens, with their choice collection of plants. The parish
church of Highclere at that time adjoined the mansion, so that
not only we, but most of the parishioners had to traverse the
whole length of the park twice every Sunday.

   "When I was at Oxford, I visited your father at Highclere
during the long vacation. I was also his guest successively at
Windsor, Llansanfraed, the Deanery of St. Paul's, Farnham
Castle, and St. James's Square. But from the time that I
became a resident Fellow at Oxford, and especially after the
rise of the Tractarian movement, I felt painfully that our intercourse was somewhat more restrained than in earlier years,
and from the time of my taking charge of Margaret Chapel in

position from anyone except Mr. Sumner, has always most generously attributed
a large share in the credit of the success he obtained at Oxford to his Highclere
training. In the first year of his residence at Christ Church he gained the college
prize for Latin verses, and subsequently the university prizes both for Latin and
English prose composition, as well as Dr. Ellerton's prize for a theological essay,
and ultimately took a second class in the Classical Schools.

1839, I felt that your father must more and more disapprove of my religious course, though I am sure without any diminution of personal regard. Hence I became shy of meeting him. The last time I ever saw him to my knowledge was about the year 1843, when I called upon him one evening in St. James's Square. I feared of course that the more decided step which I afterwards took would have completed the estrangement, but here I was happily disappointed. During the last twenty-five years, I have received from him the kindest, nay, the most affectionate of letters. The first of these was in 1849, when I wrote to him on an occasion of domestic calamity, which called forth the sympathy of all his friends, and of none more than myself, who knew better than many of them the greatness of the loss he had sustained.* The letter which I received in answer, was all that I could have desired. The next time I heard from him was in 1852, and the letter I then received is, I regret to say, the only one I have preserved. It was in answer to one requesting his assistance in putting down a public exhibition, the object of which was to hold up to ridicule the holiest institution of our religion. My reason for writing to your father on the subject was, that the disgraceful performance in question was announced to come off in two places, which I supposed to be under his jurisdiction. The following is an extract from his reply :—

    "'MY DEAR OAKELEY,

       "'I can never address you by any less familiar title, although circumstances unhappily have so much sundered us. But if I never think of you without a sigh, so can I never think of you otherwise than with much affection.

       "'I am happy to say that Newington, although in Surrey, is not under my jurisdiction, but that of the Bishop of London. Landsdowne Road is within my Diocese, but I shall not be supposed to have any control over the Binfield House Assembly

---

      * Mrs. Sumner died in 1849.

Rooms. I hope I need scarcely assure you that you cannot disapprove more strongly than myself any such ribald representation as is named in the accompanying advertisement. I return it, as you may wish to call attention to it in another quarter.'

"This letter is dated 'Farnham Castle, August 1, 1852.' I have since received several other letters from him all couched in the same terms of affectionate regard, qualified, as in the preceding extract, by a tone of natural regret, which in no case, however, took the form of reproach. This tenderness of feeling might have been expected from one who always exhibited the greatest indulgence towards the conscientious convictions of others, even when most at variance with his own. I remember a circumstance, which I will mention, not only because it illustrates this beautiful feature in his character, but because it is an instance of the delicacy with which he could administer a paternal rebuke in a case where it was needed. Once, when I was breakfasting with him in St. James's Square, somewhere about the time of the passing of the Catholic Relief Bill, the conversation turned on the personal character of Roman Catholics, against whom I was thoughtless enough to bring some of the popular charges. Your father listened in silence, and at length turning towards me, said, very calmly, 'Oakeley, are you personally acquainted with any Roman Catholic?' I replied that to the best of my knowledge I had never spoken to one in my life. 'Then,' rejoined the Bishop, 'would it not be better to abstain from talking against them?' He had a decided talent for repartee, but always exercised it with kindness and caution. I recollect a very happy instance of his readiness in meeting an opinion of which he disapproved. A young foreigner, who was at his table, had been defending some questionable principle or practice of morality, on the ground of a supposed necessity, and summed up his argument in the words ' c'est la necessité qui fait la loi.' Your father instantly rejoined, 'Pardon me, I should rather say, c'est la loi qui fait la necessité.

"And now, my dear Sir, I have finished the task you have kindly allotted me. It has been an easy, as well as a pleasant one, for the main facts of the period it comprises are so deeply engraven on my memory, that I have had little else to do than to give shape to my habitual impressions, and transfer them to paper. I must now leave those who knew him before the year 1817, and those who have been intimately associated with him during the last half century, to complete the story of a life which well deserves to be recorded as a bright example of consistent piety, ministerial faithfulness, and the diligent and conscientious use of talents and opportunities.

"Believe me, my dear Mr. Sumner,
"Yours very sincerely,
"FREDERICK OAKELEY.

"DUNCAN TERRACE, ISLINGTON, *May* 5, 1875.
"The Rev. GEORGE H. SUMNER."

It was towards the close of 1819 that the first offer of preferment was made to Mr. Sumner.

Mr. Chambers (younger brother of Dr. Chambers) was a mutual friend of both Mr. Sumner and of Charles Grant (afterwards Lord Glenelg), chief secretary for Ireland. The Lord-Lieutenant of Ireland* (Lord Talbot) was anxious to introduce Englishmen of high attainments and position as head-masters of some of the principal schools in that country, and Mr. Sumner was named to him by Charles Grant, on Mr. Chambers's recommendation, as a proper person for such a post, and he accordingly offered to him the Head-mastership of Enniskillen School. The *clear* income was estimated at about £1800 a year, and there seemed every prospect of success for a hard-working man.

He at once communicated with his elder brother, who made

---

* Lord Talbot, in October of the following year, sent one of his sons as pupil to Highclere.

inquiries for him from one capable of judging as to the desirability of the post, and subsequently enclosed to him the following letter :

"TO THE REV. J. B. SUMNER.

"My dear Sumner,

"In reply to your queries respecting Enniskillen, I have to state my opinion that the offer must be considered as very interesting, and deserving the most mature deliberation. The appointment would open a wide sphere of usefulness to any man of talents and conscience ; and at the same time would hold out to him an excellent chance, almost a certainty, of affluence and distinction. The endowment is considerable; and I have no doubt is well paid, as it probably arises out of leases granted for long periods. The contingent income of course cannot be estimated, but, from what I know of the North of Ireland, I am persuaded that a scholar of gentleman-like habits, if he chose to make his arrangements so that no boy need cost his parents more than seventy or eighty pounds a year, might at that rate have as many pupils as he chose. Provisions and all necessaries are comparatively so cheap that the master might expect to make twenty-five guineas profit from each boy.

"With respect to station, the Masters of the Endowed Schools rank with the foremost of the Clergy, and are gladly received into the highest circles. A young Englishman, coming under circumstances so favourable as those in which your brother would be placed, might expect to be received with open arms by the best people in the country. I have never been at Enniskillen, and of course am unacquainted with the peculiar circumstances of its neighbourhood ; it has the reputation of being the most Protestant district in Ireland. Its situation, so near to the romantic beauties of Lough Erne, ought not to be disregarded.

"Of course I cannot judge of the reasons which would operate against the acceptance of the offer except so far as they are of a general nature. If it should be thought desirable, I have no

E

doubt I can procure precise information on any points of inquiry.

" Be the decision what it may, ' feliciter vertat.'

" Ever yours,

" T. Turner."

Enclosing the above, his brother adds—

" I was happy to procure such information as I here send you, my dear Charles, because *we here* are as well able to judge of an appointment in the moon, as of the one offered to you, under the title of master of an endowed school at Enniskillen. Should you continue your present situation and plan, you may reasonably expect in the course of ten or fifteen years a living of £300 or £400 per ann. from some quarter or other, and that probably would be the extent of your preferment. The other is a very different opening. The *degree of sacrifice* and the comparative *loss*, is matter of feeling : on which it would be impossible to give an opinion. Such was my answer to Pearson a fortnight ago, when he asked me whether I thought you might be prevailed on to accept the appointment. If you take it, you cannot be wrong in following such a leading of Providence to a walk of great importance and usefulness ; if you decline you cannot be wrong in preferring the *fallentis vitæ semitam*, to a sphere of greater noise and ambition. I need not say that a matter of such consequence, which must colour your whole future life, demands a very solemn entreaty that you may be enlightened with wisdom from above, and enabled to decide in the way that shall prove most pleasing to God, and most favourable to the great business of our present state of living.

" Let me know as soon as you have made up your mind, as Turner would be very glad of the situation.

" Ever your most affectionate,

" J. B. S."

The following is from Mr. Chambers :

"LINCOLN'S INN, *November* 15, 1819.

"MY DEAR SUMNER,

"You must put up with a dirty half-sheet of paper for want of more, but it is gilt edged. . . . I have written to Charles Grant to-day the purport of your letter. My counsel to you is to accept the offer, for although I think he is perfectly right in qualifying his personal engagement to serve you, so as to prevent the possibility of the performance coming short of the promise, yet the situation being in the gift of the Government, it no doubt forms a step in the gradation of patronage and necessarily makes a man of merit obvious to notice, whoever may be in power : and it does not at all follow that when Charles Grant leaves Ireland he will forget those whom he has been instrumental in promoting. I can assure you that your own character and principles have been the great instrument in producing so favourable an effect in your favour; and it only convinces me that there is a great deal of rational good sense in steadily pursuing the same consistent course, and opportunities in abundance will offer assistance to the views of every right minded man."

The offer was well weighed and considered, but notwithstanding its tempting nature, as far as worldly prospects were concerned, Mr. Sumner was loath to devote the best years of his life to simply scholastic as apart from ministerial work, and declined the offer.

An entry at this date in the diary which Mrs. Sumner kept for her parents at Geneva, shows that it was no easy matter for them to make up their minds respecting the offer.

"Oh mes bien aimés parens, lorsque vous lirez ceci la décision importante sera faite, si nous restons en Angleterre, ou si nous allons en Irelande. Vous pouvez comprendre que l'incertitude dans une chose de cette importance est bien pénible—d'avoir à choisir entre les richesses, honneurs et rang, et une vie moyenne et tranquille . . ."

A few days later she adds :

"Tout est décidé! nous restons à Highclere! Mr. Sumner aurait pu devenir millionnaire. Il y a renoncé par un sentiment de devoir."

The following letter closes the history of the Enniskillen School :—

"LONDON, *December* 9, 1819.

"SIR,

"I regret that I have not been able sooner to acknowledge your letter communicating your decision respecting the Enniskillen School. I cannot but express my real concern at the result of this business ; and allow me to add that a knowledge of the motives which have influenced you, strengthens my sense of the loss which we have suffered. I must confess, too, that the reason which you are so good as to mention, completely justifies, or rather explains (for, indeed, it requires no justification), your conduct. I can only offer my best wishes for your success in your labours.

"I shall be very happy if you will favour me with an interview when you visit London.

"I have the honour to be, &c.,

"C. GRANT."

In 1820, the subject of preferment in the Church was again the topic of correspondence ; but this time in the person of his brother. Mr. Sumner was greatly pleased at his appointment to a canonry at Durham. The following letter announces the fact :—

"MY DEAR CHARLES,

"I am going to surprise you with very unexpected news, happily of a pleasant nature. I have had a letter from the Bishop of Durham, acquainting me that a stall in his church is on the point of being vacant (some arrangement for exchange), and that he has no hesitation in offering it to me as the author of, &c., &c. . . . . . You will anticipate my answer. Of course it will vacate my fellowship, I suppose at the end of the year.

"I may truly say that nothing could have been much more unexpected to me than this advancement. Certainly it may be said that there *are* encouragements to the Christian minister which I have not alluded to in my sermon. . . . . . But to return. I cannot, or ought not to feel but that my great prosperity imposes on me a most alarming responsibility. Had I been free to choose, I should certainly have conceived that my influence, whatever it is, would have been exactly in its right sphere at Eton, and should never have used any endeavour on my own part to remove from thence. But an offer of this kind seems to be a call elsewhere. As such I follow it: only praying, in which I trust my friends will join in my behalf, that I may have a measure of divine blessing proportionate to my temporal advantages . . . . I am going to put a volume of sermons to press without delay . . . . .

"Believe me,

"Your most affectionate brother,

" J. B. S."

"Eton, *October* 9."

The following is from Coleridge, referring to this subject :—

"Your brother's preferment, much as I rejoice at it on private grounds, I hardly know whether I do not rejoice more on public. It is one more stay for our good old much-abused Church that such men are so honourably marked out and placed in the posts where their lights may be most conspicuous for her glory and safety.

"Both on private and public grounds, however, I congratulate you most heartily on the event, and when you write to your brother pray make my congratulations to him. Does he keep Maple Durham? I hope he does, for else he would be very much separated from you and your mother."

Two more extracts from Highclere letters, both addressed to Mrs. Sumner, will bring us to the close of 1820.

"*August* 27.

"Yesterday (Friday) the great revolution in the house was effected, and by dint of the united exertion of White the carpenter, Elizabeth (who panted all the time like a broken-winded rabbit), and myself, we contrived to effect the déménagement and the new settlement without much difficulty. While we were in the midst of taking down beds in the nursery, I thought I heard a strange step wandering among the rooms below, and, on going down, it proved to be L——, who arrived about 2 o'clock, true to his time, and a little to my inconvenience.

"Baby has got a new lower tooth through, which caused him a good deal of fretfulness and a little fever—both of which are now gone upon the appearance of the tusk, which is next in the order to those he has already. The weather has not yet been sufficiently warm to leave off the cap, but I have taken it away several times in the drawing-room."

"HIGHCLERE PARSONAGE, *September* 5, 1820.

"I rode over to Andover this morning to the visitation, and the day was so beautiful that I enjoyed the ride in spite of myself. The Chancellor, Mr. Legge, preached himself. The text (tell my mother this, for she likes to know what clergymen talk about to each other) was from the last chapter of St. John, 'Simon, lovest thou me more than these? Feed my sheep.' Two of his topics were rather oddly chosen, but might have been not unedifying for some of his hearers—attention to dress in the clergy, and choice of and moderation in amusements and lighter occupations. Amongst other things he talked against 'boisterous sports.' Mr. ——, who races, was not there."

And so the curtain drops on what, in after years, Mrs. Sumner

often said was the happiest time that she and her husband
ever spent.   Life in the country, with all its associations and
rural pleasures, and a pastor's experience of mingled hopes and
disappointments, were soon to be exchanged for the excitement
and bustle of Court life.   The quiet country curate was destined
to be the Royal Chaplain, on the high road to offices of the
greatest distinction and influence in the Church.   Did the
Bishop of Winchester, in the stormy days of his Episcopate,
ever look back with a fond feeling of regret to the even tenor
of his life—surrounded by affectionate pupils, enjoying the
pleasures of domestic life, and working diligently as a pastor
in his curacy at Highclere?   I can well fancy that he did.

CHAPTER IV.

Is sent for by George IV. to Brighton.—Offer of a Canonry at Windsor.—Correspondence between Lord Liverpool and the King.—Offer withdrawn in consequence of Mr. Sumner only being a curate.—Correspondence thereupon.—Is appointed Historiographer, Chaplain to the King, and Librarian-in-Ordinary.—Verses composed on the top of a Coach.—Accepts the Vicarage of St. Helen's, Abingdon.—Impressions of Abingdon.—Presentation at Court.—Is succeeded at Highclere by Rev. A. Dallas.—Affecting farewells at Highclere.—Last Sermon there.—Enters on his Duties at Windsor.

IT will be remembered that Lord Francis Conyngham was one of Mr. Sumner's pupils at Highclere. In April, 1820, he was appointed Master of the Robes and first Groom of the Bedchamber to King George the Fourth. He retained such a high esteem and warm affection for his old tutor, that he lost no time in mentioning Mr. Sumner's name to his Royal patron, and sounding his praises in the King's ear. Lord Mount Charles, too, who was very much attached to Mr. Sumner, was also high in the King's favour, and heartily seconded his brother's words. The King accordingly expressed a wish to see Mr. Sumner; and Lord Francis Conyngham wrote to Highclere inviting him to come to Brighton. He at once obeyed the Royal summons, went down to Brighton, and was introduced into a reception room. There were several of the Lords-in-waiting standing about, and they at once entered into conversation with him. After a short time the King himself came into the room and expressed a wish that Mr. Sumner should dine at the Pavilion that night, and after dinner the King (he was seated on a sofa, and Mr. Sumner was standing behind it) talked with him for three hours consecutively. Those who

were about the King looked rather grave at this peculiar mark
of royal favour, but they naturally were not slow in congratulating the young curate on his good fortune in thus, at his
first interview, having so evidently ingratiated himself with the
King, and as he left the Royal presence one of them whispered
to him " Your fortune is made. There is no saying what you
may not be ere many years have passed." The King, indeed,
at once shewed that he was most favourably impressed by his
conversation with Mr. Sumner, by offering him a Canonry at
Windsor, but Lord Liverpool, the Prime Minister, while willing
to make an opening for Mr. Sumner, so strongly objected to
appoint to a canonry one who was only a curate in the Church,
that the King, much to his annoyance, was obliged to yield the
point.   The following letters give sufficiently in detail the
course of events of such intense interest to the inmates of
Highclere Parsonage.

"FIFE HOUSE, *April 12th,* 1821.

"Lord Liverpool has had the honour of receiving the letter
which your Majesty has been graciously pleased to send to him
by Sir B. Bloomfield.

"Lord Liverpool can assure your Majesty that it was his most
anxious desire to have conformed to your Majesty's wishes
respecting the vacant canonry of Windsor, as far as he could do
so consistently with his public duty. When Sir B. Bloomfield
first named to him, by mistake, Mr. Sumner, Lord Liverpool
requested that he would send him all particulars about Mr.
Sumner, and he only wished time to make the necessary
enquiries, and begged that your Majesty might not be committed on the subject until Lord Liverpool had ascertained
how far he could reconcile the selection with his official
responsibility.

"It was Lord Liverpool's conscientious opinion, upon enquiry,
that the appointment of Mr. Sumner to a canonry of Windsor,
under all the present circumstances, would be most injurious to

your Majesty's interests, and would give great umbrage to that part of the Establishment which is so strongly and deeply attached to your Majesty and your Government.

"Lord Liverpool has since received ample confirmation of the truth of this first impression, which he intended to communicate to your Majesty in his representation of last week. Lord Liverpool is most sincerely anxious to relieve your Majesty from any difficulties in which your Majesty may be involved in this most painful business: he will be desirous therefore of recommending Mr. Sumner for a valuable living in the gift of the Crown as soon as there is an opening; and it will afterwards be a matter of consideration in what degree and to what extent Mr. Sumner's further prospects in the Church can be promoted."

THE KING TO LORD LIVERPOOL.

"It is with considerable regret that the King has received Lord Liverpool's letter of yesterday, and the more, as the King feels that ever since the appointment of Lord Liverpool as his first Minister, he has not merely shewn an uniform desire not to thwart any views of Lord Liverpool or of his friends in the disposal of the different branches of the patronage of the Crown, but, on the contrary, to oblige Lord Liverpool and to give every support in his power to an administration created by himself, the King has yielded every personal feeling. In illustration of which the King need only draw Lord Liverpool's attention to two very recent events, amongst numberless others, namely, the removal of Lord Fife (a measure certainly painful to the King's private feelings) and the disregard of the King's desire, conveyed to Lord Liverpool through Sir B. Bloomfield, 'that Mr. B. Paget should succeed to the office of Receiver-General:' notwithstanding which, the appointment of another individual (however eligible) took place, without further reference to the King.

"Under so extraordinary a proceeding—did the King withhold

his signature to the warrant of appointment? Or did the King call upon Lord Liverpool to forfeit his promise or his word?

"The King might also add the instance, in which he sacrificed the most painful personal feelings and opinions to the advice and earnest desire of Lord Liverpool that 'the King would not accept the resignation of Mr. Canning, but suffer him to remain in his councils,' in despite of the very unwarrantable conduct of that gentleman (as a member of the Cabinet) in his place in Parliament.

"The question of this nomination to the vacant canonry of Windsor does not rest upon the selection which the King has made for that appointment, nor does the King doubt the sincerity of Lord Liverpool's desire to make a suitable provision in lieu of that destined by the King for Mr. Sumner. But there are principles paramount to all other considerations which will ever guide the King in his course through life. Lord Liverpool, in his desire to relieve the King from any embarrassment which the present case may occasion, appears solely to have directed his view to the policy or the impolicy of this nomination, and wholly to have disregarded that *vital part* of the transaction, which involves the *good faith and honor of his Sovereign.*

"The King therefore sees no reason to alter his determination of appointing Mr. Sumner to the vacant canonry of Windsor : and however willing the King might be to give up his own opinions to Lord Liverpool's wishes, it is no longer a question of the propriety of this little appointment as the King has already stated, but, whether *the King's word* is to be held *sacred* or is to be of *no avail.* The King acquainted Lord Liverpool that the appointment was given by himself alone, unsolicited by Mr. Sumner, or at the instance of any private friend of the King's, or of Mr. Sumner's. His merit and his character were his *only* recommendations, and the King thinks such recommendations more calculated to do honor, and to give satisfaction, than to give 'umbrage' to the Church.

"BRIGHTON, *April 13th,* 1821."

LORD LIVERPOOL TO THE KING.

"FIFE HOUSE, *April 14th,* 1821.

"Lord Liverpool has received with the most profound respect, but at the same time with the deepest concern, your Majesty's letter. Lord Liverpool must in the first instance beg your Majesty's permission to allude to the circumstances mentioned in the earlier part of that letter. He can assure your Majesty, that both with respect to the removal of Lord Fife, and to the request to your Majesty not to accept Mr. Canning's resignation in the summer of last year, he was actuated by no personal hostility to the former, nor by any regard or favour to the latter, but solely by the consideration of what appeared to him to be essential for the strength and solidity of your Majesty's Government. . . . Upon the point on which your Majesty has thought fit more particularly to communicate your sentiments and wishes to Lord Liverpool, Lord Liverpool is called upon to state that he is actuated upon the present occasion by no predilection in favour of, nor disposition towards any individual, but solely by what he is deliberately convinced is due to your Majesty's authority; and even if he should have held out expectations to which your Majesty might afterwards not be reconciled, he would feel it his duty to subject himself to any inconvenience which might arise in consequence of such disappointment. Lord Liverpool could recall to your Majesty's recollection, cases in which it could not but be distinctly admitted that the expectation which might have been personally held out by the Sovereign was subject to the responsibility of his ministers, and that it must be a sufficient answer on such an occasion that the appointment has been obstructed in a quarter which cannot by the laws of the country be passed by. Lord Liverpool can assure your Majesty that it would be the greatest possible relief to his mind, to be enabled to conform to your Majesty's wishes; but after the most painful consideration he is satisfied that he should not have effectually discharged

his duty to your Majesty by any other advice than that which
he took the liberty of most humbly submitting, in the first
letter which he addressed to Sir Benjamin Bloomfield on this
subject, and in the last which he ventured to write to your
Majesty."*

LORD MOUNT CHARLES TO REV. C. SUMNER.

"BRIGHTON, *April* 15*th*, 1821.

"DEAR SUMNER,

"I know not how to express to you the unfortunate
news, which a visit from Lord Liverpool to the King obliges me
to communicate to you. As his minister, he objects to your
appointment to the vacant canonry of Windsor, and says he
must resign if your nomination is persisted in. The voluminous
correspondence on the subject it would be useless to detail. My
feelings of what you would wish to be done have induced me
to say that you would not hesitate in returning the King's
word for the appointment, sooner than have the ministers
resign on your account. This has been done this day. And
now I have only to excuse myself from not having gone to you
in person. This, however, I did not feel at all capable of doing
on such a trying subject. I trust, however, soon to be the organ
of very different news from the present, and shall only request
my best remembrances to Mrs. Sumner.

"Yours ever truly,

"MOUNT CHARLES."

THE SAME TO THE SAME.

"BRIGHTON, *April* 16*th*, 1821.

"MY DEAR SUMNER,

"I was really in such a state yesterday when I wrote,
that I scarcely knew what I said, or what I ought to say. You
know me enough to believe that I am a bad hand at communicating bad news; the shorter that is done the better. The dis-

---

* This and the former letter from Lord Liverpool are quoted from Yonge's
"Life of Lord Liverpool," iii., 151–155.

appointment you have experienced, I need not say what I feel,
will eventually turn out much to your advantage ; this is my only
consolation. If you had seen the King on the occasion, you
would have given up all your own feelings, and have been
interested entirely by his. I never saw anything like it. He
was quite in despair. I hope in a few days to write something
which may be of more solid advantage than writing consolatory
letters, but I am for the present obliged to hold my tongue.
What hurts me most is, that the only objection Lord Liverpool found was that you were a curate. Perhaps to you it may
be matter of consolation—to me it is otherwise. My best
remembrances to Mrs. Sumner.

" Yours very truly,

" MOUNT CHARLES."

The following letter was written on the evening of the day on
which the preceding one was despatched :—

THE SAME TO THE SAME.

" MY DEAR SUMNER,

" The King has just been here. He appoints you his
private Chaplain on £300 a year. A capital house in Windsor,
opposite the Park gate. Other arrangements are in progress,
which, if they take place, will, I trust, make you as comfortable
as the canonry. I recommend you to give up the pupils, if you
have written about them, as, depend upon it, the King will
never rest until something is done. If you prefer keeping any
of the boys, you are to take them to the house at Windsor, but
I would recommend your only having Albert.* This, however, is
for *your* consideration. When I go to town I am to see your
house at Windsor. If your furniture at Highclere does not do
it is to be furnished. I can only say this arrangement is a
small relief to me for your disappointment. The King has not

* Lord Albert Conyngham had been with Mr. Sumner as pupil during the
whole of his residence at Highclere.

been himself since Lord Liverpool's visit. But you are to have
a copy of all the correspondence. The King has ordered an
express to be sent off to you, that you may not suffer more
than can possibly be avoided. His feelings have been mortally
wounded. He never will forgive it.

> "Yours very truly,
>
> "MOUNT CHARLES."

"BRIGHTON, *Monday, 6½ o'clock, p.m.*"

THE SAME TO THE SAME.

"Now that we are a little reconciled to your disappointment
by seeing good arise out of evil, I may tell you that there
never was anything which threw such a gloom of despair on all
our faces or made such an impression on our spirits. I am still
of opinion, which I wrote by the express, that I would advise
the young gentlemen to go to their respective friends; it
is true you will not be canon at Windsor this time, but as
the King most kindly quoted at dinner when he saw my
agony,

'Nil desperandum Teucro duce, et auspice Teucro.'

"You cannot conceive what he suffered on the occasion. He
is, without exception, the best hearted man that ever breathed.*
My best remembrances to Mrs. Sumner."

In consequence of this letter Mr. Sumner at once went down
to Brighton, and, whilst expressing his deep gratitude to the
King for the preferment which he was anxious to bestow upon
him, assured his Majesty that he would not suffer any private
feeling to interfere with arrangements which might be represented to him as more advisable, and would therefore cheerfully
resign all claims to the canonry.

---

* It is clear that the King's better feelings, when roused, were of no ordinary
strength. For I have been told by a friend of Bishop Sumner's, who heard it from
him, that on one occasion the King stood leaning his arms on the mantel-piece
for two hours pleading for a respite for a criminal condemned to death.

Although, therefore, the King's nomination was withdrawn, and the following letters ultimately proved inapplicable, they may properly be inserted here.

REV. J. SUMNER TO REV. C. SUMNER.

"Sunday Evening.

"MY DEAR CHARLES,

"I should not have been a whit more surprised this morning, if a letter had arrived telling me that I was canon of Windsor, than I was made by the intelligence conveyed by yours. I had not the least idea even that there was a vacancy, and from the way in which I spoke of the subject when we met at Christmas, you will judge how little I had expected that a vacancy there could benefit you. I may truly add, that I should not have been near so happy, if the information could have related to myself, and I do most sincerely rejoice in the extreme comfort which this desirable preferment throws over your future prospects . . . May you, my dear Charles, derive every advantage from it which it is capable of bestowing: you have shown yourself able to *endure hardness;* and the same light which the obscurity of a curacy has not concealed, will equally, I dare predict, prove itself a light from Heaven, now that it will shine more publicly in the sight of men. I shall not wonder if you were disappointed of some part of the pleasure which you anticipated in surprising my mother with the intelligence. It is not her nature to be suddenly elated. There were no drawbacks to *our* satisfaction, when I announced it at breakfast to-day, Mr. Bird, Mary, and Elizabeth, being added to our usual party.

"Man and wife are so much one, that I cannot congratulate Jennie as separate from you. But I delight myself with thinking of the gratification she must receive in the idea of your labours being so soon rewarded, and so likely to be abridged as they now will be.

"May the Author of every good and perfect gift bless your prosperity!

"'Give what He can, without Him we are poor;
And with Him rich, take what He will away.'

"We are all quite well.

"Your most affectionate brother,

"J. B. S.

"Cannot you take us in your way to or from Windsor ?"

R. BIRD, Esq. TO REV. C. SUMNER.

"MAPLE-DURHAM, 8 *April*, 1821.

"MY DEAR SIR,

"We were much surprised at breakfast this morning by an ejaculation from J. B. (Sumner). When will blessings cease to be poured out upon our family? What cause we have to be thankful! We were not less interested than gratified when we heard that you were the object of it in your appointment as canon of Windsor, upon which I most sincerely congratulate you and yours. Thus has your own conscientious decision relative to the Irish preferment been rewarded even in this life . . .

"Yours sincerely and affectionately,

"ROBERT BIRD."

The King was determined that Mr. Sumner should be no loser by his not being preferred to the canonry at Windsor. He at once appointed him Historiographer in ordinary, private Chaplain to His Majesty's household at Carlton House, and also Librarian in ordinary; all which offices were vacated by Dr. James Stanier's promotion. The following entry in Mrs. Sumner's journal shows what her feelings were on this subject :—

"Nous avons besoin de prier Dieu, avec plus de ferveur que jamais, que la prosperité ne nous fasse pas oublier de qui nous tenons tous les bienfaits."

Mr. Sumner went at once to Windsor in order to see his future home, and, on the top of the coach, on his way back to

Highclere, composed the following verses, describing an event which had actually happened at Windsor a short time previously :—

'Twas at the witching hour of night,
When shadowy forms have power to fright,
   And shapes unearthly rove ;
And fancy sees in every spray
That waves across the lonely way,
   Some spectre of the grove.

All silent lay and hushed in sleep
On stately Windsor's terrac'd steep,—
   Save when amid the gloom,
The pacing sentry's hollow tread
Sounds like the echo of the dead,
   Flitting around the tomb.

Pale Hecate's beam in curious cloud
In mists eternal seemed to shroud,
   Each ling'ring star withdrew,
While screaming as she left her nook
Where erst unheeded sleep she took,—
   The startled jackdaw flew.

Sudden, athwart the soldier's walk
A giant ghost appeared to stalk,
   Majestic, sad, and slow.
What seemed his arm extended high
Show'd beck'ning to the upper sky,—
   Mute harbinger of woe.

Full well, I ween, the stoutest heart
That e'er in combat played its part,
   Nor feared the battle's storm,
Had stood appall'd to see such sight,
And gazed in motionless affright
   On that unearthly form.

A moment paused the soldier brave,
The next the wonted challenge gave.—
   "Stand, ho ! Art friend or foe ?"
The echoing battlements reply,
Sole answer to the length'ning cry,—
   Then all was mute below.

One effort more the warrior made,
Forth from its scabbard drew his blade,
   Full oft in battle tried ;

> Unhurt, unharm'd, the phantom fled,
> Though the good steel had cleft his head—
> The soldier sank and died ! *

The effect of a spectral figure had been produced by a magic-lantern, and the practical joke had thus ended in the sentry's death.

The next few months were fully occupied in making the necessary arrangements for leaving Highclere. His rector was most kind in consulting his convenience in every way. He writes, on hearing from Mr. Sumner of his intention of giving up the curacy :

"I received your letter this morning, as it was delayed a day or two in Grosvenor Square. I most heartily congratulate you on your preferment, although the loss to myself and Highclere is by no one more fully appreciated."

It was necessary that occasional visits should be paid to Windsor and London. The following extract is from a letter written at this time from London :—

"All my appointments are confirmed, and I shall have a living, perhaps immediately—certainly very soon ; it is Lyme, in Dorsetshire, on the sea coast. This prospect is delightful."

The prospect, however, delightful though it may have been,

---

* The Bishop of Winchester used occasionally throughout his life to write verses. One of his sons has a "Travellers' Book," in which guests at his house write their names, with any remarks they may be pleased to append. On two occasions when the Bishop was visiting his son he wrote the following verses :—

> I came—I went,—A vision short and sweet !
> Loth to depart ; but O how glad to meet !

> ⎧ I came—I went—one intervening day,
> ⎨ Emblem of life's brief span—no lengthen'd stay—
> ⎩ In early morn a babe—at even passed away.

And again—

> Not half a day, a single night —
> Late dinner, early bed —
> So quickly sped time's rapid flight—
> I came—I slept—I fled.

was not destined to be realised, as the following letter will show :—

MR. BROCKLEBANK TO SIR BENJAMIN BLOOMFIELD.

"FIFE HOUSE, 12*th July*, 1821.

"MY DEAR SIR,

"Lord Liverpool desires me to say that the vicarage of the parish of St. Helen's, Abingdon, having become vacant, he shall be very ready to submit the name of the Rev. Mr. Sumner to the King for the living if it should be agreeable to that gentleman ; and Lord L. will be much obliged to you if you will have the goodness to ascertain this for him.   Lord L. desires me to add that he understands the value of the living is about £300 per annum, but, the parish being extensive and populous, it requires great attention and assiduity on the part of the vicar, and Lord L. is therefore of opinion that no one should accept this living unless he is so circumstanced that he can undertake the duties of it.

"Believe me to be, my dear Sir,

"Yours very truly

"J. C. BROCKLEBANK.

"RIGHT HON. SIR BENJAMIN BLOOMFIELD."

The offer, accordingly, was made to Mr. Sumner, and, after anxious consideration, was accepted in the following terms, in a letter addressed to the King's secretary.

"DEAR SIR,

"I have to thank you for the communication you have transmitted to me informing me of Lord Liverpool's wish to submit my name to the King for the vacant vicarage of St. Helen's, Abingdon.   I beg to be allowed to express, through you, my best thanks to his Lordship for his intention.

"I have taken the liberty of delaying my answer for a day, that I might have full time for considering whether I could conscientiously undertake so important a charge consistently with my duties at the chapel of Cumberland Lodge. Were the distance more considerable, I should be led to doubt whether I could fulfil the expectations of Lord Liverpool, as intimated in the last paragraph of the letter you have had the goodness to send me, but under the circumstances of the case, I think I may safely be able to promise the attention which so populous a parish requires.

" I understand His Majesty is graciously pleased not to object to my occasionally providing for the service of Cumberland Chapel by deputy at some of the times when he shall not himself be there. I should therefore purpose to reside about half the year at Windsor, and half at Abingdon, having a permanent and resident curate at the latter place as well during my own stay there as in my absence, since I feel the duties of the situation could not properly be performed without such assistance.

" I presume this arrangement, which secures to Abingdon two resident clergyman for a part and one for the whole of the year, will be satisfactory, especially since it will be necessary for me to procure a house for the reception of my family, as there is none attached to the living, and as its proximity to Windsor will enable me to inspect the parish frequently during the time when I shall be called away to discharge my other functions.

" I have therefore to request that you will take the trouble of signifying to Lord Liverpool my thankful acceptance of his Lordship's offer.

" I have the honour to be," &c.

This letter was satisfactory to Lord Liverpool; the presentation was made, and Mr. Sumner was instituted to the vicarage of Abingdon September 4th, 1821.

His brother writes :—

" *August 4*, 1821.

" I hardly know whether you wish to be congratulated on so great an accession of care as the living of Abingdon. I trust,

however, that it may be a just subject of congratulation, if not
to yourself at least to the inhabitants of the place. You will
not be five pounds richer for the benefice, but it is an important
station, where your light may shine before men, and you may
justly hope to bring others within it."

His first introduction to the place is thus described in a
letter. He had taken Lord Albert Conyngham with him to
Abingdon.

" We arrived here about three o'clock on Thursday, and immediately repaired to Mr. Carter (the curate). Upon asking him
on the subject of lodgings, he kindly went out with us, and, on
his recommendation, I saw two miserable rooms at a bankrupt
draper's, where, after some consideration, they asked two
guineas a week. This seemed so enormous that I immediately
declined any further discussion with the party, and Mr. Carter
offered to give up his own for my accommodation—sleeping
himself at his own house, which is being painted and put in
order for the reception of his family, whither he had removed
nearly everything but himself. After proper inquiries as to
inconvenience, &c., this offer was accepted, and we are established accordingly at Miss King's boarding school for young
ladies. We have a ground-floor room, of tolerable comfort, and
one large bed-room, in which there is a bed placed on the floor
for Albert. I commenced housekeeping that night by pur-
chasing a small stock of tea and sugar, and Mr. Carter drank
tea with us after we had dined at the inn.

" The church will hold, and has held, nearly 4000 persons.
The clerk has a most sonorous voice, which echoes through the
aisles in a very pertinacious manner. The induction took place
yesterday, directly after the service. I ascended the belfry, not
without much difficulty, and tolled the bell. I had scarcely
been a quarter of an hour in the town on Thursday before the
bell began to sound to summon the ringers, and in less than an
hour they had begun their peal, which was continued from St.
Helen's and the other church at intervals. Yesterday they

gave another in the morning, and on my appearance on coming
to church, struck up again, so that they had an ample claim on
my generosity.   Then called Mrs. ——, widow of the late
incumbent, who had expressed a desire to see me, and after a
little emotion—though not more than was fitting—she civilly
offered me any of the papers relative to the living which might
be of use, which were afterwards sent.   Immediately afterwards
I sallied out on my visitation, which I carried on without
intermission till half-past six, when light failed me, and I
returned home to my mutton chop.   It was destined, however,
that I should not eat it in peace, for I held a continual *levée*
from the time of the appearance of the tart with different
individuals, till a quarter before eleven, when the cheese and
celery was taken from the table.   Albert escaped up to bed, and
I soon followed him, after a short preliminary nap over my cup
of tea, at which I was literally too tired to take a book.

"I purpose issuing forth this morning immediately after
breakfast, which I am expecting every moment, and shall not
return till I can see no longer, so that I hope to be able to
report progress.   It is a great pleasure to me to find Mr. Carter
so much liked here, that it would be a great injustice both to
him and the parish not to continue him as curate.   He seems
to have made himself acceptable and useful to the upper and
lower classes, and he visits, as I understand, very assiduously.
I have not yet spoken to him on the subject, but if my
pilgrimage of to-day confirms my impressions of yesterday, I
shall not hesitate to engage with him.

"Quarter before seven.   I am just returned home, weary and
hungry, and am very glad that I had written thus far before I
went out.   I have worked without intermission since nine
o'clock, and have been to more than 100 houses."

During the last few months of his stay at Highclere he must
have been very locomotive.   The King's librarian must of
necessity be presented at Court.   His attendance at the *levée*
is thus graphically described :—

" I am now (five o'clock) this moment come in from the *levée*—as tired and hot and swarthy as an African just unpacked from a slave ship. . . . . I was sworn in this morning at the Lord Chamberlain's office. The warrants are dated the 21st of May. The King received me most kindly to-day, and gave me a five minutes audience, to the extreme inconvenience and vexation of three or four hundred people who were pressing in after me. He does not seem in the least hurt by his fatigues."

His time in London was very fully occupied, for he writes, under date August 7, 1824 :—

" Your joint letter, which I have just received, is the first cordial I have had since I left Highclere. I shall certainly constitute myself a fixture, and get myself valued in future as such, in any house in which it may be my lot to be placed. I have been walking since half past eight this morning till the present hour at least twenty miles, and have stood as many more. On my return through Lambs Conduit Street, I found John looking into the shops for my dinner, for which I am now waiting with nearly the feelings of the ogre just before he threatened to eat Tom Thumb. I see two covers laid on the table—whether Mrs. Parry means to favour me with her company, *à la* landlady,—or whether it is in mockery of my solitary meal, I know not."

The arrangements which Mr. Sumner was able to make with regard to his successor at Highclere were very satisfactory. Coleridge, then curate of Cowley, afterwards Bishop of Barbadoes, strongly recommended the Rev. Alexander Dallas, the curate of Radley, and on his recommendation the appointment was made. It is thus referred to in the "Incidents in the Life and Ministry of the Rev. A. R. C. Dallas," p. 196 :—

" He (Mr. Dallas) received priest's orders at Salisbury on the 12th of August, and preached his first sermon at his new curacy on the 9th of September. This was his first introduction to Mr. Sumner, who had preceded him as curate of Highclere; and was thus an important era in his life—the commencement of a faithful and devoted friendship, which lasted to the close with unabated affection. From this time Bishop Sumner was the adviser, the friend to fly to in every emergency. His was the tender heart to sympathise, the ready hand to help, in all the perplexities and sorrows of Mr. Dallas' future course. He was also the faithful reprover, when his more enthusiastic friend out-stepped the bounds of prudence. . . Mr. Sumner invited him to pay him a visit, and offered to introduce him to his future charge. Various arrangements as to the house, led him into much intercourse with his predecessor, and on his first visit, Mr. Dallas thus writes to his wife :—

"'HIGHCLERE PARSONAGE, *September*, 7, 1821.

" 'I passed yesterday the most affecting day I ever remember, and one at the same time that, by showing me in a most pointed manner the delightful reward that attends the execution of a clergyman's duty, has given me, if possible, a stronger excitement than ever to the discharge of my own duties.

" 'We arrived about ten o'clock, and found that Sumner had just sent off the last of his furniture.—We then mounted two ponies, for Sumner had borrowed one for me, and we went round the whole parish in spite of the rain, which set in as if it meant to last all day.—The affecting farewell of these poor people, the blessings which they poured upon the head of their pastor, the tears and sobs which followed his shake of the hand, went to my very heart.—We did not return to the parsonage till near seven : poor Sumner was much overcome.' "

The Sunday preceding the date of the above letter, had been a trying one to Mr. Sumner. It was the last Sunday that he was to spend at Highclere. His text in the morning service was taken from Deut. xxx. 19, part of 20.

"19. I call heaven and earth to record this day against you, that I have set before you life and death, blessing and cursing : therefore choose life, that both thou and thy seed may live :

"20. That thou mayest love the Lord thy God, and that thou mayest obey his voice, and that thou mayest cleave unto him : for he is thy life, and the length of thy days : "

And in the afternoon Mr. Barter, his rector, preached. He referred in the warmest possible manner, and with much emotion, to his curate's indefatigable work in the parish, and urged the people in moving terms not to forget the lessons which they had been taught by him. A few days after this, and the Highclere life is over. The whole family—parents, and four children all of whom were born there—moved to Windsor.

There are those still living in the Hampshire village who to the present day retain most affectionate recollections of the Bishop as curate in their midst. One who afterwards raised himself above the position of a labouring man, and kept a little shop in the village, gratefully traced all his prosperity, under God, to Mr. Sumner. He was but a village lad, and whilst at school was engaged on Saturday, which was a holiday, to pick stones in the parsonage field. At the end of the day Mr. Sumner was so pleased with his industry, that he gave him eighteen pence for his day's work, but instead of handing it to the lad, put it for him into the savings bank. This gave the boy the first thought of husbanding his earnings, and proved the nest-egg of what eventually turned out a moderate competency. Another, whose cottage wall is decorated by two portraits of the Bishop, loves to recall the days when she came as servant maid with the newly-married couple to Highclere parsonage, and the affectionate interest which the Bishop always took in her welfare after her marriage, which necessitated her leaving his service. "Cast thy bread upon the waters" and it shall be found after many days, was eminently true of the curate of Highclere both in temporal and spiritual matters.

CHAPTER V.

Duties at Windsor and Carlton House.—Is presented by Lord Liverpool to a
Canonry at Worcester.—Resigns St. Helen's, Abingdon.—Effects of his
Ministry there.—Is Installed at Worcester.—Extracts from Letters to Mrs.
Sumner.—His Influence over the King.—Remarkable Scene in connection
with it.—Good trait in George the Fourth's Character.—As Librarian
examines and reports upon Napoleon's Library from Elba.—Service under
difficulties.—Criticisms of a friend's Sermons.—Advice to the same on Ministerial conduct.

THE year 1821 marks, no doubt, a very important epoch in
Mr. Sumner's life. It was the first step of the ladder, up which
he subsequently rapidly mounted. At Windsor, his duties were
of a somewhat multifarious character. The King used to live
for the most part, when he was at Windsor, in retirement at
Cumberland Lodge, and it was in the chapel attached to the
lodge, that his chaplain officiated. Here, Sunday after Sunday,
a rustic congregation was gathered together. The house where
Mr. Sumner's family resided was in Windsor, but he had also
a room in Carlton House, London, where he performed his
duties as librarian. These must have been very interesting to
him as a literary man, for almost all new books of any merit
were sent to the King through the librarian's hands, and I have
often heard the Bishop of Winchester refer to the intense excitement he felt in cutting the pages of Walter Scott's novels, and
reading them some weeks before they were issued to the public.

As librarian, he was also much interested in 1822 in making
a careful examination of a number of books which were returned
from Elba after Napoleon's death. A library had been sent
out from England to Napoleon, during his stay at Elba, and on

his death these books were sent back. By the King's desire, Mr. Sumner looked through all the volumes, and selected those in which Napoleon had made any annotations. Some of the books were very much marked; "Ossian" seemed to have been an especial favourite with him, and in one of the volumes there was a parallel drawn between himself and Alexander the Great, written in a small scratchy handwriting on foolscap paper. At the beginning of this year he was summoned to Brighton, where the King presented him to Lord Liverpool, and very shortly after this introduction, when the Hon. and Rev. Richard Bagot was appointed Canon of Windsor, thereby vacating a prebendal stall at Worcester, Lord Liverpool appointed him to the latter post. Mr. Sumner felt it his duty at once to make all necessary arrangements for resigning St. Helen's, Abingdon, inasmuch as his residence at Worcester, in addition to the time spent at Windsor, would have necessitated so long an absence from his living, and accordingly, in the spring, he resigned it into the hands of his successor, Dr. Pearson.

It is most interesting to find in a letter from Mr. Sumner, dated Windsor, Feb. 14, 1823, that his influence made itself felt, even in the short six months during which he was vicar of St. Helen's, Abingdon.

"I have had another letter from —— of Abingdon. It is seldom that so short a connection as mine with that town is productive of so much pleasure. Some things have come to my knowledge since I left it, which have often inclined me to lament my separation from it, and they have taught me that the harvest must not always be estimated by the apparent measure of productiveness, for no man can count his sheaves till they are laid up in his granary."

Almost immediately after the resignation of his living, he entered on his new duties as Canon of Worcester. Under date April 13, he writes from Worcester :—

"The bells have just struck up a merry peal in honour of my installation, which they take this method of reporting to the

town ; the said installation consisted in my being introduced to
the chapter room by the sub-dean, acting for the dean in the absence of the latter, and after taking three several oaths, some of
which I had previously taken before the Bishop, I was conducted
into my stall in the cathedral, and then placed in possession of
all the rights, privileges, honours, and appurtenances thereunto
belonging, &c.   After this ceremony, the service was performed,
and at its conclusion we again adjourned to the chapter room,
where I was admitted to a vote and voice in the councils of the
cathedral, &c."

The following description of a sentimental letter is worth
inserting :—

"——'s letter is the repetition of a twice told pastoral,
and after finishing it, one is apt to ask for something to set the
teeth on edge.   A little nature is worth a world of such measured
sentimentality, and I fear both head and heart, unless she
extricates herself quickly from this mannerism, will be lost in
affectation.   It would be quite a relief to meet with a sentence
not written for effect, or which failed in its construction, but she
seems to have fallen irresistibly into the worst insipidity of
toujours perdrix."

The whole of this year 1822, as well as 1823, was spent in
his duties alternately at Worcester and Windsor, a weekly visit
being paid to Carlton House, when the king was not at Windsor.
In the early part of 1822 he was much interested in a re-
arrangement of the interior of the chapel at Cumberland Lodge,
with reference to which the King, in the most handsome manner,
gave him *carte blanche*, and the services in the little chapel,
which held about a hundred people, were very satisfactory.*

---

* The subsequent history of this Royal Chapel is as follows :—After George
the Fourth's death, Cumberland Lodge was pulled down, with the exception of
a few rooms and a conservatory, which still remain.   The chapel, too, was left
for the use of the inhabitants of Windsor Park.   On the death of the Duchess
of Kent, who was a constant worshipper at the chapel during her residence at
Frogmore, the Queen, wishing to perpetuate her memory there by a window,
caused a new chancel to be built to receive it.   This was consecrated by the

One story in connection with his duties at the chapel is so highly creditable to George the Fourth, as well as to his chaplain,* that it must be recorded.

It happened one Sunday that the King was desirous of receiving the Holy Communion. He was usually in the habit of receiving it alone and fasting at ten o'clock, but on this particular occasion, he wished to have the service an hour earlier, and accordingly desired that his chaplain should be in readiness at nine o'clock. The King was punctual to the time appointed, but no chaplain was there. An hour passed away, and still Mr. Sumner did not appear. The King grew impatient, and on inquiry ascertained that the servant to whom the message had been entrusted had entirely forgotten to deliver it. The consequence was that the King at once dismissed him from his service. When the chaplain arrived at the usual hour, unconscious of anything out of the common way having occurred, he found the whole court in dismay. The King was in a violent passion, and unable to control himself. Mr. Sumner at once went into the royal presence, and on the King expressing a wish to receive the Holy Communion, told him plainly that he did not seem at that time in a fit state to receive it; that he must learn to restrain his passion; that it was his duty to be in charity with all men, and that he must show by his forgiveness of the servant whom he had dismissed that such was the state of his mind at that time. The King took the rebuke in good part, and expressed his sorrow at what had occurred, and Mr. Sumner then further said, that if he had really forgiven the servant and bore no enmity against him, his Majesty ought to reinstate him in his service, which would afford a proof to all of his real regret at what had taken place. At this stage Mr. Sumner requested

---

Bishop of Oxford, November 3, 1863. Three years afterwards the rest of the old chapel was pulled down, and a new building erected of a more suitable character in its stead, which was re-opened for public worship on Christmas Day, 1866.

* He had been appointed Chaplain-in-Ordinary to His Majesty, January 8th, 1823, and also Deputy-Clerk of the Closet by the Bishop of Lincoln (Pelham), March 25, 1824.

the King's permission to retire, to enable his Majesty quietly
to think over the whole matter. Accordingly the King was
left alone for a short time, and when his chaplain was re-
admitted into his presence, the King told him that he would
grant the request which had been made, and that the servant
should be restored to his former place. Emboldened by his
success, Mr. Sumner urged one further point, that the King
should not receive the Holy Communion alone, but with the
rest of the household, after the service. For some time the
King demurred to this, but at last consented, and knelt at the
Holy Table with his household, the servant who had been in
fault being included in the number of the communicants. It is
only right to add, that some time afterwards the King, with
much heartiness, thanked his chaplain for the line which he
had taken in the whole matter.

Another incident connected with the royal life at Cumberland Lodge, shows Mr. Sumner's influence for good over the
King. The King one day asked his chaplain, what mark of
royal favour he could bestow upon him, in return for his good
offices towards himself. He replied that the King's kindness
towards him left nothing which he could personally desire,
but that the King had it in his power to do what would cause
him the greatest happiness, and that was to have family prayers
for his household, and after this the practice was begun for the
establishment at Cumberland Lodge.

The following anecdote as to an exceptional case of difficulty in carrying on the services at Cumberland Lodge Chapel,
is not without interest. It happened one Sunday in January,
1823, that there had been a fall of snow the night before, so
heavy as to render the roads almost impassable. Mr. Sumner
sent to the inn for a chaise and pair to take him to church, but
the answer was, that no chaise and pair could travel along the
road. "Then send a chaise and four," was the prompt reply.
But the landlord was inexorable, and would not allow a horse
to leave his stables. Accordingly Mr. Sumner had to make his

way through the snow, which was two feet deep, to the chapel. It took him two hours of hard work to get over the ground, and when he reached the chapel, he found only the clerk and one man to represent the congregation. With characteristic common sense he requested them to come with him to the house of a sick man whom he wished to visit, and read the service in the sick man's room.

His journey back to Windsor was not quite so laborious as his journey from the town, for he carefully stepped in all his old foot-marks, and thus reached his house (on the testimony of an eye-witness) more nearly dead than alive.

Mr. Sumner's sermons at Cumberland Lodge, were very simple and unassuming. His endeavour was to preach, without respect of persons, such sermons as he thought would be suitable for the whole congregation, and in order to carry out this his intention, the first sermon which he preached there was not one written for the occasion, but one selected from his old Highclere stock.. It is clear that as time passed on, his opinions on religious subjects were gradually but very strongly formed; and it is easy to gather from some criticisms on a volume of sermons sent to him by his friend Mr. Dallas for that purpose, that his views on controverted points were deeply and conscientiously held.

REV. C. SUMNER TO REV. A. DALLAS.

"Windsor, *July* 14, 1823.

"My dear Dallas,

"It was with great pleasure I finished the perusal of your sermons. I have little to remark in the way of criticism. What, however, has occurred to me you shall have freely and unreservedly. '*Simple acquiescence in the will of God*' can scarcely be conceived to be a feature in the character of the saints in heaven, whose delight it must be to anticipate His commands, and whose greatest joy to see the conversion of a sinner (Luke xv. 7) and the execution of God's purpose respecting mankind. I do not like your '*conditions;*' God's mercy is in every scriptural sense of the word unconditional. Altogether there is in this part, according to my views, too much of working, working, working, to accord with what seems to me to be delivered respecting the *gift* of salvation. You will not mistake my meaning, and suppose that I am Antinomian enough to leave out of my copy of the Bible that 'without holiness no man shall see the Lord.' God forbid! But it appears to me that there is a slight confusion and want of clearness in the expression of your ideas on this very awful and important subject. I should say that you put the cart before the horse, or in other words place sanctification in the room of justification.* We are justified freely through the blood of Christ, without condition or stipulation, and sanctification is the new life, the happy result of that unconditional and unpaid-for forgiveness. See 2 Thess. ii. 13 and Rom. vi. 23. I have always understood this very difficult clause,—so far as I have understood it—and I altogether confess great ignorance about it,—to be intended not in the way of *condition* or *compact*, for salvation would then be of works and not of grace, but in the way of connection, since the performance of the duty there enjoined, or of any other duty, only gives us a claim so far as God has engaged Himself by his promises, and not a meritorious title.

"'*Our utmost endeavours to please God.*' It should be more clearly explained that our power to please God is altogether derivative. The great Shibboleth of all congregations is the difficulty of understanding the necessity of the effusion of grace, and consequently their besetting sin is the neglect of applying in prayer for the Holy Spirit. If you talk of '*endeavours*' you should (I speak of course *opinionatively* and not

---

* Those who were ordained at Farnham by the Bishop of Winchester will remember how strongly he was in the habit of pressing upon the candidates for holy orders the necessity of their clearly understanding the relative places of justification and sanctification in the scheme of salvation.

G

authoritatively) teach at the same time in whose strength those endeavours are to be attempted, lest like the Israelites they should go up to take possession of Canaan with dependence on their own arm and power alone.

" ' *Persevering in that line of conduct which through the merits of our atoning Saviour will ultimately ensure us admission,*' &c.   I think your language here, although I am well aware that such an interpretation is very far from being an expression of your belief with regard to the doctrine in question, implies that our Saviour's merits are a sort of make-weight, a kind of additional property thrown in, to fill up some deficiency in ourselves, instead of being represented as the only and solely efficacious and meritorious cause of salvation.   If this criticism be fair it shows how necessary it is to be guarded and explicit in weighing every turn of expression which relates to the fundamental doctrines of Christianity.

" I should have liked the sermons to be more systematically divided into parts, which, however inelegant it may be as far as the mere style is considered, is the only way to imprint a sermon on the memory of an unlearned congregation."

Writing to the same friend he says :—

" Heber I hope is the new Bishop of Calcutta.   He will do for this situation.   He has zeal and some judgment, and I trust and believe much sincerity.   It is indeed a station of awful responsibility and deep interest, and the man who goes out there with right feelings may well ask ' who is sufficient for these things ? '   But if an uncultivated field for exertion—if millions of ignorant souls—if corruptions and abominations of fearful extent and deepest dye can stir up Christian energies and warm to exertion a heart which has a sense of vital religion—then the Bishop of Calcutta is a man who has before him a high and honourable course to run, in which an Evangelist even of the olden time would find full scope for his abilities and a pressing call upon his self-devotion.   Be he who he may, he will need all the prayers of the friends of Christianity."

It may be well too here to insert the following remarks to a brother clergyman who had written to him respecting a marked change in the life of one of his parishioners of high rank.

REV. C. SUMNER TO REV. ——

"The letter from —— is really couched in terms that could not have been anticipated. I see nothing to make me distrust the sincerity with which it is written, and assuming it to be the real expression of his feelings, I know not what could be wished for more at the present stage of his case. We sometimes talk of feeling a *want* of encouragement, but it rather seems to me that a tenfold measure of support is frequently given if we were but quick-sighted enough to discover it and candid enough to acknowledge it. I shall watch the progress of this business with great interest, for it seems an opening to great usefulness, and the immediate results have certainly been permitted to be seen much more clearly and promptly than is usually the case. If you find it possible to give in any delicate way a hint to —— not to feel discouraged, and above all not to suffer himself to undergo a reaction, should he find feelings not corresponding with his own among many of his former friends, it might prove seasonable. As first impressions wear off there is much danger to be apprehended if he moves much among people of a lower standard than his own to whom it would be a great object to prevent any serious and permanent change taking place in their former associate. This however is a chord which can only be touched by a master hand, which is precisely the reason why I suggest it to you."

To the same clergyman, touching the preaching of Lent lectures in a neighbouring parish, he writes :—

"I am ashamed to find on reference to your letter, that you ask me a question relative to the Lent lectures at —— and now the Ides of March are past and Lent has begun. Advice is now like that always given by 'the *late* Lord Chatham,' but had it

G 2

been offered to you at a more seasonable time, it would have been given against your *originating* any steps for preaching there. I think you would be decidedly wrong to decline any opening which might occur, or to express any backwardness, if the subject were started, but after what has occurred it seems to me that the first motion cannot in delicacy or propriety come from yourself, and that you will stand on higher and more useful ground if 'not unsought' you are 'won.' The feeling which —— evinced would probably have scarcely yet evaporated, even in a man of his apathetic temperament, and yet this in my mind is a very secondary consideration. For though I would not wantonly and gratuitously hurt the least sensitive organ in the veriest worm that crawls the spiritual vineyard, yet I hold that less respect is to be paid to individual interests than to general edification. But general edification depends much on times and seasons, and if we precipitate the 'mollia tempora fandi' there is danger lest we run too fast and overshoot the mark. But all this is trite, and will have occurred to yourself long before you read it."

CHAPTER VI.

MR. SUMNER by this time must have been accustomed to
receive letters and dispatches on the subject of preferment, but
a case of much perplexity arose in January, 1824, when greatly
even to his surprise he received the following letter from Lord
Bathurst, the Colonial Secretary :—

"DOWNING STREET, *January* 22nd, 1824.

(PRIVATE AND CONFIDENTIAL.)

" SIR,

" His Majesty's Government having in contemplation
to place the Church of England established in Jamaica and the
Leeward Islands under Episcopal control, from a full persuasion
that religious instruction is the surest foundation of any system
which may be adopted for the melioration of the black population ; and that such instruction will be most beneficially communicated according to the doctrines of the English Church,
propose to constitute two Sees, one for Jamaica, and the other
for the Leeward Islands.

" As much will depend on the character and conduct of the
Prelates to be selected on this occasion, I have felt it my duty

to consult those whose professional connections are best calculated to give me the necessary information, and it is their decided opinion, as well as that of Lord Liverpool, that you, Sir, are the person whose appointment would give the most general satisfaction and be most likely to lay the foundation of an establishment on a broad and efficient footing. Its inadequacy as at present formed, and its virtual independence of all wholesome control have been long a subject of complaint among those who have looked to the welfare of the colonies, and now that the attention of the public is awakened to the subject, the time seems propitious for any person of an active mind, and zealous for the promotion of Christianity, to take a prominent lead in so desirable an undertaking.

"It is intended that each See should be endowed with a provision of £4000 sterling annually, and that at the expiration of twelve years the bishop shall be entitled to a retirement of £1000 sterling annually. It will be expected that whoever accepts the situation should vacate whatever preferment he may at present enjoy.

"In proposing to you the bishopric of Jamaica I by no means intend to preclude that of the Leeward Islands in the event of your preferring it. It may perhaps be some inducement for you to accept this offer by being informed that a gentleman who, I understand, is in habits of friendship with you, Mr. Coleridge, is the individual to whom it is proposed to fill the other See. I must not conclude without adding that I should not have thought it consistent with my duty to the King to have given you even any intimation of what is intended until I had submitted it to His Majesty—and His Majesty has been graciously pleased to allow me to make this proposition to you.

"I have the honour to be,

" Sir,

"Your obedient humble servant,

"BATHURST."

This letter was addressed to the Rev. J. Sumner, instead of the Rev. C. Sumner, and accordingly the following reply was sent to Lord Bathurst :—

REV. C. SUMNER TO LORD BATHURST.

"I have the honour to acknowledge the receipt of your Lordship's letter, communicating the intention of H. M. Government to constitute two Sees, one for Jamaica and the other for the Leeward Islands—and proposing to me the acceptance of one of the bishoprics which it is in contemplation to establish. But as I perceive the address of the letter is to the Rev. J. Sumner, the initial letter of my brother's Christian name, and as I cannot but feel conscious how much more justly the kind expressions used in the body of the letter are applicable to him, than to me, I think it my duty in the first instance to state the mistake, and request your Lordship will take the trouble of informing me whether the offer in question was directed to me at this place by an error.

"In the event of its having been meant to propose me to fill this important post I should beg to be allowed permission to mention the subject to one or two of the nearest members of my family who seem to have a claim on my confidence in such a matter before I return your Lordship a final answer."

Lord Bathurst replied that though the initial letter was wrong it *was* the Rev. C. Sumner to whom the offer was intended to be made.

Great indeed was the difficulty and responsibility of deciding in so important a matter. In the first place the King had to be consulted. Then inquiries had to be made with reference to the climate, &c., and the subjoined letters show that the course to be adopted was simply considered as a question of duty.

REV. C. SUMNER TO SIR WILLIAM KNIGHTON.

"I have received two very kind and flattering and I may say feeling letters from Lord Bathurst, in which his Lordship has offered to my acceptance the choice of one of the new bishoprics which it is the intention of Government shortly to establish in the West Indies. I cannot but feel that in my particular situation my first duty, from gratitude and every other feeling, is owed to His Majesty. I would therefore take the liberty of requesting you to submit to His Majesty my readiness to devote myself to the proposed service, provided it is His Majesty's pleasure to permit me to undertake it."

The King sent him word to "consider all things in all ways, and to make up his mind for the best, and then before giving his answer to Lord Bathurst to come to him."

To Rev. A. Dallas, after giving the details of the proposal, he writes :—

"Such is the proposition which has just been made to me, and which, when the subject and sphere are considered to which it refers, ought to be received, by whomsoever it is sent to, on his knees. It is, of course, a strictly confidential communication, and I think myself at liberty at present only to mention it to those whose opinion I am in duty bound to consult, or to those from whom I can obtain such information as I want previous to returning my final answer. Your connection with Jamaica" (Mr. Dallas had a brother and sister there), " will enable you to give me some intelligence respecting the nature of the climate; its probable effect on European constitutions, more particularly on young children; whatever, in short, on this part of the subject, or on any other, occurs to you as material for me to know in forming my resolution. You will do me the justice to believe that these queries are not made with reference to myself. But I should be heartless, as well as

profligate, were I to overlook my immediate duty to my family
and my wife, and therefore, in the absence of any real knowledge myself on these points, I anxiously seek for some definite
information from those who are better acquainted with the
climate. You may suppose that my mind is filled with a
crowd of reflections—I hope not of an unsuitable nature to
such a call to a field of usefulness—but I cannot now indulge
in any of them.".

His brother, whom he consulted, writes :—

"MY DEAR CHARLES,—

"With respect to the offer communicated in your
letter of yesterday, I feel it impossible to give a direct opinion :
as I think it a case in which a man must decide according to
his own views and the impulse of his mind and conscience.
Here, in particular, you seem to me permitted to weigh
opposite motives. The situation is one of usefulness no doubt;
but many might question whether of more usefulness than the
one you leave. For though you might enforce the observance
of duty upon the incumbents of the West India livings, you
could not give them *souls* in the work, and those who have
seen these poor creatures perishing for years without turning
their attention towards them, are not likely to be spurred on to
useful exertion by external authority.

"Another circumstance makes the situation unpleasant.
The bishop is crammed down 'the throats of nine-tenths of
the planters, and must probably in the discharge of some
inevitable duty, or the expression of some inevitable opinion,
quarrel with the other tenth within a year, or compromise with
his conscience.

"Circumstanced as you are, the only question is whether
you see it to be a call, and upon this point I sincerely pray
that you may have direction from above, and decide in the way
that may be most likely to serve the cause of Christ.

"It is very gratifying to perceive in Jennie so much

steadiness of mind. She seems to be, in a degree which I could not have supposed, indifferent in her choice to stay or go, a circumstance which leaves you much more able to make a dispassionate determination than I should be in any similar case.

"May God direct your decision!

"Ever your most affectionate

"J. B. S.

"Monday morning.

"Two days' post to and from Worcester."

Dr. Ferguson also was consulted as to the healthiness of the locality, and after much deliberation, consultation, and prayer, it was determined that the offer should be accepted. But before acquainting Lord Bathurst with his determination, it was necessary for Mr. Sumner to go to Brighton to see the King. The result of his interview with His Majesty is best told in his own words, in a letter to an old Highclere friend :—

"After a medical consultation here respecting the probable effect of the climate on my wife and family, I went down to Brighton on Saturday prepared to accept the offer, and on arriving actually stated my view of the question, and that I felt it an absolute duty to go if the King permitted me. It then appeared that the King's own mind had been long ago made up on the subject, although he had thought it right to leave me to the unbiassed consideration of the question; that he was now advancing in years, and did not so easily attach himself to new persons, as at an earlier period of life; that he must expect many, and perhaps frequent illnesses, during which it was a satisfaction to him to know that I was at hand; that I suited him; that he had other views for me, &c., &c. In short, he entered into a detail of which you can form little idea, and left untouched no bearing of the subject which could even have passed through the mind of the man most interested on the subject. He finished by saying that if the expressions of his personal wishes were not sufficient, he should not hesitate to command.

"I, of course, immediately said, what I had felt from the beginning, that I considered it my first duty to comply with his desire, if he had any personal feeling on the subject, &c., &c. He then wrote to Lord Bathurst himself, stating that I had come prepared to accept, but that he did not choose to let me go, alleging the reasons which he had previously given to me.

"He sent up that letter on Sunday night with another from myself to him, in which I had stated my wish to accept the offer if he gave leave. I can give you a very imperfect idea of the kindness with which he entered into the whole business, and the minuteness with which he discussed every detail connected with it. It appears that the King was quite taken by surprise in the matter. Lord Liverpool, as Lord Bathurst afterwards told me, sent sixteen names to the Bishop of London, among which was mine, for the bishop to select from, and the offer made to me was the result. On my return to London on Monday I called on Lord Bathurst and Lord Liverpool and the Bishop of London to return thanks, explain, &c.

"If the feeling of envy is in any case allowable, I shall certainly feel some portion of it towards the man who is selected in my place to reap the harvest in this new field, or rather more properly speaking, to sow the seed for future labourers; but when I look at my family and think on all I should have given up, and the risk which they would have incurred, I cannot feel too grateful for having been permitted to stay without compromising my duty."

A few lines were added by Mrs. Sumner :—

"I hope and I know you think now the King deserves to be loved. He could not talk to Mr. Sumner of the possibility of his having left England and all the subjects connected with it without shedding tears. How deeply thankful do I feel that God should have found us ready to make every sacrifice for the love of Him, and that He was pleased after that not to put us to the many trials which must have accompanied the work."

With reference to the King's first sanctioning the offer and then refusing permission to Mr. Sumner to go, I may say that I have heard him state that the King allowed the offer to be made in order to test him, and see whether in practice he would act up to the principles he professed, and give up his prospects in England for a colonial bishopric. The result proved that the King had not formed a wrong estimate of his chaplain.

The following letter written from London, February 9, 1824, announces the fact to Mr. Dallas :—

"I have only time to tell you by this night's post that the King has positively refused me leave to go to Jamaica. He has behaved as he always does towards me, most beautifully and kindly; but has expressed so unequivocally his personal wishes on the subject, and has put them in such a way that, if I had not considered it my paramount duty to consult in the first instance his desire, I should have been the most ungrateful of beings had I acted contrary to it after what has passed. Coleridge goes. I have written the above in the sound of the bellman, and have no time for more now. You shall hear again shortly. In the meantime, I am quite sure it is better for me, spiritually speaking, to have been ready and desirous to go ; temporally speaking, it may be better for me to stay."

In the summer of 1824, Mr. Sumner was requested by Lord Liverpool, as Master of the Corporation of Trinity House, to preach the anniversary sermon at Deptford. With reference to this, he received the following characteristic letter from his friend Blomfield, who had just been appointed Bishop of Chester :—

"LONDON, *June 9th*, 1824.

" MY DEAR SIR,

" The preacher for the day on Trinity Monday, goes to the Trinity House, on Tower Hill, at eleven o'clock, where a breakfast is provided, after the demolition of which he proceeds (in full canonicals) in the Master's barge to Deptford. There he must continue to keep the Brethren awake for half an hour or so. He then returns to the Trinity House, and thence to the City of London Tavern to assist at a very extensive destruction of turtle—having first said grace—still in his robes.

" I do not remember to have introduced any clause into the bidding prayer, and yet I think it must be done; but you will meet the secretary at the Trinity House, who will give you the necessary information.

" Believe me, dear Sir,

" Yours truly,

" C. J. BLOMFIELD."

It is to be hoped that the preacher followed this excellent advice, and succeeded in retaining the attention of his audience. It may fairly be presumed that he did so, for at the request of the Elder Brethren of the Trinity House the sermon was afterwards printed and published.

Towards the close of this year, a very sad duty devolved upon Mr. Sumner. His old pupil, Lord Mount Charles, was lying dangerously ill at Nice, and it was the King's especial wish that his chaplain should go out to him there. Accordingly on the first of December, accompanied by Sir William Knighton, the King's physician, Mr. Sumner crossed the Channel *en route* for Nice. Travelling through France in those days was a very tedious business. The journey from Calais to Nice occupied no fewer than eight days and seven nights, the transmission of letters by post taking eleven days from Nice to Windsor.

He subsequently writes with regard to this, "I look back

upon one thing, much as Lord Byron did upon his exploit of swimming across the Hellespont—namely, that I travelled 1000 miles through the worst roads of France, in the worst month of the year, in eight days and nights—beating the mail by seventy-two hours."

On arriving at Nice, he found Lord Mount Charles evidently in a dying state. He was overjoyed to welcome his old tutor and friend, and Mr. Sumner had the great satisfaction of knowing that he was able to soothe the last hours of his old and affectionate pupil. It had been a great trial to him suddenly to be called upon to leave his home and his family, and that too for an uncertain period of time; but, ultimately, he felt amply rewarded for his self-sacrifice by the evident comfort afforded by his presence to Lord Mount Charles. In his first letter to his wife from Nice, he writes under the date of December 10th :—

"My own line of duty, putting feeling out of the question, seems to me to be evident. I cannot move from here, however gradual the sinking may be. Our comfort, therefore, for some time must be interrupted, and I assure you there are few trials which I have felt more severely than the necessity of opening my mind to the conviction that this interruption is unavoidable. It may perhaps be well to experience by the privation how great are my daily enjoyments when with my family, but I could have been well content to have remained with my former persuasion of this fact, unattended by new evidence." . . After mentioning the extreme pleasure with which Lord Mount Charles had welcomed him, he adds, "This is so far gratifying, that it proves that the sacrifice is not made in vain, so far as the feelings are concerned, and if it can be made subservient to good in a higher point of view, it will indeed be a source of pleasure to me, which will outweigh everything."

On December 14th he writes, after detailing a very interesting conversation with Lord Mount Charles :—

"I go into his room at eight o'clock in the morning, read the psalms and lessons to him, I pray with him for an hour—and again in the course of the day read the Bible and converse with him on points arising from it for about an hour and a half. On Friday I mean to administer the Sacrament to him—preparatory to which I am going through with him a regular explanation of it. . . . . ."

On Christmas Day he writes :—

"Mount Charles' state is now so precarious from hour to hour, that I never lie down at night without being prepared for seeing him go in the course of the next twelve hours."

And on the 27th :—

"I had scarcely been in bed an hour or two, and had not closed my eyes, when Conrad, his German servant, the most faithful and affectionate servant I ever saw, came into my room to tell me he thought him much worse. I rose immediately, and found the physician, Dr. Byrne, already there." . . . . (Sir W. Knighton had returned to England on the 20th). "He died in my arms at about a quarter before six. There cannot be a doubt that under all the circumstances it is a great blessing it has not pleased God to suffer him to linger through more weeks and months of an existence of great pain to himself and distress to his friends, and I shall never cease to reap the greatest comfort from the recollection that I was enabled to be with him in his last moments, and to offer him such consolation as he was capable of receiving. I have made all the necessary arrangements for his funeral, which will take place on Wednesday next. On Thursday morning early I hope to be able to start from hence, and I shall travel as fast as I can homewards."

On his return, he had the gratification of receiving the following letter from Sir W. Knighton :—

" DEAR MR. SUMNER,

"I am honoured with the commands of the King, to convey to you his Majesty's very kind regards, and to express how deeply his Majesty's feelings are impressed in all that relates to your general conduct on every occasion, both public and private. The peace of mind which your presence afforded to his Majesty's very dear friend, Lord Mount Charles, in his last moments has been the greatest consolation to his Majesty.

" I have the honour to be,

" Dear Mr. Sumner,

" Your sincere and affectionate servant,

" W. KNIGHTON."

This unexpected visit to Nice delayed for a short time the completion of a work which at the time excited very considerable interest. I allude to the publication of a translation of Milton's treatise on Christian doctrine, which had occupied Mr. Sumner's time and attention for more than a year.

Certainly, the prosecution of literary labours at Nice was carried on under great difficulties ; for under date December 18, 1824, he writes :—

" I hope to be able to make as much progress with Milton as will be possible for me without any other book but a Bible. The poverty of books here is very striking. I understand all Nice cannot furnish even a tolerable library, and there are no books for sale. This is the consequence of the intolerance of government both in religion and politics."

The carrying out of this work by the King's librarian arose in the following manner :—

Towards the close of 1823, Mr. Lemon, Deputy-Keeper of the State Papers, found a large Latin manuscript in one of the presses in the old State Paper Office. It bore the following title, " Joannis Miltoni Angli de Doctrina Christiana ex sacris duntaxat libris petita, Disquisitionum libri duo posthumi." With it were found a large number of original letters, informations, examinations, and other curious records relative to the Popish plots in 1677 and 1678 and to the Rye House plot in 1683. The same parcel likewise contained a complete and corrected copy of all the Latin letters to foreign princes and states written by Milton while he officiated as Latin Secretary, and the whole was enclosed in an envelope superscribed, " To Mr. Skinner Mercht." This manuscript, on examination, proved to be Milton's long lost essay on the doctrine of Christianity. On the matter being brought under the notice of the King, he felt that any treatise of Milton's ought not to remain buried in the State Paper Office, and entrusted the editing and translating of the work to Mr. Sumner, who took very great interest in the whole business ; and the reviewers of the day (including Macaulay in the *Edinburgh Review*) highly commended the skill and fidelity with which he had executed the task committed to him.

The editing and translating of this treatise was, however, a very laborious task. Being undertaken in addition to the ordinary duties of his post as librarian and chaplain, and his educational work with his children, it was necessary to curtail those hours which should have been devoted to sleep for this work. It was his habit at this time for several months to sit up night after night until three or four o'clock in the morning with a wet bandage on his forehead, and green tea by his side to ward off sleep.

But Mr. Sumner was not destined long to continue at this literary work. The King had made up his mind, that on the first vacancy on the bench, he should in some way be raised to a bishopric, but in June, 1825, a memorandum from Lord Liverpool to the King suggested the exchange of the prebendal stall at Worcester for one at Canterbury.

" Lord Liverpool submits to your Majesty Archdeacon Percy for the deanery of Canterbury, and Mr. Sumner for the prebend which will be vacated by the archdeacon's promotion, and will in no way interfere with any further promotion your Majesty may be pleased to confer on Mr. Sumner."

The following letter from Sir W. Knighton, revealed the King's further intentions :—

"London, 11th June, 1825.

" Dear Mr. Sumner,

"Let me tell you that Lord Liverpool has been most kind in everything relating to yourself, and when I mentioned to him His Majesty's wish that you should be *next* bishop, he made not the slightest difficulty. This has been repeated by his Lordship this day to the King in the most agreeable manner. Now, my dear friend, you must begin to do everything as if you were at this moment a bishop. . . . Be so good as to get rid of your shirt-frill and your trousers. It is the King's wish that you *immediately* take your doctor's degree.

" Believe me,

"With great affection,

" Your most attached friend,

"W. K."

Accordingly on June 27, 1825, Mr. Sumner resigned the stall at Worcester, and was instituted to one of the prebends of Canterbury, and in the next month was made D.D. by Royal Mandate.

Hitherto he had been spared domestic sorrow, both in his own family and in connection with his brothers and sister, but in January, 1826, his sailor brother died. With reference to this, an intimate friend writes to him :—

"It is not too much to say that your brother Henry seems to have been brought home to you last year that you might all know of a surety his state of preparedness for the change that awaited him, and be enabled from your inmost heart to apply such words as Bishop Heber's :—

'Thou art gone to the grave—we no longer behold thee,
    Nor tread the rough path of the world by thy side ;
But the wide arms of mercy are spread to enfold thee,
    And sinners may hope, since the Sinless has died.'"

Mr. Sumner undertook the painful task of breaking the sad news to his mother, at Milford, and on his return thence wrote to a friend :—

" I little thought when we parted how severe a blow was hanging over me. It has fallen indeed most awfully and most unexpectedly, and I hope not without profit. Our family has been of late years so much spared, that on looking into myself, I find that some such visitation was not unnecessary to awaken me from that state of unthinking security into which a long continued series of mercies tends to plunge us. The late illness of my eldest brother and this sad event have been sufficient to raise me to a full sense of the short-lived tenure by which we hold all earthly things. I am most happy to be able to say that my mother and sister are supported wonderfully in this trial. All the affections of the latter were centered in him, as was natural in her situation, without nearer objects of affection. But she bears the blow as I had anticipated, from my knowledge of her religious feelings."

" WINDSOR, *January* 31, 1826."

From letters written at the time, it is evident that Henry Sumner's death coming so unexpectedly was very much felt by every member of the family, and cast a gloom over them all which they found it difficult to shake off.

CHAPTER VII.

Translation of Bishop Van Mildert to Durham.—See of Llandaff and Deanery of St. Paul's thereby vacated, offered to Dr. Sumner.—Letters upon the subject. —Mrs. Sumner, with four children, goes to Geneva.—Letters to her from Dr. Sumner.—Confirmation at Bow Church.—Consecration at Lambeth.—Commences his Duties as Dean of St. Paul's.

THE King's librarian must have been more than mortal not to have mentally formed expectations of further preferment in the Church in consequence of his Royal Patron's avowed intentions respecting him. Nor had he to wait long for their realisation. For in March, 1826, Bishop Barrington of Durham died, and Bishop Van Mildert was appointed to succeed him, thus vacating the see of Llandaff, and the deanery of St. Paul's, which was at that time held *in commendam* with the Bishop-rick. In the following terms Lord Liverpool offered this preferment to Dr. Sumner.

"FIFE HOUSE, *March 25th,* 1826.

"MY DEAR SIR,

"Although I have little doubt that His Majesty will have communicated to you his gracious intentions in respect to you in consequence of the death of the late excellent Bishop of Durham, I think it nevertheless right to apprize you that he has conveyed to me his royal pleasure that you shall succeed to the Bishoprick of Llandaff and the deanery of St. Paul's, upon the translation of the present Bishop of Llandaff to the see of Durham.

"I have the greatest satisfaction, I can assure you, in making

this communication, as I feel myself justified in entertaining
the strongest conviction, from your past conduct, that you will
do credit to the preferment which His Majesty has determined
to bestow upon you.

"I am, with great truth,

"My dear Sir,

"Your very faithful, humble servant,

"LIVERPOOL."

The reply was as follows:—

"MY LORD,

"It is with feelings of great gratitude that I beg to
acknowledge the kindness with which your Lordship has communicated to me His Majesty's gracious intentions in my
favour.

"In undertaking the responsible duties to which I am about
to be called, my first desire is to be enabled to fulfil them with
a constant remembrance of Him to whom I shall one day be
accountable for the due discharge of such important functions.

"But, if to this high impulse I may be permitted to join
any secondary motive, I shall find the strongest incitement to
future exertion in the favourable opinion of my conduct which
your Lordship has expressed in a manner so gratifying to my
feelings on this occasion."

Lord Liverpool in connection with this writes to Sir William
Knighton:—"I shall leave London with my mind more at ease,
this business being settled and *well* settled."

The following extracts from the letters of congratulation
which poured in upon the Bishop elect are, for various
reasons, interesting:—

FROM HIS BROTHER, THE REV. J. B. SUMNER.

"This moment, five o'clock, Tuesday, I open your letter for
the first time. . . . Most heartily glad I am for your own

sake, and for the Church's sake, that you are safely seated on
the bench, and may there be many *tui similes!* You have so
conducted yourself in every situation which you have yet filled
that I feel a certain confidence for the future. You will be an
instrument in promoting both the glory of God and the good of
mankind. Marianne* regrets that she cannot write herself this
afternoon; but you and Jennie will give her credit for all she
feels on this occasion. The girls are already pleasing themselves with familiarising to themselves the phrase 'My uncle,
the Bishop.' I will write further about the Consecration
sermon at an early opportunity.

FROM THE SAME.

"*March* 31.

"MY DEAR CHARLES,

"I was obliged to write in such a hurry the other
day, in order to save the post, that I feel as if I had not said
half what I wished to say. Indeed, one advantage of a case
like yours is, that the more it is reflected on, the more satisfactory it appears; whether we consider the receiver, or the good
received. If it were possible to fly across the twenty-five miles
which separate us how much time might be saved by a few
hours' conversation.

"I should like to know many things concerning your See, as
whether it has any palace or *domicile*—for *palace*, I am sure it
has none. I remember seeing an old castle-like place at Cardiff,
in a state of dilapidation, which I think pertains to the bishoprick; but Llandaff is two or three miles distant, and as the
country about it is flat and comparatively uninteresting, I did not
deviate so far from my route, little thinking that I should ever
have reason to regret this lack of curiosity.

"I see that you have half Welsh and half English clergy to
deal with, if Monmouthshire may be rightly called England. I

---

* In 1803 Rev. J. B. Sumner had married Marianne, daughter of Captain
George Robertson, R. N. She died in 1829.

had a very kind letter from the Bishop of Gloucester congratulating me on your advancement, and speaking of you in the
most handsome terms.   Indeed, it is fortunate for your patrons
and yourself that your character silences jealousy.   About the
sermon—if on mature deliberation you decidedly wish me to
preach, I readily consent.   With kindest love to Jennie and
the bairns, believe me always, my dear Charles,

"Yours most affectionately,

"J. B. Sumner."

FROM THE SAME.

Writing on April 4, he says,—

"The sentiments with which you take your high office are
most satisfactory pledges of the manner in which you will
fulfil it; and you have a great advantage with you.   For
Raikes, in a letter just received, repeats what I have heard
from all other quarters.   'A singular felicity seems to attend
his sudden rise.   I hear of no cavil, no murmurs against the
appointment, and as far as my opportunities extend, all parties
acquiesce in the propriety of his advancement.'"

FROM THE HON. AND REV. R. B. STOPFORD, CANON OF
WINDSOR.

"I hope that some confidence may for once be placed in a
common report, and that your friends may venture to congratulate you on your elevation to the Bishoprick of Llandaff
and Deanery of St. Paul's.   I must confess that our congratulations are not wholly unmixed with some little selfish considerations of sorrow on your *possible* removal from Windsor,
although I am not without hope that you may continue to have
duties to perform in that neighbourhood which may detain you
there.   I sincerely hope this may be the case, and that we may
not be deprived of (I do not mean to flatter) the *élite* of our
society."

FROM THE BISHOP OF ST. DAVID'S (JENKINSON).

"Having heard that you are to succeed the Bishop of Llandaff, I cannot help troubling you with a very few lines to offer you my best congratulations on an appointment which I am sure will give universal satisfaction. For your comfort, also, I am happy to tell you that much as I was annoyed by the wig at first, I have now got quite used to it and feel no inconvenience from it."

FROM JOHN PATTESON (Afterwards a Judge of the King's Bench).

"The papers tell me, and for once I am disposed to give them implicit credit, that you are to be Bishop of Llandaff. I heartily hope that this information may be correct, and if it be, congratulate you on it with all my heart. I think the last time I saw Mrs. Sumner I told her you would be on the bench before I saw her again, but did not suspect that the words would be literally true. . . . You have thoroughly got the start of James, Coleridge and myself, and we must whip up, or we shall be altogether distanced. Coleridge is doing great things upon the Western Circuit, and will very soon become a person of some consequence in my profession."

FROM REV. A. DALLAS.

"I endeavoured, while in Oxford, to ascertain the feeling there about the episcopal arrangements; but as it was vacation, Shuttleworth was almost the only influential man with whom I conversed. He says that his own feeling, and he thinks the general one at Oxford, is that your whole conduct has been so respectable as to command the general approbation at your elevation. This he said in a manner which gave me no reason to judge that his expressions were influenced by a knowledge of my friendship for you."

FROM LONSDALE (Afterwards Bishop of Lichfield).

"I have just heard of the high elevation which immediately

awaits you, and cannot delay a moment to express to you, in a few words, the hearty congratulations of an old friend. Most rapid as your rise has been, and singularly in some respects as circumstances have led to it, you have the invaluable satisfaction of reflecting, and the general voice too bears testimony, that it has sprung from the *solid foundation of merit.* To me, who have *long* known what that merit is, the event which now prompts me to address you is, even independently of the consideration of friendship, gratifying in a degree which I will not attempt to describe. Long, very long, may you adorn the high station to which you are called by Providence, and which gives the friends of the Church so much cause to rejoice."

FROM REV. C. WORDSWORTH (MASTER OF TRINITY COLL., CAMBRIDGE, FATHER OF THE PRESENT BISHOP OF LINCOLN).

"I feel something that the choice of the Crown has fallen upon a Trinity man, but I assure you I feel much more when I consider who the person is upon whom the choice has fallen, and how highly endowed with the requisites for filling the highest stations in the church."

FROM THE BISHOP OF CHICHESTER (CARR).

"Pray accept my most hearty and sincere congratulations on an event that has given the most sincere delight to your friends, and has received the unqualified approbation of the public at large. . . . You will want the attendance of two Bishops at your consecration at Lambeth. I shall be most happy to render you my services on that occasion."

FROM DR. KEATE.

"The very welcome news of your great and well-merited preferment met us on our return from Hartley last night, and I must be allowed to express the unfeigned satisfaction which I, in common with all my family, have experienced upon this occasion, and the wish that you may long live to wear these honours with as much comfort and satisfaction to yourself and family as I am convinced they will be worn with advantage to the Church.

FROM THE PRESENT SIR JOHN TAYLOR COLERIDGE.

"MY DEAR CHARLES,

"Perhaps it is for the last time that I shall be able, or at least think it right, to address you with that appellation of boyhood. I had intended, before I received your kind letter, to have written to you upon the rumours which I saw in the papers, and thought very credible, and yet hardly knew whether they ought to be treated as authentic or not. Nothing that I have heard for a long time has given me so much delight—that such a responsibility, so many new duties, and such unaccustomed prominence, should make a thinking man anxious, and a religious man look beyond himself for support, is all perfectly natural; but I have every belief that in your new situation you will do honour to yourself, and good to the Church. God bless and support you. . . .

"My dear friend,

"Your affect.,

"J. T. COLERIDGE."

It had been arranged previously that Mrs. Sumner should, in the course of the early summer, pay a long-promised visit to her relations at Geneva, and, notwithstanding all that had occurred, it was thought better that this project should be carried out. Accordingly, at the beginning of May, she left with the four elder children for a three months' visit to Switzerland, the two younger children being left at Offley near Hitchin, under the care of their uncle and aunt McNiven. The following extracts from Dr. Sumner's letters to Mrs. Sumner will sufficiently show the course of events.

"CARLTON HOUSE, *May* 12, 1826.

. . . . "I have not been able to stir out of London since I last wrote. Nothing can exceed the number of ceremonies

through which it is necessary to pass in order to obtain
possession of St. Paul's. All other preferment which I have
held previously is as nothing to it. To-day I am to be confirmed and installed, and on Sunday I read in and preach . . .
That over, I have completed everything for the Deanery. On
the following Thursday I am to be confirmed as Bishop, when
the wig is put on for the first time. On Sunday, the 21st, the
Consecration takes place, the Bishops of Chichester and St.
David's attending, and the Bishop of St. Asaph in the place of
the Bishop of London, who holds an ordination on that day.
John comes up the day before, and perhaps Marianne will be
with him. . . . . Thus far I got when I was interrupted, and
since that time I have been spending a very long morning at
St. Paul's, undergoing the two ceremonies of Confirmation and
Installation. I keep the programme of all the proceedings, as
you will like to see the nature of them. I could have wished any
one who took an interest in me to have been present this morning,
for the effect of the whole was very fine. After the preliminary
business at the Chapter House was concluded, a procession was
formed, consisting of singing boys and men, Minor Canons,
Prebendaries, Residentiaries, civilians, etc., all in their gowns,
wigs, and other costumes. Then came the beadles with their
maces, vergers, etc., preceding me ; and in this mode we
marched from the Chapter House, which is on the North side
of St. Paul's Churchyard, round the yard, and then within the
rails, ascending the steps and entering by the large West door,
and thence walking up the nave to the choir, where, after
installation, the service was performed, with an appropriate
anthem : we then returned in the same order as before, to the
great amusement of a very large body of spectators all round
the church. I have now only to read in, which I do on Sunday
next . . . . I dined on Saturday at Lambeth with the Archbishop . . . . I am at present rather going the rounds of
Episcopal dinners: to-day with the Bishop of Chester, to-morrow
with the Bishop of St. Asaph, Monday with the Bishop of

London, and at the end of the week with the Bishop of Durham."

. . . . "On Sunday I am consecrated. I hope I mentioned in my last letter the possibility of the ceremony being fixed for that day. Mrs. Sutton sent me a message inviting you to be there, and if it could have been it would have been a great delight to me. But, on the whole, I think you give up less by your absence now, than you would have done at any other time.

. . . On Sunday last I read in at St. Paul's and preached there for the first time without fatigue . . . . During residence it is customary to give a dinner between the services to the members of the Church, which, considering the day, is a most disagreeable part of the duty."

The 21st of May, 1826, was therefore an important epoch in his life, for it was on that day that Charles Richard Sumner was consecrated Bishop of Llandaff at Lambeth by the Archbishop of Canterbury, being assisted by the Bishops of Chichester and St. David's (Carr and Jenkinson).

The text of his brother's sermon was from 1 Tim., iv. 16. "Take heed unto thyself, and unto the doctrine; continue in them : for in doing this thou shalt both save thyself, and them that hear thee."

The "Theological Review," in noticing this sermon, added the following remarks : "The present Monarch has signalised his reign by great and patriotic diligence in the selection of the most distinguished for literature and virtue among the clergy. The peculiar situation of the present Bishop of Llandaff gave his Royal master opportunities of close investigation : no man in the realms, perhaps, is better able to judge of the qualities for high office, whether in Church or State, and we believe that whether on the ground of learning and ability, of amiable manners and temper, or of Christian piety and knowledge, it would be difficult to point out a more popular promotion than that of the late librarian to His Majesty."

The following letter from George the Fourth to Lord Liverpool * will show that the "Theological Review" had good grounds for crediting His Majesty with conscientiousness in the matter of patronage.

"CARLTON HOUSE, *Thursday Night* 12.30, *May* 16, 1822.

"DEAR LORD LIVERPOOL,

"I have been thinking very seriously on the subject relative to the Primate of Ireland, and I cannot make up my mind that either you or the Lord Lieutenant are right in the conclusion which you both seem disposed to come to as to the individual to be exalted to that sacred station. I am too far advanced in life not to give subjects of this description the most serious and attentive consideration. It is, alas, but too true that policy is too often obliged to interfere with our best intentions; but I do think when the head of the Church is concerned, especially at such a moment, we ought alone to be influenced by religious duty. Do not be surprised at this scrupulous language, for I am quite sincere. I think that you would do well to inquire of the Archbishop of Canterbury if no English Bishop on the Bench can be found fitting and suitable for such an important trust, and if not, if no dignitary of the Church in this country can be selected for that purpose (for you will remember that Dr. Howley was *most justly* at once made Bishop of London) let us have piety and learning if possible. Besides, I do not like, I cannot reconcile myself, to have the Primacy of Ireland filled by an Irishman, for let us not forget the particular circumstances in which we are at present placed. I have no confidence in Lord Wellesley's opinion on this subject. I shall say no more, but I desire you to give this your deliberate consideration.

"Believe me your sincere friend,

"G. R."

Dr. Sumner, under date May 19th, thus writes with reference to his confirmation as Bishop at Bow Church. On this

* Yonge's "Life of Lord Liverpool," iii., 9, 10.

occasion I sallied out for the first time equipped in my wig,* though without the loss of my hair, as I have reserved to myself the comfort of wearing it for these last two days.   On Sunday morning it finally falls, and you must prepare your eyes for a transmogrified head on your return.   However I am more and more convinced of the propriety of it, and you will be soon reconciled to the sight of it."

With reference to his consecration, the Bishop writes to his mother.

"CARLTON HOUSE, *May* 22*nd*, 1826.

"I cannot permit so solemn a day as yesterday to pass without requesting your prayers that the duties to which it devoted me may never be absent from my mind during my future life. The awful and devotional nature of the ceremony is well calculated to make an impression on the most unthinking heart, and I earnestly desire that its influence may be permanent on mine through the grace of Him to whose service I have been so solemnly devoted.   John exceeded himself on this occasion. He preached from 1 Tim. iv. 16, in a manner which is beyond all praise.   You will not expect more from me at present, but

---

* The gradual abolition of the Episcopal wig is thus accounted for in Bishop Blomfield's "Memoirs," vol. i., p. 97 :—"It was not till the reign of William IV. that the wig was dispensed with.   On this subject the following anecdote has been communicated by Sir George Sinclair : soon after the accession of King William, Sir George happened to be at Fulham Palace just before paying a visit to his Majesty at Brighton.   He asked the Bishop whether he could deliver any message from him to the King.   The weather was extremely hot, and the Bishop jocularly replied : 'You may present my duty to His Majesty and say that at this tropical season I find my Episcopal wig a serious encumbrance, and that I hope he will not consider me guilty of a breach of court etiquette, if I am induced to lay it aside.'   Sir George repeated this message for the amusement of the King, who, however, took it up seriously, and replied, 'Tell the Bishop that he is not to wear a wig on my account : I dislike it as much as he does, and I shall be glad to see the whole Bench wear their own hair.'   The result was that Bishop Blomfield took the hint ; other Bishops followed his example, and the Episcopal wig was gradually discontinued."   After the Bishop of Winchester's serious illness in 1832 he left off wearing his wig habitually, and allowed his hair to grow again.   But for several years afterwards he wore it whenever he was performing episcopal functions.

I could not satisfy my feelings or my sense of duty, without saying thus much to you by the first post after so eventful a day in my life."

The new Bishop's old Eton feelings led him to ask for a whole holiday for the school, which was most graciously accorded by Dr. Goodall.

"Most heartily shall I give the present Etonians an opportunity of rejoicing at an event which has given so much real satisfaction to their elder brethren of all ages.

"Yours ever, my dear Lord,
"Most faithfully,
"And, remembering that age has its privileges, I will add,
"Most affectionately yours,
"J. GOODALL."

And so his time at Windsor came to a close. This, like his life at Highclere, had been very pleasant. The vicinity to his old haunts at Eton, his intimacy with the families of the Stopfords and Cannings (Canons of Windsor) and the nature of his duties as Librarian being singularly congenial to his own taste and feelings, must all have helped to endear life at Windsor to him. Add to this his varied occupations at Abingdon, Worcester, and Canterbury, and the extreme kindness of the King both to himself and family, and it is impossible not to suppose that he severed his connection with Windsor with very great sorrow. He had not however much time for indulging regrets as to the past, for the present brought plenty of work day by day. He writes to Mrs. Sumner :—

"CARLTON HOUSE, *May* 29, 1826.

"I see more and more every day the wisdom of the plan by which we settled that you should now pay your visit to Geneva. Had you been here, I could have seen little more of you than I now see ; for it so happens that as the whole ecclesiastical business of the year is transacted at this time, every day brings its employment, and leaves me little leisure for domestic comfort.

However, I expect to be ready to receive you back again long
before you are ready to return, or your friends to part with you.
The account of your arrival at Geneva was very gratifying, and
since the receipt of your letter Coode has returned, who has
given me some more particulars. I can hear but of one inconvenience—the smallness of the carriage—and considering the
length of the journey, it is well to have but one thing to complain of. . . . . I am going down on Wednesday to Offley;
partly for the pleasure of being with Louisa and the children,
and partly for the purpose of writing a sermon, which I have to
preach on Thursday week at St. Paul's, on the anniversary of
the meeting of the charity children.   This office has been delegated to me at very short notice, in consequence of Archbishop
Magee, of Dublin, who had engaged to preach it, not being well
enough.   It comes, however, at a most inconvenient moment,
for it is an important sermon, and as it is printed it must not
be negligently written.   On the day after the sermon, I give
my inaugural dinner at the Chapter House, to all the members
of the Cathedral ; on the next day, Saturday, I propose going
to Windsor ; on Sunday I preach a charity sermon at Kensington, for Archdeacon Pott; and on Monday I consecrate a new
church in the City, which is under my peculiar jurisdiction as
dean. . . . . John's sermon at Lambeth yesterday week was,
as I had anticipated, an excellent one.   The text was 1 Tim.
iv. 16.   It is to be printed, and I shall send out a copy by the
first opportunity.   The day was a most solemn one, and every
part of the ceremony was conducted in the most impressive
manner. . . . . With regard to myself, I am to do homage to
the King to-day, which is the last ceremony, with the exception of taking my seat in the House of Lords.   This I shall not
do till the next Parliament, as the Houses are on the eve of a
dissolution.   My wig is admitted on all hands to be a good one
of the kind.   The opinions of its effect upon me are various.
Some say it makes no alteration in my age—others report that
I look like the elder brother of the Bishop of London.

" Louisa will probably give you her judgment upon it in her first letter after she sees me, and you will learn by that what you have to expect. My head is now becoming a little more accustomed to it, and I have less the sensation of feeling it always in a pillory."

The following is Mrs. McNiven's judgment upon the wig referred to :—

"OFFLEY PLACE, HITCHIN, *June 5th*, 1826.

" Avant de te diré adieu, il faut te dire un mot sur la terrible perruque, que tu seras bien aise d'apprendre n'était pas si redoutable. Je ne sais si au premier abord ce que je vais ajouter te plaira ou te choquera, mais cela n'en est pas moins vrai—perruque, habit, tablier de soie, et tous les etc. qui forment le costume épiscopal, siégent si naturellement et si bien à celui qui les porte qu'on dirait qu'ils étaient faits pour lui. Nous sommes tous frappés de l'ensemble admirable de l'habit, des manières, et de l'homme."

"CARLTON HOUSE, *June* 14, 1826.

" I know not whether you have the same hot weather at Geneva as we have been subjected to here for the last ten days. For myself I wonder that I bear it so well, considering all the circumstances. On Thursday I preached in the nave of St. Paul's to above 18,000 people, it being the anniversary of the Charity Children. On Friday, gave dinner at the Chapter House to sixty-five. On Saturday, visit to Windsor. On Sunday, charity sermon at Kensington. On Monday, consecration of a chapel in the city, where sitting room for 1500 was converted into standing room for 3000. And all this with a thermometer at 85°! For the last two days, my time and mind have been much occupied with a most delicate and difficult matter at St. Paul's, which I have at last arranged to my satisfaction, though not without much anxiety. You may judge, therefore, whether I am not very desirous of the rest and fresh air of the country."

I

CHAPTER VIII.

The Bishop and his Family go to Llansanfraed—State of the Church in Llandaff
—Visitation of the Diocese—Statistics as to its present state—Curious Scene
at Trillick—School Sermon at Chepstow—Manner of Life at Llansanfraed—
His Popularity—Reminiscences by Archdeacon Jacob of his first introduction
to and Ordination by the Bishop—Visitation at Newport—Consecration of
Dowlais Church—Rev. E. Jenkins' Reminiscences—Summons to Windsor—
Is offered the Bishopric of Winchester—Mrs. Sumner's feelings on the
Appointment—Congratulatory Letters.

THERE was no Episcopal palace at Llandaff, and the first
thing therefore which the new Bishop had to do was to provide
himself with a suitable residence in Wales. He who opposed
non-residence of the clergy, must be the first to set a good
example himself. He was fortunately able to rent a very
convenient house at Llansanfraed, between Abergavenny and
Monmouth, and here in July 1826 he took up his abode, and
was joined in the early part of September by Mrs. Sumner and
his children. He had hardly more than sufficient time to make
all necessary arrangements in connection with this matter, and
to hold his first ordination at Llandaff, "a most busy and
anxious week," before he was obliged to go to London for a
month's residence at St. Paul's. It is indeed a happy thing for
the Church, that the system of holding an office or benefice *in
commendam* has been abolished. For the case of the Bishop of
Llandaff, holding with that see the deanery of St. Paul's, was
only one out of many similar cases. In 1826 the Bishop of
Bristol was Master of Christ's College, and Regius Professor of
Divinity, Cambridge. The Bishop of Chichester was dean of
Hereford. The Bishop of Chester was rector of St. Botolph,

Bishopsgate. The Bishop of Exeter was a prebendary of West-minster. The Bishop of Gloucester was rector of Kirkby Whiske, in Yorkshire. The Bishop of Hereford was Warden of Winchester College. The Bishop of Lichfield and Coventry was dean of Wells. The Bishop of Lincoln was canon of Chichester. The Bishop of Oxford was Warden of All Souls', Oxford. The Bishop of Peterborough was Lady Margaret's Professor of Divinity, Cambridge. The Bishop of Rochester was not only canon residentiary of Wells, but also prebendary of Peterborough. The Bishop of St. David's was also dean of his own Cathedral, and a prebendary of Durham. And lastly, the Bishop of Sodor and Man was also Vicar of Broad Windsor, Dorset.

How was it possible that the duties of these several posts could be adequately performed? In the case of Llandaff for example, Bishop Sumner had to reside more or less continuously at St. Paul's, from December 1826 till June 1827. If the duties of the one post were efficiently carried out, it must be to the detriment of the other.

No sooner however had he come down to Llansanfraed, in the summer of 1827, than he set about the visitation of his diocese in earnest. Searching enquiries were made of every incumbent as to the state of his parish. Nor was it a day too soon. In that part of Glamorganshire which was in the Llandaff diocese, sixty-two out of one hundred and seven incumbencies were without any house of residence for the clergy, and in Monmouthshire the case was worse still, for while fifty-five incumbencies were provided with glebe-houses, seventy-two had none, and in the whole diocese, one hundred and thirty-seven out of two hundred and thirty-four parishes were without a resident clergyman—and one hundred and forty-one parishes had neither Sunday nor day-school. It is difficult to transport ourselves back in thought to such a state of things, when the Holy Communion was sometimes administered without any offertory collection; when the alms were constantly dis-

tributed after the administration of the Lord's Supper to those
who had just knelt at the Holy Table ; and when the clergy
themselves, if by chance they desired an interview with their
Bishop, were in the habit of coming to the back-door of the
Episcopal residence, and expected to be regaled in the servants'
hall.   It is hardly necessary for me to say on what a different
footing matters are now placed.   But half a century ago the
Church in Wales had sunk to a deplorably low condition, and
earnestly and heartily did the Bishop of Llandaff endeavour to
rouse the clergy of his diocese from a state of lethargy and
indifference.   His rule over the diocese was too short for him
to see the result of his labours, but he sowed seed which, no
doubt, bore fruit in due time.*

Two incidents connected with the conduct of divine service
reveal such a curious state of things that they deserve to be
recorded here.   One occurred at Trillick, about fourteen miles
from Llansanfraed.   The Bishop had promised to preach in aid
of the fund for the restoration of the church, and, "arrayed in
his gown and dress wig," was waiting patiently at the parsonage
for a summons to come to the church.   No summons came, and
at length the chaplain was sent to report on the state of things ;
on his return, he said that the congregation were all broiling in
the sun, as the churchwardens would not open the doors.   The
curate was then sent to request that the congregation might be
allowed to enter, and he brought back a suitable apology to the
Bishop, in which the churchwardens excused themselves by

---

* The following statistics show the existing state of things in the diocese.
Since the time referred to, "55 new churches have been built, 124 parish churches
rebuilt or restored at the cost of not less than £278,950, and 106 parsonages
provided.   In the county of Glamorgan, in 1867, there was only one parish with
a population exceeding 1000 which had not its own school or was supplied with
religious instruction in adjoining parishes."—*Conv. Rep. Chron.*, 1870.   By returns made to the Llandaff Education Board in 1870, with which the Rev. G. C.
F. Harries has kindly furnished me, it appears that in 219 parishes, with a population of 439,308, accommodation was provided in church schools for 27,750.
The Bishop of Llandaff informs me that in 1874 the total number of schools
inspected by the Diocesan Inspector of National Schools was 143.

saying that they were afraid the church would not have been clean for his Lordship, if the people had all been allowed to enter before him! The congregation, however, do not seem to have resented this treatment, for "though there was not a single gentleman's carriage" the collection amounted to nearly £50. After the service the Bishop won all hearts, not merely by his friendly intercourse with the clergy* and by speaking to the school-children, but especially by stopping in the lane which led from the church, without his hat (being unable to put it on over his dress wig) to talk to a good old schoolmaster of the neighbourhood, " a very little bent man, with grey locks, dressed in a long, coarse, white coat, with the most happy expression of countenance."

The other incident took place at Chepstow. The Bishop was preaching a sermon on behalf of an infant school, about to be established there. It had been arranged that the collection after service should be made from pew to pew, but the churchwardens had omitted to inform the congregation of their intention. When, therefore, the Bishop had offered up a prayer at the close of the sermon, he paused before delivering the blessing; the collectors came forth from their seats, the organ struck up a voluntary, but the congregation rose *en masse* to leave the church. The Bishop, seeing the state of things, requested the curate to leave the reading desk, and go and shut the doors of the church. At this juncture the curate's wife fainted, still the poor man endeavoured to carry out the episcopal injunction, but when he got to the church doors, instead of shutting them, he seized hold of the first thing that came to his hand, in which he might receive the alms of the

---

* A new Bishop must have had some difficulty in connecting together names and faces, owing to the well-known identity of nomenclature in Wales. On one occasion, at a dinner where there were many clergymen present, the Bishop asked a Mr. Williams, whose eye he thought he had caught, to drink wine with him. Unhappily, the poor man had an imperfection in his eye, and was looking the other way, but seven clergymen of the name of Williams, seeing that nobody responded, at once each took the compliment to *himself*, and simultaneously acknowledged it

congregation, which unfortunately turned out to be a school-
boy's hat without a crown! At last the Bishop succeeded in
stopping the organ, and dismissed the congregation with the
blessing, and retired to the vestry. The churchwardens, when
they came to the Bishop, expressed their regret that the collection would so greatly suffer in consequence of the mishap, but
the Bishop took the opportunity of saying that there were
far higher things at stake than the amount of the collection
—that the services of God's house should always be carried
on decently and in order, and that he trusted arrangements
would be made to prevent such a state of things ever occurring
again.

The Bishop's manner of life at Llansanfraed was very simple
and unaffected. From a journal kept during a visit there by
Miss Bird, a cousin of the Bishop's (to which I am indebted
for many of the facts mentioned in this chapter, and from
which various extracts have already been given), it appears that
at this early stage his habits were very similar to those which he
adopted throughout his Episcopate. After an early* breakfast
it was his wont to retire to his study, where, unless summoned
away by diocesan business, or in order to receive any of the
clergy who might wish for an interview, he remained until
luncheon time occupied with his correspondence. The afternoon was devoted either to a walk with Mrs. Sumner, or a
drive to some one of the neighbouring parishes, in order to inspect the church and school, and make acquaintance with the
incumbent. In the evening it was his habit at this time,
though he gave it up in after life, to read aloud books or
reviews of the day, and occasionally poetry. Miss Bird describes
the conversations which arose from the topics suggested by the
reading as most interesting—the Bishop freely criticising the

---

* Though not such an early riser as his brother, yet the Bishop was very exemplary in this respect. Even when he was living in London, and necessarily,
at times, keeping late hours, the time for assembling for morning prayers was
never changed. Punctually at half-past eight throughout the year the gong
sounded to summon the household.

books read, and giving his opinion without reserve on the subjects opened out by them.

"The conversation," Miss Bird writes, " is remarkably lively and discursive. Something is started by some one, which the others take up and canvass. To-day we had the difference between maternal and paternal love. Of course the ladies took one side, the gentlemen the other."

In this journal I find abundant proof of the manner in which the Bishop at once made his way in the diocese. High and low, rich and poor, were alike attracted by him. The case was the same with Mrs. Sumner. She soon made herself acquainted with the poor people in the neighbourhood of Llansanfraed, and was indefatigable in ministering to their necessities.

I am indebted to Archdeacon Jacob,* who was through life a valued and faithful friend to Bishop Sumner, for the following reminiscences of his first introduction to him at Llandaff in 1827. Some unavoidable delay had occurred in the summons to the examination reaching him, and he consequently was not able to be at Cardiff, where the examination was held, until the afternoon of the day before the ordination in Ember week, September, 1827.

"I found myself in the midst of the candidates for orders at the Cardiff Arms, which hotel the Bishop had taken (as there was then no Episcopal residence in or near Llandaff) for the reception of the candidates, all of them dining with him and his chaplain and other invited guests, including some of the clergy of the neighbourhood, during the three days' examination. When I arrived, the Bishop was just about to deliver the Charge wont to be given at such times to those who were to be admitted to the offices of Priest and Deacon.

* The Rev. Philip Jacob (whose rector at Newport singularly enough was Mr. Isaacson) followed the Bishop of Llandaff to the Winchester diocese as domestic chaplain, and after a few years was appointed to the rectory of Crawley, and subsequently to a canonry at Winchester. On Archdeacon Wigram's appointment to Rochester in 1860, Lord Palmerston nominated him Archdeacon of Winchester.

" The novelty of the scene, so unlike anything I had ever experienced, was soon forgotten in the tones of earnestness and
fatherly counsel addressed to us.   One thing, and one thing
only, I can now recall, was the advice given as to attempting to
introduce family prayers into lodgings, where so many young
clergy would have to reside.   Houses of residence were not contemplated or supposed.   After the Charge, my own examination
by the Chaplain was preceded by a short conversation with the
Bishop himself.—' What are your inducements for seeking Holy
orders ?—What do you consider to be the chief doctrines which
should pervade your pastoral teaching ?   How much of your
duty as a clergyman do you consider you have discharged
when you have performed your Sunday duties ?'   Here I recollect I was helped in my answer by the Bishop—' One
seventh ?'   I will now pass you over to my examining
chaplain'—Chancellor Knight, who, for, it seemed if it was not
so, two full hours at least orally examined me.   It was now
time for dinner, and Mr. Bruce Knight put into my hands a
thesis for a Latin Essay which I must write, leaving the dinner
as soon as I well could for the adjoining concert room, where
the examination had been held.   The dinner and its whole
party were novelties of another kind, wholly foreign to my experiences.   I had once in my life as a boy been addressed not
unkindly by a Bishop—Fisher, of Salisbury, on his visit to the
Channel Islands for Bishop North, 1818, but I had never been
so near a Bishop of such friendliness and courteousness of
manner as Bishop Sumner.   I saw that in him, which was
always so striking in all future dealings with his candidates for
Orders, only more and more developed, the desire of placing
them at their ease, and calling out their confidence.   I am not
aware that at this time any Bishop was in the habit of gathering his candidates around him at the time of ordination, as the
then Bishop of Llandaff did.   It was not only that the candidates' necessary expenses were greatly lessened thereby, but
the Bishop and his future clergy were brought together in com-

parative familiarity, and thus a foundation was laid for future intercourse.

"The Cathedral of Llandaff, in which the ordination was held, at that time was a poor specimen of a church, much more of a Cathedral,* instruments of music led the singing, which was neither ancient nor modern. But all else was done decently and in order. I do not recollect the text of the morning sermon, but the subject treated of was in strict accordance with the rubrical direction—how necessary is the order of Deacon and Priest in the Church, and how the people ought to esteem them in their office. We all dined with the Bishop between the services, in the neighbouring Chapter House, and the Bishop assigned to different candidates different parts of the afternoon service. The Bishop preached from St. John iv. 24. 'God is a spirit: and they that worship Him, must worship Him in spirit and in truth.'

"Next day at the visitation at Newport, I heard for the first time a Bishop's Charge to his clergy. I had read many Charges. I may have been unfortunate or limited in my reading, but this Charge seemed idiosyncratic. It was one of a new order of things as it seemed to me. In one word it was diocesan. The wants of the diocese, and how to meet them—a most pressing topic. So new was this sort of episcopal Charge, that I was assured by one the editors of a church magazine, that he and his co-editors solemnly deliberated in council, whether such a line of episcopal topics was to be tolerated or countenanced; and, after deep deliberation, they happily agreed: 'it was to be encouraged.'†

---

* The Cathedral of Llandaff is now in a very different condition from what it was in the days referred to by Archdeacon Jacob. The present Bishop of Llandaff has informed me that when, some years ago, the Bishop of Winchester came to Llandaff to preach on the occasion of the opening of an organ, as he stood at the west door and was just about to enter the building, the western end of which in his time was roofless, the eastern a Grecian inclosure within the ruin, he turned round with a feeling of astonishment at the change, and said, "Had you any notion that there was such a place?"

† Bishop Coplestone, who succeeded Bishop Sumner at Llandaff, writes subsequently concerning this charge: "It lays open more of the state of the diocese

To revert to the visitation. It *was* a visitation. Clergy were seen privately—much needed reformations in the number of services—(for plurality of curacies was then too common an order of things), ensured by command or earnest request, and all was done in the best of spirit and temper. I heard conversations in proof of the acceptance of their new Bishop. The visitation dinner, at which the Bishop spoke frequently, was not without its good effect and kindly influence.

"In my intercourse with the Bishop, I was very much struck with the knowledge which he had even then gained of his diocese. No one seemed unknown to him. The appointment for special conversation, after the formal visitation, with many of the clergy implied that the Bishop had read and studied the answers to his visitation queries. Not long after entering upon my new duties as curate at Newport, I called at Llansanfraed in obedience to the Bishop's directions, in order to report progress, and then I heard that he had left that very morning for Windsor on a summons from the King, with reference to his translation to Winchester. A few days after, however, I met him by appointment at Dowlais.* Here I was first introduced to your mother, my first impressions of whom partook of the rapturous. Your

than I ever saw attempted in any similar address. Its value will be permanent, both to the clergy and their diocesan." Visitations, however, were conducted in a very different manner then to what they are now. Some things which were then little thought of would now, doubtless, greatly shock our ideas of ecclesiastical propriety. Truly strange, for example, must it have been to hear the apparitor with a dismal voice cry out before the clergy came up from the body of the church into the chancel,—"O yes, O yes. All good people, and especially the clergy of this diocess, are to listen to the primary visitation of Charles Richard, Lord Bishop of Llandaff. God save the King, and his Lordship the Bishop!" And then immediately before the delivery of the Charge, the chapter clerk further announced,—"All persons are requested to keep silence while the Bishop of Llandaff delivers his Charge."

* The Bishop was at Dowlais for the consecration of a church. The Rev. E. Jenkins, who was appointed incumbent of the benefice by the Bishop, thus writes to me respecting his intercourse with his diocesan : "In the year 1827 the good Bishop appointed me to the living of Dowlais, Glamorganshire. The consecration of Dowlais Church was the last official act performed by the Bishop. On his way from Dowlais that day—Nov. 27th, 1827—I went with him about six or

father was consecrating a church at Dowlais. He preached the sermon. It was the first service of the kind at which I had ever been present. What an ideal did I then form of your father's character as a Bishop of the Church, and as a Christian gentleman. How fully was that ideal realised during an intimacy of more than forty years,—but of this I dare not trust myself to speak. I know not how far my judgment of Bishop Sumner's person or mien—that whole outward appearance of a man which includes the very dress—may interest anyone, but I confess that I was very much taken by it on my first introduction to him. My acquaintance with Bishops was confined to having heard about seven in the pulpit, and having been present once at the administration of confirmation when that rite was performed without a single word of admonition or encouragement, and once when I was taken kindly by the arm by Bishop Fisher, in Guernsey. Age and infirmity were the chief ideas in my mind in connection with a Bishop. How could I be otherwise than impressed when I stood in the presence of episcopal youth and vigour? A new idea possessed me. It was not that anything like condescension was visible, or that I was over-awed, but I certainly felt intense respect for the Bishop in whose presence I stood. Those who knew him in early days, will remember how remarkable even then he was for dignity and composure of bearing, coupled with winning manners. It is impossible but that many thoughts should crowd into the mind of one just ordained when in the presence of his Bishop. Does he inspire confi-

seven miles. I shall never forget his parting patriarchal and fatherly address to me. He had my hand in his two hands, and he said : 'My young friend, good-bye. I commend you to God and to His Grace. You have an important sphere to labour in—do not be discouraged—look up to God. He will be your friend and guide. He will not leave you. I leave you as a missionary in the heart of Africa. God be with you. May He bless and prosper you! Good-bye, my dear young friend.' The Bishop's words and manner made an impression upon me which I can never forget. During the short time he presided over the diocese of Llandaff he did much real good. He gave much encouragement and impulse to the faithful ministry of the Gospel. The blessed effects of his Episcopate are felt till this very day."

dence? Does he call forth your sympathies? Is he a real
father in God? It was impossible to be in Bishop Sumner's
presence without answering these questions unhesitatingly in
the affirmative. I at any rate was so impressed from the
first, and the long experience and greater intimacy of nearly
half a century, only confirmed and deepened those first impressions."

It must indeed have awakened keen anticipations in the
minds of the earnest clergy of Llandaff, to find that the Bishop
set over them in the Lord was thus anxious to be their fellow-
helper and fellow-worker. Before the Bishop's eye also a well
governed diocese, with organizations duly set on foot for the
furtherance of the Church's work, would rise clear and distinct,
but such anticipations were not destined to be realised, for
Bishop Sumner's primary visitation of the clergy of Llandaff
in the autumn of 1827 was also his last, for at the beginning of November, Tomline Bishop of Winchester died, and
the following letter from the King conveyed the tidings to
the Bishop of Llandaff, of his destined translation to the vacant
See.

KING GEORGE THE FOURTH TO THE BISHOP OF LLANDAFF.

" MY DEAR BISHOP,

" The very moment I was informed of the death of
the Bishop of Winchester, I nominated you his successor. In
doing this, I have not only consulted that which is most agreeable to my own feelings, but which my conscience tells me will
be most beneficial for the See of Winchester, and also for the
good of the Church in general.

" Yours sincerely,

" G. R.

"ROYAL LODGE, Nov. 18th, 1827."

Lord Goderich, who had been appointed Prime Minister
after Mr. Canning's death on August 8th, wrote as follows :—

"My Lord,

"I yesterday, by the King's command, gave the necessary directions for conferring upon your Lordship the vacant See of Winchester, but by some strange omission, for which I owe your Lordship very many apologies, I did not at the same time communicate to you His Majesty's gracious intentions in that respect. I hope, however, that I may now be permitted to express to your Lordship the great satisfaction with which I have executed His Majesty's commands, not only on account of the personal feeling of the King towards your Lordship, but also on account of the manifest fitness of the appointment itself, whereby one of the highest posts in the English Church will be filled by one of its most virtuous and distinguished ornaments.

"I have the honour to be,

"My Lord,

"Your Lordship's most obedient, very humble Servant,

"Goderich.

"The Lord Bishop of Llandaff."

The following entry in Mrs. Sumner's diary announces the offer :—

"Jeudi, 22.—Quel événement inattendu! L'Évêque avancé à un des premiers Évêchés! Le Roi le lui a annoncé de sa propre main. Le diocèse est très grand, et il a grand besoin d'un bon Évêque, mais hélas !—je n'ai vu que des yeux mouillés de larmes et même des sanglots dans ce diocèse. Je regrette notre délicieuse retraite, ces montagnes Suisses ; tout ici aidoit au bonheur,—tous les jeunes ministres—tous les pauvres—tous les habitans des environs, sont en larmes. C'est Lundi passé que l'Évêque a reçu la nouvelle, et il est parti immédiatement pour remercier le Roi. Il revient demain. Je ne sais encore si nous serons obligés d'aller à Londres la semaine prochaine.

Les lettres de félicitation pleuvent, mais les habitans de ce diocèse me félicitent en pleurant."

The subjoined letter from Mrs. Sumner to a friend gives us a further insight into the feelings with which the change was contemplated by her.

"LLANSANFRAED, *November* 21.

"MY DEAR FRIEND,

"I knew how you would feel, and I cannot tell you the pleasure it has given me to receive your kind note to-day. The feeling of regret at leaving this country and diocese prevents my giving way to joy: humility fills my mind. My prayer is most earnest, that we may be kept humble and ever feel, that so many more talents added to our charge calls for redoubled vigilance and activity. The idea of a *splendid* residence does not delight me. I loved our little house and beautiful mountains, and the only point for which I like the idea of a large house is that we may have more of our friends together. Pray for us, my dear friend, that we may never forget that true happiness does not consist in meat and drink, but in doing the will of God and using His blessings and mercies to His glory.

"I am always your most affectionate Friend,

"J. SUMNER."

Bishop of Winchester! It was indeed so. At the early age of 37* the son of the retired country vicar was appointed to the See of Winchester, over which in the good providence of God he was destined to preside for upwards of forty years. Congratulations, as was natural, poured in upon the Bishop. A few letters are subjoined.

FROM LORD CONYNGHAM.

"MY DEAR BISHOP OF LLANDAFF,

"His Majesty has this instant informed me that you

---

* John Ponet or Poynet was appointed Bishop of Winchester, 1550 (on Bishop Gardiner's deprivation), when he was only about 34 years of age.

are to succeed to the See of Winchester. From the very bottom of my heart I sincerely wish you and the whole Church Establishment joy. I cannot add another word, I feel so delighted at the appointment. May you and dear Mrs. Sumner long, very long enjoy your promotion is the prayer of your most attached friend,

" CONYNGHAM.

"*Sunday, Nov.* 18*th,* 1827."

FROM HIS BROTHER, REV. J. B. SUMNER.

"*Friday.*

"MY DEAR CHARLES,

"I have been trying but cannot recollect any event which I consider more beneficial to the great interests of the Church of Christ, than your promotion to Winchester. In that light we see it here, and in that light we most cordially rejoice in it. Besides which it is impossible not to feel private gratification at the enjoyable nature of the diocese and residence; and its nearness to Mapledurham" (of which Mr. Sumner was rector) "and to every other seat of civilisation, and its fixing you without fear of change till you become Archbishop of Canterbury. All these are no small sources of felicitation, therefore be assured of our exceeding satisfaction.

"I need not add that you have my earnest prayers, that with your prosperity grace may be continued to you, and that you may serve God as faithfully at Winchester as you have at Llandaff. 'Poor picturesque Llandaff'—exclaimed Dukinfield —'I pity it—all things seemed going on so prosperously.'"

FROM SIR JOHN COLERIDGE.

"MY DEAR FRIEND,

"I have been watching the daily papers with intense anxiety, believing from the probability of the thing, yet hardly daring not to doubt the truth of the statements I read there, till they came confirmed by your hand. Upon every account I rejoice most sincerely and heartily at your translation, and I

should not do this as I do, unless I also sincerely and heartily
believed you will perform the high duties of your station as
well as any other Bishop on the Bench—and thinking as I do
of two or three, I need not say more. While these rumours
have been afloat, I have rather made it my business to collect
men's opinions on the subject, and you will be pleased I think
to know that although men are at first startled, as might be
expected, at the rapidity of your advance, and with many a
king's appointment is an obnoxious thing, yet I have heard no
single dissentient opinion as to *the person* chosen. This was
not said to please me, but is a just tribute to your united discretion and activity since your elevation to the Bench. .. May you
long live to enjoy your future in health and happiness, and to
perform its attendant duties with good acceptance and effect."

FROM LORD CLARENDON.

"THE GROVE, WATFORD, *Nov.* 29, 1827.

" MY LORD,

" I cannot help offering your Lordship my warmest
congratulations upon your recent promotion, which I only just
now learn from the *Gazette*. To a mind like your's, great
honours and great success in life call forth many feelings besides
those of actual enjoyment in their attainment. Upon such a
point as any duty I need hardly say it is the farthest from my
intention to think of touching. But I may be permitted to
suggest one reflection which would be among the last to occur
to yourself. It is the well earned satisfaction and most gratifying feeling that the whole tenor of your life, the understanding
and the disposition with which it has pleased God to bless you,
have made you worthy of your success, and likely to do credit
to the elevated station in which the judgment and kindness of
the King has placed you. I do not say this lightly. I must
prove my own sincerity by mentioning that since I became
acquainted with your conduct and deportment in Wales, I
have often said to Lady Clarendon that sooner or later your

Lordship was sure of being selected from merit and character
alone, for some promotion on the Bench. I should have felt
my confidence in this prediction much confirmed by the excellent Charge which I beg to acknowledge your Lordship's
kindness in sending me, even if his Majesty had not already
established its accomplishment.

"I have read the Charge with the greatest satisfaction in
every respect as far as its author is concerned, but with very
sincere regret as to many of its details.

"Something effectual must be done both to ameliorate the
condition of the poorest clergy in the Principality, and to
enforce the provisions of our Constitution and of our Church
Establishment for a better administration of religious ordinances
and religious instruction than exists at present. Your Charge
will be an invaluable guide upon this subject, and I am
persuaded that however extensive your new duties may be, you
will be called by the regrets of your late flock, as well as by
other motives, to render every assistance in your power.*

"I have not forgotten the little library which you wished to
found, and to which I promised to contribute my mite. I
mean to connect my gift with your name in some such words
on each book as these: 'Given by the Earl of Clarendon at
the suggestion of C. R. Sumner, Lord Bishop of the diocese.'
It will therefore be fit that I should first show you the list,
which I will do when we meet in town.† Though I have

---

* Lord Clarendon was quite right in his supposition, for up to the very last
the Bishop of Winchester took great interest in the Diocese of Llandaff, notwithstanding the fact that he was connected with it for so short a time. Throughout
his life he subscribed annually to some of the diocesan charities, and took in a
local newspaper. The gossip of such publications soon ceases to have much interest for those who have left the particular locality, and I remember some years
ago the Bishop determined that he would take the paper no longer, and wrote to
the publisher to that effect. The editor replied that the newspaper hardly supported itself pecuniarily, and that in all probability the loss of the Bishop's
subscription would decide the question as to the continuance or non-continuance
of the paper. The Bishop's heart was touched by the editorial appeal, and up to
his death he continued to take in the paper.

† No wonder the Bishop was anxious to form a diocesan library, for the two

K

troubled your Lordship with so long a letter, I must yet add the sincere congratulations of Lady Clarendon to Mrs. Sumner and to your Lordship, with the assurance of every sentiment which is so due to both."

FROM THE REV. D. WILSON (AFTERWARDS LORD BISHOP OF CALCUTTA).

"MY LORD,

"I beg leave with the utmost sincerity to assure you of the pleasure I have received in hearing of your Lordship's translation to a see where so wide a sphere of usefulness in the Church and of influence in the councils of the realm is presented to you. It will, I am persuaded, be the fervent prayer of all who know your Lordship personally and have read your most admirable Charge that grace and wisdom may be granted to you continually from the God of our salvation, to meet the new and arduous duties, and repel the insidious and numerous temptations of the spiritual adversary which your exalted station must bring upon you. What the Marquis de Fénelon is said to have suggested to Harlai, when raised to the Archbishoprick of Paris, has often occurred to me as most worthy of recollection by all in somewhat similar circumstances. 'The day on which you are receiving the congratulations of all France on the elevation to your new dignity is very different from that, when you must give an account to God of the manner in which you have administered your office.'"

FROM THE REV. J. W. CUNNINGHAM, VICAR OF HARROW.

"I venture to hope that I shall obtain your Lordship's pardon for giving expression to those feelings with which I may truly

divinity schools in Wales which were frequently resorted to by Welshmen instead of the universities, were singularly deficient in this respect. At one of these schools the only books at the time referred to were D'Oyly and Mants' Bible and Wheatley on Common Prayer, the last of which at the time of the Bishop's visit was locked up because one of the students had unfortunately injured it. The other school had no books at all.

say my heart is labouring when I contemplate the appointment
which has recently taken place, and in consequence of which so
exalted and extensive a sphere of duty is assigned to one so
anxiously desirous of fulfilling the will of the Great Head of
the Church. . . . . It will be pleasant to you to know that,
such as they are, my earnest supplications to the Author of our
mercies follow you in every step of your career. One bright
feature of the present case appears to me to be—and I am sure
you will forgive me for referring to it—that you have reached
this high station by no one compromise as to opinion or
practice. Your larger work on 'The Character of Christ'* and
the Charge which I have read to-day, appear to me to be
written in the simple and honest spirit of a faithful servant of
our Lord and Saviour. You will I am sure acquit me of
anything so base as an intention to use the language of flattery.
God knows my heart, and knows that I wish to speak the truth
in the utmost simplicity. I cannot say how much I venture to
promise the Church of England and the more extensive and
glorious Church of the Redeemer from your Lordship's appointment to a high and independent station such as this. We have
long needed some individual of high authority and influence to
take a middle point between the two classes in the Church,
and instead of siding distinctly with either, to rebuke the faults
and cherish the excellences of each. Your Lordship well knows
what is 'wanting' to each party. May your labours be blessed
so as to lead them both to lower the petty flags of contention,
and to raise that great broad banner of the Cross under which
we were pledged at baptism to muster and to fight. One of
the difficulties which every honest mind has to encounter is
the temptation to yield to the particular prejudices or errors of

---

* This refers to a work published by the Bishop soon after he had entered on
his duties at Windsor, "The Ministerial Character of Christ." This volume
was the expansion of lectures delivered in the Chapel at Cumberland Lodge,
and treated of Christ in His successive offices of Prophet, Priest, and King.
It passed through two editions.

the body of whose general principles and practices we cordially approve. Our friends are often more formidable than our enemies. . . . . May you, my dear Lord, be enabled to become not merely a bulwark against the crimes of the bad, but against the extravagances of the good."   · · ·

One other letter of a different character may be inserted here.

"The Archbishop of Canterbury presents his compliments to the Lord Bishop of Winchester elect, and hereby signifies to his Lordship that he makes choice of the next presentation to the prebend or canonry founded in the cathedral church of Winchester now in the possession of Philip Williams, clerk, whenever the same shall become void for his option.

"LAMBETH PALACE, *Dec.* 12, 1827."

It was the custom in those days for the Archbishop of Canterbury on the appointment of any Suffragan Bishop within the province of Canterbury to select some particular piece of preferment as his option, and on a vacancy occurring in the preferment so chosen, the Archbishop had the right of nomination for that turn. The canonry selected by the Archbishop became vacant in 1831, and his nominee accordingly was appointed by the Bishop. The right of selecting an option in this manner no longer exists. A few words inserted in the Cathedral Reform Act of 1840 were subsequently held by lawyers to have made all such assignments of patronage illegal.

On the 12th of December the Bishop of Winchester was confirmed, on the next day paid homage to the king, who placed round his neck the badge of the Order of the Garter,* and at the beginning of 1828 the whole family moved to Farnham Castle, Surrey.

* The Bishops of Winchester have been Prelates of the Order of the Garter since the reign of Edward III., William De Edyngdon being appointed Prelate by the King in 1350.—Cassan's "Lives of the Bishops of Winchester," i. 187.

CHAPTER IX.

Description of Farnham Castle.—The Bishop's Reception at Farnham.—Population of the Diocese.—Enthronization at Winchester.—Purchase of Winchester House, St. James' Square. — Support to Missionary Societies.—
Preaches the Anniversary Sermon at St. Bride's.—The Bishop's First Ordination at Farnham.—Relative Advantages of private and public Ordination.
—Character of the Bishop's Examination.—Testimony from those Ordained.
—His Brother accepts the See of Chester.—Letters thereupon.—Clothing
distribution at Farnham.

FARNHAM CASTLE, situated on the borders of Hants and
Surrey, is one of the most delightful residences that can be
conceived. It stands on a height overlooking the town of
Farnham, and has been in the possession of the See of Winchester since the middle of the twelfth century. A deer park,
of about 300 acres, lies immediately behind the castle, and the
garden is formed around the ruins of the old keep.

It was built originally by Henry de Blois, Bishop of Winchester, in the year 1129. Nearly a century later (1216) Louis
the Dauphin of France, possessed himself of it, but it was
recovered by Henry the Third shortly after. It was not,
however, considered of importance as a fortress until the reign
of Charles the First.

The neighbourhood of Farnham was in 1642 the scene of
many a sanguinary encounter, and the Castle was partially
blown up by Sir W. Waller, one of the Parliamentary generals,
in that year. In the middle of the seventeenth century it was
dismantled as a fortress, and has ever since been used only as
an episcopal palace. Bishop Morley (1662—1684) is said to

have expended some eight thousand pounds in repairing and
improving the Castle.*   Each Bishop in succession

"Diruit, ædificat, mutat quadrata rotundis,"

and the consequence is that at the present time Farnham
Castle, while retaining some of the characteristics of an old
baronial residence, for comfort is equalled by few houses in the
country and surpassed by none.

To this castle the Bishop came in January, 1828. His
reception was of the most enthusiastic character. He had
posted from London, a distance of forty miles, and when the
party arrived about a mile from the castle, they saw through
the dim light that the sides of the road were lined with men.
Suddenly the carriage was stopped, surrounded by large masses
of persons, and, before anything could be said or done to prevent
it, the horses were unharnessed and their places taken by some
forty or fifty men, who drew the carriage at a brisk pace through
the town up to the castle door, a crowd of people running along-
side, cheering and shouting. At the entrance to the castle the
Bishop spoke a few kind words to them, and expressed a hope,
on the part of himself and Mrs. Sumner, that their intercourse,
thus happily begun, would always be of the most friendly character. He entered the castle and the people gradually dispersed.

But who shall say what thoughts at that moment filled the
Bishop's heart? He was raised on a pinnacle of worldly
prosperity; wealth, and all that is incidental to high station,
lay before him; but to his mind's eye the difficulties to be
surmounted were surely present also. The diocese of Winchester opened out, before an earnest godly man, such a
prospect as might well have daunted the bravest heart. It
extended from the banks of the Thames to Jersey, and
included Surrey (with the exception of a few parishes), Hampshire, the Isle of Wight, Jersey, Guernsey, Alderney, and
Sark.† The population of Hampshire and Surrey, according to

---

* See Manning and Bray's "History of Surrey," vol. iii., pp. 134 *et seq.*

† The Channel Islands originally formed part of the see of Coutances, in Nor-

the census of 1821, was 615,349. In Surrey 340,735. In Hants 274,614.* To this must be added, for the Channel Islands, 55,070 souls, making a total of 670,419. For this population the number of churches and chapels provided by the Established Church amounted to 491; 142 in Surrey, and 319 in Hampshire, and thirty in the Channel Islands.

Additional churches were required in every direction, and more especially in the populous parishes in the neighbourhood of London. Eighty-eight parishes had neither Sunday nor day-school connected with the church. Diocesan organizations were at zero. But Bishop Sumner came with vigour both of mind and body to this vast diocese, and under a deep sense of responsibility and in entire dependence on His Master, whom he faithfully served, showed what a Bishop could, under God, be enabled to effect. It is not too much to say that, during the term of his tenure of the see, a revolution was effected in the episcopal office. Prelates with wigs, great state, and corresponding haughtiness of manner gave place to real overseers of the clergy, sympathising in the pastors' struggles, cheering them in their disappointments, counselling them in their difficulties. Bishops Blomfield, Kaye, and the two Sumners were in the van of this movement.† The perfunctory discharge of customary duties was felt to be no longer the ideal of perfection to be aimed at. Real hard work was the order of the day.

mandy. King John had it in contemplation to place them under the episcopal supervision of the Bishop of Exeter; and Henry VII. actually procured the Pope's bull for placing the islands within the jurisdiction of the diocese of Salisbury, which he cancelled, and obtained another, transferring them to Winchester. But this last never took effect, and it was not till the reign of Elizabeth that they were finally annexed to the diocese of Winchester.—See Berry's "Hist. of Guernsey," p. 241; and Falle's "Hist. of Jersey," p. 152.

* In 1831 the population of that part of Surrey included in the diocese had increased to 413,764, and of Hampshire to 314,313. In 1871, Surrey is returned as having a population of 1,091,365, and Hampshire, 544,684.

† The Rev. J. B. Sumner was, on Blomfield's translation to London in 1828, appointed to the see of Chester.

One more ceremony had to be gone through before the Bishop could be considered to have entered into full possession of the See, and that was his enthronisation at Winchester.

It was on the 18th of January that he went to Winchester for this purpose. As it had been at Farnham, so it was at the Cathedral city. The citizens were most cordial in their welcome of their new Bishop. A short distance from the town some fifty of the tradesmen met him on horseback, and with a band of music at their head, preceded him into the city. The people were anxious themselves to draw the carriage, but the Bishop, being probably more on the alert owing to his Farnham experience, was able to dissuade them from carrying out this part of the programme. As the cortége passed through the crowded streets of the city the bells from the Cathedral and the various churches of the town struck up merry peals, and the whole scene was one of much enthusiasm. Still more so was this the case when, on the next day, the actual enthronization took place. No Bishop of Winchester, since the Reformation, had been personally enthroned, and there was therefore not unnaturally a great desire on the part both of the clergy and of those living in the immediate neighbourhood of Winchester to witness the scene. The Cathedral service began at half-past ten, but long before that time the cathedral precincts were crowded with a vast influx of people. It is the custom at Winchester (I know not how it may be elsewhere) that, until the conclusion of the first lesson, the Bishop with the Dean and Canons should remain in the Chapter Room. It was not therefore until the early portion of the service was concluded that the Bishop came forth into the Cathedral. St. Lawrence's Church, in which, as the mother church of Winchester, the actual induction of a Bishop takes place, stands a few hundred yards from the western entrance of the Cathedral. A procession was formed, and the Bishop, preceded by officials and the members of the Chapter, flanked on either side by the

Jurors of the Bishop's Liberty of the Soke, and followed by the Collegiate body and such of the clergy of the diocese as were present, passed at once through the nave of the Cathedral to St. Lawrence's Church, singing the 100th Psalm. Here he was met by the Mayor and other city officials, and the usual ceremonial connected with induction having been carried out, and the bell duly tolled by the Bishop, the procession returned to the Cathedral. At the western entrance the Hon. and Rev. A. C. Legge, as Commissary of the Archdeacon of Canterbury, administered the oath touching the good government of the See : and the Bishop was then conducted by the Commissary and senior Canon (Dean Rennel being absent on account of age and infirmity) to the Holy Table, where he knelt for some minutes in private prayer. Before he entered the Bishop's Throne, the oaths of supremacy and allegiance were administered; and the service then proceeded as usual. It is said that as he walked up the nave of the Cathedral, a tall erect figure,* thin and pale, his whole demeanour all the while showing that he was conscious of the solemn duties devolving upon him as Bishop of so vast a diocese, there were some there present who were so struck by his delicate appearance that they ventured to prophesy that before a year had passed his place would be filled by another. Slight and somewhat fragile looking he may have been, but happily for the Church this prophecy proved as false as that of the Cambridge don had proved to be, and the year's tenure of the See which the prophets foretold, was prolonged in fact to upwards of forty years' presidency over the diocese.

In the evening of the day a large party were invited by the Mayor to meet the Bishop at dinner at St. John's House.

---

* Bishop Sumner must at this time have presented a strikingly handsome appearance. He stood exactly six feet high, and had a well-proportioned figure. His manners were most courteous, and his whole demeanour that of a Christian gentleman. I have been told that the soubriquet was applied to him of "the beauty of holiness."

Toasts of the usual character followed, and the Mayor, on behalf of the citizens of Winchester generally, greeted with great cordiality the new Bishop.

One of the first matters of business connected with the diocese which occupied his attention was the purchase of Winchester House, St. James's Square, as a town residence for the Bishops of Winchester. As there seems every probability that ere long this house will pass away from the See, it may be well to record here the history of its connection with Winchester. At the beginning of the 12th century Giffard, then Bishop of Winchester, built a house for the See in Southwark. This is said to have been a very magnificent palace, with a park of sixty or seventy acres. In 1642 it ceased to be the Bishop's residence, and some time after was converted into factories. In 1663 an Act was passed which enabled Bishop Morley to lease out Southwark Park (the house having been destroyed), but also obliged him to lay out £4000 for the purchase of a convenient house within three miles of London for the residence of himself and his successors, and accordingly in 1664 he purchased from the Duke of Hamilton a new brick house at Chelsea. This continued to be the London residence for the Bishops of Winchester till the year 1821, when Bishop Tomline obtained an Act enabling him, in consequence of the inconvenient distance of Chelsea from London, to sell and dispose of the house, and enacting that the proceeds should be applied "for the purchase of a freehold messuage or mansion-house, offices and buildings, suitable for the residence and use of the Bishop of Winchester for the time being, to be situated in the city of London, or the suburbs thereof, or in the city and liberties of Westminster or in the suburbs thereof." Chelsea House, accordingly, was sold, and the proceeds placed in the hands of trustees, and on Bishop Sumner entering upon the See this fund had accumulated to the sum of £7200. It was ascertained that much more than this sum would be required to purchase a house suitable for the diocese of Winchester. The Bishop was informed by his woodward that "a vast quantity" of timber on the See property was annually going to waste for want of being felled—only sufficient being cut for repairs and for supplying the demands of the various tenants under leases. It occurred to the Bishop that without detriment, but, on the contrary, with positive advantage to the Episcopal property, timber might be cut in sufficient quantities to provide the sum necessary to complete the purchase-money for a new townhouse. Accordingly, after obtaining the cordial consent and approval both of the Archbishop and the Lord Chancellor, the Bishop obtained an Act empowering him to cut sufficient timber for this purpose. This was done, and Winchester House, St. James's Square, was purchased with the accumulated fund arising from the sale of Chelsea House and the produce of the sale of timber.

As soon as the Bishop was fairly installed in Farnham Castle, he was very urgent in requesting his mother (now seventy years old) to take up her abode with him. Mrs. Sumner heartily backed his request, but his mother thought that on the whole it would be a more comfortable arrangement for all parties concerned if she were to occupy a house of her own, and a suitable house was therefore rented at Godalming, about twelve miles distant from Farnham, where she at once took up her abode. There was one fixed day of the week on which some one or more of the party from the Castle regularly visited her up to the time of her death in 1846.

One of the first objects to which the Bishop turned his attention was the miserable support afforded throughout the diocese to the missionary societies of the Church. In order that due interest should be aroused in the subject, he felt that it was essential that district associations should be formed, and accordingly beginning at Farnham (where the meeting was held in the noble hall of the castle), he was instrumental in forming local committees, and framing the details of such organisation as were found necessary at Winchester, Droxford, Christchurch, and Alton. In his speech at the meeting at Winchester over which he presided, he said that the income of the Society for the Propagation of the Gospel only amounted to £6,000 a year, and that only £70 was sent in support of the Society annually from the whole diocese. In contrast with this, it may be stated that in 1866, at the close of the Bishop's Episcopate, the amount contributed to the Society for the Propagation of the Gospel by the diocese was £4061 11s. 5d. In the same year, Hants, Surrey, and the Channel Islands contributed to the Church Missionary Society £8964 1s. 10d.

The Bishop had also been called upon to preach the annual Church Missionary Sermon at St. Bride's on the 5th of May in this year. To preach at St. Bride's was a very different thing then from what it is now. It stamped a man at once. Much more would this be the case when the preacher was not only a Bishop, but the first Bishop who had ever preached the Anniversary Sermon. Missionary Societies, it must be remembered, were then supported very languidly, and those who were urgent in the cause, dwelling on the responsibility devolving upon this nation as entrusted with the truth, were looked upon as little better than misguided enthusiasts. One who was present on the occasion has told me that the Bishop looked and acted as one who was fully conscious of the decided step which he was taking. He looked pale * and somewhat anxious, but preached with great animation and vigour. His text was Rom. xii. 5, "We, being many, are one body in Christ, and every one members one of another," and he argued that though the relative duties between man and man were universally allowed, yet it belonged to Him who first gave an enlarged meaning to the word "neighbour" to recognise the universal brotherhood of nations, to inculcate a spirit of Catholicity, and to show the oneness of the various members of the body. A solemn duty devolved upon all who themselves had drunk of the well of life,

* This may have been partly owing to his having sat up the greater part of the previous night, preparing his sermon.

and if the members of the Church at home would be like-minded with Christ they must show Christian charity to their brethren scattered throughout the world.

By thus publicly coming forward on behalf of the Church Missionary Society, the Bishop very distinctly and decidedly allied himself with the Evangelical party. Very erroneous ideas were current at that time with respect to missionary work. The idea was very generally entertained that the fact of taking an interest in missionary work, and showing that interest by pleading the cause of the various societies at meetings, almost necessarily argued an absence of zeal in home work on the part of the speaker. As an instance of this, I may mention that in 1833, when the Bishop of Bristol (Gray) was staying at Farnham Castle, and heard Gerard Noel, who was then curate of the parish, preach, on his return to the castle from church he asked, with much interest, who the preacher was, and on being told that it was Mr. Noel, expressed great surprise. "I thought," he said, "that Mr. Noel was a very different preacher —very impetuous, and with much gesticulation. I find it nothing of the sort—very good indeed—quite temperate. Pray does he attend to his ministerial duties?" On the Bishop of Winchester asking why he supposed he would be likely to be deficient in that respect, the Bishop of Bristol said that he had often seen his name at meetings, and that he supposed that "he and all similarly circumstanced had no time for anything but the platform."

The Bishop's first ordination was held in July. During the whole of his Episcopate, with the exception, I believe, of two occasions, the ordinations were held twice a year in the chapel at Farnham Castle. On one of these exceptional occasions, the ordination was held in the Cathedral, and on the other, in the parish church of Farnham. It was not without much deliberation that the Bishop came to the conclusion that, on the whole, it was desirable that the ordinations should be held in the chapel at the Castle. It is, of course, more conducive to the interest of the individual members of the Church at large that ordinations should be held in various central towns, so that the solemn rite may be witnessed more generally than can be the case when the ordinations are invariably held at the same place. But as regards the effect on the candidates themselves, the Bishop felt that the advantage lay on the side of the quiet service in the little chapel. Any friends of the candidates, any from the town who desired to be present, were always heartily welcomed ; and the candidates' minds were not disturbed by the oftentimes irreverent thronging of the multitude of gazers. None, I am sure, can have been present at the ordinations as conducted by the Bishop, without feeling that all was done that could be done, as far as outward arrangements were concerned, to solemnise the hearts of those most deeply concerned in the service. The examinations began on the Thursday morning preceding the day of ordination. The candidates were lodged either in the Castle or in lodgings selected for them in the town (which were under a sort of collegiate surveillance) ; and the candidates spent the whole of each day at the Castle. The examination began at ten—two examining chaplains taking respectively the paper work of the deacons and priests, and another the *vivâ voce* examinations. Each candidate went in turn to the Bishop, who commented on special points in his examination, on his work during the year of his diaconate, or on the sermons sent up for inspection by the candidates for the priesthood. To each was said some words appropriate to his special case. With the exception of a short interval for luncheon, the examination was continued each day till four or five. Dinner was at seven. A general invitation was given to some of the neighbouring clergy, whom the Bishop thought likely to influence the candidates for good, who, if they wished to dine, simply left their names at the porter's lodge.* A service was

---

* In the later years of the Bishop's Episcopate he found it necessary somewhat to abridge this privilege, owing to the increased number of candidates for ordination.

held in the chapel at ten o'clock, at which the Bishop always expounded some appropriate passage of Scripture. On Saturday afternoon, when the examination was concluded, he delivered a more formal charge, generally touching on some of the topics of interest in discussion at the time.

There was one point, the importance of which he never seemed weary of impressing upon the candidates—the necessity of "preaching Christ." Archdeacon Jacob on the Sunday after his death referred to this as one of his characteristics. "How often has he said, especially to his candidates for holy orders, 'Preach Christ;' and, in answer to one who replied 'I *have* done this,' he rejoined, 'Preach Him again, preach nothing but Christ.' All doctrine, all precepts, and sacraments circulate around Him. He is their sum and substance. His person and office are the grand centre of the Christian system. Any teaching which would compromise the great doctrine of our righteousness or justification in and by Christ through faith (*solâ fide*, as our article has it) he deemed 'another—an alien—gospel.' The sacramental system, in the interpretation which has been given it—that 'the end of all preaching is the exaltation of the sacraments' in all the different shades of this sentiment—was, in his view, disloyalty to Christ and to His Church; and, as such a bar, so far as he could raise it, to admission into the ministry of our Reformed Church. He quotes, with evident approbation, from Bishop Wilson on Colossians II., v. 5—'I am jealous over myself when I am called to speak so much of external order and discipline. I fear lest I should over-value them. My constant desire is that you should exalt Christ, preach Christ, magnify the grace of Christ, follow Christ, love Christ, bear the cross of Christ, live and die for and with Christ.'"

At the ordination service he selected some well-known clergyman as preacher who might be likely, in his opinion, to say a word in season to the candidates at so solemn a moment in their lives. The evening service was always wholly con-

ducted by some of those newly ordained. One who was ordained
deacon in 1830 writes to me thus : " I still retain a very vivid
remembrance of the solemnity which reigned throughout the
whole of the arrangements. Each day of the examination the
candidates dined at the Castle, care being taken that some of
the elder clergy should be intermingled with the young men at
dinner, and the conversation was ordered so as to afford profitable topics for thought. . . . At the beginning of 1831 the
same honoured hands admitted me to the office of the priesthood. The ordination, also conducted at Farnham Castle, being
under the same solemn auspices. . . . I think it impossible that
any of the candidates could ever forget the simple solemnity of
the occasion, or the paternal tenderness and wisdom of him who
bore himself among us as a true father in God."

Another, ordained a few years later, writes :—

" When I was ordained priest at Farnham (June 30, 1844),
I was struck by the evident care with which the Bishop had
perused the three MS. sermons which each candidate was
desired to forward for inspection before the examination. He
made remarks and criticisms on each, pointing out defects,
reading himself aloud and with emphasis a somewhat homely
passage in one of the sermons, which he approved as well suited
to arouse the attention of a country congregation, and pleasantly
noticing some extracts from the memoir of a physician recently
dead, whose experience I had quoted in another sermon on the
subject of inattention to the church prayers, on the part of some
who are quite alive to a stirring sermon. I certainly left the
Bishop's study quite convinced that my sermons had not been
sent as a mere form, and that it would be my own fault if I did
not profit largely by his kindly criticisms.

" On the day of the ordination Gerard Noel preached the
sermon, and after dinner the Bishop asked him before us all
what sermons of the day he would recommend as models of
style. Mr. Noel said that on the whole he would say Mr.
Charles Bradley's, to which the Bishop replied, " In conference

you have added nothing. It is the very book I have already named." After the evening service at the Castle Chapel (at which Downton, afterwards at Geneva, was preacher), when we met for tea in the drawing room, the Bishop appeared to make an opportunity of saying a seasonable word to each; and I think he gave to most or to all a text to remember in connection with the day, to me 1 Tim. iv., 14, 15, remarking that we should meet again very shortly, as he was just going to hold a confirmation at Newton Valence, and enquiring how I had succeeded in the instruction of my candidates for this first confirmation and speaking very pointedly of his own experience of the great importance of confirmation, and what a crisis it often proved in the young Christian's career.

"During the four years I remained in my first curacy, I always had a kind and sympathising friend in the Bishop, and used to look forward with pleasure to the occasions of meeting him, even though there might sometimes be little more than the opportunity of a passing word, or a gracious smile of recognition; and when I had to leave my curacy on the appointment of a new rector, and was in much uncertainty as to my future position, the Bishop wrote me the most encouraging and reassuring letter, bidding me not be over anxious, and quoting the passage in Philipp. iv., 6, $\mu\eta\delta\grave{\epsilon}\nu$ $\mu\epsilon\rho\iota\mu\nu\hat{a}\tau\epsilon$, and his letter was speedily followed by further proof of his fatherly care. Whilst I was incumbent of Hale,* my intercourse with him and dear Mrs. Sumner was very frequent, and I have a lively and

---

* Hale was a district separated from Farnham. During the term of the Bishop's Episcopate he was enabled to originate and carry through, with the hearty co-operation of the Archdeacon of Surrey and others, the formation of three separate districts—Wrecklesham, Hale, and Tilford—each of them with church, school, parsonage house, and ultimately an endowment from the Farnham great tithes. Arrangements were also made for service in a school chapel at the Bourn, which, since the Bishop's death, has been made a separate district, with its own church, school-buildings, and glebe house. When the Bishop first came to Farnham he found the vicar non-resident, and one curate in charge of the whole parish. At his resignation of the See, eight clergymen were working in this same district.

grateful recollection of the deep personal interest they both took in church and schools, club and lending library, and in all that concerned the cottagers of the district. The Bishop was a frequent visitor in the cottages on the Common. Those were not days for the artificial warming of churches, and the Bishop used often to tell me that '*the proper place for the stove was in the pulpit !*'

"I had more than one walk with him across the park and over the Common in deep snow. He knew every hollow and drifty place, and pioneered the way like an Arctic hero. On one of these occasions he took Archdeacon Allen (then lately made one of H.M. Inspectors of Schools), and two or three more of us (some of whom fell away on the road) to visit the Common School. Such was the weather that we found but six or eight children there." *

The present Archbishop of Dublin thus writes to me :—

"I received priest's orders at your father's hands ; but it is now forty years since. I remember well his desire to make the time one of spiritual profit for us ; for example, the way in which after dinner he sought to draw out some clergyman whom he considered to have something to say on some important aspect of the pastoral office, and in this way to establish a general conversation, from which all might be gainers. One of these subjects, as I can well recollect, was on the subject of revivals, and how best to bring these about in our country parishes, in which the Bishop naturally took the lead, and others, who have now with him past to their rest, shared ; we the younger, fitly occupying the place of listeners only."

The following letter, referring to this subject, appeared in the Record newspaper, some time after his retirement from the See :—

---

* The Common School here referred to was a school started and wholly supported up to the time of his death by the Bishop for the district of Hale. On the establishment of Aldershot Camp, about a couple of miles from this school, it became of considerable importance.

"EPISCOPAL ORDINATIONS.

" SIR,

"I venture to hope that you will permit an old and attached reader to make a few observations on an article entitled 'Ordination Examinations,' which appears in your impression of Oct. 19.

" The subject is of great importance, and several of your suggestions are valuable, but in the thirst for reform which exists in these days, and with the disposition to find out all kinds of defects in existing institutions, there is a strong temptation to ignore what is really good, and to forget those who have been quietly and faithfully carrying out, during many years, the very principles and practices recommended. I have a strong feeling that it is so in the present instance, and a few simple facts will, I trust, tend to confirm this view.

"It was my happiness to be admitted to Holy Orders (both deacon and priest), on letters dimissory, by the now venerable Bishop Sumner, then the devoted and beloved Bishop of Winchester ; and although the long period of thirty-five years has intervened since that time, I have not forgotten, and never can forget, the deep impression made upon my mind by the paternal welcome given to a total stranger, the godly counsels of the Bishop and his excellent chaplains, and the admirable arrangements of these solemn occasions.

" The candidates met at Farnham Castle on the Thursday morning, and did not finally separate till the Monday following. Several were accommodated in the Castle, and others were lodged in the town, but all were entertained by the Bishop with the most liberal hospitality.

" The direct examinations lasted for six hours daily, and were not only conducted with great ability by the Bishop's chaplains, but many of the questions proposed were of a most searching description, evidently intended to convey to the candidates a solemn feeling of their responsibility, and to lead them to a farther study of the great truths so prominently brought before them.

"The Scriptural character of the polity of our Church, and the distinctive dogmatic teaching of our Articles were admirably brought out, and were well calculated to make those who enjoyed these instructions attached Churchmen, as well as earnest Christians.

"On each evening experienced clergymen were invited to the Castle, whom the Bishop, in his peculiarly happy way, drew out in conversation, to the great edification of the young men.

"On the Saturday afternoon, the Bishop delivered his earnest and impressive charge, and on the Sunday the Ordination sermon was preached by a pious and able clergyman selected for that purpose. On the first occasion of my being present the preacher was the late Rev. Henry Blunt, and on the second the late Rev. Francis Cunningham.

"Nor did the Bishop's kindness and Episcopal care end with these sacred seasons. Those who were ordained by him have ever found him their faithful friend and counsellor, easy of access at all times, and ready to assist them in difficulties, and to encourage them in times of trial. May it please the great Shepherd and Bishop of souls to watch over and bless that venerable Prelate in his retirement and old age, and to grant that he who has so faithfully watered others, may himself be watered.

"I think, sir, that I have said enough to show what some Episcopal Ordinations have been, and what all may be (without any Church reform whatever) where there is a sincere desire to serve Christ, and to be taught and guided by his Spirit.

"I feel it right to add that I have never held any appointment in the diocese of Winchester, and that I offer you this plain statement of facts as an act of justice.

"I am, Sir, your constant reader,

"A Sexagenarian."

Such testimony as this to the value of the examination week at Farnham might be multiplied indefinitely. Many a candidate has been known before leaving the Castle to contrast the not unnatural dread with which he had entered its precincts, with the grateful recollection which as he alleged he would carry away with him of the time spent there. The Bishop's own sense of the responsibility of ordination seasons is expressed in the following extract from his Primary Charge :—

"The episcopal office is beset with many anxieties; but none press so heavily on the mind as those which are caused by the seasons of ordination. Well and forcibly have they been described by one who himself had felt them. 'It must be the greatest joy of a Bishop's life, who truly minds his duty in this weighty trust of sending out labourers into God's vineyard, to ordain such persons, of whom he has good grounds to hope that they shall do their duty faithfully in reaping that harvest. He reckons these as his children indeed, who are to be his strength and support, his fellow-labourers and helpers, his crown and his glory. But, on the other hand, how heavy a part of his office must it be to ordain those against whom perhaps there lies no just objection, so that, according to the constitution and rules of the church, he cannot deny them; and yet he sees in them nothing that gives him courage or cheerfulness. They do not seem to have that love to God, that zeal for Christ, that tenderness for souls, that meekness and humility, that mortification and deadness to the world, that becomes the character and profession which they undertake; so that his heart fails him, and his hands tremble when he goes to ordain them.'* To the same purpose speaks Archbishop Leighton :—'There is,' says he, 'an episcopal act that is above all others formidable to me, —the ordaining of ministers.'"†—*Primary Charge to the Clergy of the Diocese of Winchester*, pp. 27—29.

* Bishop Burnet's Pastoral Care. "Clergyman's Instructor," p. 172.
† Pearson's "Life of Leighton," p. 115.

In the autumn of this year, his brother, who had in the course of the previous year been appointed to a canonry at Durham by Mr. Canning, and had subsequently declined the bishoprick of Sodor and Man, accepted the see of Chester vacated by Blomfield's translation to London.   Coleridge as usual is one of the foremost in his hearty congratulations.

"TRELARKE, NEAR LAUNCESTON, August 4th, 1828.

"MY DEAR FRIEND,

    "I hear that the public papers announce the elevation of your brother to the see of Chester, and I cannot but conclude that what is so probable, and would be so proper, is true. If it be so, accept my hearty congratulations to you as a brother and a Christian.   In both characters you will feel what I mean when I say that there is no other brother in the kingdom that I know of, whose elevation to the bench after your own, and while you are there, could be received generally with so much pleasure, and with so little alloy of that kind of misliking which will always attend great instances of human felicity. This is owing to his great and allowed merit, and if I were not writing to you, I should add that your own had a little to do with it.   There will be some who will *exult* in the elevation from party feelings, there will be others who will regret it from the same—both, I am satisfied, mistakenly—but the great mass of sincere well wishers to Christianity, will rejoice in it as a probable source of unmixed good to religion ; and *also* as a pledge, that in appointments of this kind it is intended to act upon upright and Christian motives. . . . . I do not know where your brother is, and if I did, I am hardly entitled to write to him myself, but pray do not forget to let him know for me how truly I rejoice on every account on what has befallen him—and pray say the same for me to your mother, who has reason indeed to be thankful. . . . . Our circuit has been beyond measure light and unproductive—and we have had more time than I could have wished for pleasurable excursions.   Erskine and I got three or four days for a run through the New Forest, to the back of the Isle of Wight, and so by Christ Church, Poole and Wareham to Dorchester. I had never been in the Island before. Some of its sights, such as Shanklin Chine, I thought much over-rated, but the Undercliff itself, Bonchurch and Steep-hill are amongst the most beautiful summer views I ever saw or can conceive. Whenever you visit there, you must let Mrs. Sumner go that little round—it is very accessible, and done in a very short time. The beauty of the church at Christ Church was a surprise to me—what a county yours is to have three such churches as that, Romsey and St. Cross! They are doing a good deal to it very liberally, and very well *in general*, but there are some things which an Archdeacon should look at, while the repairs are in progress, as to pews and galleries. . , . . . If I am able and you are disengaged towards the end of September or beginning of October, I should like much to come to you for a few days. I long much for the *unius ambulationis sermo*, which it is so long since I have enjoyed ; you will suspect by my scrap of Latin what I have been about on the road—reading a good deal in the carriage. I had never read more of Cicero's Epistles than what we picked up at school, and I am amused with them generally and much gratified by some—but instead of saying as some one did, what gentlemen those Romans were, I should say what coarse vulgar fellows they were! It is clear that in the senate and in the forum, and in private, Cicero indulged in a strain of language which would be tolerated in no gentleman now, but which he thought witty enough to be repeated in his letters to one of the most polished men of the day.

" It seems to me that the heathen authors are not enough studied with this view of showing the *universal* influence of Christianity on the mind and morals by this comparison. I have been reading a good deal of Tacitus too on the circuit, and the same remark struck me—if anyone would but make a statement from him in his most moral passages, of what positions he lays down, and what he assumes as principles in moral conduct, and consider what would be thought of *such* a man now, I think the objection of how little has been done by the Gospel would not be lightly made again.

"I must leave off, for my young cousins are at my window clamorous for a sight of my wig and gown, and a mock trial. . . .

"My love to Mrs. Sumner—and your children—God bless them all and you.

"Yours affectionately,

"J. T. Coleridge."

And thus the two brothers were united in fraternal bonds, episcopally as well as naturally. They had always lived on the most intimate and affectionate terms, and a great comfort it was to the Bishop of Winchester to be able to confer confidentially with his brother of Chester, junior on the Bench though senior in years, on all points of difficulty which arose in the management of his diocese. It was afterwards a mutual source of gratification to the brothers when, by the Bishop of Chester's translation to the Archbishopric of Canterbury in 1848 their opportunities of intercourse became more easy and frequent. Their close intimacy continued uninterrupted until the Archbishop's death in 1862.

The following letter from Bishop Blomfield, in reply to a letter from the Bishop congratulating him on his appointment to London, refers to the same subject :—

BISHOP BLOMFIELD TO THE BISHOP OF WINCHESTER.

"London, *July* 30.

"My dear Lord,

"Many thanks for your kind congratulations upon the approach of an event which it would be affectation to say I do not contemplate with pleasure, but which you will be sure that I do not regard without a fearful apprehension of the responsibility which it will lay upon me. Yet perhaps I ought not to say *fearful*, knowing in whom I have trusted, and shall continue to trust for that sufficiency which I never can have of myself; the complexion of the times is such as to tell us that, while we labour individually in the several departments of His household over which the Lord has placed us, we must cordially co-operate as brethren in strengthening and extending His Church. I am *told*, but not on certain authority, that your brother is to succeed me at Chester. I have not seen the Duke of Wellington, so that I will not yet congratulate you upon that of which I am not *assured*. I have left Mrs. Blomfield and my children at Chester, where they will remain till we can go to Fulham. I beg my kind remembrances to Mrs. Sumner.

        "I am, my dear Lord,

            "Faithfully and sincerely yours,

                "C. J. CHESTER.

     "P.S. His Majesty having desired to *see* the Bishop of London and myself, I conclude that he still honours me with the same favourable consideration which he was pleased to intimate some months ago."

At the close of 1828 the Bishop was much occupied with arrangements connected with the division of the diocese into rural deaneries. Hitherto the office of rural dean had not existed in Winchester diocese, but the Bishop had found the benefit arising from the system at Llandaff, and was desirous of availing himself in the working of his new diocese of the co-operation of such fellow-workers. Hampshire was first dealt with, and subsequently Surrey. That the matter was not without some difficulty may be inferred from the following very cautious letter, in which he instructed the rural deans as to their inspecting the churches in their several deaneries :—

     "I send herewith the first set of annual queries, which I shall feel greatly obliged to you, as rural dean, if you will answer by

the first of August, after personal inspection of the churches at
such times as your convenience may permit.   You will perceive
that there is a separate paper for each church, and I hope the
inquiries have been so framed as to give you little trouble in
collecting the necessary information for making the replies.
Wherever repairs or alterations in your judgment are required,
it will be best for you rather to *suggest* them than to *order*.
Should opposition be offered in any instance, you will content
yourself with simply reporting in your answers what is at fault,
and it shall be enforced through the Chancellor, which will
spare you an invidious task.

"Where much requires to be done, I am anxious to proceed
gradually, that the burthen may fall in the least onerous
manner possible on the parishes; and in all cases where it can
reasonably be required, I would allow such time for the completion of the work as may be consistent with the safety of the
building and the decency of public worship.

" Any remarks which you may desire to subjoin to the replies
on matters not touched upon in the queries will be received
with due attention by me."

But, while the Bishop was thus occupied with diocesan
matters, parochial affairs in the parish of Farnham were not
neglected.   The following anecdote has been related to me by
an inhabitant of Farnham, who was present on the occasion.
It had for some time been the custom for the Bishop of Winchester to distribute bedding and clothing at Christmas, and
Bishop Sumner gave orders that at Christmas, 1828, this should
be done as usual.   "When the day came, the Castle was literally
besieged by applicants, the court-yard so crowded that it was
difficult for those who had received their blankets to pass
out to make way for others, and this continued during the day.
There was a great deal of grumbling and no gratitude, for all
looked upon 'the gift,' as it was called, as a right.   The Bishop
and Mrs. Sumner were both present themselves during the
greater part of the distribution, and determined that such a

scene should never be enacted again. And before another Christmas came round, a Clothing Club (which was then very far from being a general institution, as at present) had been established. The parcels of goods selected by the depositors were at Christmas time to be distributed to their respective owners at the school. Mrs. Sumner was asked by the clergyman to be present at the distribution. Accordingly, at the time appointed, she went thither, but found it so surrounded by the five or six hundred depositors, that it was with great difficulty that she could make her way into the room; and, when at last she did reach the door, she found the scene within still worse than without. The clergyman, mounted on a table, was endeavouring to make himself heard above the clamour of voices, as he called out the number of each parcel and the name of the person to whom it belonged. As there was no attempt at any classification, the probability was that the person called was at the outside of the crowd, and had to push and elbow his way through it before he could get near enough to have his parcel tossed to him over the heads of others. As may be supposed the distribution lasted the whole day, and was nothing but a scene of confusion. Mrs. Sumner was greatly disturbed, and begged to be allowed to undertake the arrangement the next year. The clergyman only too thankfully accepted her offer. The parcels were all to be sent to the castle, where they were arranged in the large hall in hundreds, each hundred again in tens. The subscribers had different coloured cards given them, each hundred having its own colour; flags were provided of the same colours as the cards, and men with these flags were posted in different parts of the yard; the depositors being told to arrange themselves round the flag, the colour of which was the same as their card. The first hundred were then admitted into the castle hall, the number and name were called out, the bundle placed in Mrs. Sumner's hands, who gave it to the owner, the Bishop standing by and saying a word to each as they came up for their bundle. When all the hundred had received their bundles, they followed their flag-bearer out at one door, while the next hundred came in at another. There was no confusion of any kind, the whole was over in a couple of hours, and the clergy were obliged to allow that the lady had shown herself to be the best general."

CHAPTER X.

Roman Catholic Relief Bill—Letters from the Bishop of Chester, Bishop of Winchester and George the Fourth on this subject.—Bishop's Opinions changed in 1845.—Views on making Promises of Preferment.—Payment of Tithes in kind.—Visitation of the Diocese.—Extracts from his Charge.

DURING all this time difficulties and embarrassments in the political world were "looming in the distance." The battle which was to be fought out in 1829 with reference to the Roman Catholic disabling Acts had already begun, and the generals on each side were marshalling their forces. It was of course impossible that the episcopal bench should keep aloof from the fray. In a matter of this kind it would have been the veriest cowardice and the betrayal of an important trust committed to them, if the Bishops had hesitated to declare themselves on one side or the other.

After what had taken place in the House of Commons in 1828, it was evident that the matter was ripe for decision, and the Bishops of Winchester and Chester were in constant correspondence on the subject. Towards the close of 1828, the Bishop of Chester writes :—

"I did not wait for the second letter this evening (both reached me together) to open the Duke's packet, and have given it such consideration as the time allowed, and will send the remarks which occurred to me with the parcel on Monday. As I set out for Manchester on that day, I cannot keep the papers longer with advantage.

"It happened curiously that I had a long talk with our dean (Philpotts) on Tuesday, upon the subject, and found that he fully expected the measure to be carried, and had written so to friends, who urged him to pamphleteer: and that he thought the only question, now, was how we might be best secured. A declaration against abuse of political power, and prohibition of ecclesiastical titles clashing with our own, were the only two things he insisted on. He has no doubt that the Archbishop of York, the Bishops of London, Lincoln, Rochester, Llandaff, and Lichfield, would all be *for* the measure.* But there is a dense mass of ignorant resistance in the country: of which specimens are sent me every post, and I foresee that the question will shake us as corn is shaken in a sieve. Nay, it will divide friend against friend, and brother against brother, in a way that has never been known. Since writing the rest of my letter, I have finished the remarks which occurred to me, and shall therefore send the parcel by this night's mail. I have been obliged to consider the subject under every conceivable disadvantage of interruption, engagements, diversity of business, and distraction of thought."

Again, on December 25, 1828, he writes :—

"I believe that our respective ordinations have kept us equally engaged, and now that they are over, I wish that I had the use of a balloon, and could have a few hours' conversation with you. But as this cannot be, you must write me something of what you know, if you know any more than I do of the sentiments of our brethren respecting the proposed Bill. I despatched on Tuesday a second paper on the articles respecting licence and salary, strongly deprecating them both, on the ground of their recognising the Roman Catholic clergy as a body within the state (surely of dangerous precedent considering

---

* The Dean was not quite right in his prophecy. The Archbishop of York and the Bishops of London and Lincoln voted against the measure ; the rest, as he foresaw they would do, in its favour.

their claims, disposition, and union), and also sanctioning by
public support the teachers of unsound tenets.   I really do not
think that part of the measure could be carried, or ought to be
carried ; it would arm against Government every denomination
of conscientious Protestants.   Neither do I see why the measure
should be encumbered with such an adjunct, though the Duke
seems to have paid great attention to it as if a favourite part of
his project : I suspect from the imaginary dependence on the
State which would result.   You would observe in my first
thoughts that this objection struck me : but I felt it far more
seriously when I had more time for reflection.

> ' Bella, horrida bella,
> .   .   .   .   .   cerno.'

".   .   .   .   .   Really Blomfield has done wonders for this diocese,
and the height to which he has screwed the preparation for
orders, joined to his previous interview and intercourse with
the candidates, is the highest credit to his memory.   By the
grace of God this shall not decline. . . . . The dean is here.
His mind is full of the Popish question.   He was dining with
some of the wits the other day, and they gave him Protestant
Ascendancy, on which he thought it advisable to preach moderation.   I keep clear of all this, and by this means keep not
only alive but well."

George the Fourth's sentiments on this subject are well
known.   He never altered his opinion with respect to the
impolicy of the Roman Catholic relief bill, but from first to last
he was opposed to any relaxation of the stringent laws then
existing.   He had been most anxious that the question should
not be mooted at all during his Regency, and afterwards had
constantly assured both the Archbishop of Canterbury and other
Bishops that he had insuperable objections to any repeal of the
disabling laws, in consequence of his coronation oath.   On the
6th of March, however, the House of Commons decided by a

majority of 188, " that this House resolve itself into a Committee of the whole House, to consider of the laws imposing
civil disabilities on His Majesty's Roman Catholic subjects,"
and immediately after this, the King seeing which way matters
were tending, made some communication to the Bishop, to
which he sent the following letter in reply.

After the usual preliminary matter, he thus addresses himself
to the point :—

" I consider the proposed measure as one of *political expediency*; but it does not belong to me to discuss it in this point
of view. . . . .

" I could not, however, consent to support the measure, if I
believed that it tended to injure the Protestant, or strengthen
the Roman Catholic religion.

" If, for instance, it had been proposed, by the introduction of
vetos and *concordats*, to acknowledge an authority which ought
not to have any power in a Protestant country, I should have
objected to the measure as inconsistent in this respect with
Protestant principles ; or had it been intended to incorporate
the Roman Catholic religion with the State, by paying its
priesthood from the public purse, or by any other mode of
national recognition, direct or indirect, as a conscientious Protestant I must have opposed a measure which would have
incurred the guilt of countenancing and supporting a corrupt
Church.

" But in the measure actually brought forward by your
Majesty's Government, I can see nothing which is at variance
with the true principles of Protestantism, or which will take
away one real bulwark from the Established Church.

" On the contrary, I believe that the settlement of the
question in the way proposed will remove the chief obstacle
which now impedes the conversion of the great mass of all classes
of the Irish people.   The disabling statutes have unquestionably
tended to prevent Roman Catholics of rank and influence from
opening their eyes to the errors of their Church, by the dread of

appearing to forsake what they consider a persecuted cause and a party in disgrace. The same causes, operating in a different way, place the lower ranks in Ireland under a like disadvantage. Experience proves that there is little prospect of succeeding on any great scale in promoting the education, or diffusing scriptural knowledge among the people, while the present irritation between the two contending parties renders every agent of Protestant benevolence an object of suspicion, and makes it a very dangerous matter to incline to the Reformed Church. The projected measures will give, for the first time, fair play to the Protestant religion in Ireland, and I can trust to its truth for its extension. I think, therefore, that in promoting an arrangement likely to diminish the number of the opponents of the Reformed Church, I am doing what is most likely, at the present day, to maintain the Protestant religion as by law established, in the true spirit and letter of your Majesty's Coronation Oath.

"Your Majesty will perceive that my opinion is so settled, that this is a benefit to the Protestant Church, and especially to the Irish branch of it, that if I vote at all, my conscience will not permit me to vote against the measure. The question therefore is, whether, considering the high station in which your Majesty has been graciously pleased to place me in the Church, I shall do justice to myself, if I give no vote on the introduction of this bill into the House of Lords. If not to myself, it is impossible that I should do justice to your Majesty's selection. It cannot be concealed that if the Bishop of Winchester takes no part in so important a discussion either by vote or otherwise, the public must know that his private opinion favours it, but that the command of His Royal Patron bids him be silent. This would be alike injurious to the honour of your Majesty, and to this necessary measure of your Majesty's Government. May I venture humbly to add, that it would be destructive in the judgment of the religious world of my own character as a Christian Bishop."

M

To this letter George the Fourth replied as follows :—

"MY DEAR BISHOP,

"I am sure in all that you do you are influenced by the best and most conscientious motives ; I shall, therefore, only add that I am always,

"Your sincere friend,

"G. R.

"WINDSOR CASTLE, *March* 10*th*, 1829.

"THE BISHOP OF WINCHESTER, &c. &c."

It is not necessary here to detail the history of the passing of the Roman Catholic Relief Bill. Suffice it to say, that on the tenth of April the bill was read a third time in the House of Lords, and was passed by a majority of 109, the Bishop of Winchester voting with the majority. His brother the Bishop of Chester, also voted on the same side. It must indeed have caused the Bishop many a struggle thus to give a vote at first sight contrary to the strong Protestant principle which he had always professed ; and it is evident that it was not without anxious consideration that he felt himself constrained to do so. The question, as will have been seen, had been fully discussed between himself and the Bishop of Chester. They had in concert corresponded with the Archbishop of Canterbury (who took the opposite view), on the subject. The Duke of Wellington too had come over from Strathfield-saye to Farnham—a distance of about twenty miles—and had been closeted with the Bishop for two hours, so that there was no doubt but that he had looked at the matter under debate from all sides. His conduct, however, on this occasion, undoubtedly cooled the King's feelings towards him. His Majesty took very strong views himself on the subject, and was but little able to brook those whom he had favoured with his friendship viewing the matter in a different light. The consequence was, that the Bishop was never on the same terms with the King afterwards as he had been before, and in 1830, during the King's last illness, it was the Bishop of Chichester (Carr), who ministered to him as chaplain, instead of the Bishop of Winchester, whom it would have seemed more natural that he should have summoned to his bedside.

When, in the autumn of this year, he delivered his charge to the clergy, he added, in some places at any rate, the following words with reference to this subject—words which do not appear in the charge as published.

" I must say one word on this subject, opposed as I have been in opinion on its merits to many whom I reverence, honour, and respect. In a question of such importance I could follow the leading of no human authority : I felt that my decision must be my own : that my conclusion must be formed in the closet on my knees before God. With these feelings I have taken my part, and can leave the result with confidence to Him whose never failing Providence ordereth all things in heaven and earth, humbly hoping that it will tend to the advancement of His glory, the safety, honour, and welfare of our Sovereign Lord, His kingdom, and His dominions."*

The Chaplain (Mr. Jacob) in writing to Mrs. Sumner, bears witness to the interest excited by these words. Having mentioned the emotion visible in the faces of many of the clergy, (and of some laymen who had come from Farnham to Basing-

---

* In subsequent years the Bishop regretted the course which he took with reference to this Bill, and candidly confessed it. In his Visitation Charge of 1845 he says : " To the Roman Catholic Relief Bill I gave my assent on grounds simply political. It seemed to me that it might be viewed as involving civil privileges only, and those legitimately following on the concessions made successively in 1774, 1778, 1782, and, above all, in 1793. The objections urged on religious considerations did not appear to me to be necessarily consequential upon its principle. As a political measure, it has been hitherto a signal failure. It has not restored tranquillity to the country—it has not lightened the difficulty in the councils of the state—it has not contributed to the safety of the branch of our church in Ireland—it has not opened the way to converts from Popery. I owe it to you and to myself to avow that, if I could have read that measure by the light of the fifteen years which have elapsed since its enactment, I could not have given, in 1845, the vote I gave in 1829."

stoke, a distance of fifteen miles, to hear the charge,) he thus
continues :—

"I observed Dr. W.'s countenance, particularly in the part
when the Bishop referred to the line he had taken in the
Roman Catholic Relief Bill. You know Dr. W. took a very
warm part in the opposition. His attention was deeply excited in a moment, it was at first the excitement of enquiry,
curiosity, interest, and when the Bishop said, 'I felt I could
follow no human guide, that in this affair my judgment must
be peculiarly my own, in this spirit, on my knees before God,
God knoweth I took my part,' Dr. W. gently drew his hand to
his face ; a deep blush suffused his countenance, and for a few
seconds he seemed absorbed."

Another matter occurred at the same time which could not
but cause the Bishop some annoyance. An old friend of his
requested him to promise to prefer a particular clergyman in
his diocese, in order to make an opening in the small living
thus vacated for a friend who was about to be married to a
daughter of the squire. The Bishop, after explaining why, in
the particular instance, the course suggested could not be
carried out, said, "I ought to add, with respect to promises,
that it is my invariable rule not to make any, and it is only
by strict adherence to it that I can avoid causing disappointments in ninety-nine cases out of a hundred. The applica-
tions made to me within the last year are more than 400
in number ; some from individuals having almost irresistible
claims, and very many from persons of whose services I should
be most glad to avail myself. Now, my predecessor, during the
seven years he was Bishop of Winchester, had opportunities
of preferring seven persons only. He was originally very
scrupulous in never raising expectations, but latterly became
less strict in this respect, and the consequence was disappointment to many deserving persons whose hopes had been excited,
and who have applied to me to satisfy pledges which, in the
common course of things, never could have been fulfilled."

I remember once hearing the Bishop say that whenever he received a letter which, from whatever cause it might be, made his heart beat a little faster than usual, he always slept over it before sending an answer. His experience was that twenty-four hours' calm reflection often smoothed apparent asperities. The letter referred to above must, I think, have been of the class which required twenty-four hours to elapse before the writing of the answer. So too must the letter, which called forth the following reply some twenty years later, to a private friend who had written to ask, with extreme urgency, for a living for a particular person. ". . . . . . . I cannot be led by any considerations to swerve from the rule from which I have never yet departed since I have been responsible for the disposal of preferment. I never will lead others to entertain expectations which it may never be in my power to realise. Nor can I consent to fetter myself by any such engagement. If I were to do so, I could not discharge my duty towards the seven or eight hundred clergy of my diocese, some of whom may have paramount claims at particular times, or towards the parishes to which I am called on to present, as I am bound to consider, not only whether the place will suit the person, but the person the place. . . . . . Considering that it is not the first time that I have written to you on this subject, I have felt it necessary to speak explicitly; but I beg you not to think that I write in an unkindly spirit; nothing, believe me, is farther from my intentions, or would be more repugnant to my feelings."

Speaking at the Church Missionary Society's meeting at Exeter Hall in May, the Bishop showed that he still retained a warm feeling for the Welsh. One who was there, after referring to a slight indisposition of the Bishop, thus writes to Mrs. Sumner:—

"After the meeting he seemed much revived. His speech to-day was peculiarly effective. Allusion had been made in the report to a dearth of bibles at Aberdare. The Bishop took up this statement, and pressed the obligation of assisting the Welsh. He was now indeed by situation and affection united to another clergy, but he could not divest himself of his Welsh associations, and found in his deep interest for that people, that however separated he had indeed a Welsh heart. Llewellyn, who was behind me, glowed with generous emotions ; my own eyes as were those of others were turned towards him, and we beheld him swelling with joy and patriotic enthusiasm. He could say nothing when I pressed his hand."

A curious incident occurred this summer illustrating a state of things which now has happily passed away for ever. It was before the commutation of tithes, and the Bishop, when about to pay a visit to a rector in his diocese, found to his surprise as he entered the grounds of the parsonage, a flock of 102 lambs just being driven in at the gate. On enquiry it turned out that one of the tithe-payers of the parish, wishing to spite the rector, insisted on thus paying his tithe, knowing that the rector had no food for the lambs. "Just right, my dear friend," said the Bishop. "It so happens I can get you out of this difficulty. My steward said to me as I left the castle that we had food and wanted stock—let them be driven to Farnham to-night." The bargain was struck, and the lambs at once despatched to Farnham to the rector's satisfaction and the discomfiture of the tithe-payer.

In the autumn the Bishop was called upon to appoint to the vacant Archdeaconry of Winchester. None felt more than he did the importance of this post. Far from considering an Archdeaconry a sinecure he looked upon it as one of the most laborious offices in the Church. And throughout his Episcopate he was most faithfully, zealously, and affectionately aided in his duties by the successive Archdeacons both of Winchester and Surrey. To the vacant post he preferred the Rev. C. J. Hoare, Vicar of Godstone. The following letters show the Bishop's mind on the subject.

THE BISHOP TO REV. C. J. HOARE.

"FARNHAM CASTLE, *Oct.* 26*th*, 1829.

"MY DEAR SIR,

"The lamented death of Archdeacon Heathcote has placed at my disposal the Archdeaconry of Winchester. It is my most anxious desire to place in this responsible post one in whom the diocese and myself will have confidence; and I think I cannot take any step more likely to ensure the fulfilment of this wish under the Divine blessing, to the utmost, than by requesting you will give me the benefit of your services in the vacant Archdeaconry.

"I am,
"My dear Sir,
"Your faithful Servant,
"C. WINTON."

Mr. Hoare in his reply appears to have expressed some hesitation as to accepting the post, and the Bishop writes again.

"FARNHAM CASTLE, *Oct.* 31*st*, 1829.

"MY DEAR SIR,

"As far as regards myself I have nothing to re-consider. Since I entered the diocese it has been. my most earnest prayer that I might be directed in the appointments which it might fall to my lot to make, to the choice of the fittest men for the respective vacancies. I will not knowingly deviate from this principle; and I have little doubt that all, save yourself, will unite in acknowledging that I have acted upon it in proposing the vacant Archdeaconry to your accept-ance. ......"

"I am,
"My dear Sir,
"Your faithful Servant,
"C. WINTON."

The following is added as showing the sort of communications passing between the Bishop and his Archdeacons.

"FARNHAM CASTLE, *Dec. 2nd*, 1829.

" MY DEAR SIR,

" My first communication after your installation into the Archdeaconry must not reach you without conveying the expression of my earnest hope that you may long prove in it an instrument of extensive usefulness to the glory of God and the good of His Church.

" My present business has reference to your rural deanery.

" *In re*—

" A glebe house seems most desirable, and with a view to endeavouring to procure it, can you give me information respecting the present gross value of the living? You are probably aware the incumbent is insane. Is ——, Esq., the patron, his brother? What is his address? Do you know anything of his character? Is there any waste land suitably situated in the parish which might be obtained for building under the authority of the act enabling lords of manors to grant not exceeding five acres for such purpose? Or in default of any such land, is there any specific piece of land held under Jesus College, which that body might fairly be asked to alienate with a probability of success?

" 2ndly. Do you know anything of Mr. ——, the curate? His character? respectability? pursuits, &c.? There is only one service at present (population in 1821, 585), and it will be necessary for me to call on him for a second; but I should like to know confidentially something about him first.

" I am, my dear Sir,

" Very faithfully yours,

" C. WINTON.

" P.S. Mr. ——, in his replies to the circular queries, says:— ' Public school much required.' Why does he not bestir himself in its establishment? He states no obstacle. Your sermon duly reached me—by *the waggon*—a conveyance for which Hatchard seems to have the unconquerable predilection of the last century. I have read it with still more satisfaction than I heard it, for there is much which gives occasion for thought. Your notes are very interesting and valuable, and so they are considered by all with whom I have conversed respecting them."

The Bishop lost but little time in making a personal visitation of his diocese. He was anxious to obtain that knowledge of localities, churches, schools, and clergy, which can only thus be gained after previous circulation of formal and minute inquiries. No queries had been officially issued in the diocese since 1788. The month of August was set apart for this important matter. During the previous century, each Bishop of Winchester in succession had only officially visited the diocese once during his episcopate. In fact, whilst there are only records of eleven previous visitations altogether, Bishop Sumner during his tenure of the See, visited no fewer than ten times. The Bishop's Primary Charge was received by the clergy with the greatest possible interest. They probably expected, from what had occurred at Llandaff, that his utterances would be something more than a mere formal and dignified address, and they were not disappointed. I have thought it well to subjoin a considerable portion of the Charge, showing, as it does, the feelings of the Bishop with reference to the office which he held :—

"Accustomed as I have ever been to regard the first official interview of a bishop of our Church with his clergy, as an event fraught with deepest interest for himself and for them, I have found it impossible to look forward to my own personal meeting with those who are now connected with me by such dear and solemn ties, without experiencing feelings of great emotion. . . . It can never pass from my remembrance, that in this diocese my own post of ministerial duty was first appointed,—here I first statedly entered upon the practical discharge of the functions belonging to our sacred profession,—here I first knew the alternations of hope and disappointment, of joys and fears, with

which the ministrations of the pastoral office, in whatever
sphere, are inseparably attended, — here I first learnt, by
personal experience, the trials and difficulties of that order of
men who, as messengers, watchmen, and stewards of Christ, are
to teach and to premonish, to feed and to provide for the Lord's
family.   Recollections of this kind, never absent from my
memory, and pressed upon my mind with unusual force by the
various details of parochial duties, which in my present situation are daily brought under my notice, cannot but enhance
my feelings of attachment towards that valuable body of
labourers in the Lord's vineyard, who, as parish priests, are
striving to save their flocks through Christ for ever.   Gladly
would I encourage the belief that something of a reciprocal
feeling will be entertained by those whom I, on my part, unfeignedly wish to honour for their work's sake.   My heart's
desire is, that mutual confidence may distinguish our intercourse ; that I may receive from them those ready communications and friendly suggestions which experienced and willing
counsellors are prompt to give ; that they may find in me not
an indifferent and apathetic witness of their spiritual toils, but
a fellow-servant and friend, and helper of their joy ; not a check
on what is done decently and in order for the furtherance of
the great object of their ministry, but a co-operator in all useful
and proper measures, tending to promote the glory of God, and
the knowledge of his salvation." *

After giving some details as to the population, church accommodation and church deficiency of the diocese (the number of
churches and chapels being in Surrey, 142 ; in Hampshire, 319),
he adds,

"Let me say on this subject, that wherever a new church or

* "It is the misfortune of the modern English Church, that the Bishop is too
often regarded by his clergy, not as the master-spring, but as merely a controlling
power ; a *remora* to check too ardent zeal, rather than an agent to further improvement ; a censor of measures already adopted, rather than a guide in measures proposed."—*Bishop Heber's Charge to the Clergy of the Diocese of Calcutta,*
p. 30.

chapel is erected, it is of extreme importance to carry into effect the sub-division of parishes for ecclesiastical purposes. It is the principle of the Church of England, to commit definite portions of the people to definite ministers. To provide places of worship without assigning parochial districts to them, is a departure from this system of such questionable propriety, that it can be excused by nothing but the palpable necessity of the case. It certainly accommodates those who are 'hearers only,' but at the expense of degrading the parish priest into the Sunday preacher. It seems to make the public ministrations of the clergy every thing, and to cast into the shade the more unobtrusive, though not less efficient pastoral duties—the domestic visitation of the sick and ignorant,—the preaching of the gospel to the poor from house to house,—attention to the young,—and all that general parochial superintendence which is implied in what is termed the cure of souls."

But the churches internally require much care, attention and adornment :

" It is not fitting that the house of God should be connected in the minds of the people with associations of neglect and discomfort; or that the officials of the church should ' dwell in an house of cedars, while the ark of the covenant of the Lord remaineth under curtains.'* It is not too much to say, that no very inaccurate judgment may be formed of the state of religion in a parish by the care with which the decent appearance of its church and churchyard is maintained. There should be such a reverential regard for preserving the appropriate character of the sacred precincts, as would indicate, even to the eye of a stranger, 'this is holy ground.' It seldom happens that the inner temple of the heart is swept and garnished, where the visible house of the Lord and its courts are suffered to lie waste."

The law referring to pews with respect to which flagrant abuses prevailed is next given, the establishment of a second

* 1 Chron. xvii. 1. See also Haggai i. 4.

service urged when practicable in the 161 churches in which there was only one service on a Sunday :

"And if there be some to whom the long interval between Sabbath and Sabbath would be passed unprofitably, without the provision of some public weekly ministration, let not this additional kindness towards our people be grudged at our hands, for the sake of those who are hungering after the bread of life. The saying of the Psalmist becomes well the mouth of a Christian minister, 'I was glad when they said we will go into the house of the Lord.' Let our earnestness in the work be made manifest by the willing and ready mind with which we lay ourselves out for usefulness, sparing not our ownselves, in the hope of multiplying the channels of grace, and drawing down a more abundant blessing on those who forsake not the assembling of themselves together for the refreshing work of prayer and praise. I am persuaded that none will think themselves absolved from this duty, in any practicable case, by reason of the smallness of the congregation. God has vouchsafed to promise, that where two or three are gathered together in his name, he is in the midst of them, and will grant their requests; and none of his servants will consider it becoming their calling to place an obstacle in the way of those, few though they may be, and of small account in man's sight, who desire with one accord to make their common supplications to the throne of grace.'"

Care in the selection of curates, the necessity of their being duly licensed, and the need of additional glebe-houses, come next under review. Educational statistics are then given, 30,461 children being under education in church schools :

"Every parish should have, if possible, its own proper school; and such an arrangement should only be relinquished because unattainable. I trust I am not too sanguine in hoping, that the time will come when no church in the diocese however small its population, will be opened for public worship where a little class of Sunday scholars may not be found within its doors, forming, perhaps, not the least intelligent, nor the least hopeful portion of the congregation."

*   *   *   *   *

Confirmation is the next topic. If health and strength allowed, the Bishop would visit every part of his diocese at least once in every three years, for the purpose of administering this rite, and in the large towns, and in the neighbourhood of London more frequently.

"My belief is," he goes on to say, "that the parochial minister will find no season of intercourse with his parishioners so blessed in its results, as that communication with his catechumens by which, in obedience to the canon, he 'uses his best endeavours to prepare and make them able' for confirmation. Whatever be the standard of qualification which he proposes to his own mind, he cannot bring them satisfactorily to any degree of fitness without much and frequent familiar instruction, much individual converse, many personal examinations into the grounds of the faith of each, many close and searching inquiries into the meaning they assign to their baptismal obligations, which, in the presence of God and the congregation, they are desirous of ratifying and confirming in their own persons. No one can have long entered upon this interesting task, without perceiving how much of gross and dangerous misconception, worthy only of the darkest ages of superstition and ignorance, is prevalent on this subject. If the candidate for confirmation be asked the motive of his desire, he will sometimes refer it to a vague notion of benefit to be derived from the bishop's blessing, or of the propriety of submitting, with or without personal fitness, to a form prescribed by the Church. Sometimes the rite is considered as a mode of relieving sponsors from responsibility; sometimes as a mere preliminary step to admission to the Sacrament of the Lord's Supper. Sometimes errors are found prevailing even yet more debasing and absurd; errors which degrade the ordinance itself to a mere *opus operatum*, a formal and influential ceremony, and the recipient of the rite to a passive agent, charmed, as it were, by the performance of some outward visible sign, the token and pledge of no inward and spiritual grace. To infuse clearer views into minds thus darkened, is no easy part of ministerial duty. How much of forbearance does it require! how much of singleness of mind and faithfulness! how much of skill to probe, and of love to bind up the contrite heart! how much of vigilance to detect the self-satisfied and formal spirit! how much of ready application of the word of God to the consciences of each! above all, how much of special and earnest prayer, that at this solemn time no member of the church or congregation whom we serve, may take any hurt or hindrance by reason of our negligence! The errors themselves are grounded on such utter ignorance of religious truth, as indicates the necessity of going to the root of the matter, and laying afresh the whole foundation, beginning with the very elements of Christian faith;—and this, not in the ordinary mode of pastoral instruction, but by patient, personal, individual address, alarming some, awakening some, affecting some, undeceiving and reasoning with some; according to the degree of hardness or carelessness or blindness which, in different cases, the heart evinces.

"But, difficult as this work of preparation may be, and attended as it often is by its own peculiar trials, by much doubt and perplexity and fear, lest in our inexperience and want of discernment we should slay some souls that should not die, and save some souls alive that should not live, should make sad some hearts whom God hath not made sad, or speak peace to some whom it behoved us to reprove and warn, I cannot but believe that many of my reverend brethren reflect upon these periods of their ministry as the special seasons wherein a more abundant blessing seems to have been vouchsafed to their labours, a more gracious influence given to their teaching. They are doubtless enabled to look back upon these times with thankful feelings, as epochs whence they may date the first sowing of the seed, the first opening of the bud of promise, the first dawn of new light on the souls of those of whom they have good hope as their future 'crowns of rejoicing' and 'glory and joy,' in the Lord.*

"The Sacrament of the Lord's Supper calls for the discharge of functions often not less difficult and delicate. I observe by the returns, that the communicants in this diocese very rarely exceed one-tenth part of the congregation; and in the great majority of instances, the proportion is still smaller. This suggests a fearful consideration : 'Were there not ten cleansed, but where are the nine ? ' What judgment is the minister to form of that part of his charge who live in the habitual neglect of this ordinance ? What hope can he entertain of being able to render up his account of them with joy ? How is he to deal with them so as to preserve the proper mean between bidding presumptuously and discouraging a scrupulous brother, sincere, but weak in faith ? In populous parishes, sacramental meetings, with the special view of preparation for this ordinance, have been found useful. They admit of a more simple and familiar exposition of the rite than can generally be introduced into addresses from the pulpit, and enable the steward of these mysteries to grapple more closely with the personal objections which hinder the young Christian from discerning the Lord's body."

In many cases, a more frequent administration of the Holy Sacrament is much to be desired, so that the well-disposed part of the pastor's flock may have many opportunities of drawing near to the table of the Lord.

Local evils are next touched upon—"the profanation of the Sabbath," "the practice of keeping shops open sometimes to an extent which makes the Sabbath literally the market day, the payment of wages, the habits of cricketing, village festivals," &c. ; "the payment of the poor in church after divine service," the deficiency of cottage accommodation for the poor, and the consequent overcrowding of the inmates—Matters of this kind

* 1 Thess. ii. 19.

ought not to be supposed to be beyond the province of the
stewards of Christ's mysteries. Nothing is too trifling to be
turned to account, if it may be rendered conducive to the great
object of those who watch for souls that by all means they may
save some.

Dissent moreover is very active :

" Others are in the field who are ready to pick up the glean-
ings of the spiritual harvest, wherever a handful has been left,
whether on the top of the mountains, or in the valleys, which
stand so thick with corn below. They will, doubtless, put in
their sickle first, if the appointed husbandman is absent ; or
will go into some neglected part of the field, if the labourers
already employed are too few to reap it. Under these circumstances the parochial clergyman must be ever at his post, and
in his work. He must gird himself up to the difficulties
attendant upon an increased and increasing population. He
must be in the midst of his people, listening for ' the voice of
the Lord, saying, Whom shall I send, and who will go for us ? '
and ready to answer, ' Here am I, send me.'* The entire
week must be too short for the purposes of his ministry. He
must have no time for amusements and recreations, which are
not in keeping with the gravity of his sacred character. He
must ' use both public and private monitions and exhortations,
as well to the sick as to the whole within his cure, as need shall
require and occasion shall be given.' If he stands on a vantage
ground less high than formerly, he must be animated with a
spirit of more entire and simple reliance on the blessing of Him,
whose grace is sufficient for bringing all hearts into subjection
to himself. He must preach more earnestly, more simply,
more affectionately, the great doctrines of our church, one God,
one Saviour, and the Holy Spirit. He must have wherewithal
to answer the close and touching inquiry of the great Shepherd
and Bishop of souls, ' Where is the flock that was given thee,
thy beautiful flock ? ' He must not speak his own words, but

* Isaiah vi. 8.

adhere simply and literally, as an agent, to his instructions, that is, to deliver the message of. God to men, as one sent in the name of Christ, and by His authority to treat respecting reconciliation and peace. He is to proclaim—not himself— that would be a breach of allegiance to his kingly Master; but Christ Jesus, and Him crucified. His language is to be, 'Now then we are ambassadors for Christ; as though God did beseech you by us, we pray you, in Christ's stead, be ye reconciled unto God.' He must say nothing coldly or carelessly, but with the warmth and earnestness of a man who feels that, while he speaks, souls are at stake ; not like an heathen philosopher or mere essayist, without any serious views of eternity, but as a preacher of the New Testament, conscious of being the depositary of vital truths, and that life or death is in the message of his lips."

And would a reward be withheld from such labour as this ? Assuredly not. But then "The Christian minister, above all other men, should be a man of prayer. If he be not a man of prayer for others, where will be the seals given to his ministry in the conversion of souls to God ? God forbid that he should sin against the Lord in ceasing to pray for them. If he be not a man of prayer for himself, how shall he stand in his own strength ; how bear the weight of that heavy trust committed to his unworthy keeping ; how advise, or exhort, or rebuke, or console, or humble, in his ministerial visitings, day by day, the several members of his charge ?"

"May He," concluded the Bishop, "who is the great Head of the Church in earth and heaven watch over all its members ; protect, strengthen, bless them, with His perpetual care ! To those especially whom He has called to the ministry of His holy word may He grant grace in more abundant measure, that their labours may be made effectual to the great purposes of the gospel ! May He enable them so clearly to discern the truth as it is in Jesus, and so faithfully to maintain it, that in doing this they may both save themselves and them that hear them."

N

It will thus be seen that in his Primary Charge, the Bishop, though recognised as belonging to what was then called the Evangelical party, earnestly recommended, amongst other things, what some may have supposed to be almost the monopoly of the opposite school of thought—which so shortly after developed itself—the restoration and adornment of churches, reverential regard for "God's acre," an increased number of services in the church both on weekdays and Sundays, more frequent administrations of the Holy Communion, and earnestly deprecated degrading the parish priest into the mere Sunday preacher. It was impossible but that the utterance of such earnest exhortations, enforced as they were by a very impressive delivery, should awaken much interest. The Charge passed rapidly through three editions, and letters from all quarters showed the wide-spread influence of the Bishop's words.

Simeon of Cambridge writes :—

"Were your Lordship's Charge of an ordinary kind, I should feel that in presenting to your Lordship my humble and grateful acknowledgements for the honour conferred upon me by the gift of it, I should properly discharge the duty incumbent upon me. But it is not of an ordinary kind. It has humbled me in 'the dust, and filled me with contrition.' My own judgment goes along with it; and if my life were to come over again, I would endeavour more than I have done to conform to it. My only comfort is that there is a fountain opened for sin and uncleanness, and that I am yet at liberty to wash in it. With most respectful and unfeigned gratitude to your Lordship, both for the gift and for the wounds inflicted by it, I remain, your Lordship's most devoted servant, C. Simeon."

Coleridge, in writing to ask about the Charge, under date October 15, 1829, thus refers to a sermon preached by the Bishop at the anniversary of the Society for the Propagation of the Gospel:—

"Your sermon before the Society for Propagating the Gospel,

&c., I have just read in my report. It was a subject I knew
preached on *con amore*, and the sermon delighted me. I
think you have put the cause on the only true principle—the
authority of the precept, not the success of the practice, and if
I may talk of approval in matters so out of my way, I should say
that it is useful, especially in these days, to look at that subject
as *to its results* soberly, and not for the sake of attracting
temporary and unsound support, either to diminish the
difficulties or their obstinate enduring nature, or to exaggerate
the degree of success with which they have been, or probably
for years will be, encountered. It seems to me in the present
day, that in the zeal of some for the promotion of good objects,
the motives of the contributors are too little regarded; if subscribers can be got, no matter upon what principle they subscribe. I daresay you know numerous instances where contribution to a charitable society is merely subscription to one
supposed party rather than another. One mode of making the
mean blessed to the end is to try to purify the motive; and that
may be done, among other ways, by setting the duty forward
always upon the right principle, and fairly stating the probable
result. John Keble says, that we had more charity when there
were fewer subscribers, fewer meetings, and fewer and less
powerful societies. These things perhaps are *necessary* incon-
veniences in advancing the good cause, but I think those who
are influential should be aware of them, and labour to reduce
the evil while they profit by the good."

CHAPTER XI.

Visit to the Channel Islands.—Bishop Sumner the first Bishop of Winchester who had gone there.—Guernsey.—Sark.—The Bishop's Party "in Perils by Waters."—Jersey.—Church Matters in connection with the Islands.—Alderney.—Abolition of Hop Sunday at Farnham.—Bible Society Meetings.—The Bishop presents Rev. S. Wilberforce to Brighstone.

THE visitation of the clergy and churchwardens in Hampshire and Surrey was no sooner concluded than the Bishop, according to previous arrangement, paid his first visit to the Channel Islands. He was accompanied thither by Mrs. Sumner, his two eldest children, and two chaplains, the Rev. A. Dallas, and the Rev. Philip Jacob.* Government placed a steamer, "The Lightning," at the Bishop's disposal, and the early autumn found the Episcopal party *en route* for Guernsey. So long as the Channel Islands form part of the diocese of Winchester, it is most desirable that the Bishop should be a good sailor. Certainly in this respect Bishop Sumner was well fitted for the post which he occupied. The sea never seemed to affect him. He enjoyed the rough weather off the Caskets, or the boiling waters of the Swinge off Alderney, and when, after twelve hours' tossing, his chaplains have been utterly unable to take their proper part in whatever might be the business of the moment, Bishop Sumner used to land fresh and cheery, with a kind word for old friends, and a genial recognition of old faces, ready at once to begin his Episcopal work by a general reception of the clergy, confirmation of candidates, or consecration of a

---

* Mr. Jacob, at the Bishop's request, had given up his curacy at Newport in 1828, and had taken up his residence in Farnham Castle, as domestic Chaplain, the duties of which office he fulfilled till 1831.

church, as the case might be. It is very rarely indeed, that the passage to the Channel Islands is smooth. The tides run very strongly, and the sea is almost invariably more or less rough. But all is soon forgotten when Guernsey is reached. St. Peter's Port, the only town in the island (which contains a population of about thirty thousand), presents a very beautiful appearance from the sea. It is built on the slope of a hill, and the gabled houses rise one above the other in a very picturesque manner. Very lovely it looks, when, on a summer's morning, you see it emerging from the waters, like Genoa in the sunny South. Here, at the beginning of September, the Episcopal party landed. About eleven years previously, Fisher Bishop of Salisbury, had spent some little time on the islands, on behalf of Bishop North, but as far as I can ascertain no Bishop of Winchester had visited this portion of the See before Bishop Sumner. It was then only natural that the inhabitants should welcome with much warmth their own Bishop, who thus early in the days of his Episcopate gave this practical proof of his interest in their well-being. His daily progress from village to village was of a *quasi-regal* character, and crowds followed the carriage, frequently expressing their feelings by hearty cheers.

Nature in the Channel Islands is very prodigal of her richest favours. Fruit and flowers are magnificent, and the inhabitants have a pretty custom of sending presents of both to those whom they wish to honour. Not a day ever passed without the Bishop and the members of his party being loaded with such gifts. The upper classes in the Channel Islands speak English, but the labouring classes almost invariably speak French or a sort of patois. It was therefore necessary that the Bishop should, in the country villages, administer the rite of confirmation in French. His connection with Switzerland here stood him in good stead, for he was a capital French scholar, and moreover had the advantage of being able to submit his French addresses to the catechumens to Mrs. Sumner for correction previous to their delivery. In the visits to the Channel Islands which, from this time forth the Bishop paid periodically about every fourth year, it was his habit to arrange for all the clergy of the particular island in which he was, to meet him immediately after his landing, and then a programme was drawn up, to suit their convenience, of confirmations, and whatever other Episcopal functions he might be called upon to perform. The visitation of the clergy was always his final act, after which he hospitably received them at dinner. About ten days was usually allotted to Guernsey and Jersey respectively, and a day or two, according to circumstances, to Alderney and Sark.

In connection with his visit on this occasion to the latter island, the Bishop incurred really considerable danger. Sark lies some half-a-dozen miles east of Guernsey, and is about three miles long, by one-and-a-half broad, containing a population of between five and six hundred souls. The island is protected on all sides from the invasion of man by rocks and cliffs. On the north-east side there has been a tunnel cut through the solid rock by which the adventurer gains the table-land, but small boats must be used for landing at this spot, for the steamers dare not come too near the beach. The inhabitants of Sark are, as may be supposed, somewhat primitive in their manners and customs, but singularly free from vicious habits. I remember on one occasion asking the Lord of Sark (for it belongs to one proprietor called "Le Seigneur"), whether a species of *Lock-up* which we were just passing was often used. He told me that he only remembered one occasion on which anyone had ever been incarcerated there. A young girl had it appeared called out in a mocking manner after the clergyman* of the island "vous

---

* The present incumbent of St. Mary, Sark, the Rev. J. Cachemaille, has not left the island for thirty-nine years. He was on one occasion the witness of a terrible scene when a cutter, carrying some friends of his from Sark to Guernsey, was wrecked, and all those on board drowned. He has never been able to nerve himself since that fatal day to quit his island-home. The Bishop in vain, by summoning him to his visitation in Guernsey, endeavoured to break the spell. When the day came, "unavoidable circumstances" were sure to prevent his making an appearance.

avez les jambes de coq," and for this very heinous offence was sentenced to twenty-four hours' imprisonment in the "lock-up." But when she was duly barred and bolted in, the authorities, to their dismay, discovered that the place was absolutely air-tight, and that if the girl were left there she would be suffocated. The crime of which she had been guilty was thought hardly sufficient for so extreme a penalty, and accordingly a compromise was entered into between the parties, and on the culprit's giving her *parole d'honneur* she was allowed to sit for twenty-four hours in the open doorway, carrying on during the daytime her usual vocation of stocking-knitting! It was to this little island that the Bishop went in "The Lightning," landing as I have described on the north-east coast, and entering through the tunnel. He had to consecrate a small church, and subsequently hold a confirmation. The intercourse between Guernsey and Sark is somewhat infrequent, owing to the dangerous character of the coast, and the extraordinary vehemence of the tides, and the Bishop, having offered to take a few friends over for the day, the party on the island consisted of more than the usual number of Episcopal followers. Mrs. Sumner, the two children, and the chaplains, were of course included in it. The Bishop had scarcely finished his duties, before the Captain sent word that the wind was rising, the tide contrary, and that if the Bishop and his party did not go on board at once, they would be obliged to remain on the island all night. Hurriedly they made their way down to the beach, for the prospect of a night in Sark, without any accommodation for so large a party having been previously provided, was not of the most agreeable character. Two boats were in readiness to convey the passengers from the shore to the steamer. The Bishop, Mrs. Sumner, and their daughter, Dean Durrand (an old and infirm man, who had been originally urged not to join the party, but in vain) and his daughter Mrs. Kershaw, Mr. Dallas, and several other gentlemen, entered the first boat. The second boat-load, consisting only of gentlemen, took a short cut through the surf, and

reached the steamer first. The sea was now very rough, and
as the boat in which the Bishop was approached the steamer,
a wave caught it, and violently dashed it against the other.
Ropes were let down from the steamer, and the gentlemen in
the boat which had first arrived urged to spring on the deck as
rapidly as possible. Glad indeed were the party in the second
boat to hear the cry "shove off" and see the empty one glide
away. But now their turn came. The gentlemen seized the
ropes, and by springing at the exact moment, succeeded in
gaining the deck of the steamer. These were young and active,
but there still remained in the boat the Bishop, Mrs. Sumner,
their daughter, the Dean, Mrs. Kershaw, Mr. Dallas, (with his
arm, which had been broken a short time before, in a sling) and
Ainsley, the Bishop's valet.* The Captain foreseeing the difficulty they would have in springing at the right moment, ordered
the ladder to be let down. Hardly had this been done, when the
swell carried the boat close under the steamer, so that the hooks
of the ladder became entangled in the boat, which was sub-
merged by the rolling of the steamer. Ainsley attempted to
disengage the ladder, which, however, fortunately broke, and
released the boat, but he had not time to loose his hold of the
ladder before the vessel rolled away, and the Bishop, to his
horror, saw his servant at one moment hanging in mid-air over
the stormy sea, at the next plunged down into the waves.
Happily he clung tight to the ladder, but a new danger presented itself, for the boat was again seized by a wave, and was

---

* The old adage that no man is a hero to his valet-de-chambre was singularly
untrue in the case of the Bishop. His successive valets were throughout his life
most faithful and attached followers. Ainsley, referred to above, in due time
became butler, and remained in the Bishop's service nearly forty years until his
death in 1866. His successor, J. Higgate, after eleven years' faithful service was
appointed one of the clerks at the Cathedral, was unswerving in his affection for
the Bishop and every member of his family, and died much regretted at the close
of 1875. J. Powell, who succeeded Higgate, was promoted on Ainsley's death to
be butler, and was a most trusted servant until the Bishop's death ; and J. Read,
Powell's successor, nursed the Bishop through the last six years of his life with a
devotion which could not be surpassed.

on the point of being dashed against and doubtless crushing
Ainsley, when a sailor swung himself down, took firm hold of
the collar of his coat, dragged him out of reach of the boat, and
was himself pulled back with his burden on to the deck. The
boat by this time was half full of water. The old Dean who was
very deaf, stood up bewildered. "Sit down, Sir," they shouted
from the steamer, but he only stretched out his hands in much
alarm. His daughter began to scream, and Mrs. Sumner, with
considerable presence of mind, pulled him down at her knees
and held him there in the water, till he could be hoisted up by
two sailors. And so, in succession, each one was dragged on to
the deck, and when all were safe, the crew and passengers
gathered together; there was a general hand-shaking; the
gentlemen uncovered their heads, and a fervent thanksgiving
was offered to God for what was felt on all sides to be a preservation from imminent danger.

Jersey, with a population of about 50,000, lies some twenty
miles south-east of Guernsey, and vies with its sister island in
loveliness. To Guernsey, perhaps, the palm must be given for
its rocks and cliff scenery, but there is nothing in Guernsey to
equal the bay of St. Heliers. It is the Bay of Naples in minia-
ture. The Bishop's reception here was no less enthusiastic than
it had been in Guernsey. Dissent has always had a very strong
hold upon these islands, but general rumour had spoken before-
hand of the Bishop as a liberal-hearted, earnest, God-fearing
man, and all parties joined together in giving him a hearty
welcome. Church feeling was then at a very low ebb in the
island. The surplice was a vestment almost unknown. The
communion table was sometimes in the centre of the church,
sometimes hidden away in a side-aisle, and the churches themselves disfigured by large square pews and hideous galleries in
every direction. These matters required and received very
gentle handling. Rigid orders or rough dealing would have
raised a storm which it would have been very difficult to allay.
But this state of things has been gradually changed. The erec-

tion of new churches with comely and orderly arrangements
has put to shame the hideousness and un-ecclesiastical character of the old buildings, and now you will find as hearty and
as well-conducted services in many a Channel Island church as
in England itself. In connection with this visit an interesting
anecdote is recorded in Dr. Marsh's Life.

Miss Marsh writes :—

"The Bishop of Winchester kindly preached for him" (at
Beckenham) "on Sunday, June 29th, (1862) and my father
much enjoyed his society. He had a natural reverence for
authority ; and when he had, as in this case, perfect confidence
in and sympathy with his diocesan, it was an especial pleasure
to him to welcome him under his roof. There were many pleasant events in past years to recall together ; and foremost in
their memories, seemed to be a visit which the Bishop had paid
to the Channel Islands when my father was residing in Guernsey for part of the summer of 1829. It was the first time that
a Bishop had been there for years, and it produced quite an
excitement of interest amongst the inhabitants. The Bishop
was accompanied on that visit to Guernsey by his chaplains, the
Rev. Alexander Dallas, and the Rev. Philip (now Archdeacon)
Jacob. They all united in promoting, in every way in their
power, the work of the Lord. The Bishop carried on his own
special office of ordaining and confirming, and also united with
his two excellent chaplains in preaching, visiting, and address-
ing schools. It was a time of great interest, and doubtless of
much blessing. One remarkable instance of conversion may be
recorded here. In the island of Jersey an unhappy young man
was at the time in prison, and under sentence of death for
murder committed in a fit of passion. There had not been an
execution in the island for twenty-four years, and the case
excited painful interest among the inhabitants. Mr. Dallas and
Mr. Jacob visited the poor criminal, and earnestly pointed him
to the Saviour. He became truly penitent, and their conversations and prayers were made the means of leading him to cast

himself as a guilty sinner on the Lamb of God who taketh away the sin of the world ; thus he was enabled to trust in that Saviour's pardoning love, and to meet without dread the awful fulfilment of his sentence." Life of Dr. Marsh, pp. 446, 447.

Alderney, with a population of nearly 3,000 souls, distant from Guernsey about fifteen miles, is the nearest of the whole group to the French coast, lying only seven miles west of Cape La Hogue. It is chiefly known in England in connection with Alderney cows (most of which come from Jersey) and the building of the breakwater for a harbour for English vessels.

These four islands the Bishop always visited periodically, and in no part of his diocese was he more cordially welcomed.

A correspondent of the " Guardian " writes, in the issue of that paper for September 22, 1875 :

" Distance from England has not simply isolated us from the rest of the English Church, but we were thereby debarred for 200 years from the personal superintendence of our diocesan, and consequently from the rite of confirmation. It will scarcely be credited, perhaps, at the present day, that the first Anglican Bishop who ever visited Jersey in an official capacity was Bishop Fisher of Salisbury, who visited the islands at the desire of Bishop North in 1818. On that occasion crowds of cate-chumens of all ages showed their eagerness to avail themselves of the opportunity. The late Bishop Sumner (to his honour be it said) was the first diocesan who deigned to visit this distant part of his diocese, and I have more than once heard him state that in one parish he had at one time kneeling before him six catechumens who had passed their eightieth year. I believe that these Episcopal visits, which have been repeated every fourth year since 1829, have had much to do with the establish-ment of chancels and altar-rails, for it is a fact that these improvements were first carried out in those churches in which confirmation was administered."

On the Bishop's return from the Channel Islands to Farnham, it was a source of much gratification to him to find that certain

local evils connected with what was called " The Hop Sunday "
were greatly diminished.   Farnham, as is well known, is the
centre of a hop district, and during the time of picking it is
filled to overflowing by an imported population of roughs and
their belongings.   The following description of the scene on
Hop Sunday, and the successful attempt which was made to do
away with it, has been kindly sent to me by the Rev. Charles
Hume, who was then curate of Farnham.

"It was the mid Sunday of the hop-picking season, when
the town of Farnham was handed over to the dominion of the
hop-pickers.   Booths for the sale of vast quantities of fruit,
stalls piled with cakes of every description, and presenting
mountains of gilded gingerbread, were erected early on Sunday
morning, as close as they could stand, along both sides of the
street, leaving only room for a carriage or the old road-waggon
of the period with its eight horses and tinkling bells to pass
between them.   The Hop Sunday was a sort of Carnival for
the neighbourhood miles round.   The country folk in gigs or
carts, or on foot, flocked into the town, while in Farnham itself
there were thousands of hop-pickers congregated from far and
near.   The streets were thronged with the idle and profane ;
and it was no uncommon thing to see people as early as nine
o'clock on that Sunday morning drunk in the booths, or stagger-
ing on the crowded pathway.   Such a state of things was
extremely distressing to the Bishop, and I remember it was one
of the first efforts to which he directed my attention when I
entered on the duties of the curacy of Farnham.   Catching the
inspiration of his zeal, I endeavoured to carry out the earnest
wishes of my Bishop, and commenced operations suggested or
sanctioned by him, and in which we earnestly sought the
guidance of Almighty God.   Copies of the statute of Charles II.,
prohibiting the sale on Sunday of things other than necessary,
were printed and posted up conspicuously through the town.
Every public-house in Farnham and its outskirts was visited,
and the landlords were earnestly requested to co-operate with

us in bringing about a better state of things. On the preceding Sunday notice was given in church that at the evening service on Hop Sunday a sermon would be preached on the subject of remembering the Sabbath-day to keep it holy. The time drew on, and on Saturday the clergyman received a visit from Admiral Sir John Ommaney, a neighbouring magistrate, telling him that he had been informed of a design to maltreat the clergyman on his return from the service, and that in consequence of this information some special constables had been sworn in, who would be ready to act on the first appearance of violence. Every preparation was made at church to accommodate the roughs, and they filled the church to overflowing. The text chosen for the sermon was 1 Peter iii., 15, ' Sanctify the Lord God in your hearts,' and throughout the service those rough-looking men were rapt in earnest attention. When the service was over and the congregation broken up, the clergyman and his wife, who insisted on accompanying him, left the church. It is some distance from the church-door to the gate of the churchyard. Throngs of people lined the pathway. The special constables, though not conspicuous, were ready to spring into action, like Roderic Dhu's men, at a moment's notice. But it needed not. No word was spoken—no hand raised against them, and quietly they walked home through the midst of the multitude, and from that hour to the present, Hop Sunday at Farnham has been numbered with the things that are passed away."

One other parochial event connected with 1829 deserves to be recorded. The Bishop was throughout life a staunch and firm supporter of the Bible Society. He never wavered in his allegiance to it. He felt that just as persons of very different creeds might well join together in subscribing for the erection of a light-house for the purpose of warning vessels of sunken rocks or hidden shoals, so those who differed with regard to Church discipline or doctrine, but yet consented to abide by the teaching of Scripture, might unite together in order to spread

abroad copies of the Word of God, which should warn men of
the danger of sin, the value of their souls, and of the redemp-
tion which Christ had wrought out for them. In the winter
of 1829 the first Bible Society meeting was held in the hall of
Farnham Castle. There was considerable excitement about it
in the town, the novelty of the whole proceeding, as well as the
interest of the occasion itself, attracting numbers to it. So large,
indeed, was the attendance that it was found necessary in subsequent years to hold the meeting either in the schoolroom or the
Assembly rooms of the town. The Bishop usually arranged to
have these meetings on the Monday after the ordination had
been held. This secured a supply of good speakers, and those
interested in the work were invited in the evening to dine at
the Castle. The drawing-room was thrown open afterwards for
the reception of a larger number than could be accommodated
at the dinner-table, and at ten o'clock the party adjourned to
the Chapel, when a hymn, an appropriate exposition of some
passage of Scripture, and prayer, brought the evening to a close.

It is interesting to find in a letter from the Bishop, dated
June 8th, 1830, an allusion to one who was afterwards destined
to play so important a part in the Church of Christ, and to be
the Bishop's own successor in the See of Winchester. Writing
to Mr. Dallas, he says : " Samuel Wilberforce, now curate of
Checkendon, succeeds to the vacant living of Brighstone, and I
trust will prove an useful man in a sphere of considerable
importance. It is now exactly one hundred years ago since
Isaac Walton was collated to that living, A.D. 1730. He was
succeeded in 1780 by Digby, so that the two last incumbents
have filled the ground for a century." Only eleven years, however, did Samuel Wilberforce hold this benefice, for in 1841 the
Bishop presented him to the rectory of Alverstoke, having
previously, at the close of 1839, appointed him Archdeacon of
Surrey, and in 1840 a Canon of Winchester.

CHAPTER XII.

IT is sad to have to turn from these scenes of Episcopal and
parochial work to the record of stirring events and political
strife and disaster. But the close of 1830 ushered in a time of
great anxiety and disquietude. From one end of the country
to the other men's minds were unsettled. The agricultural
districts were inflamed by the introduction of machinery; the
political horizon was disturbed by the agitation connected with
the Reform Bill; and the minds of ecclesiastics were kept on
the stretch by the whisperings concerning contemplated
changes in the Established Church, and by a very generally
expressed dissatisfaction at the existing state of things. And
so it came to pass that no interest or class of society was free
from trouble and anxiety. Landlords and farmers received
threatening letters. "Swing" was a familiar signature forebod-
ing evil, and incendiary fires blazed on high night after night.
The Bishop was anxious, if possible, to prevent evils arising in
the neighbourhood of Farnham in connection with the introduction of machinery and the rate of wages, and accordingly
summoned in November a meeting at the Castle of all the
farmers and rate-payers of the district. Discussion was long

and animated. For three hours, matters in dispute between the employers and employed were debated, but at last the Bishop succeeded in obtaining a general promise, that the rate of wages throughout the district should be raised. It is evident, however, that there was a very strong feeling of discontent abroad, for it was not thought safe that Mrs. Sumner should drive out except in the park, and the following sentence in a letter from her to Mrs. McNiven shows the general state of the country :—

"The Duke of Gloucester came to Bagshot, to be at the head of his household, who are all armed. The threats have been very dreadful against his residence."

The Bishop in writing to Coleridge thus refers to the subject :

"FARNHAM CASTLE, *Nov.* 27*th*, 1830.

"I was in town for a day this week—a grudged day, and given only of necessity, for my presence was very requisite here, inasmuch as the ochlocracy has been ruling in all the neighbouring villages. I am happy to say, however, that an excellent spirit has been shown here in all classes, and they have not only not risen against ourselves, but have actually ventured to volunteer a march at eleven o'clock at night against a mob from the neighbourhood reported to be meditating an attack upon us.

'Impius hæc tam culta,' &c.

But it has been a fearful week for the county, and we only now respire."

It was only a few days after the meeting above mentioned, that the party at the Castle were alarmed whilst at dinner by a message being brought in, to say that a mob of men were outside the Castle gates, anxious to come in and have an interview with the Bishop. What was to be done ? The Bishop at once determined to go out and speak to them, and accordingly, accompanied by Mr. Jacob, Mr. Robert Maunoir (Mrs. Sumner's brother), and one or two of the servants, he passed outside the Castle gates, which were immediately closed behind him, and he found himself confronted by the angry faces of the mob.—A parley ensued.—The men were encouraged to state their griev- ances, which consisted chiefly of a supposed want of compliance on the part of the farmers with the agreements entered into at the previous meeting at the Castle, and the Bishop promised that he would do all he could to redress their wrongs, and was able after some time to persuade them to separate peaceably.

This, however, was only the beginning of troubles. It is not necessary now, to say much about the Parliamentary battles, which issued in the ultimate passing of the Reform Bill, the dif- ficulties which the Reform party had to encounter, the opposition persistently maintained by the House of Lords, or the violent feelings excited on all sides, for these are matters of history. But undoubtedly, the general feeling of unrest to which the Reform discussions gave rise, awakened in the public mind con- siderable opposition to the Established Church. Nor can it be denied, that there were at that time a great many evils con- nected with the organisation of the Church which called loudly for reform. Insufficiency of income, and the fact that so many livings were without glebe houses for the residence of the in- cumbents, rendered pluralities almost a necessity, and a great evil they were. It was no uncommon sight to see the officiat- ing clergymen hurry from the morning service in one parish to the afternoon service in another, whilst the mud-besplashed boots *would* appear from under the ill-washed and iron-mouldy surplice. The payment of tithes in kind formed, moreover, a constant source of disagreement between the clergyman and his parishioners. May I not add that cathedral bodies were, in many cases, the centres rather of lethargy and repose, than of life and activity ? Around the dean the canons clustered in goodly numbers ; but capitular revenues, and it may be a gene- rous hospitality occupied more of their time and thoughts, than plans for the spiritual welfare of the diocese of which with the

o

Bishop they formed the ecclesiastical centre.   The month's
residence in the well-kept Cathedral close, was an agreeable
relaxation after parochial duties.   Bishops too, were beyond all
others, a mark for popular abuse.   They were accused of living
in purple and fine linen, and faring sumptuously every day; they
were supposed in many cases to be hinderers, rather than promoters, of pastoral activity, and the mind of the common people
was therefore stedfastly set against them.   The accession of
William the Fourth had given an impetus to those in favour of
movement.   It was thought that he himself was more disposed
to changes in the Church than George the Fourth had been,
and hence the party was stirred up to increased activity.   An
interview between the King and some of the Bishops on Sunday
July 3, 1830, is graphically described by the Bishop of Chester.
The Bishop of Winchester was unavoidably absent in consequence of his ordination being held on the day appointed by
the King.

"Before I set out for Leicester," he writes, "I must give you
a brief account of our interview yesterday, because it will be
gratifying to know that Episcopal heads are safe on their
shoulders.   The *entrée* was a little *farouche*—no grace nor
much tact; could not think of Bishop of Carlisle's name. 'Who
is *this* Bishop? I remember him at Oxford—Bishop of
Rochester—O, this is the Bishop that was an ensign! Bishop
of Chester—Sumner—brother of the Bishop of *Durham!*' All
this being despatched, we stood round and about the room, the
three Archbishops, ' the Primate of all England, the Metropolitan of England, the Primate of Ireland,' in front.   And then a
longish speech, in which we were told of the most cordial
attachment to the Church of England.   ' No country could be
great without an established Church.   It is impossible to
survey the world and not to see that England is, and is intended
to be, a great country; and therefore it must have an established
Church—and that Church must be supported—and it is my
determination to support it with firmness, yet with moderation.

Nothing so unfair as the attacks which have been made on the revenues of the Church, and those who hold them. Is a man, who in any other garb would be held up to respect and honour, to be insidiously assailed because he is a Churchman, and has a sufficient income! So far from thinking the revenues of the Church too much, I should be glad to see them increased. All the subjects of the realm being now freed from all restraints, &c., toleration has its bounds. I know the principle which placed my family on the throne, toleration—but this must not become licence, and I am resolved to uphold the Church of England, to follow the example of George the Third. I have only deviated from it in calling you together this day' (supposed to allude to the Sunday assemblage), 'because I would take the opportunity, the earliest afforded me, of assuring those whom I see before me, men whom I admire, I revere—if I may say it —I love, of the sentiments with which I ascend the throne.' Then His Majesty alluded to his having that morning received the sacrament, and seemed to forget that it was no longer a test.* He desired that his having received it might be recorded in the registry of the Chapel Royal—that he above all might show obedience to the law, and his conformity to the Protestant Church. He also thanked the Bishop of London (Blomfield), for the good advice which he had given him, instead of fulsome flattery, and desired to have a copy of the sermon 'fairly transcribed,' that he might 'keep it by him.' 'And now, my lords, I have nothing more to say to you. You are going, I doubt not, as soon as Parliament breaks up, to your respective dioceses, and the sooner you go the better.'

"Upon this we prepared for a march in quick time, but were recalled by the trumpet of our leader, which reminded us that all this grace must not be without its reply. The Archbishop gave a very proper one, but in an unusually embarrassed manner, which I did not wonder at, thinking the whole business

---

* It will be remembered that the Repeal of the Test and Corporation Acts had been carried in 1828.

rather awkward. He also apologised for your absence, together
with the Bishop of Durham and others, which was graciously
·received and properly understood. Altogether, I think there
were seventeen of us, so we made a goodly show. As we
retired, I met some judges coming in, who I presume, received
a lecture upon law. There was all the cordiality about the
·Church, which seemed to proceed from a conviction of its
importance to the State, and there was an evident disposition
to be well thought of by those who worship God. I should have
been happy to hear some acknowledgment of the importance of
Christianity to the individual. Farewell. Breakfast calls."

It will be seen by the foregoing letter, that the King was
not only favourable to the Church, but to the Church Establishment as then existing ; but notwithstanding this support in
high quarters, the feeling of the country was very unmistakeably
expressed in favour of some Reform in the Church, as well as
in the constitution of Parliament. Towards the close of the
year 1831, this feeling broke out into overt acts of violence.
Riots took place in various parts of the country. In Bristol
the mob was inflamed by the presence of Sir Charles Wetherell,
the Recorder. He had made himself very unpopular with the
Reform party, for according to Lord Russell (" Recollections
and Suggestions," p. 78), he with Sir Edward Sugden tried to
unpick the Reform Bill, thread by thread, leaving no remnant
of the original texture. His appearance at Bristol was the
signal for a fearful outbreak of violence. The rioters got complete possession of the town, the Mansion House was burnt, the
gaol broken open, the prisoners freed, and the prison burnt.
The Bishop's palace too was set on fire, and completely destroyed.

It was just at this time that Archbishop Howley went
down to Canterbury, purposing to hold a visitation there. It
was intended that he should be received by the Mayor and
Corporation, who had invited him to luncheon at the Town
Hall. The Archbishop's carriage drove up, Archdeacon Croft
sitting by him, and some persons who were friendly to him

came to the carriage and begged that he would not go to
luncheon, adding that there was a mob of persons in the town
who seemed bent on mischief, and they could not answer for
the consequences if the Archbishop carried out his intentions
of holding his visitation. The Archbishop acted in accordance
with this advice, and remained in his carriage, and told the
postilions to drive to the Deanery. The postilions did not
know the way thither, and drove backwards and forwards about
the streets of Canterbury, the mob following the carriage
vehemently hooting. The consequence was, that at length the
Archbishop was actually obliged to leave Canterbury without
holding his visitation, and, as it is said, at once gave notice to
the Government that he, at any rate, should not oppose the
issuing of a Commission of Inquiry respecting the revenues and
other circumstances connected with the Established Church.
Accordingly, the very next year a commission was issued under
the Great Seal, " authorising and directing the commissioners
therein named to make a full and correct inquiry respecting
the revenues and patronage belonging to the several archiepis-
copal and episcopal sees in England and Wales, to all cathedral
and collegiate churches, and to all ecclesiastical benefices
(including donatives, perpetual curacies, and chapelries), with
or without cure of souls, and the names of the several patrons
thereof, and other circumstances therewith connected."

The spirit of opposition to those holding high office in the
Church, which thus confronted the Archbishop at Canterbury,
also showed itself at Farnham. Here the mob had for a time
almost complete possession of the town, and it was much
feared that they would actually attack the Castle. They did
indeed march in large numbers up the Castle Hill, and took
possession of the open space in front of the entrance lodge, but
the ponderous gates of the Castle effectually stopped their
onward progress, and they retreated with the intention of burning the Bishop, who had made himself unpopular with the mob
by his opposition to the Reform Bill, in effigy in the market-

place.* This was, however, on that occasion prevented by a worthy inhabitant of the town, who, in concert with some of the tradesmen of the place, succeeded in rescuing the figure destined to the flames, pacified the mob by giving them five shillings, and by burying the effigy in his own garden effectually prevented its suffering any further ignominy at the hands of the rioters. The Bishop writes with reference to this, as indicating the state of the country at large: "I have no doubt that we have already gone through several pages of a volume of revolution. Miserable are they who cannot look beyond it or over it. What happened here was nothing, absolutely nothing, a mere handful of rabble—nothing to what might have been expected, and to what probably will be, ere matters are finished. But this in my mind is as nothing compared with the unsettled and excited state of religious minds— which is dividing us daily, and is the feature above all others which makes me fear for our Church—and the only consideration which at present gives me real anxiety."

An incident connected with this time has been mentioned to me, by one who was then an inhabitant of Farnham. It appears that an unruly spirit of the day came into the bank with a bundle of papers under his arm, and with a knowing wink called the banker's attention to his bundle, and informed him that it was composed of placards abusive of the Bishop and of the Church. The banker looked him full in the face and said, " Mr. ——, are you aware how you stand with us ; do you know the state of your account here, and how much you are in our debt ? I here distinctly tell you, that I will proceed to the utmost of my power against you, unless this very instant, you put your whole bundle of placards which you intend posting all over the town into the fire, and burn them in my presence."

---

* One who actually was present on the occasion has told me that it was a very common custom with the Farnham roughs to burn in effigy anyone who at the moment had made himself unpopular with them. A few nights after the rescue of the Bishop's effigy described above, they constructed another figure and succeeded in burning it.

The owner of the placards, it need hardly be said, under this threat at once succumbed, burnt the papers and speedily effected his retreat.

But in the midst of these riotous demonstrations, a grievously heavy blow fell on the inmates of the Castle. The Bishop had been for some time over-taxing his strength; the anxiety connected first of all with the Roman Catholic Relief Bill, and then with the Reform Bill, told upon him, and in November 1831, he was prostrated by a severe attack of fever. For some weeks he lay hovering between life and death, and at one time his strength had so completely given way, that it was supposed that death had actually taken place. Dr. Chambers, Sir William Knighton, and Mr. Newnham, the local medical man, were in constant attendance upon him. Intense anxiety was expressed on all sides, that a life so valuable should be spared, and earnest supplications were offered up on his behalf. The church at Farnham was opened daily for the special purpose of enabling the parishioners to commend their Bishop to the loving mercy and care of God, and on his ultimate recovery it was acknowledged by many that never had there been a more evident answer to the fervent prayers of his people for one they loved so well.

The Rev. Charles Hume, who was at that time still curate of Farnham, has kindly furnished me with the following reminiscences of this sad time :—

" There never was a house where domestic happiness was more beautifully seen, or where the intercourse of friends was more genially enjoyed, than at Farnham Castle. It was the very home of affection. The Bishop himself, formed in the very 'prodigality of nature,' adorned the society which he drew around him. And who that was ever intimate at Farnham Castle, can forget the joyous radiance of Mrs. Sumner, of whom it may be truly said, that she was the centre of a system of gladness, which influenced the whole circle as it moved harmoniously around her. The very clouds of anxiety which here must pass over us all, seemed to catch a brightness as they

passed over her.   To thoughtful observers it may have seemed
too full a cup of joy to be safely permitted to continue.   And in
the midst of it all, the Bishop was struck with sickness which
soon became somewhat alarming, and advanced to a complica-
tion of symptoms so formidable, as to create the saddest apprehensions for his life.

"A heavy gloom, as of the shadow of death, came over
that sunny home. 'All joy was darkened.' The mirth of the
house was gone, 'and the gate seemed smitten with desolation,'
as the cloud, deeper and deeper still, increased.

"Daily I passed all the time I could spare from work in
Farnham Castle.   Never can I forget the *utter silence* of the
house, when alarm was the expression on every countenance,
and they moved about in distress with cautious step, and spoke
with bated breath.

"At this crisis, when the physician had given up all hope, I
requested the permission of Sir Wm. Knighton to see the
Bishop *once more*.   In the delirious state of the Bishop, Sir Wm.
Knighton could not allow any new person to be introduced
within his observation.   Ainsley suggested that I might see the
Bishop, if, while he himself stood in the door of his room, I were
to look over his shoulder.   And thus I took what I fully believed
would be my farewell of the Bishop.   He was lying on his back
—his head considerably raised by pillows—the expression of
his countenance *supremely happy*—his hands and arms up-
lifted, as though reaching toward some one with whom he was
in delightful communion.

"That same evening I received a request from Mrs. Sumner,
that I would take the Bishop's carriage early in the morning
to bring the boys home from their tutor's, near Reading.   I set
out before daylight, with the melancholy persuasion, that on
my return with the boys, we should find their father dead.

"As soon as it was light enough to read, I took out my pocket-
testament, and opening it my eyes fell upon the words 'Lord,
if he sleep, he shall do well.' I read the whole chapter, and

with great comfort got my thoughts away from death, to Him who is 'the Resurrection and the Life.'

"On my return with the boys, and as I drew near the Castle, I recognized some friends of mine taking their usual walk. There are some who think that intense excitement so quickens the faculties, that under its influence the ear catches sounds, and the eye has the power of distinguishing objects at a much greater distance than usual. Whether this was the case or not in the present instance I cannot say, but certain it is that, while my friends were yet a considerable way off, I thought I perceived as we approached them an air of cheerfulness in their general bearing, which acted as a charm upon me, and at once lifted up my heart from the depths of despair. Stopping the carriage I quietly said, 'How about the Bishop?' The answer was—and I could not help thinking of those first verses on which my eye had fallen at break of day—'This morning, about nine o'clock he went into a natural sleep. He is sleeping still, and Sir William Knighton says it is the turning point of his recovery.' And so through God's infinite mercy (and shall we hesitate to believe it was His answer to the effectual and fervent prayers which had been 'made of the Church to God for him'), the Bishop recovered from that hour. Thus was his valuable life divided into two nearly equal portions by this most solemn event of all God's dealings with him. And not fifteen years, as with Hezekiah, but more than forty years were added unto him."

During the whole of this illness Mrs. Sumner nursed the Bishop with an amount of care and attention which nothing could exceed. No trained nurse of modern times could execute the duties connected with a sick room more skilfully than she did. The Bishop, to use her own words in a letter to her sister, was "a most gentle and docile patient." And all the time, whilst nobly fulfilling her duties by her husband with an aching heart, she found time from day to day to send details of the existing state of things to those most deeply interested. A report of his death, which appeared in the evening newspapers at the beginning of December, greatly added to her necessary correspondence. The Bishop of Chester writes to Mrs. Sumner under date November 16:—

"I know not how it is, my dear sister, but domestic events seem to interest me more than public alarms, and present certainties more than the uncertain future. I have scarcely thought so much of the cholera as I have of dear Charles' fever, and more especially because fever is a strange thing in our family. I *trust*, however, and shall be most anxious for the next accounts. I fear this must be traced back to the odious Bill which has already so much to answer for. I regret our distance of separation, but you have assistance within reach, and comfort always nigh. Do not suppose me insensible to the times or the signs of the times. I see them in an awful light. But our confidence is that our God reigneth, and though I have neither the gift of prophecy nor interpretation, I hope to be found among those who are watching and keeping their garments."

And again on November 21 :—

"In the sort of suspense which disturbs me at this moment I know not how to write to you, still less do I like that a post shall go without a line from my pen and from my heart, which would try to express how much it feels. With what anxiety am I waiting for to-morrow evening which will bring me tidings from Farnham—tidings how infinitely important to myself and to multitudes besides. Oh, may the fervent prayers which I am sure are offered from a vast variety of quarters prevail at the Throne of Grace. We deserve, indeed, nothing but judgment as a nation, and have little to expect as a Church in the way of mercy: and yet I cannot bring myself to believe that God is so angry with us as to take away my brother in the midst of his days! I cannot bring myself to anticipate so great and unexpected a calamity. . . . You will not wonder that I cannot add more under present circum-

stances. I rejoice to hear that you are supported according to
your need, and so I feel sure you will be; but, O Lord, have
mercy upon us! for indeed the time is come when we have
need of mercy."

On the 26th he writes:—

"I cannot enough thank you for your great kindness in
writing to me so constantly and fully, and every fresh letter
brings additional cause of gratitude to the Author of all
mercies for the wonderful interposition which he has vouchsafed in this case. It is indeed an answer of prayer: it is
indeed a gracious favour to His Church: and the Church, at
least the true and genuine Church, is justly sensible of it; its
supplications were heard, and now its thanksgivings are not
silent. I shall be deeply interested, you may suppose, in the
memoranda to which you allude. The case must have been
very remarkable of recollection of mind, united with raging
fever and excessive pain. I do trust, indeed, that your own
health will not appear to have been injured by the fatigue and
anxiety which you have undergone. Hitherto the support
which you have received both to body and mind appears
wonderful, and, as you say, I doubt not but stedfastly believe
that it will be continued."

Once more, the Bishop of Chester writes:—

"Thank you, my dearest Jennie, for the enclosed, in
which you may believe I found great interest. You must be
so bewildered with letters of a like strain that I do not send
you mine, or I could add largely to your heap both from the
north and from the south. Now will come one of your
difficulties—how to keep the convalescent from business.
Both parties must consent to use moderation. To preclude it
entirely would be injurious, as much as to allow it too freely.
I may add now my kindest love to Charles."

The Archbishop of Canterbury writes most sympathisingly:—

"I have been this morning (Nov. 23) relieved from a
feeling of the deepest concern by the statement which appeared

in the evening papers of yesterday, that the Bishop is pro-
gressively recovering from his late severe attack. At the
same time I feel so much anxiety on his account that I cannot
forbear requesting you will have the goodness to desire any
gentleman, who may be in the house, to give me a few lines to
inform me how he is going on. I am sure you will excuse this
trouble, and with sincere prayer for the speedy and complete
restoration of the Bishop's health,

"I am, dear Madam,

"Your faithful servant,

"W. Cantuar."

Coleridge writes to the Bishop on December 6 :—

"Mrs. Sumner's note to my sister tells me I may write a
few lines to you direct. I was going to have done the same to
her, but I will not deny myself the gratification of writing to
you. I congratulate you and all near around you, my dear
friend, most heartily upon the merciful dispensation which has
spared you to them, and will, I trust at no great distance of
time, restore you to us, and the heavy duties of your station. I
should do you no good, in your present state, if I were to dwell
on all I felt when I heard your danger was so imminent, or on
the general anxiety which I have witnessed from day to day
wherever I went, and could be asked questions about you as to
your state and progress to recovery. I will say no more than
that I heartily thank God for raising you up again. May He
grant you many many years of usefulness abroad and happiness
at home. One word only more, do not try your strength too
soon with business, and even months hence, when you may
find yourself as strong as ever, do not, I earnestly beg of you,
undertake more than you can do with regard to your health,
and *if* you have been in the habit of going beyond the duties
of the diocese, which I cannot but think you have, I would
press on you, as matter of obligation, to cut all that off with
an unsparing hand. *You* are likely to receive at all times

numerous letters from people who have no business to address
you, who have no connection with you either personally or
officially, and no *right* to call on you for advice or direction ;
if you were sufficient for all this, of course, as a minister of
Christ, you would attend to it ; but experience, my dear friend,
shows you are not, and, therefore, you must limit yourself to
the household. God bless you, my dear friend, love to your
dear wife and children."

The following letter from Rev. W. Brock, who was at that time
curate of Highclere, will show what anxiety was felt by the
Bishop's old parishioners. The letter is addressed to the Rev.
P. Jacob, the domestic chaplain. After detailing his own feelings of distress and sympathy, he writes :—

" It will rejoice Mrs. Sumner's heart and yours to know how
the people here have felt—the feeling has been intense. It
was truly cheering to me at the lecture to-night to observe the
countenances beaming with joy, and the eyes filled with tears
at the mention of the name of the dear Bishop. I of course
told them all, and many who had come with heavy hearts went
away with a song in their mouths, and I hope prayer in their
hearts. And it was gladdening to me to have such an opportunity to-night of leading upwards of sixty people of this parish
in united praise and prayer for their once pastor at this time.
. . . . And as to dear Barter " (rector of Highclere) " I love the
man the more I see him. This morning the tears ran down his
cheeks as he spoke of the Bishop. He had come with heaviness
in his heart to condole with us, but learnt by the way the glad
news. He said, with all his feeling energy—' This is the happiest moment of my life.' Dear Miss Bull* was present too,
and but one feeling filled all our hearts. Tell dear Mrs.
Sumner this, and also about the interesting scene at the lecture,
and the incense that ascended there. I must now conclude with
earnest prayers for our dear Bishop and all his family. .Do give

---

* The lady who had treated the Bishop in so hospitable a manner on his first
entrance into the curacy of Highclere. See page 32.

my sincere and hearty remembrances to Mrs. Sumner—Dallas —and say the kindest things in your kindest way. What a consolation to have a praying wife, praying children, friends, and servants."

The Channel Islands, too, were not behindhand in sympathy. The Dean of Guernsey's daughter, Mrs. Kershaw, writes:—" I can give you no idea of the extreme anxiety felt by all classes here for your precious invalid. I knew and had told you how great an impression his many virtues had made here, but I knew not by many degrees its extent." And another Guernsey friend, Miss Jacob, writes:—

"Those prayers, which have been offered by the flock of our pastor's diocese here and elsewhere, have met acceptance at the Throne of Grace. The intense, the anxious interest which the first alarm occasioned does credit to the hearts and minds of our Islanders. . . . Our good old dean could scarcely be persuaded from walking up at the early hour of post-time, Thursday, to us. Mrs. Kershaw brought him, having first been to us to know the result. We had in succession Mr. and Mrs. T. Brock, Mrs. Condamine, Lord De Saumarez with the Courier paper which had so much relieved him. Our harbinger of glad tidings was hailed with joy by the succession of callers and senders. But I have gone full far ere I express my feelings to that Almighty Being who hath evinced such feelings towards us in preserving such a life as our Bishop's to his family, to the Church, and to us. As I have inwardly wept so do I now rejoice that his dear widowed mother's heart may sing for joy."

Sir William Knighton, on November 30, writes :—

"The inquiries since my return have been almost universal. I will begin with the highest—the Duke of Wellington, whose letter I received yesterday, and end with the lowest—a poor man in a hovel who had heard your good and excellent husband preach in our little parish church. The feeling has been universal—the regret in some instances very great, and among those who knew the blessings of true Christian piety an alarm and suppression of spirits not common! All this will, I trust, work together for good, and if it ends in the pouring out of the indwelling Spirit within, it may lead to much and lasting glory."

Lady Acland, on Dec. 7th, thus expresses her feelings :—

"We do, indeed, my dearest Mrs. Sumner, not only from motives of private regard, but as members of the Church, thank God for His mercy in the preservation of your excellent husband, and O may he yet be long spared to his country ; for to him I look as to one of the ten righteous for whose sake the city may be saved ! These are indeed awful times, and I confess I look with far more comfort to the prayers of the good than the counsels of the great."

The Rev. C. Morgell, an old pupil, writes :—

"It is altogether impossible to describe my feelings at the glance I just allowed myself to take of Jacob's postscript in the letter announcing ' no hope ! ' I am sure it would be equally vain my attempting to express the thankfulness of my heart at the wonderful and most unexpected mercy extended to us. I think it scarcely possible for me to be more agonized by any bereavement with which the Lord my gracious God may visit me, than I was by the distressing intelligence of Sunday week last. But He has been, how much ! better than all my fears. Certainly He must have some great thing for our Lazarus to do."

The following, from one of his old clergy in the diocese of Llandaff, must be added to complete the circle of sympathy :—

REV. JOHN LLEWELLYN TO MRS. SUMNER.

"MY DEAREST MADAM,

"Soon after I wrote to you, as I was sitting one evening at my rector's, the melancholy news arrived of the demise of my best of friends in the whole world. My distress was indeed such as could scarcely be exceeded in his nearest and dearest relation. I never felt the like, except at the melancholy news of my dear father's death on the day I was ordained priest.

Mr. and Mrs. Harding seemed to feel much with me. I immediately left, and on calling on my way home at the post-office
for my own paper, the *Record*, I could not open it for some
time, knowing it would aggravate if possible my distress by a
doleful confirmation of the sad report. But you may easier
conceive than I can express my contrary feelings when, having
opened it, instead of a confirmation I met with a most joyous,
and, as it appeared to me, well authenticated contradiction of
the melancholy news. On this occasion, indeed, if ever I
praised God in my life for any mercy, I *did* praise and magnify
him with a gladdened heart and joyous lips. Though late at
night, I sent word directly to Mr. Harding, that as he seemed
to participate in my grief, he might participate also before he
slept in my joy. And it affords me no small satisfaction to
think that both my joy and grief were felt, and deeply felt, by
thousands far and near. . . ."

In looking through the voluminous correspondence connected
with the Bishop's illness from which the above extracts have
been selected, there is nothing more striking than the almost
unanimous feeling of the writers of the letters to the effect that
the Bishop's recovery was a special answer to prayer. He did
indeed seem to be restored to the Church by the unceasing
supplications of the faithful from the very jaws of death. Sir
William Knighton at one time actually retired from the room
where he was lying, as, to use his own expression, "he could not
bear to see him die." And yet God raised him up for many
years of useful labour in His Church. The diocese at large was
not slow in recognising with thankfulness the hand of God
stretched forth in behalf of His servant, and as earnest prayers
had been offered up for his recovery, so now on all sides the
voice of thanksgiving was heard. A general wish was expressed
that there might be a portrait of the Bishop painted and presented to Mrs. Sumner in remembrance of the trying time
through which she had passed, and to Judge Patteson and Dr.

Dealtry, who had been deputed by the subscribers to address
the Bishop on the subject, he replied as follows:—

"FARNHAM CASTLE, Feb. 1st, 1832.

"MY DEAR MR. JUSTICE PATTESON AND DR. DEALTRY,

"It has not been without much emotion that I have
received the intimation conveyed in your letter of the affectionate feelings entertained towards me by the friends whose
kind proposal you have undertaken to communicate. In
looking back upon the many mercies never to be forgotten by
me, which have been recently vouchsafed to my family and
myself, I reflect with unfeigned gratitude on the warm manifestations of attachment shown by all my friends during the late
illness with which it pleased God to visit me. I have felt these
tokens of their regard most deeply, and the recollection of those
prayers to which you allude, offered up for me in the time of
my sickness, will bind me to them, still more closely than
before, by fresh and more endearing ties of affection and
Christian esteem. I cannot but acquiesce with much willingness in the proposal contained in your letter. Such a memorial
will be very grateful to Mrs. Sumner and my family, as a means
of reminding them of the graciousness of their Heavenly Father
in sparing the life of one dear to them: and in disposing the
hearts of so many friends to sympathise with them alike in the
times of their joy or sorrow.

"I am,
"My dear Mr. Justice Patteson and Dr. Dealtry,
"Your very affectionate and faithful friend,
"C. WINTON."

This portrait was painted by Sir Martin Shee, and on Bishop
Sumner's death was presented by the family to the See in
remembrance of the Bishop's long episcopate, and now hangs
in the noble hall at Farnham Castle side by side with the
portraits of some of his predecessors.

P

The following letter, written to Sir John Coleridge, will fitly close in his own words the subject of the Bishop's illness and recovery :—

"FARNHAM CASTLE, *Jan.* 23*rd*, 1832.

" Time rolls on rapidly, and I am conscious makes me appear ungrateful to the kind and affectionate sympathy with which you have regarded me and mine during my late illness, and my dear wife's still more recent confinement.* But the truth is that till very lately writing has been a considerable effort to me, and now that my fingers have regained something of their wonted strength they are kept in such continual exercise by replying to the daily influx of letters from the clergy in all parts of my diocese that I have neither time nor power nor franks for correspondence not absolutely necessary. I must tell you, however, my dear friend, that I have heard, not with dry eyes, of all your kind anxiety for me, and of your rejoicing with my wife on the unexpected turn which it pleased God to give to my disorder. I have been brought indeed from the very bottom of the grave, and I hope I shall retain a permanent impression of the singleness of devotion to which such a dispensation binds me. The affection of my personal friends (manifested with a warmth and tenderness which I can never forget), and I may say of my clergy universally, has left a very grateful sentiment on my mind, and will bind me to them with fresh and still more endearing ties."

* Emily, the Bishop's youngest child, was born at Farnham, January 6, 1832.

CHAPTER XIII.

The Bishop's Correspondence.—Fast Day for the Cholera.—Reform Bill carried, the opposing Bishops refraining from voting.—Confirmations in Hampshire. —Number of Centres.—Importance attached by the Bishop to Confirmation. —His powers of Conversation, and Punctuality.—Visits to Highclere, Bonchurch and Wolvesey.

IN the words quoted at the close of the preceding chapter the Bishop speaks of the daily influx of letters requiring answers. It may be well here to say a few words as to his habits with regard to letter writing. No one could have been more punctual than he was in answering his numerous correspondents. It has been said that everybody thinks himself at liberty to write to a Bishop on any matter whatsoever, and there is some truth in the saying. From all parts of the diocese letters flow in daily. The writers naturally enough think the subject on which they write the most important topic that can occupy the Bishop's attention, and enlarge upon it accordingly. But any letters which required attention were invariably answered by him with his own hand. Much to the regret of those who were about him, an amanuensis was very rarely made use of, except for the mere copying of letters. After Mr. Jacob left Farnham Castle for Crawley, he had no domestic Chaplain. His children were either too young or, because of their absence at school, unable to render any help in this respect, and Mrs. Sumner was necessarily much occupied in her own department of work. The Bishop therefore acquired the habit in his early Episcopal life of writing all his letters himself, and he was unable afterwards to make any

change in this respect. But the tax upon his time and strength
was enormous. Life at Farnham Castle was carried on, as it
had been previously at Llansanfraed, with clock-work regularity.
Chapel at half-past eight, luncheon at one, dinner first at six
o'clock, but gradually getting later and later till half-past seven
was reached, were the order of the day. A quarter of an
hour's stroll after breakfast through the garden and hot-houses
(for the Bishop was passionately fond of flowers) took him to his
study, whence he seldom emerged till luncheon time. Two hours'
exercise followed this meal, and he was again to be found in the
midst of his letters till dinner, and for another hour and a half
in the evening, until the later hour of dinner rendered this
unnecessary. I find that in 1867, the year before his resignation, the Bishop wrote upwards of three thousand five hundred
letters on matters of business. Many of these of course
required a great deal of thought. In these days of free
publication the Bishop always feared lest he might see his
letters printed, and it was impossible that they could be written
off *currente calamo*. But up to the very last his epistolary
industry never flagged. Not a church was built, not a new
district formed, not a school erected, not a curate selected without the Bishop being consulted at every step. And the answer
was always promptly given and to the point. Not many words
were used, but there was no mistake about their meaning.
The oracle never spoke vaguely or indefinitely. Mr. Pringle,
one of the secretaries to the Ecclesiastical Commissioners, writes
to me "that the Bishop was in the habit of writing so large a
number of letters during the time when he was giving attention
to the business here as to excite our wonder, and I remember
his telling me one day, *à propos* of my expressed astonishment,
that he had in one day once written ninety letters with his own
hand."

And yet, notwithstanding this vast amount of business correspondence, enough, one would have thought, to dull the intellect
of the brightest, the Bishop would find time to write in his

study letters of condolence and sympathy whenever such were needed. Occasionally too he would write a sparkling *jeu d'esprit*—sometimes English and sometimes Latin verses. His birthday letters, whether congratulatory to his children or grandchildren, or in answer to those written to himself, were models of what such letters ought to be.

In addition also to family and Diocesan letters, his position as visitor of no fewer than five colleges at Oxford and Winchester College, involved occasionally much correspondence : knotty points were continually brought before him, differences between the reforming and Conservative bodies within the walls of the particular college, had to be adjusted, and at one time the disputes arising in connection with one college were so frequent that the Bishop would say playfully that he almost dreaded taking a drive without having with him the statutes of that particular college, lest he should be called upon by some special messenger to give an opinion on some disputed point. Writing to a friend in 1833, he says, " Another appeal from —————— College. Having been more than a month without one I might fairly have expected it." Difficult questions had over and over again to be decided by him as visitor, and it is here acknowledged thankfully that his friends on the Judicial Bench, and especially Coleridge, were always ready to help him confidentially in these matters with their advice, and to give him the full benefit of their legal knowledge. There was free and full intercourse between them, both on diocesan and these collegiate matters, as, with reference to the former, the following letter to Coleridge will show :—

"FARNHAM CASTLE, *May 2nd*, 1832.

" There is not a word of truth in your circulating story. I have never heard of any clergyman in my diocese changing the lessons or omitting the litany, or assigning as a cause the length of the service, his sermon generally exceeding an hour ; much less has any complaint been made to me respecting any individual whatever on all or any of these points. And now my dear friend, let me hope you will never offer a word of apology for advice or enquiry. Next to your love and esteem I desire to enjoy the advantage of your judgment and candour in its fullest freedom."

The year 1832 opened somewhat gloomily for the nation at large. The cholera (or, as it was then almost universally called, cholera morbus) had first appeared in England at the close of the preceding year. The suddenness of the attack, and the extreme rapidity with which the sufferers succumbed to its violence, alarmed the nation and stirred it to its very depths. A fast was proclaimed for the 21st of March, in order that supplications might ascend from England as a nation to Almighty God that He would be pleased to remove the scourge from the land. The day of humiliation was wonderfully well observed throughout the whole country. The Bishop preached at Farnham to an overflowing congregation from Dan. ix. 8, 9.

"O Lord, to us belongeth confusion of face, to our kings, to our princes, and to our fathers, because we have sinned against Thee.

"To the Lord our God belong mercies and forgivenesses, though we have rebelled against Him."

Meanwhile the prolonged agitation with respect to the Reform Bill continued to embitter political parties. The Bishop, owing to his recent illness, did not, as was his usual habit, spend the spring and early summer in London. It was thought better by his medical advisers that he should be spared the fatigue and anxiety necessarily connected with town life. The Bishop of Winchester, owing to so important a portion of his diocese being situated within the limits of the metropolis, must necessarily be incessantly occupied in London. In addition to such work as would naturally fall to his lot as one of the senior Bishops amongst his Episcopal brethren, South London would occupy a great portion of his time and labour. During the whole of his tenure of the See, the Bishop invariably preached

in some church or churches in the suburban portion of his
diocese on every Sunday during his stay in London, and in the
earlier portion of his Episcopate he was one of the few Bishops
who took a prominent part in the Exeter Hall missionary
meetings. It was thought well that he should be spared all
this additional fatigue, and therefore he was not present at the
exciting debates and no less exciting negotiations connected
with the ultimate passing of the Reform Bill. His opposition,
however, to the measure was as strong as ever. On the fourteenth of April, when the House of Lords passed the second
reading by a majority of nine, the Bishop voted by proxy in the
minority, while his brother of Chester's name is found amongst
the majority. Then came Lord Lyndhurst's amendment proposing the postponement of the disfranchising clauses of the
bill. Some of the Tory peers who had voted for the second
reading joined the Opposition, and the consequence was that
the amendment was carried by a majority of thirty-five. Lord
Grey's resignation followed, but on the Duke of Wellington's
inability to form a ministry on the principle of an extensive
Reform in the representation of the people, he resumed the
reins of Government with a distinct understanding from the
King that if necessary he would create a sufficient number of
peers to carry the bill in its integrity through the House of
Lords.* This being the case, the Duke of Wellington used all
his influence to prevent any further opposition to the bill, and
in the division which took place on the 4th of June, when the
bill passed the third reading by a majority of eighty-four, the
Bishops, who had hitherto opposed the bill, abstained as a body
from recording their vote at all.

Shortly after his summer ordination the Bishop confirmed
throughout Hampshire and the Isle of Wight. He was always exceedingly happy in his confirmations. It was marvellous how he
was enabled day after day to hold two confirmations in churches

* "Correspondence of King William IV. and Earl Grey," vol. ii., p. 464,
referred to in Lord Russell's "Recollections," p. 108.

some five or six miles apart, and addressing the candidates with
a freshness, vigour, and reality which would give the hearer
the notion that the whole thing was an exceptional occurrence
in his life.   He would oftentimes take the hymn which had
been sung in the preceding service, and make it the backbone
of his exhortations; but whatever it might be, whether hymn,
confirmation service itself, single verse, or passage of Scripture,
which he might take as the basis of his address, his words were,
from first to last, fresh from the heart, and were listened to with
eager attention.*

I find from old records of the diocese, that in 1797 the number
of centres for confirmation in Hampshire was sixteen.   This list
had not been enlarged in 1822.   In 1832 Bishop Sumner
increased the number in Hampshire to forty-five, the circuit
occupying a little over a month.   In 1868 the list had swollen
to the number of sixty-nine centres.   In 1830 the number of
centres for confirmations in Surrey was twenty-four, and in 1863
increased to fifty-six.

The Bishop was urgent in impressing upon his clergy the
great importance of a season of confirmation, and the necessity
for the utmost care in the presentation of candidates.   It is
absolutely impossible to guard against the intrusion of some
unworthy candidates, but both in private and in public the
Bishop did all in his power to raise the general standard of
qualification for the catechumens.

These confirmation tours, though refreshing to the spirit of
the Bishop, were undoubtedly very laborious.   His habit was

* Archdeacon Jacob, preaching on the Sunday after the Bishop's death, thus
refers to his confirmation addresses :—" During the years that I attended him in
his confirmations, held mostly twice a day, not excepting Sundays, I never remember his asking me the effect of any of his ministrations and addresses.   I
knew he cordially disliked any comment in the way of admiration.   Once I do
recollect that by my expression of opinion, from seeing much emotion and attention (it was at Christ Church, Hants), that his address seemed specially forcible,
I drew from him these words, very marked in one who so rarely described his
inward feelings, ' I am at times overwhelmed with the sense of my responsibility
at these seasons, and I can't help fearing how many opportunities I lose.'"

to stay each night at the house of some friend either lay or clerical, and thence on the succeeding morning take the confirmation in the neighbouring church. It was only natural that a party of guests should be invited to meet the Bishop, and consequently, after the labours of the day, he was almost invariably called upon to make himself agreeable to his fellow guests. But in this respect the Bishop always seemed equal to the occasion. With a large store of general information, and a well-furnished mind, he was able to hold his own with any competitor for conversational pre-eminence. On one occasion, in the time of the second Lord Ashburton, he was staying with his Chaplain at the Grange. Lady Ashburton had collected around her, as was her wont,* many literary celebrities, and at dinner there was a conflict of wit amongst those well able to take part in the contest. I have been told by the Chaplain on that occasion, that when the guests were assembling for breakfast the next morning, there was an universal agreement of opinion expressed that the Bishop had on the previous evening carried off the palm. "Only think," said Thackeray, "that we who are wits by profession should have been outdone by the Bishop last night."

The Bishop's punctuality throughout the confirmation tours was very remarkable. The distance between the several localities selected as centres, the nature of the roads, the probable number of catechumens at the preceding confirmation, were all well considered before the list was definitely fixed, and the consequence was that true to the minute the Bishop was sure to appear at the Church-yard gate. On two occasions, in the early days of his Episcopacy, his punctuality was put to a somewhat severe test. It was before the days of railroads, when he posted in his own carriage throughout the diocese. It happened one day, that in the middle of a stage the pole of the carriage broke. What was to be done? The Bishop was due at a particular place at an assigned hour. "If you will trust me,"

* See Lord Houghton's "Monographs," pp. 232, 248, 255.

said the post-boy, "I will take your Lordship safely there."
After a short parley the Bishop agreed to do so, and the post-
boy, by judiciously starting at the top of each hill at a walk,
and gradually increasing his speed, so as to keep his horses in
advance of the carriage till they were at full gallop, kept his
word, and the Bishop was able to carry out his proposed
arrangements. On the other occasion a post-boy was found to
be so intoxicated that he was utterly unable to control the
horses. "Do you think you could manage to ride and drive,"
said the Bishop to his valet—before referred to—Ainsley. "I
will do the best I can, my Lord," was the prompt reply. And
accordingly the post-boy was left by the side of the road, and
much to the surprise of the incumbent of the village to which
the Bishop was bound, his carriage appeared at the proper
time, with the servant occupying the post-boy's place !

Throughout the confirmations held by the Bishop in the
course of this autumn, he was much cheered by the visibly
improved appearance and demeanour of the catechumens.
Naturally enough, it reflected itself in his addresses. The
Chaplain writes to Mrs. Sumner, "I could not help expressing
to the Bishop on our returning here (Winchester) how
deeply he seemed *in* the confirmations now, widened in the
varied nature of his addresses, the warmth and stirring of his
appeals. He told me he felt himself *in* his work—never more
so—it was profitable. Never a better opportunity for people
and ministers. And surely I can say the improvement in
manner and spirits of the candidates, compared with the last
confirmations, is very striking. The young *men* are more than
ordinarily devout and serious. Well, therefore, may the dear
Bishop expend himself."

The following extract shows the spirit of the Bishop :—

Referring to a confirmation in the Isle of Wight, the Chaplain writes—"To the question in the confirmation service the
candidates did not answer, and the Bishop was obliged to speak
to them, and to put the question again. He spoke in serious

sadness, and in a tone very softening and touching. I could not help saying to him in the carriage afterwards, "I was hardly sorry the candidates did not answer at first, for you obtained a more distinct one than if some had answered the first time, and you spoke so very nicely, so very tenderly." "My dear friend, there's a hint to me," the Bishop replied, "now I do entreat you will give a *hem* if on similar occasions you observe a sharp spirit breaking out in me. I do confess I am sometimes provoked by the apathy of unanswering people."

One confirmation must have been of special interest. On Sunday, the 19th of August, he revisited his old curacy, High-clere. Mrs. Sumner came over from Farnham, and two of his old pupils, Oakeley and Matheson, met him there, and when the Bishop reached the Church-yard gate, he found two rows of parishioners, bare-headed, waiting to welcome their former curate with hearty cordiality. The Bishop, it need hardly be said, had a kind word of greeting for all, and recognised many of his old friends. The service was deeply impressive, and in preaching from the words, "Ye shall be my sons and daughters, saith the Lord Almighty," the Bishop expressed his keen interest in the welfare of those to whom he had formerly ministered, and referred to the fact that many of those whom he had just confirmed had been dedicated to Almighty God in holy baptism by himself. After the service he was able personally to visit some of his former parishioners.

The Bishop succeeded in accomplishing this confirmation tour with a degree of comfort which he had hardly anticipated. He still felt the remains of his recent severe illness, but was able to write in the middle of his tour, "To-morrow is another very busy day—indeed all days are so busy that I continually wonder I am so strong, but I feel thankful for it—as I ought—though not enough so. Yet I am thankful." Writing to Mrs. Sumner from the Isle of Wight he says, "The Wilberforces are very dear persons," and again from Brighstone, of which S. Wilberforce was Rector, "I much want you to know the

Wilberforces more. They are exactly what you would like, and really among the very nicest people in spirit and agreeableness, and amiabilities as well as in talent, &c., that I know. . . . . . . Every moment of my time is closely employed, and all wonder how I can get through so much. . . . I have been interrupted in these last sentences by Samuel Wilberforce, who is talking to me, and to whom it is impossible not to listen. . . ."

As soon as the confirmations were over the Bishop took Mrs. Sumner and his family to Bonchurch, in the Isle of Wight, where he thoroughly enjoyed change of air and scene. It was usually his habit in the autumn to take a month or six weeks' rest, and no one enjoyed a holiday more than he did. Mrs. Sumner, writing from Bonchurch to a friend, says, "We are greatly enjoying ourselves here by walking and rambling over the rocks, inhaling the sea air, admiring the exquisite views, and still more by being alone with our children, and permitted to enjoy their society as we can never do at home. To be so much with my husband, and see him thus surrounded with his children, and delighting to hear them converse freely, are sources of happiness which you, my dear friend, will be able to appreciate. It is a happiness which I fear not to enjoy. I can ask God's blessing upon it; His love sanctifies it, and although He may see fit to interrupt it, it will only be an interruption. . . During part of the time spent in the Isle of Wight, the Bishop took Mr. Wilberforce's duty at Brighstone. Hearing much from the parishioners of the zeal and energy with which Mr. Wilberforce carried on his work at Brighstone, the Bishop wrote to his father, thinking it would be a gratification to him to hear of his son's work, and received the following grateful reply :—

"BATH, *September 28th*, 1832.

" MY DEAR LORD,

"You are yourself a father, and therefore I need not assure your Lordship what a cordial drop your kind letter has infused into my cup, and I derive a special pleasure from your

Lordship's communication, because it supplies a fair, indeed, quite a fit occasion for my returning your Lordship my cordial thanks for the mention to me of your favourable estimate of Sam's services.

"The circumstance also appears to me not only to warrant, but considering the expediency of your Lordship's being made acquainted with the qualifications and character of your clergy, really to require my stating an incident which lately took place. I cannot find a letter which I had rather have enclosed than have related to your Lordship the substance of it.

"Some few weeks ago, I forget exactly how long, I received a very friendly letter from Lord Spencer, with whom, though I knew him pretty well some fifty years ago, I have had little or no intercourse for many years, telling me that he coveted the pleasure, or some such sentiment, of informing me that on the preceding Sunday at Ryde he had the service of the communion table (not the sacrament, but the ordinary service), and that also of the pulpit, performed with very superior ability, and that on enquiry he had the gratification of learning it was one of my sons. He added that he had availed himself of the circumstance of Sam's having been a college acquaintance of his domestic physician, Dr. Calvert, to ask him to become his guest while at Ryde, an obliging attention which he renewed on the only other occasion of Sam's visiting Ryde during his Lordship's stay in the island. I trust I need not assure your Lordship that though I value this lordly testimony to my dear boy's services, I am not the less, in some points of view, more gratified by your assurance of the attention of his humble parishioners at Brighstone.

"Let me beg your Lordship to present Mrs. Wilberforce's and my own respectful and kind remembrances to Mrs. Sumner, as well as to accept them yourself from,

"My dear Lord,

"Your Lordship's obliged and affectionate

"W. WILBERFORCE."

At the close of the year the Bishop stayed for some weeks at Wolvesey* Palace, Winchester, in order that he might become better acquainted with the clergy and laity of his cathedral city and its neighbourhood, and exercise hospitality, as was his wont, with an ungrudging hand.

---

* Wolvesey, as well as Farnham Castle, was built by Henry De Blois. At the date of its erection, 1138, it must have been of considerable extent and magnificence. The origin of the name is disputed, some deriving it from the Saxon "Ulf" or "Wolf," a lord, and "Ey" an island; others supposing that the name is connected with certain wolves' heads, which were delivered as an annual tribute by the Welsh to King Edgar on the site of the Castle. Here Queen Mary was lodged before her marriage with Philip of Spain. In the civil wars during the reign of Charles the Second, it was entirely destroyed by Sir W. Waller's army, but was rebuilt by Morley, Bishop of Winchester, 1684, the greater part of which palace was pulled down by Bishop North in 1820, and since this time no Bishop of Winchester has permanently occupied Wolvesey Palace.

CHAPTER XIV.

LIFE AT FARNHAM—*continued.* 1833—1834.

The Bishop attends Mr. Wilberforce's funeral.—Visits Mr. Gurney at Earlham.
—Death of his Niece.—Visitation of the Diocese.—Extracts from his Charge.
—Mrs. Sumner goes to Geneva.—Doubts whether Mr. Wilberforce will leave
the Diocese.—Illness of Mrs. Sumner at Godalming.—Confirms for Bishop
Gray in Dorsetshire.—Animosity between Churchmen and Dissenters.—
The Archbishop's reply to an Address from the Clergy of the Isle of Wight.

THE Bishop seems to have long felt the effects of his severe
illness in 1831. It was with some difficulty that he was able
to carry on his usual work in London, even in 1833. Twice in
the course of his residence there he was obliged to refresh
himself by a week's rest in the country. I mention this
because it is so singularly in contrast with his usually robust
health and almost herculean power of enduring work, which
was so manifest to all in the later years of his Episcopate.

It was in the autumn of this year that Mr. Wilberforce died.
He was buried in Westminster Abbey, close to the tombs of
Pitt, Fox, and Canning. The greatest respect was paid to his
memory, the members of the two Houses of Parliament attending the funeral in their official capacity. Amongst the number
was the Bishop of Winchester, who thus paid the last tribute of
respect in his power to one whom he highly honoured and
revered. Writing to a friend he says :—

"I have just returned from paying the last public tribute of
affection to dear Mr. Wilberforce. It is something to have
been permitted in these days of rebuke and blasphemy to have
seen his Christian spirit brought again before the nation's eye,
purified of aught of sordid and debasing mould ! It was a

solemn and most affecting service—to all—and, I need not add,
to me. It was impossible to look unmoved on the three sons
standing over the grave with so much of filial affection and
reverence, and at the same time so much of the spirit of those
who sorrow not as men without hope in their whole demeanour.
There was a very large concourse of all whom Wilberforce would
most have wished to have respected his memory."

Shortly after this the Bishop went with Mrs. Sumner and
Mr. Dallas to Cromer and Lowestoft, staying *en route* with Mr.
Gurney at Earlham.   His intercourse with the *friends* is thus
described :—

" Gurney is an extraordinary man, and showed himself to
great advantage.   Mrs. Opie is also very agreeable, and
Catherine Gurney full of kindness and attention.   Other
friends I saw, many, but none of a character to be cared for at
first sight. You will like to know the course of our ministrations
while there.   Before the first day's dinner, after sitting silently
about twenty seconds, Gurney gave (I will not say was moved
to give, lest it should look like levity) a very good Establishment grace.   After dinner silence for a space.   Neither prayers
nor exposition at night, whereat I marvelled.   Second day
morning Gurney expounded beautifully Eph. iv., and prayed
well.   Before dinner silence, after dinner an oral grace again
(was not this well managed ?).   At night Gurney expounded
Ps. ciii., and then called on Mrs. Cunningham for a hymn, in
which all but the friends joined, ' O for a heart to praise my
God !'   No prayer.   Third day morning I expounded and
prayed. . . . Scarcely had I arrived here (Cromer) when the
landlord entered with ' Our *little reverence* is here, and wishes
to know when he may wait on,' &c., &c.   It seems that the
annual missionary sermon is to be preached to-morrow, and
they have actually been circulating bills the past week with the
preacher's name in blank, in hopes of being able to fill it up
with mine.   I have consented accordingly, and Dallas preaches
in the afternoon.   This morning I have had the clergy with

me, all beseeching sermons in their churches, and pointing out the special reasons of importance which exist in each case."

From Lowestoft, where the Bishop stayed with the Francis Cunninghams, and where he first made acquaintance with one who till his death was a true and faithful friend, the Rev. W. Carus, fellow of Trinity College, Cambridge, and afterwards preferred by the Bishop to a canonry in Winchester Cathedral, he writes :—"This house is quite delightful. It is pervaded throughout, from the attics to the cellar, and in every hour of the day and night (by the bye, there is very little of the latter here) by a truly Christian spirit."

No sooner had the Bishop returned from his stay in Norfolk than he was called upon to make preparations for his second visitation of the diocese. Returns had to be obtained from the various parishes and tabulated, and his charge prepared.

Mrs. Sumner, under date Oct. 10, speaks of his imprisonment :—"Since yesterday he has been locked up in his study, coming out five minutes at lunch and ten minutes at half-past seven to take a basin of soup and chop in the green drawing-room. You can have but little idea of the moral torment to a wife. If I could I might not go in the study." (Mrs. Sumner had been very ill for a short time previously). "To-day I did walk down, and was wheeled three-quarters of an hour on the lawn. Twice I passed the study door in silence, though I have not entered it for six weeks, and had not seen the Bishop for several hours. You guess his *charge* is to be charged with all this cruel bondage."

But before starting on his visitation tour he was called upon to mourn over the death of his niece, the Bishop of Chester's daughter, wife of the Rev. J. A. Colpoys. The two following letters show more of the Bishop's feelings than he was wont to manifest openly. The first is written to a friend on the anniversary of his correspondent's wedding day :

"FARNHAM CASTLE, *October* 10*th*, 1833.

"I presume you felt it was unnecessary to remind me *of the*

Q

day. Twelve months have rolled away in a course, as I trust, of happiness and usefulness, and have brought with them, I do not doubt, to both your hearts an increase of love and tenderness and mutual confidence and affectionate sympathy. But we are warned to rejoice in these gifts with trembling. Monday next, which is probably the day when the grave will close over all that Colpoys loved on earth, will be the anniversary of the day when, five years ago, I joined them in marriage. So closely united, as I remember Mr. Noel once observed, are our happiest and our saddest hours. May God be with you, and —— and grant you, if He see fit, many days of comfort together here, and then never-ending union in eternity."

And on the day after the funeral :

"October 13th, 1833.

"Yesterday was a very trying day to me, rendered more so by the number of clergy present, which, though gratifying, was affecting to my feelings. But I was comforted and edified by the sight of Colpoys so much sustained—bowed down, and yet upheld by everlasting arms—afflicted, yet not cast down, and able to show forth the power and reality of religion to console in the midst of the heaviest of earthly sorrows. I know not any loss that I have ever felt more tenderly. It makes me remember an observation of the Archbishop of Canterbury as we went together some years ago to a state funeral, that as years advanced I should feel the trial of separation from those I loved as amongst the severest of earthly sorrows. He has since verified the truth of his own remark in following to the grave his only son."

Immediately afterwards the visitation began. There were thirteen centres, at each of which the Bishop delivered his charge, and entertained the clergy at dinner. At Newport, the Rev. S. Wilberforce was the preacher. Throughout the whole diocese the Bishop was much gratified at his reception both by laity and clergy. Nothing could be more cordial or encouraging to him than the way in which he was greeted on all sides

as one who united the office of a friend with that of the
Bishop. His charge was thoroughly practical. After a brief
reference to those who had appeared amongst them at the previous visitation, but " whose books have since been closed, who
have gone with their staff broken and their censer quenched to
render up an account of their stewardship and await the scrutiny
of the Chief Shepherd at his appearing," he went on to vindicate the usefulness of such meetings as those of the Bishop
and clergy at visitations ; some thought them superficial and
perfunctory, and asked whether the brief space allotted by
custom, or rather necessity, to these periodical visits, would
suffice for the correction of disorder or the encouragement of
good. But such critics forgot that what was before the public
eye at the visitation was really but a part of the whole matter.
Details of the various parishes throughout the diocese had
been previously furnished to the Bishop, and he was able to
say that there was not a single parish of which the spiritual
statistics had not been passed before him in review with painful
and laborious reference to its wants and capabilities of improvement. There was not a hamlet, however remote or insignificant,
which was not mapped, as it were, in the tablet of his mind.
And it was because the Bishop thus valued the opportunity of
meeting his clergy at the visitation that he broke through the
previous custom existing in the diocese, by virtue of which one
single visitation was supposed to suffice for the whole of an
episcopate.

"I have been unwilling," the Bishop said, " to debar myself
the privilege of renewing more intimately my bonds of fellowship
with those who are bearing the burthen and heat of the Christian
year in the work of the parochial ministry. I have desired to
participate in the fruits of your experience. I have wished to
meet you again, for our reciprocal benefit in our allotted spheres
of duty ; as a helper of your joy, and a sympathizer in your
difficulties ; as a co-partner in your labours, and a fellow-worker
together with you in the extension of the Redeemer's kingdom.

And I venture to claim with confidence your affectionate and
faithful co-operation in an endeavour to extract from our meeting the materials for edification and mutual comfort; and, in
reliance on the Divine promises, with the view of strengthening
each other's hands in all that relates to the efficiency, the spiritu-
ality, and the influence of the pastoral office in this diocese."

From statistics which had been given to the Bishop, it
appeared that since the previous visitation twenty-five churches
and chapels had been added to the number previously existing
in the two counties, and that there were resident clergy in
thirty-seven more parishes than in 1829.   The clergy officiating
in the diocese numbered 527 (323 incumbents and 204 curates).
The number of schools too had considerably increased, for 426
churches had schools in connection with them (as compared with
373 in 1829), and there were only sixty churches (as compared
with eighty-eight in 1829) reported as having no schools affiliated
to them; but, notwithstanding all this, the Bishop was far from
satisfied with the state of things, and he was therefore most
earnest in his exhortations to the clergy to increased diligence
on their part.   Had all efforts been made, all expedients tried—
district visiting societies, bible classes, adult teachings, cottage
readings?   The time was gone by when it was sufficient to rest
on prescriptive claims for respect.   The apostolical commission
of the clergy was to be vindicated as need might require, but
no personal inconsistency must defeat the weight of their
argument.   To little purpose would it be to trace their
genealogy in its lineal descent, unless it were also written "in
fleshy tables" on the hearts of their people.   Their hereditary
succession must stand manifest before the world in incontro-
vertible evidence to be read of all men, whether friends or
gainsayers—in their apostolical wisdom, their apostolical prudence, their apostolical meekness, their apostolical zeal and love.
Wise admonitions as to the mode and manner of dealing with
their several congregations brought the charge to a close with
the following characteristic remarks:

"The preacher, therefore, must not be wise at the expense of his faithfulness. Essential and fundamental doctrine must not be sacrificed, to accommodate the taste or indulge the prejudices of our people. Imperfect or clouded views of truth must not be put forth under the pretence of ministerial discretion. If the trumpet give an uncertain sound, it will not effectually warn the wicked, arouse the careless, or instruct the ignorant. Scripture must be preached scripturally. 'The gospel is a mighty engine, but only mighty when God has the working of it.' * The affecting details of our Lord's matchless condescension and grace must be represented to the heart in all their necessary relations to the salvation of man, before the soul will be melted into repentance or quickened into love. It is only in proportion as the true word of the Lord is prophesied upon the dry bones, that 'a noise' and 'a shaking' are heard among them. 'God, in His providence, seems to make but little account of the measures and contrivances of men, in accomplishing his designs.' † All our best arguments are worth nothing, unless they are founded upon the distinguishing doctrines of the Cross, and honour the Saviour by a faithful exhibition of His grace and love. But when Christ is exalted, and the Gospel preached in its integrity and simplicity, in the spirit of a sound mind, Satan falls, 'like lightning from Heaven,' and is dethroned effectually from his empire in man's heart."

The year 1834 was a somewhat gloomy one for the Bishop, as far as his domestic life was concerned. In the early spring he was called upon to mourn the loss of his only sister, Mrs. Wilson, and for nearly six months Mrs. Sumner and four of the children were absent in Switzerland with Mrs. Sumner's relations. The Bishop was singularly dependent for his happiness upon his domestic circle, and there is no doubt that the time of separation seemed long and weary to him. He unselfishly wrote to Mrs. Sumner :

"I am afraid you will scarcely send me letters often enough,

* Adam's " Private Thoughts."   † Cecil's " Remains," p. 310.

but I hope you will remember that they are doubly valuable to me in my desolate situation, for it is very desolate to be here alone. I know few things more trying, than to be seeing people in succession the whole day on business, and then to have no one for friendly or domestic intercourse by way of relaxation. But I do not mean to dwell on this—because I particularly wish you to enjoy to the full your visit—and having alluded to the subject once, that you may not think I am indifferent to your absence, I do not mean to allude to my own solitude again."

Shortly after Mrs. Sumner had left, he was in some doubt and anxiety as to whether he should not lose S. Wilberforce from the diocese. Mr. Simeon offered to him for his acceptance the living of St. Dunstan's in the West. Mr. Wilberforce hesitated for some time as to whether he should accept the offer or not, but finally decided against it. The Bishop thus refers to the matter.

" May 10th.—Samuel Wilberforce has the offer of a living in the city of London from Mr. Simeon. It is St. Dunstan's, close to Temple Bar, and he has come up to London to see whether he ought to take it. It is thought he may become influential among the London clergy, &c. . . . The two principal streets of the parish are Fetter Lane and Chancery Lane, and it seems sad to bring his fragile wife and young children to be immersed in such an atmosphere. I have advised him to ascertain how far it is safe to expose them to it. The value of the living is about the same as Brighstone. I do not yet know how this affair will terminate, and I cannot give much opinion on it, though strongly pressed, but I shall be most unfeignedly sorry if he leaves my diocese."

"May 16.—There is nothing absolutely settled yet with respect to Wilberforce's acceptance or rejection of St. Dunstan's, but I think he will not take it. His friends urge it."

" May 23.—Wilberforce has not yet finally decided. I have written to him by this day's post, giving my advice to him to remain at Brighstone, and I think he will acquiesce in it. He has pressed for my opinion so urgently and repeatedly, that I could not avoid giving it, although I had much rather have been spared, as it is a point on which I may seem little able to give a dispassionate judgment. But I have thought it my duty to speak."

"May 30.—S. Wilberforce declines St. Dunstan's."

In July the Bishop went to Lavington, "to marry Henry Wilberforce to Mary Sargent."

"The Samuel Wilberforces," he writes, "were there, old Mrs. Sargent, a most magnificent old lady of eighty, in full possession of all her faculties and full of life and vigour, the very picture of a venerable and happy old age—Mrs. John Sargent, cheerful and full of sweetness in her widow's dress, and evidently never forgetting her loss for a moment, but entirely acquiescent and not incapable of entering into the happiness of others—Mr. and Mrs. Henry Manning, the youngest daughter, looking quite like a child, extremely pleasing, and said to have much talent. He is the successor of Mr. Sargent in Lavington and Graffham, two adjoining parishes, and seems to be worthy of his father-in-law both in spirit and talent."

The Bishop had no sooner returned to Farnham than he was summoned to Godalming, by the alarming illness of his mother. She was seized with a paralytic stroke, and for some time lay in a very precarious condition. The Bishop was of much comfort to her in her illness, and ministered most faithfully to her in spiritual things. A friend writes respecting her thus:

"Among her many mercies she must, I am sure, consider it a very special one, that she has such a son as the Bishop of Winchester within so short a distance. No mother could, I think, be blessed with one more affectionate and attentive to her comfort. I count it no small privilege to have been permitted to be present at his spiritual ministrations in his mother's sick chamber."

And the Bishop himself writes:

"Although without any use of the whole left side, arm, and

leg, she has not so much as expressed a sentiment of regret, much less of murmur, at the privation. Her mind is in the best possible state—full of peacefulness and trust in her Redeemer, and nothing can be more striking or consoling than the clear expression of her views to which she is continually giving utterance. She retains perfect possession of her faculties. She desires me daily in praying with her to particularize the dear children."

Mrs. Sumner ultimately, however, gradually recovered from the severity of the seizure, and lived in comparative comfort for several years afterwards.

The Bishop much hoped that he might have been able, as the summer wore on, to pay a visit to the Channel Islands, and thence go on to Geneva to fetch his wife and children (for the three boys, who had been left at school, had gone there for the holidays) home again. But he could not do so. Work pressed so much that he could not absent himself from his diocese, and the only relaxation which he seems to have had during the whole year was a change of scene by undertaking a series of confirmations in Dorsetshire. The Bishop of Bristol (Gray), who was in infirm health, had asked him to help him by officiating in his stead in that county—(Dorsetshire being then in the diocese of Bristol)—and the Bishop had consented to do so. But before the time came Bishop Gray died. All the preliminary arrangements, however, having been made, the Bishop felt that it would be such an extreme inconvenience to the clergy that the confirmations in their several parishes should be postponed, that he obtained special authority from the Archbishop of Canterbury to hold the confirmations, as arranged, during the vacancy in the See. The clergy of Dorsetshire very warmly expressed their gratitude to the Bishop for his having thus carried out the plans formed previously to Bishop Gray's death. From Sherborne his Chaplain writes, " The afternoon confirmation was very satisfactory—the congregation very large—the church very large and beautiful, and yet all was conducted with

the most impressive stillness.   Strangely enough, a pamphlet
had just been circulated in the town, among other things
speaking of the ' disorderly ' confirmations.]   How soon has a
visible contradiction been given to this calumny of the dissenter
who circulated the pamphlet ! "

There seems at this time to have arisen an unusually strong
feeling of animosity between Churchmen and Dissenters.
Churchmen feared that the privileges which they possessed as
members of the Established Church were being gradually ceded
to Non-conformists, and addresses from all parts of the country
on the subject poured in both upon the King and the Archbishop of Canterbury.   Amongst these addresses, one from the
Isle of Wight, transmitted to the Archbishop through the
Bishop, elicited the following reply from Archbishop Howley,
which is interesting as showing the general feeling of alarm
which pervaded the minds of Churchmen from the highest to
the lowest.

"ADDINGTON, *October 17th*, 1834.

" MY DEAR LORD,

"I shall be much obliged to you, on my behalf, to
acknowledge the address from the clergy of the Isle of Wight,
transmitted to me through your hands, and to assure them that
no exertion consistent with prudence will be wanting on my
part to effect a permanent and satisfactory settlement of the
matters referred to in their address, so as to secure to the people
the benefits which they reasonably expect from a Church
Establishment, and to relieve the clergy from the suspense and
anxiety which they cannot but feel in the present very unsatis-
factory position of things.

" I trust they will not be dissatisfied with this general answer.
I could not, with any discretion, either promise to accede to
their desire, or state my reasons for declining to do so.   In confidence, I may say to your Lordship, that considering the sentiments in regard both to the Church and religion so frequently
expressed in the House of Commons during the last Session, the

number of members pledged to the Roman Catholics, the
Dissenters, and the Radicals in avowed hostility to the Church,
and the unwillingness of ministers to run the risk of offending
these powerful factions, I look forward with great apprehension
to the next session. It is even doubtful whether Government
would engage to support measures originating with the Bishops
for Church Reform, or if they did, whether they could keep
their word ; for though, by the assistance of the Conservatives,
they might, if they put forth their strength, command a
majority on such questions, they would lose the support of
numerous friends whom they could ill spare. I will not, however, detain you on these matters, which must be discussed at
the proper season. . . . . It is very satisfactory to know
that every mark of respect was paid to the late Bishop of
Bristol's memory. My acquaintance with him was of very long
standing, and I can bear conscientious testimony to the kindness of his disposition, his disinterestedness and liberality in
pecuniary concerns, and his inflexible integrity. Believe me,

" My dear Lord,

" With great regard,

" Very truly yours,

" W. Cantuar."

The end of the year was marked by the death of the Duke
of Gloucester, at Bagshot. The Bishop's intercourse with the
Duke had always been of a happy character, and several times
he had stayed at Bagshot Park with Mrs. Sumner. It was
therefore with much satisfaction that he received a most interesting account of his last hours from the Rev. T. Snell, the
Rector of the parish. Some portions of the letter are of too
private and sacred a character to be transcribed here, but a few
extracts may be given :

" November 23rd, 1834.

" On Thursday afternoon great apprehensions were entertained
on his account, as he became suddenly extremely feeble. He

passed a restless night, but was better in the morning. On Friday it was settled that he was to receive the Sacrament on the following day, with the Duchess, at four o'clock. . . . . The Duke desired to see me alone.

*   *   *   *   *   *   *

"When the service was concluded, he requested me to read 'I know that my Redeemer liveth,' but added, 'come to-morrow and read it, for I feel fatigued, and the Duchess must be much fatigued after all her exertions and kind attentions to me. Go with her and compose her.' The Duchess conducted herself through the whole trying service with great composure and firmness of mind, for indeed it was very affecting. I must add, the Duke expressed his gratitude for all the comforts he enjoyed—for the great attentions he had received from the Duchess, his medical adviser, and all about him—adding, 'by doing this' (laying his hand on the table), 'I can have the first physicians from London, and every comfort to alleviate my sickness, whilst the poor man in the village is taken ill, thrown out of work, and his family in absolute distress.' He did not forget the poor in his alms."

Writing on December 3rd, after the Duke's death, Mr. Snell adds, "The Duke maintained his composure and strong religious feelings quite to the last few hours of his existence, when he became insensible,—the same humility, repentance, and implicit faith in the atonement of his Saviour. He received the sacrament with his sister on the Thursday previous to his death. On the Saturday evening, being unable to pray, he desired me to go and pray for him; though some time after this I heard him distinctly offer up this short but effectual prayer to the Father of Mercy, 'God be merciful to me a sinner.'"

CHAPTER XV.

LITTLE has hitherto been said with reference to the
Bishop's political opinions. He almost invariably voted with
the Conservative party. In early life he was perhaps more of
a Tory than in later years. Political differences were then more
clearly defined than they are now, and a Radical was looked
upon by a Tory Churchman as little better than a rabid
revolutionist. Men were therefore obliged, more or less, to join
a party and act ordinarily in agreement with it. But as years
rolled on, the Bishop felt that the boundary line between the
old political parties was less clearly defined, and in a liberal
conservative spirit looked rather to measures than men to
guide his political conduct. The following letter, referring to
the King's speech at the opening of Parliament in 1835, just
before the commencement of the long administration of Lord
Melbourne, shows at any rate the Bishop's feelings respecting
Sir R. Peel's administration. It is addressed to Mrs. Sumner.

"ST. JAMES'S SQUARE, *February 24th*, 1835.

"Half-past three. I have this moment come back from the house, having been to the opening of Parliament. You will see the speech in the papers, and it is difficult to judge of it from hearing it once read, but it seemed to me to be likely to be satisfactory to any who *will be satisfied;* holding out much promise, and yet in a tone and spirit likely to inspire confidence in the Conservative party. The crowd was immense, but so far as I saw remarkably orderly. I went down in my carriage, but finding it would be some time before it would be drawn up, after all was over I walked back. The King appeared to me to be cheered throughout the whole line as we passed very warmly. It is expected there will be an amendment moved to the address in the Upper as well as the Lower House. I wish the event was as certain in the latter place as in the former. . . . I had the pleasure of seeing Coleridge in the house with the other judges (Patteson among the rest), and congratulating him. He looked as if he had been a judge all his life."

A stormy session followed in connection with the defeat of Sir Robert Peel and the return of Lord Melbourne to power. Anxious questions were raised with reference to the Irish Church, and it must have been a great relief to the Bishop to return at the end of June to Farnham for his midsummer ordination, respecting which he was able to write to a friend:

"FARNHAM, *July 6th*, 1835.

"I had begun writing this yesterday, when Cunningham (Francis) unexpectedly entered my room to take leave, the coach being in the act of passing through Farnham. His assistance at the ordination has been truly valuable ; all his conversation consistent, his sermon* simple, affectionate, and

---

* Writing on another occasion to Mrs. Sumner, the Bishop gives his idea of what an ordination sermon ought to be. "—— preached—a good sermon, but

most useful, and I believe felt as I could have wished it to
have been by those who heard it.   On the whole it has been
an ordination of much comfort to me ; and I have the satisfaction of believing that none of those sent forth are going
without much serious impression, and the majority of them
with more or less of the true ministerial spirit implanted in
them.   May the great Shepherd and Bishop accompany them
with His blessing."

September found the Bishop once more in the Channel
Islands.   He engaged a cutter, with special pilots for each
occasion, which took him in succession to Alderney, Guernsey,
Sark, and Jersey.   He was throughout much favoured by the
weather, and the various voyages were much more happily
carried out than on the occasion of his previous visit.   He was
accompanied only by his chaplain and secretary.   Mrs. Sumner,
much to the regret of those whose acquaintance she had made
in 1829, was not able to accompany the Bishop.   As usual,
much work was crowded into the time allotted to each island.
The Bishop writes from Guernsey under date Sept. 7th :

"Yesterday was a very fatiguing day.   After preaching at
St. James' to a most crowded and hot church, we went to the
Sunday School, which you recollect was so fine a sight when
we were last on the island, when I examined and addressed the
children.   We then dined with the De Saumarez family at his
town house, where I take up my quarters in the town, and am
now writing.   2 o'clock.—Since writing the above, I have been
to the town Church, held a confirmation, returned and received
the Directors of Elizabeth College *en masse*.   I now hear the
bell ringing for St. James' Church, where I am about to

not enough of feeling for the occasion. A sermon at such a time should be full of
feeling, and lead to a burst of feeling.   They " (the candidates) "have been for
the three previous days indoctrinated even to satiety, and they come broken
down and humbled, and ready for an impulse, if it be given. You must not
suppose, however, from what I say, that the sermon was not very good. *Tout au
contraire.*"

confirm in English at half-past two. This evening we dine with the Dean."

Referring afterwards to the confirmation at St. James' he says, "We have had a very hot and crowded confirmation at St. James' Church. It seems to me as if people flocked together both in church and out of it, more this time than in 1829. Perhaps the heat of the weather makes it more perceptible."

And from Jersey on Sept. 10, he writes:

"Hitherto we have been well prospered, and though there are difficulties here in many things, and some very awkward spirits to deal with, yet I have good hope that we shall be well brought through here. My public duties here are as follows:—Wednesday, consecration of All Saints' Chapel at 4 o'clock p.m.; Thursday, French confirmation at 11 a.m. in town Church; English confirmation at half-past 2 in All Saints' Chapel; Friday, visitation at 2 p.m., and dinner to the clergy afterwards; Saturday, visits to the schools in the morning, confirmation at St. Saviour's at 3 p.m., dine with the Governor; Sunday, consecration of Gorey Chapel at half-past 10 a.m., preach for infant school at town Church at half-past 2 p.m.; Monday, confirm at St. Martin's at 10, at St. Laurence at 2, at St. Peter's at 4 o'clock. On Tuesday morning I hope to sail for Guernsey at the earliest moment. . . . I have been writing a charge all the morning, and have not yet got a single one of all my business letters written."

One more extract from a Jersey letter to show the Bishop's extraordinary energy and powers of work. It is written to Mrs. Sumner.

> "JERSEY, *Sunday night.*
> "*Half-past* 10 *o'clock.*

"You must not be surprised if I can only send you a line. But I am just told that letters must be put in the post to-morrow night for the next packet. I must rise at a quarter past 7 to set out for my three confirmations, and do not expect to reach home again before seven at night, so that all I can write must be done before I go to bed.   That the *all* cannot be *much* you will readily believe when I give you the history of my day. At 9 o'clock we set out for Gorey, where, after consecrating the church and preaching, I took a hasty lunch with Sir Hilgrove Turner" (whose acquaintance the Bishop had previously made at Ryde), "who has a cottage there, and returned hither just in time to reach the town Church at half-past 2, where I preached to a most overwhelming congregation.   Then I went to the girls' school and boys' school successively, when I had to address them both—as there are so many gratuitous teachers employed that it was desired I should pay some attention to them.   I got back here about a quarter past 5, and after eating some hasty dinner, much in the manner of the passover, returned again to the town at 6 o'clock, as I was engaged to preach at St. James' Chapel.   My work finished little before 9 ; and I am now, as you may imagine, thoroughly fatigued, with the prospect of a most heavy day before me to-morrow."

His work, however, was not labour in vain, for one well able to judge, writes with reference to this visit to Jersey :

"The more I reflect on the probable effect of the Bishop's ministrations here, their influence over men of high party views, the more I feel how thankful we ought to be to God for this visit.   All has been perfect."

Another writes from Guernsey to a brother clergyman :

"I require rest after the excitement of our dear and revered Diocesan's visit, which I trust has been greatly blessed to us all. He is indeed a Bishop! a pastor after God's own heart—commanding the respect and winning the heart and confidence of every one.   I have seen him at all hours and in a variety of positions, and such a man I had never yet seen or known.   He has been most kindly received here by all ranks: his ministrations have delighted everyone, and I trust edified many. Nothing could go off better than our confirmations; the Charge was excellent, came home, and at the united request of the

Jersey and Guernsey clergy, is to be published." Memoirs of Rev. T. Brock, p. 101.

Almost immediately after the Bishop's return to Farnham, he received the following letter from the King :—

"The King having been informed by the Queen, that Sunday, 4th next October, is the anniversary of the Third Century of the Reformation in Europe, and being fully sensible of the advantage that the entire world, and Great Britain in particular has received from this event, is desirous that the Bishop of Winchester, if not professionally engaged on that day, would come to the Castle to dinner on Saturday 3rd Oct., preach on Sunday 4th, and remain that day with their Majesties. The King of course will lodge the Bishop.

"WILLIAM R.

"CASTLE, WINDSOR, *September 20th, 1835.*"

In accordance with his Majesty's command the Bishop preached at ·Windsor Castle, and his sermon was printed at the King's desire. His text was 2 Thess. iii. 1,—"Finally brethren, pray for us, that the word of the Lord may have free course, and be glorified, even as it is with you." It was evident that the prayers of the Church in successive centuries for the free course of the word, had been signally answered. Three hundred years ago, there was a famine of the word of the Lord throughout the land. Men hungered after the Bread of Life and were fed with the chaff and husks, instead of the solid and nutritious truths of the Gospel. For the great mass of the people revelation was shrouded in mystery. Then God raised up his instrument, (Coverdale,) to print, for the first time in the English tongue, a version of the entire Bible. The publication of Cranmer's Bible followed, and year after year "the word enjoyed a freer course, the single impression became the parent of many and improved editions, restrictions were removed, the costly price was lowered, a royal injunction was issued to al

incumbents "to provide a book for every parish church, and lay
the same in the quire, chained to a desk for every man that
willed to look and read thereon." After the lapse of three
centuries, what was the result? The waters of life no longer
flowed through a narrow channel, streams had broken out in the
desert, the parched ground had become a pool, the thirsty land
springs of water. In the preceding year, the Society for the Promotion of Christian Knowledge, had sent out into the parishes of
our own country alone, 173,000 Bibles and Testaments. During
the same period the British and Foreign Bible Society had expended nearly £60,000 for Bibles and Testaments. So too, a
further evidence that God had listened to the prayers of the
Church for the free course of the word would be found in the
blessed effects of the spread of that word. In our own land,
however low or imperfect was the state of Christianity, yet our
power and strength as a nation, the pleasantness and peace of our
domestic relations, whatever is of good report either in our
public or private life, is due to the unfettered circulation of the
word of God through the length and breadth of the kingdom.
Another evidence would be found in the preservation of its
doctrines pure and unadulterated, and in their effectual working
for the salvation of individual souls. What then was the
present duty? To acknowledge the gracious hand of God, to
cherish the fundamental doctrines of the Gospel, and individually
to enter upon self-examination, to see whether that word influenced every thought, word, and work.

The visit at Windsor was followed by a long series of confirmations throughout Hants. Two incidents connected with
this tour must be recorded; the first, the Bishop's visit to
Highclere on Sunday, October 10. The Chaplain, the Rev. P.
Jacob, thus writes to Mrs. Sumner:—

"We went to Highclere parsonage, reaching it half an
hour before church time. Mr. Escot was gone, and as the
Bishop knows, I believe, the localities, he did not need to
ask the servant to show him over the house. He looked all

over it. I accompanied him to the garden; and truly it is a
wilderness. The rhododendrons of the Bishop's own planting
are beautiful, and as the appearance of things was not as bad
as we had been told, the Bishop did not see sufficient desolation
to give him a feeling of sadness. The Bishop robed in his own
bed-room, and we got into the carriage for church. The park
looked beautiful; a few minutes earlier, perhaps, we should
have seen it enlivened by people. But their eagerness had
hurried them to Church . . . Old Howell (the clerk) was about
to take two lighted candles into the pulpit; for the Church
owing to the trees about it, was very dark, but the Bishop told
me to stop him. 'What will he do without 'em?' asked old
Howell in astonishment. The text was John iv. 23. It was
an extemporaneous sermon throughout . . . It was just that sermon which I can fancy the Bishop used to preach at Highclere.
His voice was altered, and there was more expostulation and
less of authority, more of appeal and less of oratory, than any
sermon I have ever heard the Bishop preach. 'The hour
cometh and now is' was adapted to the aged, and then to the
young. His heart was poured forth; he not only alluded
distantly to, but directly spoke of his feelings at the present
moment, his associations, his constant remembrance. It must
have been a strong heart which did not feel the touching
address . . . The Bishop went to unrobe. I felt a pull at my
sleeve. It was old Howell. He took me aside, ' Mr. Sumner
—my Lord—used to be very fond of my grapes; now I've
brought 'm some, do you think he'll have them?' 'Yes,
surely, Howell.' 'Well, there 'm be in the vestry. Shall I
put 'm into the carriage?'"

From Lymington, where the Bishop was staying with Henry
Wilberforce, under date Oct. 14th, Mr. Jacob thus refers to a
meeting between the Bishop and John Henry Newman.

"Whom should I see among the invited but Mr. Newman of
Oriel College, Oxford, the great advocate of apostolicity. The
Bishop was a little surprised to see him, but expressed pleasure,

and exchanging a few kind and rapid enquiries, went to his room . . . The Bishop liked his manner and tone and expression. And this morning the Bishop and Mr. Newman took a turn together before breakfast, pleasing and pleased."

On the Bishop's return to Farnham he was glad to welcome to the Castle his old friend Dr. Hawtrey, who, after he had left, sent the following graceful letter to Mrs. Sumner, enclosing a volume written by himself, and a German Bible, won by her eldest daughter in the game of "Bonjour Philippine."

"HASTINGS, *December 28th,* 1835.

"My Dear Mrs. Sumner,

"I have not forgotten a single day of our delightful visit at Farnham, and as this inclosure will prove have honestly recollected the forfeits which were so fairly lost on Monday last.

"It is a happy circumstance for German readers that the richest mine of that language (as well as of our own) is to be found in the translation of the Bible, and I hope, therefore, that these little volumes may be graciously received in payment of my debt.

"At the same time I have ventured to add for your acceptance a very trifling volume, of which the author has given away a very few copies, and to which he has not affixed his name. He happens to be a very old friend of mine, which must account for my looking with some partiality upon the production of his idler hours. I can assure you that he is not always so ill employed.

"We shall look forward with great pleasure to seeing you and the Bishop again in our house at Eton, and do not mean to forget your renewed promise. Among many agreeable recollections connected with that house, I often recall the day when I congratulated my friend on the commencement of his happiness; and though there is no one who has had the good fortune to know the Bishop, who does not also know how well

he deserves that happiness, I do not think that any can see
it with sincerer pleasure than the Eton friends of Charles
Sumner.

" I am, my dear Mrs. Sumner,

" Very faithfully yours,

" E. C. HAWTREY."

The next year, 1836, was as usual busily occupied, but in the
autumn the Bishop was able to take a run through the Midland Counties to the Lakes, and to Durham, where he was his
brother's guest for ten days. Not the least interesting part of
his trip was a visit to Kenilworth, where he was glad to find
his old nurse still living, and whose recognition of him was of
the most cordial and motherly character. It was a pleasure to
him, on his return to Farnham, at the beginning of October, to
welcome there the Archbishop of Canterbury and Mrs. Howley.
The Archbishop was on his way to Winchester, where he was
to preach at a festival service in the Cathedral on behalf of the
County Hospital. The Bishop was anxious to do honour to the
Archbishop, and invited all the clergy of the neighbourhood to
meet him at dinner. Seventy-four guests sat down in the
noble old Castle hall, of whom sixty-six were clergy. After
dinner the clergy took the opportunity of presenting, through
Dr. Dealtry the Chancellor of the diocese, a congratulatory
address to the Archbishop, to which he responded with great
cordiality. After referring to the assaults which were continually made upon the Church, and the confidence which
he had that God Himself would defend the cause of truth
and right; he adverted to a part of the address which spoke
of his fellow-labourers in his appointed work, and he stated
that it had not been unusual to hear the Bishops spoken
of as negligent of their duty, unconnected by any kindly ties
with their clergy, and considering their own interests only.
When any such charge was made by anyone against the
Bishops of our Church, he would send such a one to Farnham

Castle, where he would find evidence of diligence in duty, of friendly and affectionate intercourse with the clergy, and of enlarged liberality, which ought to silence the calumny . . . .

The Bishop replied with much heartiness to the Archbishop's speech, and was thankful to be able to say that as the Archbishop had stated, the utmost cordiality existed between himself and his clergy.

Unfortunately the Bishop was not able to accompany the Archbishop to Winchester as he had intended, for he was seized with a sudden attack of illness which confined him to his room for three weeks. His absence from Winchester was very much felt. S. Wilberforce writes to the Bishop, giving the particulars of the Archbishop's visit under date Oct. 18 :—

"First I must express the extreme anxiety with which I have waited for the daily account from Farnham and the delight (and I trust gratitude) with which I have heard of your convalescence. May it please God to accomplish and confirm it." After describing a dinner to the Archbishop, he adds, " It was a very sad change from what we had all expected, and so indeed is it continually, and not the least when the throne was filled this morning in the cathedral with a multitude of ladies. . . . N.B.—When the Mayor marched up the choir towards his seat, and the red-coated apparitor preceded him, Miss —— was heard to question Mrs. —— ' Mamma is *that* the Bishop in the red coat ?' meaning either the Mayor or the apparitor."

After speaking warmly of the Archbishop's sermon as interesting, written very carefully, and the style for the most part chaste and beautiful, he adds :—

"There was a very considerable number of clergy, but their effect was lost. I should have marshalled them in their gowns at the Western door to meet the Archbishop, and let them march up behind him into reserved seats. But there are very *few* Protestants who understand such forms. I hope that in those who do, there is nothing of a Popish leaven (as our friend

—— would assert), for I could not help observing the want of it in a consecration last Thursday at Chichester compared with those I have witnessed in the diocese of Winton."

Writing on Oct. 19, he refers to a dinner given by the College in honour of the Archbishop :—

"The hall was excellently lighted and furnished for the occasion—a high table—a long table, and a small side table for the overplus, contained a party of rather more than eighty. . . . Soon after dinner the warden (Barter) gave the health of the Archbishop in a short and very beautiful speech. Indeed all that he said throughout the evening was said with such an admirable grace—so naturally and with such a glow of healthy feeling that it was quite inimitable though it was without the smallest claim to anything of oratorical skill. . . . The warden next gave 'the better health of the Lord Bishop of the diocese' in a speech of as nice feeling and expression as the last, briefly alluding to the general affection of the clergy of this diocese for their Bishop, an affection in which the members of this society were in no respect behind the rest of his clergy, more especially as they acknowledged in him a kind upright judicious and able visitor."

Writing to a friend on the same day, he says referring to the public dinner. "The Archbishop spoke better than I ever heard him before. There were many allusions to our dear Bishop and all in nice taste—all showing *real* affection and respect. . . . Lord Palmerston" (who was then Foreign Secretary) "was called up as Vice-President and made one of the best, if not the best speech, as speech, that was made at all. There were curious intimations of political feeling struggling through the proclaimed neutrality. The Duke of Wellington and Mr. Fleming" (M.P. for the southern division of Hants and a Conservative), "were the two toasts which excited the most acclamation. Lord Palmerston looked whitish amidst the returning bursts of cheers. He himself had a considerable amount of applause. . . . I cannot make you think, who are afar from all, what our Bishop's absence has been throughout. It is 'sunshine without the sun and nothing else ;' the festivals as festivals are most 'abject ;' even yesterday at a good place in the crowded hall I felt that if He was there, there would be something."

At the beginning of the year 1837 the Bishop was very busily occupied in arranging for the formation of a Church-building Society for the diocese.

In the course of the previous year he had gathered together all the Rural Deans of the diocese at Farnham Castle for three days' conference, and the question of the advisability of starting such a society was fully considered. Hitherto there had been none, and the Bishop was most anxious that an impetus should be given to Church-building in the diocese generally by the working of a central body conversant with the wants of the various localities and endeavouring to raise subscriptions for the purpose of supplying those wants. It was in the large towns that the deficiency in church accommodation was most apparent. Since the commencement of the century the population of Hampshire had increased $38\frac{1}{2}$ and that of Surrey 65 per cent., so that the new population constantly accruing more than swallowed up any additional church room provided. Since 1830 thirty-three new churches had been built in the diocese, twenty more had been materially improved and enlarged so as almost to deserve the name of new buildings; and in addition to this, additional accommodation for 14,000 souls had been provided in 130 churches in the two counties. The total number of churches in Hants and Surrey at this time was 470. But notwithstanding that a move had thus been made in the right direction, very much still remained to be done, and that with more systematic support than had hitherto been accorded to the work. Accordingly the Bishop put himself into communication first of all with some of the principal laity of the two counties. The Duke of Wellington sent an exceedingly characteristic reply to the Bishop's letter which is subjoined.

It will be seen that his views respecting "free and open churches" were very considerably in advance of his day.

"STRATFIELD-SAYE, *December* 22nd, 1836.

"MY LORD,

"I have had the honour of receiving your Lordship's letter of the 19th instant, and its inclosure of the 10th ; and Mr. Wellesley * has spoken to me on the subject of these papers.

"I have frequently reflected on this interesting topic ; and I have in this parish done everything in my power, at some expense and at some sacrifice of personal convenience, to afford additional accommodation in the church ; and it does not appear at least that there is any want of room in the church of this parish.

"At the same time I am aware that many do not attend regularly who are in communion with the Church of England. Yet there are in this parish, besides the higher motives for attendance, others of a worldly nature ; such as the uniform and regular attendance of all the gentry residing in the parish ; a convenient accommodation in the church for nearly every farmer in the parish, and for his family, besides free sittings for the poorer classes and their children ; the church is at no great distance from any part of the parish, and the roads to it by no means bad ; the church is well warmed ; and I must in justice add, that we have the advantage of the instruction of a clergyman, who, in the short time that he has been here, has acquired the favourable opinion of all his parishioners and neighbours.

"I am convinced, that whatever may be the proportion of church room to the population of this parish, we do not here require church room. If the whole population of the communion of the Church of England was to attend, we might require church room, unless some other distribution of the space was made. But attended as the church is now, there is more space than is required.

---

* The Hon. and Rev. Gerald Wellesley, then Rector of Stratfield-Saye, now Dean of Windsor.

"It has frequently occurred to me that, where church room is required, the first thing to do is to prevail upon individuals to give up the pews which they cannot use; which was the course which was adopted in this parish last year. This, and a new arrangement of the pews, gave much accommodation.

"If more space was required, I should propose that all pews should be given up; that the whole space of the church should be laid open for the accommodation of all the parishioners indiscriminately, separate chairs of a cheap description with arms, being provided for their accommodation. This being done, and space being still required for the accommodation of the parishioners in their attendance upon Divine service, I would propose to consider of the mode of enlarging the church, or if that could not be effected, of building another church or chapel. It must never be forgotten that another church or chapel would require the attendance of another clergyman, who must live, and must be remunerated. He can be remunerated only by the sale or hire of the pews and places in the new place of Divine worship; and here again would commence the evil which has, in my opinion, been the most efficient cause of the non-attendance at Divine worship of the lower classes of the people of this country.

"I have ventured to submit these ideas to your Lordship. I admit that they are applicable only to a country parish. But it appears that that is the immediate object which your Lordship has in view. If I am right, but little is required in Hampshire. At all events, whether right or wrong, I am ready to support your Lordship's views, and in case any subscription should be entered into in this county, I beg your Lordship to put down my name for one hundred pounds.

"I have the honour to be, my Lord,

"Your Lordship's most obedient humble Servant,

"WELLINGTON.

"The Lord Bishop of Winchester."

He wrote again in the spring of the year, 1837, as follows :—

"STRATFIELD-SAYE, *March 7th*, 1837.

"MY DEAR LORD BISHOP,

"I think that the Church Building Question is taking a new appearance in consequence of the motion of the Chancellor of the Exchequer in the House of Commons on Friday.* It is true that whatever may be the result, it may be desirable · to encourage by subscription the building of new churches. But I never can put myself forward as a promoter of a plan for leasing pews in country churches—until I see what is the result of this plan, I must beg leave to decline to put myself forward as presiding over a meeting in the county of Hants for the purpose of organising a Church Building Society. I shall have company in my house during Easter; and although I will attend the meeting at Farnham at one o'clock, on the 29th of March, if I should find that circumstances should be such as to enable me to do so, and I am much flattered by your Lordship's invitation to pass the day at the Castle, I hope that you will excuse me if I should find myself under the necessity of returning home after the meeting.

"I have the honour to be, my Lord,

"Your Lordship's most obedient humble Servant,

"WELLINGTON.

"The Lord Bishop of Winchester, Farnham Castle."

The Bishop was able to satisfy the Duke with reference to the future action of the proposed society, for at the end of March the Duke, as Lord-Lieutenant of the county, presided over a largely attended and influential meeting at Winchester, where a Diocesan Church Building Society was duly organised. The Bishop's address at this meeting bristled with telling statistics, and with a true prophetical spirit he expressed his

---

* The Chancellor of the Exchequer (Mr. Spring Rice) had moved for a Committee of the whole House on the Church Rates Abolition Bill.

fears that in carrying out the objects of the society " every pew would be found a Saragossa, and every church a Badajoz." The Bishop headed the subscription list with a donation of £300 and an annual subscription of £100, in addition to £300 to the Metropolitan Fund for the Deanery of Southwark (which was then united to the London district for church-building purposes), and £500 to churches actually in progress in the diocese.

The society was very warmly taken up in both counties. At an inaugurating meeting at Epsom in May, Lord Arden, the Lord-Lieutenant of Surrey, took the chair, and at the first annual meeting held at Winchester in July, 1838, the Bishop was able to state, that in the preceding year nine new churches had been built, and that twelve more were in progress, and that the society had contributed very nearly £3000 in aid of the funds raised locally. That much of the success of the new society was owing to the exertions of the Bishop may be gathered from the fact that in the course of the twelve months he attended no fewer than twenty-four meetings in various parts of Hants and Surrey for the purpose of forming district associations in the several rural deaneries. The return made in 1875 to the House of Lords of the sums exceeding £500 expended since 1840 upon the building or restoration of churches, shows that the zeal for church-building, thus happily awakened, was not a mere temporary feeling, for the total sum expended in Hampshire amounted to £864,419, of which only £40,952 was derived from public funds. The sum expended in a like manner in Surrey amounted to £1,178,454, of which £192,697 was derived from public sources. So that the grand total for the diocese was reported to be no less a sum than £2,042,873.

It was in June of this year that William the Fourth died. The succession to the throne was regarded, if possible, with more than usual interest, owing to the youth of the Princess Victoria. The young Queen met the Lords of the Council at Kensington Palace the morning after the King's death, and the next day, at St. James' Palace, received the Archbishops and Bishops, amongst whom was the Bishop of Winchester.

These men, venerable both from their years and station, stood at one end of the room looking eagerly towards the door through which the youthful Sovereign was to enter. She then numbered only eighteen years, and had been somewhat rarely seen by her future subjects, and there was, therefore, considerable curiosity and excitement felt as to the manner in which she would comport herself in a position of so much difficulty. The door opened, and she entered alone—the Duchess of Kent remaining behind. The door closed behind her, and the young Queen, with her slight, graceful figure dressed in black, advanced towards the expectant prelates, quietly, simply, and alone, with perfect self-possession. There was no apparent nervousness, but only sufficient emotion perceptible to show how fully she realised her position. The Bishop, when describing this scene, often said that he, for one, found it impossible to watch her unmoved—she looked so sweet, and graceful, and dignified. It was a strange scene—this lovely child-like Queen alone in the midst of a group of Ecclesiastics. She bowed to them, and then spoke in a soft, silvery voice, very quietly and naturally, and expressed a hope that she might be able to fulfil rightly the great duties which would devolve upon her, and thanked them for their loyal greeting. They were filled with astonishment and admiration, and as in succession they kneeled to kiss her hand, their chivalry and loyalty reached the pitch of enthusiasm.

None knew better than the Bishop did, from his former experience, the anxiety and labour which fell to the lot of royalty, and cordially did he press upon his clergy in his visitation charge, which he delivered a few months afterwards, the duty of special prayer for their youthful Sovereign. "If," he said, " there be one prayer more fitting to us than another at this juncture, it is that God might be pleased to direct and prosper all the councils of our gracious young Queen to the advancement of His glory and the good of His church." In this charge, which was one of great interest, the Bishop speaks prophetically of religious considerations in matters affecting the national polity being so separated from civil, that in the plausible assertion of an unbounded tolerance we might be in danger of losing sight of essential principles; of the progress of the Church of Rome, and of the education of our youth being dissociated from religion, and the families of the working classes left to collect their creed as best they might without direction or authorised teaching. He was able to report that thirty-two new schools and twenty-one new churches had been built, and at the close of his address the clergy were earnestly warned to look to their own individual ministrations, and see why, in many cases, all still continued cold and stationary, why the fleece remained unmoistened, and why the dry bones were motionless, with no breath in them. They would do well to seek with zeal, earnestness, and unweariedness, to carry out their high and holy mission, always remembering that, after all, the real source of all ministerial success is external to ourselves. "Not by might, not by power, but by my spirit saith the Lord."

In the course of his visitation tour throughout the diocese an incident occurred which might have led to serious consequences. He was staying with his chaplain, the Rev. C. J. Boyles, at Brighstone Rectory, and the adventure is thus described by Mr. Boyles in a letter to Mrs. Sumner :—

"It was very important for us to be at Black Gang Chine yesterday about twelve. Mr. Wilberforce went alone on the box of his carriage, I with the Bishop inside. We had some little difficulty in making a start again as on a former occasion, but the coachman had good confidence in himself and horses, and the Bishop in him, and I in them all ; and so, after a little struggle, we went on, and were discharged safely at the hotel above the Chine. There was only a boy to act the part of ostler, who seemed inexperienced in that line of business, so

Wilberforce and I took a horse apiece into the stable, and when I came out I saw the Bishop pushing the carriage under a shed. We descended at a full pace down the Chine—the wind offering, however, a considerable force to us. Wilberforce was well attired for the expedition in a foul-weather hat and waterproof cloak. The Bishop also had taken the precaution of attaching strings to his hat. We had anticipated breakers, but when we were really on the strand, and, as it were, under the mountains of sea and spray, a simultaneous burst of 'How magnificent! What a sea!' came from us. Wilberforce said he had never seen the effect more grand. But there was a point round which we desired to get, and having succeeded in evading the approach of the waves, which every now and then made us take to our heels to escape a washing—we feared nothing more, and proceeded to weather the point; a mighty wave came rolling in, which we stood to admire, but not long, for on it came, and we found that we were within its reach—not a moment was to be lost; up we scrambled, but the cliff was no protection. I felt the water rising to my middle, and I stuck my stick in the ground to prevent being dragged back. I had seen the Bishop mount into a cavity of the bank just behind me, and when I recovered my recollections, I looked hastily round, but the wave hid everything from my sight. That was an anxious moment, but the next brought my two companions again by my side, and we found that we all shared alike, except that, perhaps, my head and shoulders had escaped rather more of the sea than the others. Mr. Wilberforce had been just by my side at first, but with great presence of mind he thought that the Bishop's was the least secure place, and was quickly by his side, lest his foot should have slipped. We were all wet to the skin—at least, as far as our lower extremities were concerned, but all agreed that we had been more than repaid by the glorious sight of the ocean."

On the Bishop sending his charge to Archbishop Howley, he received the following letter in acknowledgment, the latter clauses of which have been singularly verified by the subsequent history of the Church as regards legislative action :—

"My dear Lord,

"I should have thanked you sooner for your kindness in sending me your Charge; but I received it only on Friday last, and had no opportunity of reading it till Sunday. With many parts of it I have been much gratified, and have derived pleasure from all, with the exception of the remarks on the Commission, in respect to which I do not coincide in your Lordship's sentiments; though there is nothing in them inconsistent, either in matter or expression with the kindness which I have always received from you, or with our ecclesiastical relations to each other. In the present state of the Government, I do not expect any measure directly hostile to the Church; unless on compulsion from the Dissenters and Radicals. The operations will be confined to sapping and mining if the latter are satisfied with this slow process : a process really more dangerous in its nature than open attack, which if it chances to fail is ultimately disadvantageous to the assailants.

"The Committee of enquiry into the possible improvement of Church property without any limitation of object, but in reality with the intention of finding a substitute for Church rates will be re-appointed, and attempts will be made to tamper with public education, and to disconnect the schools from the Church. Of course we shall resist to the utmost of our power : but schemes which appear monstrous at first sight are familiarized to the public mind by continued discussion, and may at last be realized almost as matters of course.

"I remain My dear Lord,

"Your Lordship's most faithful servant,

"W. Cantuar."

CHAPTER XVI.

THE year 1838 seems to have passed, as far as the diocese
was concerned, without much of interest and excitement, beyond the ordinary routine of ecclesiastical work. The Bishop
in his capacity as Prelate of the Order of the Garter, was called
upon to take part in the coronation of the Queen on June 28th.
It was the second coronation which he had witnessed. On the
occasion of that of their Majesties King William and Queen
Adelaide on Sept. 8, 1831, the Bishop had supported the
Queen, with the Archbishop of Armagh (Beresford) on the
other side. On the present occasion, he carried a large quarto
Bible with massive gold clasps, on which the Queen took the
oaths, the Bible, according to custom, becoming subsequently
the property of the Bishop.

In the procession up the Abbey the Bishop immediately
preceded the Queen, with the Bishop of Bangor (Bethell) bearing the Patina, and the Bishop of Lincoln (Kaye), on his left,
bearing the Chalice. The following extracts from the Bishop's.

s

letters to Mrs. Sumner (who was nursing a sick daughter at Chester), show the state of excitement which existed in London. S. Wilberforce and his family were staying at Winchester House.

"June 24, 1838. Samuel Wilberforce and Robert" (the Bishop's son), "are gone to-night to hear Melvill, having sat under Hook in the morning."

"June 27th. Anything like the sort of confusion and excitement in which London is cannot easily be imagined. It appears that the illuminations are to be general in this part of the town, so that I have mounted a star in the centre of the balcony, and the said balcony is at the present moment in the act of being shored up with planks erected from the area to make it safe to hold any number of occupants. This morning I went out on to the top of the house, and perceive we shall have a good view of the fireworks in the Park from thence. As for going out at night in a carriage, it will be out of the question, from the state of the streets. It is extremely difficult to pass either driving or walking at present. Mrs. Wilberforce had a ticket sent to her this morning for the North Transept, and Samuel has succeeded in getting one for the same part of the Abbey to which Robert is going, so they will be together. John" (his eldest son) "in court dress with bag-wig and sword will be rather amusing."

"Half-past seven. Thursday. I am just setting off. I hear the rest of the party were off by half-past four, and got into the line in Waterloo-place. It is a fine morning."

"June 29th. I find after all, the letter which I left to be sent yesterday was not posted. In the confusion I suppose it was overlooked, and I am sure I cannot be much surprised, though I am very sorry. I did not get home myself till half-past seven. Nothing could go off better than the whole ceremony, although it was very fatiguing. All had good places and seemed satisfied. The illuminations at night were very splendid, but it was impossible for any to go out, as the streets were literally impassable. We saw the fireworks let off in the Green Park, (which by the bye did not begin till eleven o'clock at night), from the top of the house, where the Bishop of London and all his family, including children and servants, were all placed. They were most brilliant."

Almost immediately after the coronation, the Bishop went for a day or two to Godstone to stay with Archdeacon Hoare, and the following letter to Mrs. Hoare in answer to one from her, is inserted as a sample of the playful letters which it was his habit to write to intimate friends :—

"I hope to arrive at your house on Monday the 2nd of July, before your dinner-time, so that if you think fit to put on your 'entertaining gown,' according to the Mansion-house phrase, on that day, I shall be able to profit by your hospitality. With respect to your kind question whom I would wish you to invite, I am sure you will excuse me if I leave you to your own sense of what is

"Firstly, right.

"Secondly, necessary.

"Thirdly, convenient. And

"Fourthly, agreeable.

Only I would ask you to remember that *I do not* reply as a certain bishop is said to have once done to a hospitable layman in answer to a similar inquiry 'Not the Clergy.' On Wednesday the 4th I must return to Farnham for the ordination."

Mrs. Sumner was much missed at the ordination, and at the usual Church Missionary gathering, which took place on the Monday following. The Bishop writes :—

"We had in the hall 'Jesus shall reign,' and in the chapel 'O'er the realms,' but you were specially wanted in the last to soften and polish it up. Mrs. John Cunningham led, and —— followed at the top of his voice, to which he contrives to give strength by shutting his eyes all the time."

The Bishop seems at this period of his life, to have been very frequently laid by from illness during the autumn. It

was so this year, and his indisposition came on at a peculiarly
unfortunate time, for he was in the midst of a confirmation
tour in Hants, when he was seized by a violent attack of quinsy.
The Bishop of Barbados, however, (Coleridge), kindly came to
the rescue, and prevented the postponement of the confirmations,
which would otherwise have been unavoidable.   As soon as he
was able to do so, he went with his family to Cowes to recruit
his strength.   It must have rather amazed him to receive there
one morning the following letter from Newman, whom, it may
be remembered, the Bishop had met at Lymington, in 1835.

" MY LORD,

"I have just received by post a number of *The Record*
newspaper, containing a report of my having expressed myself
to the following effect, with relation to the sees of Chester and
Winchester : 'that the sees of Chester and Winchester are,
from the unfitness of those who occupy them, *ipso facto* void,
and that the clergy of the dioceses cannot be justly called to
render their nominal diocesans canonical obedience.'

" I am perhaps unnecessarily intruding myself and the paper
in question on your Lordship's notice, when I briefly state,
which I beg leave to do, that the above report is untrue in all
its parts, and that I deny it as thoroughly as I can deny anything.   Nor can I fancy any conversation of mine which has
given rise to it.   As far as I can recollect, I have not been
expressing any judgment at all about any bishop whatever.
And I think I may add, I have thought no opinion about any ;
except indeed such opinion about conduct as we spontaneously
form concerning whatever comes before us.   The idea expressed
in the report above given is to me quite a new one.   I have
addressed a copy of this to the Bishop of Chester.

" I am, my Lord,

" Your Lordship's obedient servant,

" JOHN H. NEWMAN.

"ORIEL COLLEGE, *November* 30th, 1838."

The Bishop's stay at Cowes much refreshed him, and he had intended to have paid a few visits to friends before returning to his ordinary work at Farnham, but his plans were disarranged by the death of Mrs. Sumner's mother at Geneva, at the end of November, and he returned quietly to Farnham, and immediately commenced the somewhat arduous task of organising a Diocesan Board of Education. The first step towards this desirable object had already been taken. The National Society had, in the earlier part of the year, appointed a committee of enquiry as to the best mode of helping on the cause of national education throughout the various dioceses of England, and in consequence of the report of this committee the society issued certain " suggestions," which were approved by the Archbishop, and sent with a recommendatory letter from the Bishop to the Dean and Chapter. One of these suggestions was the formation of a Diocesan Board of Education for the purpose of originating and carrying out such measures as might be generally deemed desirable for the promotion of education in the diocese. Meetings accordingly of laity and clergy were held at Winchester on the invitation of the Dean and Chapter, and a Diocesan Board consisting of certain official and elected members was formed at the beginning of 1839, after many and somewhat anxious questions had been discussed at the preliminary meetings. The following letter from S. Wilberforce to the Bishop shows that there were rocks and shoals, which threatened the safety of the newly launched institution.

"Brighstone, *January 5th*, 1839.

" The main feature of our doings was the desire of certain parts of our body to make the terms of union, &c. very stringent, and to have a select few join us, and the opposition to this on the other side. There were three points on which this one principle was debated. First, Keble proposed that the schoolmasters be required to be members of the Church of England *and communicants.* For many reasons this was judged objec

tionable, as savouring of a sacramental test, &c. I suggested
that the schoolmasters be in communion with the Church of
England, 'Mr. Mayor' seconding me as a singular pheno-
menon! It was, however, apparently more the will of the
meeting to gain the same result by the simple 'apocope' of the
words 'and a communicant,' so the other form was not pressed,
and on a division Keble alone adhered to 'and a communicant.'
The second point was as to books. Keble proposed as a term of
union, 'that no books be employed in any school in union but
such as have been approved by the Board.' Objection—that
no middle school would join, if compelled, e.g., to give up old
geography books; the master would never find his way to
Winchester in the new one, &c. I proposed, and Jacob
seconded, that the present rule for National schools be continued, only adding the licence of using in such schools any
books not on the lists, of which the Bishops shall have approved,
and that for middle schools it be merely that the lists of the
books they now use should be sent into the Board—the purpose
of which was to avoid beginning threatening—to get them into
union, examine their books, and meet difficulties in detail ; not
alarming a timorous class by an initial obligation of whose
tendency they could not be well aware. I think we should
have carried this, had not —— and —— brought strongly up
the old sore of the Christian knowledge restriction, which
immediately turned a certain number the other way. However, we carried a middle resolution, namely, that no books be
used of which the Board disapprove. This must of course be
verbally altered into—have signified their disapprobation—and
then the result is doubtless right : though it be not I think the
best way of reaching it.

"The third point was,—on visiting and inspecting. We put
it forth as one of our advantages offered to middle schools and
others—visitation and inspection tending to the improvement of
the school, and increase of confidence in parents. Keble proposed that we should *also* make it a condition of union, that

they should engage to submit to such inspection. This I think objectionable for the very same reason. It needlessly alarms the timorous beginners of an untried union. It is like asking a man to let you tie his hands down. If you did not he might never raise them, but the proposal makes him suspicious. This, however, was carried by two, I think. Such were our only important points."

It will thus be seen that there were many knotty questions to be discussed and determined before the Board could commence operations. The Bishop, though at one time matters looked so complicated that he wrote with reference to a meeting at Winchester, " I propose to be present on Thursday next, with the hope of righting matters which seem to me now suicidally wrong," was able to carry matters to a successful issue ; and in the spring of the year the Board was fairly launched, and commenced operations by endeavouring to enlist the sympathies of the diocese. One of the most important matters which they took in hand was the establishment of a Training College for masters. A house in Winchester was rented, where, in conjunction with the choristers from the Cathedral, the students were placed under the superintendence of the Rev. D. Waugh as Principal. The Board arranged that the Training School at Salisbury for Schoolmistresses should be common to both dioceses, a like arrangement being entered into with regard to the Winchester Training School for Masters. Very energetic measures were taken to promote the spread of education through the means of the Board. Meetings were held at Farnham Castle, under the presidency of the Bishop, and at his request in the various rural deaneries of the diocese. That it was an occasion on which energy was needed is clear from the fact stated by the Bishop at the meeting at Farnham, that at that time there were in daily schools under the superintendence of the clergy 37,644, leaving as was calculated 102,176 not under instruction, at any rate in Church schools. Parliamentary returns showed that only 3,714 were under instruction by dissenting teachers, leaving a net deficiency of instruction of 98,462 children.

That all was not straight sailing in the establishment of the Board will be clear from the following interesting letters from the Duke of Wellington to the Bishop. It does not appear from the subscription list that the Duke ultimately ever saw his way to joining the Society.

"WALMER CASTLE, *October* 30*th*, 1839.

"MY LORD BISHOP,

"I have had the honour of receiving your Lordship's letter of the 28th instant.

"I have already made known in detail to the Archbishop of Canterbury, and have stated in Parliament my opinion regarding private subscriptions to enable Diocesan Societies to establish in the several dioceses additional means of religious education.

"I am not only ready but anxious to contribute towards the promotion of this object, but it is to establish real religious education under the superintendence and control of the clergy of the Church of England.

"The State may think proper to establish another system, that is to say, to provide for a system of eleemosynary secular instruction, omitting altogether religious instruction ; or to provide for the instruction of the people in the doctrines of Popery, or any other not those of the Church of England.

"As Member of Parliament, as one of Her Majesty's subjects, I may, as I should, object to the adoption of such system or systems. But I must submit to the law, when such should be adopted by the State.

"That which I decline to do is to contribute by voluntary subscription to carry into execution such systems. It appears to me that the Government have determined that the Committee of the Privy Council shall have the power of employing inspectors to inspect the schools established or maintained by the aid of public money.

" Doubts have been entertained regarding the intention and extent and nature of this inspection ; and endeavours have been made at different times in various modes, verbally and in writing, to remove these doubts. The last explanation of the intentions of the Committee of the Privy Council which I have seen, is in a pamphlet circulated by authority of that Committee.

" These various explanations, and particularly the last one, tend to convince me that the consequence of the proposed authoritative inspection of the schools must be to place them under the direction and control, eventually, exclusively of the Government.

" Under these circumstances, I am anxious that the Diocesan Societies should avoid to expose themselves or the schools under their management to such inspection ; and I feel this anxiety so strongly, as to have determined that I will not contribute a subscription to the fund of any Diocesan Society which shall not decline to accept assistance from the Committee of the Privy Council, excepting on the condition that the proposed inspection by the officers of the Government shall be accurately defined, and limited to the proof that the funds received have been expended for the purpose for which they were granted, and that a school, having been established, is conducted under the superintendence and control of the clergy of the Church of England.

" Your Lordship will perceive that I am by no means prepared at this moment to attend, much less to preside at a public meeting. Government will probably hereafter explain more fully their intentions, and I will then most readily contribute my aid to promote the views of the Diocesan Society, on the principles laid down in this letter.

" I have the honour to be,

" My Lord Bishop,

" Your Lordship's most obedient humble servant,

" WELLINGTON."

"LONDON, *November 23rd*, 1839.

"MY LORD BISHOP,

"I have had the honour of receiving your Lordship's letter and the newspaper enclosed—the former dated the 18th instant.

"It is quite clear that the Committee of the Privy Council, that is the Government, intend to persevere, and to render efficient the inspection of the schools which may be established under the direction of Diocesan Associations, in aid of which funds may be granted by the Committee of the Privy Council, either direct to such Diocesan Associations, or through the National Society.

"It is quite obvious from the proceedings of the Committee of the Privy Council on the subject of the formation of a Normal school, and from the contents of the pamphlets published by their authority, that the views of the gentlemen now composing the Committee of the Privy Council are not identical with those of the Diocesan Associations in general.

"I feel a confidence that the gentlemen now composing the Committee of the Privy Council will not exert the powers which are undefined; and unlimited right of inspection into all schools established by the exertions of the Diocesan Associations, aided by public money, will undoubtedly give them opportunity to introduce systems of education not approved of by those who may have contributed to make up the funds at the disposal of the Diocesan Associations.

"But it must be observed, that although the powers assumed by the Committee of the Privy Council, and intended to be maintained, are permanent, the gentlemen composing the Committee are not permanently appointed. These may be changed on any day. Others may be appointed in whose opinions and sentiments the same confidence could not be felt; and it would be found that a number of individual subscribers called Diocesan Associations, would have given their subscriptions to establish in their several dioceses and parishes, not a system of education founded on the doctrines, system, and practices of the Church of England, but any other that should be thought expedient by the members of the Committee of the Privy Council.

"Under these circumstances I feel that there is no course left for the Diocesan Associations, excepting to decline to accept aid from the Committee of the Privy Council.

"As an individual, I must decline to take part in any meeting which may have for its object to raise subscriptions for establishing schools ; unless on the condition that such Diocesan Associations shall engage that they will not receive aid from the fund at the disposal of the Committee of the Privy Council.

"If this should be clearly understood, I shall be ready to attend at any time that your Lordship may appoint.

"I have the honour to be,

"My Lord Bishop,

"Your Lordship's most faithful and obedient humble servant,

"WELLINGTON.

"The Lord Bishop of Winchester, Farnham Castle."

"STRATHFIELD-SAYE, *December 11th,* 1839.

"MY LORD BISHOP,

"I have had the honour of receiving your Lordship's letter of the 9th inst., and the enclosure.

"I quite concur in the first resolution of the Winchester Diocesan Board of Education of the 6th Dec. instant.

"I concur likewise in the first member of the second resolution ending with the words, 'a claim of inspection.'

"In my opinion, the last words of the resolution tend to convey a notion that it is contemplated that there may be an inspection on authority not that of the Church, sanctioned by the Bishop.

"I am very unwilling to decline to do that which your Lordship is disposed to recommend. But I confess that I feel very unwilling to attend, and above all to preside over, a public meeting upon this subject.

" " We must be sensible that those who think as your Lordship, and as I do, upon this subject, however numerous, do not compose the whole society. The Roman Catholics, and all the Dissenting sects in the country, and the members of the Government and their friends and supporters throughout the country, are of a different opinion. The doors of any meeting must be wide open, and all must be admitted who desire admission ; and the consequence must be a discussion, which will end as such discussions generally do, by sending every man home with the same opinions and intentions as influenced him when he came to the meeting.

" The meeting may determine what it may, but I for one will not subscribe for schools which are to receive aid from the Government through any channel, and are in consequence to be liable to an inspection by an officer of the Government, of which the exact nature and limit are not clearly defined and expressed, before I put down my name.

" That being the case, I don't see what I have to do in a meeting.

" I can write down what I have to say at the bottom of the first resolution, or of the first and second modified and explained as I have suggested in this letter ; and I think that you will find that more benefit to the cause of education will result from this mode of proceeding than from any meeting.

" I have the honour to be,

" My Lord Bishop,

" Your Lordship's most obedient humble servant,

" WELLINGTON.

" The Lord Bishop of Winchester."

In the autumn the Bishop again visited the Channel Islands. On the occasion of his visit to Sark Mr. Fosbery (afterwards incumbent of Sunningdale) accompanied him. On returning to Guernsey, after a confirmation held in Sark, the Bishop pointed to a solitary rock, round which the waters were wildly dashing, and suggested that it would be a very fit subject for poetry, adding a few thoughts in connection with it.　Mr. Fosbery acted on the suggestion, and wrote the following beautiful lines, which were afterwards published in his volume of " Hymns and Poems for the Sick and Suffering."

There is a single stone
　　Above yon wave—
A rocky islet lone,
　　Where tempests rave.

What doth it there? The sea
　　Restless and deep
Breaks round it mournfully
　　And knows no sleep.

The sea hath hung it round
　　With its wild weed,
No spot could there be found
　　For better seed.

Storm-beaten rock—no change
　　'Tis thine to know
Only the waters' range
　　In ebb and flow.

The happy sounds of earth
　　Are not for thee ;
The voice of human mirth,
　　Of children's glee.

No song of birds is thine—
　　No crown of flowers ;
Say, dost thou not repine
　　Thro' long lone hours ?

Yet stars for thee are bright
　　In midnight skies,
And tranquil worlds of light
　　Around thee rise.

These smoothe thine ocean bed,
　　Its heavings cease ;
While those, from o'er thine head,
　　Breathe on thee peace.

The wearied man of grief
Like thee I deem,
To whom comes no relief
From life's dark dream.

No human ties are left,
Earth's hopes are gone ;
He dwells, a thing bereft,
Blighted, alone.

Yet o'er him, from above,
Bright spirits bend,
And One with voice of love
Calls him His friend.

And then he thankful learns
Why grief was given,
And trusting—peaceful turns
To God in Heaven.

S. Wilberforce also acted on the Bishop's suggestion, and wrote the following :—

There is a lonely rock in the wide sea,
The waters roll
About it with wild moan unceasingly :
It is the goal
The sea bird reaches with a weary wing,
When the fierce storm
Thwarts his free course with ruthless buffeting :
But human form
Was never seen on it ; no friendly bay
In the wave war
Meets there, upon his vexed and fearful way,
The mariner.
But the rude surf beats alway mountains high
And threatens death—
Yet upon it, from out the evening sky
In summer's breath,
Bright stars look mildly down : to it the wave
With gentlest flow
Then chaunts, as ebb and flood its rough sides lave—
And even so
Is man set lonely in an ocean tide
Of outward things,
Which chafes and roars around his vexed side
Nor rest e'er brings.

But there is bent upon him from above
　　Earth's storm and haze,
Watching his weary strife with thoughts of love,
　　A Father's gaze—
And if he dare look up to that mild Eye—
　　The storm-winds cease,
The waters' roar is lulled to melody—
　　He is at peace.

From the Channel Islands the Bishop went on to join Mrs.
Sumner and his family who had previously gone to Geneva. It
was here that he heard of Lord Walsingham's death, which
vacated several important pieces of preferment in the diocese,
amongst others the Archdeaconry of Surrey. The filling up of
this post required much thought. The Archdeacon of Surrey
was by virtue of his office the appropriator of the great tithes
of Farnham, Surrey. These tithes were of very considerable
value, and the Bishop was very anxious in conjunction with the
Archdeacon to restore the tithes to their original use, as an
endowment for the clergy of Farnham and its dependencies.
To the Archdeaconry of Surrey, the Bishop, after much and
anxious deliberation, appointed S. Wilberforce, Rector of Brighstone. Throughout his tenure of the Archdeaconry he loyally
co-operated with the Bishop in steadily refusing to renew the
leases and thus foregoing a considerable sum which legally was
the property of the Archdeacon for the time being.

As Prelate of the Order of the Garter, the Bishop was called
upon to be present at all the principal state ceremonies. In
the marriage of the Queen which took place on the tenth of
February 1840, he took the most loyal interest. The Bishop
was always greatly impressed with the exceeding grace and
dignity with which the Queen comported herself on state occasions. And it was impossible not to take a more than usual
interest in witnessing the youthful sovereign of these realms
plight her troth to one, who, then almost unknown in England,
proved himself afterwards fully worthy of her choice. Few men
were so much misunderstood during their life-time as the

Prince Consort, but now, owing to the publication of the Queen's journals and letters and the light of history, the memory of none is dearer to the people of England.

> " We know him now . . . .
> . . . . A Prince indeed
> Beyond all titles, and a household name
> Hereafter through all times Albert the Good."
>   TENNYSON's Dedication to "The Coming of Arthur."

The Bishop was much occupied during the Parliamentary session of this year with a very troublesome question, referred to above—namely the settlement of the Farnham tithes. He tried to bring the matter to a successful issue by himself introducing a bill into the House of Lords—the Rectories of Farnham, &c., bill, the object of which was to re-endow the rectories of Farnham and its dependencies with the alienated tithes, and to annex to the Archdeaconry of Surrey, in lieu of these tithes, a prebend in the Cathedral Church of Winchester.

The bill having passed the House of Lords on the sixteenth of June, was sent down to the House of Commons, and on July 3rd Sir Robert Inglis moved the second reading, which was carried, notwithstanding the fact that considerable opposition was raised against the bill, mainly on two grounds ;—first, that " public property" was being dealt with by a private bill ; and secondly, that it was unfair to the lessees to decline to renew the leases as the lives fell in. Ultimately, however, in consequence of certain clauses being introduced into the bill which gave compensation to the lessees, (to which the Bishop declined to assent, as forming a bad precedent) the bill was withdrawn, and on the motion of Sir Robert Inglis the order for the third reading was discharged. The Bishop then made up his mind that he would endeavour to carry out privately that which he had failed in accomplishing through the intervention of Parliament, and by the hearty co-operation of the successive Archdeacons, Wilberforce, Dealtry, Hoare, and Utterton ; who all declined to renew the leases to the lessees, the endowment of the various districts was carried out in 1864.

By a bill which was passing through Parliament at the same time, entitled "An Act to carry into effect with certain modifications the fourth Report of the Commissioners of Ecclesiastical duties and revenues," Winchester was allowed to retain five canonries instead of four, which would, under the general arrangements of the bill, have been its natural complement, and this fifth canonry has always been looked upon as a sort of endowment for the Archdeaconry of Surrey in lieu of the income arising in old times from the appropriation of the Farnham tithes. It is true that the fifth canonry was left to Winchester under the supposition that the Farnham Rectory Bill would have become law, which absolutely endowed the Archdeaconry with the canonry. That bill not having passed the Houses of Parliament, the legal obligation fell through, but the Bishop always carried out what was obviously the intention of Parliament, by promoting each successive Archdeacon of Surrey, when necessary, to a Canonry in the Cathedral. The bill itself, however, the Bishop uncompromisingly opposed. It was in consequence of his motion in the House of Lords that on July 23rd and 24th, counsel (Knight-Bruce and Hope) were heard at the Bar to speak against the bill; and on the second reading being proposed by Lord Melbourne on July 27th, the Bishop spoke at considerable length, and, as was acknowledged by the other side, with much eloquence and force, against the bill. It was, however, carried by a majority of fifty-one, and ultimately passed on the sixth of August. It was this Act which finally appointed the Ecclesiastical Commissioners on the basis on which they have since carried on their extensive operations. It may be well to state here, as indicative of the Bishop's character, that though he had thus as far as was in his power withstood the original formation of the Commission, yet when he found that opposition was of no avail, no Bishop more loyally endeavoured to make the act beneficial to the highest interests of the Church. In 1856 he was appointed a member of the Church Estates Committee, on whose recommendations

T

the principal measures of the Commission are founded, and continued a member of the Committee till 1864.*

In thus acting, the Bishop was carrying into effect his own words when speaking in his Charge in 1841 of the measure passed the previous year: "As it has pleased the Legislature to pass it into a law, it now becomes our duty to assist in making its provisions as efficient as possible for producing the utmost amount of beneficial result which can be derived from it."—*Charge*, 1841, p. 19.

* The Church Estates Committee consists of five members, namely: three "Church Estates Commissioners," two of whom are appointed by the Crown and one by the Archbishop, and two of the Ecclesiastical Commissioners appointed annually by the Board itself.

CHAPTER XVII.

Charge delivered in 1841.—The Bishop's opinions on the Tractarian controversy.
—Confirmation Tour.—Baptism of the Prince of Wales.—Letter as to the
position of the Episcopal Church in Scotland in relation to the Established
Church in England.—Diocesan Training School.—Government Inspection of
Schools.—The Bishop's hearty Support of it.—Correspondence as to the Introduction of a representation of the Virgin Mary into a Painted Window.
—Visit to the Channel Islands.—Incident at Alderney.—Letters to the Rev.
V. Ryan.—Assists in the Consecration of the Bishop of Lichfield.—Reasons
for peculiar interest in it.—Speech at the Consecration of the Colours of the
49th Regiment.—Formation and Success of the Southwark Fund for Schools
and Churches.—£30,000 raised.—Charge delivered in 1845.—Consecration of
the Bishop of Oxford.

IT was in the year 1841 that the Bishop made his first public
utterance on the subject of the Tractarian controversy. It so
happened that in the ordinary course of events it became his
duty to deliver a Charge to his Clergy in the autumn of that
year, and it was impossible that one in the prominent position
of the Bishop of Winchester should pass over the subject in
silence. And yet, throughout his life, controversy was very alien
to his spirit. He was a man of peace, and loved peace; but
when he felt that principles were at stake which it would be
treason to abandon, no man could stand more firmly, at whatever cost or hazard to himself, than Bishop Sumner. And he
felt that in 1841 such an occasion had arisen. In the spring of
that year Tract 90 was published. The ecclesiastical atmosphere was violently disturbed by the memorial of the four
tutors addressed to the editor of the series, speedily followed by
the condemnation of the Tract No. 90 by the Hebdomadal
Board. The publication of the tracts was stopped, but their

influence had spread far and wide, and the Bishop felt strongly
that the germ of much evil was contained in the teaching developed by them, and did not hesitate to take his stand distinctly
on the protesting side. He saw dangers looming in the distance, and, as a watchman, warned those over whom he was set
with no uncertain voice.

"Is there heard," he said, "as it were, something of a con-
fused sound of voices at a distance, which might make some Eli
sitting in the gate to tremble for the ark of God? If there be
in the horizon as much as the earliest rising of a little cloud,
you have a right to expect from one in the position which the
duty of my office bids me fill this day, the explicit declaration of
my fears."

Very characteristically the first point pressed is the danger
incurred by the Church,

"If a cloud be raised again around that great doctrine, which
involves the mode in which we are 'accounted righteous before
God,' if it be even called in question whether 'the Protestant
doctrine of justification' be 'a fundamental of faith,' if, instead
of the satisfaction of Christ, singly and alone, as the ground of
acceptance, a certain inherent meetness of sanctification be so
connected with the qualification *ab extra* as to confound the
operation within with the work of Christ without."

There was ground, too, for fear " if a system of reserve in communicating religious knowledge be introduced—if we derogate
from the exclusive supremacy of the Word as containing all
things necessary to salvation, by a phraseology which, in effect,
gives a co-ordinate authority to the interpretation of antiquity,
instead of making the Church with our article a witness and
keeper of holy writ."

There was "ground again for fear if, on the one hand, it
becomes habitual among us to extenuate and speak in soft language of the deep corruptions of the Church of Rome, dwelling
upon her 'high gifts and strong claims on our admiration,
reverence, love, and gratitude' . . . and if, on the other hand,

in the same breath we accustom ourselves to speak slightingly
and disparagingly of those great and venerable names of the
sixteenth century . . . or if we learn to designate the blessed
Reformation itself as ' that great schism ' which ' shattered the
sacramentum unitatis,' since which era ' truth has not dwelt
simply and securely in any visible tabernacle,' or if we under-
value our own liturgy, and formularies, and homilies ; or put
interpretations on our articles at variance with what has been
generally received as the intention of their compilers, and
inconsistent with the royal declaration, that no man shall put
his own sense or comment to be the meaning.

"And, lastly," he said, "I cannot but fear the consequences for
the character, the efficiency, and the very truth of our Church if
a system of teaching should become popular which dwells upon
the external and ritual parts of religious service, whilst it loses
sight of their inner meaning and spiritual life . . . which speaks
of the sacraments, not as seals and pledges, but as instruments
of salvation in a justificatory and causal sense . . . investing
them with a saving intrinsic efficacy, not distinguishable by
ordinary understandings from the *opus operatum*, which tends
to substitute, at least in unholy minds, for the worship in spirit
and in truth, the observance of ' days, and months, and times,
and years '—for the cheerful obedience of filial love, an aspect
of hesitation, and trouble, and doubt,—for the freedom of the
Gospel, a spirit of bondage,—for the ways of pleasantness, and
the peace which passeth all understanding, the valley of Baca,
and a body of death—which works out salvation indeed with
fear and trembling, but without any foretaste of the rest that
remaineth for the people of God, and without joy in believing."
—*Charge*, 1841, pp. 30—39.

It will thus be seen that the trumpet blew no uncertain
sound, and that the Bishop unhesitatingly placed himself in the
van of the movement in opposition to the Oxford party.*

* It will be remembered that this and other Episcopal Charges were not without effect upon the author of Tract 90. In Newman's " History of my Religious

The Bishop must have been more than fully occupied this autumn, for immediately on the termination of his visitation of the Clergy and Churchwardens, he set out on a Confirmation tour throughout Hampshire and the Isle of Wight.   Two incidents it may be well to record : one, the confirmation of a curate in one of the towns in the diocese, who, though of course a constant communicant, had never been confirmed ; the other, the case of a young girl at Bishopstoke, who did not arrive at the church until the conclusion of the address after the administration of the rite.   The Bishop saw her evidently much concerned, sent for her, questioned her: " Why was she so late ?" " She had lost her way over the downs," was the answer; and on reference to the clergyman of her parish, who gave her a very high character, the Bishop administered the rite to her alone.   The Chaplain's comment on the incident is not unnatural : " She seemed most thankful ; and I thought that a good many would wish that they had come late."

Soon after his return to Farnham, the heir to the Crown was born, and at the beginning of 1842, as Prelate of the Order of the Garter, he was called upon to be present at Windsor at the Baptism of the infant Prince.   The admission of the King of Prussia as a Knight of the Most Noble Order of the Garter took place at the same time as the baptism of the Prince of Wales.   Royal baptisms, we are told by Martin in his " Life of the Prince Consort," had hitherto been, as a rule, celebrated within the Palace.   The Queen happily broke through the established custom, and expressed a wish that her son—England's future King—should be baptised in a consecrated building.   St. George's Chapel, Windsor, was selected for the purpose ; and

Opinions "—a book which I suppose none can read unmoved—he writes with reference to 1841 : " I was in the misery of this new unsettlement, when a second blow came upon me.   The Bishops, one after another, began to charge against me.   It was a formal determinate movement. . . .   They went on in this way, directing charges at me for three whole years.   I recognized it as a condemnation ; it was the only one that was in their power.   At first I intended to protest, but I gave up the thought in despair."—*History of my Religious Opinions,* pp. 139-40.

there, under circumstances of peculiar state and splendour, the rite was performed at 10 A.M. on the 25th of January—the baby Prince behaving, according to the *Times* reporter, " with truly princely decorum." . . . " It is impossible," says the 'Queen's Journal,' " to describe how beautiful and imposing the effect of the whole scene was in the fine old Chapel, with the banners, the music, and the light shining on the altar. . . . There was a full choral service at the Christening. A special anthem had been composed by Mr. (now Sir George) Elvey for the occasion. On the Prince being told of this, and asked when it should be sung, he answered, ' Not at all. No anthem. If the service ends by an anthem, we shall all go out criticising the music. We will have something we all know—something in which we can all join—something devotional. The Hallelujah Chorus : we shall all join in that with our hearts.' The Hallelujah Chorus ended the ceremony accordingly."*

On the Bishop's return from Windsor, he was not unnaturally called upon to give a full account of all he had seen, and the following letter, written at the time from Farnham, gives his impressions of the whole ceremony :—

" The Bishop reached this to-day about four o'clock. He had taken precaution to order horses to be sent for him from Bagshot, or he could not have got away so early from Windsor. The whole party met immediately in the small drawing-room, and then he gave, in a very interesting and playful manner, a full account of the Christening. The whole arrangements were made, except the placing of persons in the Chapel, by Prince Albert himself. Lord Delaware and his subordinates had merely to carry into effect H.R.H.'s orders ; and nothing could have been better as to grandeur and comfort than the whole. Lord Delaware had been up superintending from half-past five. He could almost have burst out crying when first he went round at that early hour. It was his first discharge of office. The weather was most unpropitious. There seemed a contest be-

---

* Theodore Martin's " Life of the Prince Consort," I., 129-30.

tween frost and snow and rain and wind, which should have
the mastery. Not a workman was at his place; nothing seemed
done. However, everything was marvellously accomplished
long before the time required. As each guest arrived, he was
at once led off to the place he was to occupy until called thence
to his next position.

" The Queen on entering the Chapel knelt down at her chair
in secret devotion, and remained so for some time, in a manner
perfectly unaffected and devout. The King of Prussia is a fine
specimen of a King; in every respect his bearing was kingly.
To a figure lofty, robust and well formed, was united a manly
grace which would at once have attracted attention, were there
no other cause for interest in His Majesty. His countenance is
fine, open, noble, intellectual, more English than German, and
full of suavity and good humour. He appeared so completely
pleased throughout, that his eyes seemed to glisten with enjoyment. He joined in the Baptismal service devoutly in appearance, audibly and with excellent accent; making all the
sponsorial responses clearly and fully.

" When receiving the garter, there was a dignity of manner
which the Bishop never witnessed in any knight before. There
is generally a great awkwardness, amounting to an unmanliness
and *gaucherie*, at that part of the ceremony. But His Majesty
put out his leg with self-possession and grace, which, combined
with an expression of pleasure, rendered the moment one of
unwonted interest. Even the little difficulty in adjusting the
garter did not cause the smallest impression of anything
untoward.

" The Queen finding the officer do it with difficulty, reached
out her hand, and putting the strap through the buckle with
much adroitness, she drew it with force, and fixing the tongue
of the buckle, set all to rights in an instant.

" The young Prince of Wales is a beautiful child, quite like
one hired for the occasion. His mantle was splendid. He behaved remarkably well, awake all the time, but did not cry.

The Queen was very attentive to His Majesty of Prussia. The acolade or royal kiss was administered by her with audible heartiness. The only awkwardness which occurred, was owing to a stupid apparitor of the Bishop of London having stood at the Baptism in front of the royal personages of Gotha, and in vain did Prince Albert frown upon him ; he kept his place. At length the Gothas wormed their way in front of him, and he was literally squeezed into the background. ——— ——— was also very awkward. He sat upon the kneeling cushion, to avoid turning from the Queen, when all others knelt down.

"The Queen placed all the personages in the Chapel, and gave to Sir Robert Peel the place of special honour. It was not that which belonged to him as Premier, but chosen for him by Her Majesty as of special favour. This was evident to all. The Queen Dowager sent all her servants for the day to Windsor, so that there were a hundred servants in royal livery at the banquet. The candelabra sustained above 300 wax-lights on the table. There were besides 90 Argand lamps. All was gold. The Bishop had some chat with the great traveller, Baron Humboldt, who said such a magnificent display could only be equalled at St. Petersburg, if even there. . . . .

"The Bishop, after his return from the Garter Chapter to Frogmore (where he dressed and slept) and back again to Windsor, found himself too late for the King's levee. Lord Denman and the Bishop of Norwich were in the same case. One of the Prussian equerries perceiving this, advanced and said, 'The King has retired, but I am sure he will return to the levee room to receive you.' They were then led upstairs, and presently the King entered. He spoke in French to the Bishop, and in a mixture of French and English to the others. To Lord Denman he said, 'I have been in your court; I should like to see it in activity.'

"After the Banquet, while the music was going on in the Waterloo Gallery, the Queen occupied one end of a long sofa, and the Duchess of Kent the other ; looking very royal and unapproachable.   Presently, pages came in with immense copper-gilt vessels, containing mulled claret, which was poured into a vast vase of gold, holding at least a hogshead! It stood upon a table, and by its side a huge cake eight feet high. Gold cups being placed at the disposal of the company, each guest, the King and Prince Albert among the number, approached with his cup, into which a page standing upon the table, ladled out the royal nectar.   The King and Prince Albert seemed to take deep interest in the brewing, and to enjoy the flavour of this excellent liquor.   There were only thirteen ladies present.   At first these ladies seemed unwilling to admit the cup to their lips; but when once they tasted, they seemed spell-bound, and the cup refused to abandon the eminence it had attained.

"When the king came through Eton, hearing the cheering of the boys he stopped his carriage and alighted : instantly he was surrounded by the boys. 'I thank you for your kind reception; I admire your voices very much.' He then shook hands with as many as possible and returned to his carriage. Prince Albert and the Gothas were dressed in large Jack Horse-Guard Boots at the Banquet."

I have before referred to the Bishop's letter-writing as singularly clear and to the point.   A distinct and unevasive answer was always given to a distinct question.   As an instance of this, let me cite the following correspondence with Bishop Terrot of Edinburgh.

BISHOP TERROT TO THE BISHOP OF WINCHESTER.

"*Nov.* 29, 1842.

" MY LORD,

"A painful event in my diocese, with the details of which it is unnecessary for me to trouble your Lordship, induces me to intrude upon you with two questions, answers to which I am very desirous of procuring from as many of the heads of the English Church as will favour me with their judgment.

The questions are :—

"1. Does your Lordship hold the Episcopal Church in Scotland to be in full spiritual communion with the Established Church of England ?

"2. Can a congregation in Scotland, separated from the Episcopal Church there, be considered as in communion with the Church of England ?

I must take the liberty of adding, that answers to these questions, in order to be available for my purpose, must be accompanied by permission to make public use of them.

"I have the honour to be,

"Your Lordship's very obedient servant,

"C. W. TERROT, Bp."

The Bishop answered as follows :—

"I have no difficulty in replying, according to your request, to the two questions which you have placed before me in your letter of the 29th ult.

"1. Considering the Episcopal Church in Scotland to be a pure branch of the Universal Church of Christ, being a 'true' Church, 'in the which the pure word of God is preached and the Sacraments are administered according to Christ's ordinance' (23rd Article of Religion)—the doctrines of the Church being the same with those of the United Church of England and Ireland, the Bishops and clergy of both Churches subscribing the same articles of religion, and the Apostolical succession of the Scottish Bishops being the same with those of the Bishops of the Church of England,—I hold the Episcopal Church in Scotland to be in full spiritual communion with the Church of England.

"2. If the view taken in the preceding answer be a correct one, it follows necessarily that a congregation in Scotland separated from the Episcopal Church there, cannot be considered as in communion with the Church of England. Such, it is well known, was the opinion of Bishops Horsley and Horne.

"On this subject the arguments of the late Bishop Sandford, in his ' Reasons for uniting with the Scottish Episcopal Communion,' appear to me quite unanswerable on ecclesiastical principles. 'Memoirs,' Vol. II. Appendix No. I. p. 231. See also his letter to a friend, written ten years later. Appendix No. II."

The Bishop of Edinburgh appreciated his straightforward answer, and replied :—

"EDINBURGH, *December 8th.*

"MY LORD,

"I can neither omit nor delay to thank you for the clear, satisfactory answer you have returned to my questions ; and perhaps I feel the more, because from answers received from English Bishops to the same questions, I was led to suspect that there was something unreasonable in putting them, and that a precise answer was not reasonably to be expected. I shall not make any public use of your Lordship's letter, though I shall show it with much gratification to those most interested in the subject. I did hope that something like an unanimous answer would have been given by the English Bishops, but in that I have been grievously disappointed. Only one other has answered in the same spirit and to the same purport as your Lordship.

"It may be that grave legal considerations are involved in the answers, and that practical difficulties might occur to an English Bishop who wished to act in consistency with your judgment. But surely, still graver Ecclesiastical difficulties attend the waiving of the question : for if the Established Church be not in full spiritual communion with us, with what portion of the Church of Christ beyond the realm of England and Ireland is she in communion ?

"But I did not mean to argue. I took my pen only to return my grateful thanks, and subscribe myself,

"Your Lordship's very faithful servant and Brother,

"C. W. TERROT, Bp."

If the preceding letter was appreciated by the Bishop of Edinburgh, so too must the following have been welcomed by Coleridge, mourning over the loss of his brother.

"FARNHAM CASTLE, *January* 29, 1843.

"MY DEAR FRIEND,

"On my return home last night from the Western extremity of my diocese, I found your letter awaiting me with the affecting tidings of the actual occurrence of that event which has been so long hanging over you—or rather, let me say at once, in more Christian phrase, of your brother's *death*—for why should we, for whom Christ has died and risen again, shrink from the word, and hide it under the euphemisms of Gentilism? Why especially, when, as in your brother's case, we are not sorrowing as men without hope, but can look upon his removal, as so lately upon that of your dear sister, as a departing to be with Christ, which is far better. We are both of us beginning to realize the lapse of years, and the fast running of the sand in both our glasses, by witnessing the fall around us of many a relation and friend and contemporary. And we may begin to take note of time by the snapping asunder of many a tie of affection. My very dear friend, let us learn by our losses, as the first lesson they are designed to teach us, to gird up our loins, and to stand ready and waiting—and then, as the second, to prize the more dearly those loved ones who are left. I am not now finding out for the first time that old friends are better than new, but as one and another are snatched away, I think I perceive myself clinging the more closely to those who remain. And this makes me think of dear Patteson and yourself with more than common tenderness—quite apart from the demands which both of you are now making upon my best sympathy. Give my true love to him.

"Ever, my dear Coleridge, most affectionately yours,

"C. WINTON."

At the beginning of the year 1843 there were two matters

connected with educational progress in the diocese which required somewhat tender handling. The first was connected
with the Training-school. Attempts had been made to combine
two objects in one—namely, a school for the choristers of the
Cathedral and College, and a training-school for masters. This
plan had not been found to work well, and there was some
thought of giving up the Training-school altogether. The
Bishop, however, was urgent in advocating the retaining of the
Training-school, but the gradual elimination from it of the
middle-class character. Accordingly, it was arranged that the
choristers both from the College and the Cathedral should be
withdrawn from the school, although for the time being a
limited number of other pupils, both boarders and day-scholars,
were to be admitted.

The other matter was none other than the introduction of the
thin end of the wedge of Government Inspection of Schools. The
Bishop had made application to the Government that Mr. (now
Archdeacon) Allen, one of Her Majesty's Inspectors of Schools,
might be directed to inspect such schools in the diocese as the
managers might throw open to him. The Bishop had a very
high opinion of Mr. Allen, and the Committee of Council on
Education, much to his satisfaction, at the close of 1843, directed
Mr. Allen to inspect the schools in the diocese of Winchester.
He was able to report at the end of the first year that he had
inspected 182 schools in the diocese, and pays the following
tribute to the Bishop's zeal in the matter :

" In the diocese of Winchester, the Bishop has recommended
his Clergy to apply for inspection, and has done all in his power
to facilitate the work. My most respectful thanks are due to
his Lordship for the mode in which he introduced me to his
diocese. Certainly, if the work of inspection does not prosper
in the district that has been allotted to me, the fault will lie
only with myself."

The following letter to a clergyman in his diocese, respecting
the introduction of a representation of the Virgin Mary with

nimbus and a lily into a painted window, is singularly instructive when viewed by the light of subsequent events as connected
with the cultus of the blessed Virgin in the English Church.

"St. James' Square, *January 15th*, 1843.

"As regards the representation of the Virgin Mary, I must
again state that I consider it inadmissible for a reason which I
need not specify, and which is not applicable to the other
figures. It will be easy for you to introduce instead of it, if
you think fit, a central figure of our Lord, without deranging
the remainder of your plan, or deviating much from your
original intention, which, it seems, you have already modified
to avoid misconception. I hope it is unnecessary for me to say
—and yet I cannot satisfy myself without assuring you—that I
press this upon you with the greatest reluctance. Indeed it
has been with the greatest personal pain that I have interfered
at all in the matter. I know too well the pious and devoted
spirit in which the building of this church has been undertaken,
and the cost of it defrayed, and I honour and respect that spirit
far too highly to place willingly, or on light grounds, the
smallest obstacle in the way of the fulfilment of your wishes.
And while under the influence of these feelings I give up my
own opinion, as far as I think I may, to your desire, I earnestly
hope you will bear with me in this expression of my objection
to that part of your design, which seems to me to be more than
merely dangerous or inexpedient."

The clergyman did not fall in with the proposed substitution
of the figure of our Lord for that of the Virgin, and the Bishop,
having occasion to answer his letter, thus wrote :—

"I have not the least wish personally in reference to the
representation of our Lord as the central figure. I suggested it
precisely because its position seemed to me to take off the
equality.* But if it seems otherwise to others, it is an addi-

* The clergyman had expressed a fear lest a representation of our Lord
amongst other single figures would lower Him to a level with the rest.

tional proof how very easily misconceptions are created on subjects of such delicacy, and involving *now* considerations of so much importance. My objection to the figure of the Virgin would not be obviated by the removal of the nimbus and the lily."

Ultimately it was arranged, before the consecration of the building, that a representation of St. Luke should be substituted for that of the Virgin Mary.

In his visit to the Channel Islands in the autumn of this year, the Bishop had the pleasure of renewing acquaintance with the Rev. Vincent Ryan, who had recently been appointed incumbent of St. Anne's, Alderney. Little did the Bishop then think that Mr. Ryan would at a subsequent period come forward to help him in episcopal work as quasi-"suffragan." But so it was. For Mr. Ryan, of Alderney, was afterwards appointed, on the Bishop's recommendation, to the bishopric of Mauritius; and after his return thence, in consequence of ill health, was enabled, in the Bishop's failing condition, to render him essential and heartily-appreciated services. The Bishop's parting from Mr. Ryan at Alderney was of a very peculiar character, and has always been remembered in the island as an instance of episcopal pluck. Bishop Ryan has kindly, at my request, described it in the following lines :—

" The visits of the Bishop of Winchester to Alderney are among some of the happiest recollections of a very happy ministry of six years in that island. The impressions produced by his noble presence, his genial and kindly bearing, his warm interest in the welfare of the people, were of a very deep and pleasant character ; and the landing-place was thronged with crowds who went down *pour voir l'Evêque arriver.*"

After alluding to the Bishop's speech at a missionary meeting, and the administration of the rite of Confirmation, he adds :—

" We returned to an early dinner under the hospitable roof of the Judge Gaudion, where a large party was assembled. The steamer from Guernsey to Southampton was expected to call

for the Bishop, by special arrangement, between six and seven
o'clock, as he was engaged to consecrate a church at Portsmouth
the next day, and had formed other plans for immediate resumption
of his work in England. Soon after we sat down to dinner
a dense fog came on. We all concluded that it would be impossible
for a steamer to come up through the dangerous passage
of 'the Swinge' in such weather ; and as missing that opportunity
would involve a detention of several days, and the necessity
of returning to Guernsey by a sailing vessel to meet another
steamer, there was much uneasiness and anxiety felt. At last
it was proposed that we should go to an elevated spot, not far
from the house, to see if there was any prospect of the weather
clearing up. We went, and were but confirmed in the conviction
that no steamer could possibly come up that evening. We
could not see ten yards ahead. Just as we were talking of the
utter hopelessness of the case, some one said he heard a bell
from the direction of the sea. All listened intently, and presently
the sounds came clear and unmistakable. The effect
was electric. Some hurried off to return the signals and get
the boat ready, others returned to the town for the luggage, and
the Bishop with his party, and the Judge, went with all speed to
the harbour. The boat was soon manned ; we got into it, and
those who do not know the islands will find it difficult to conceive
that the instant we pushed off from the pier we could see
nothing whatever in any direction. In the hurry no compass
had been put into the boat, so that we rowed by guess, and
came close upon a rock, which we knew to be in the direction
of the roadstead. A few minutes after passing the rock we
were close upon a large indistinct object, which proved to be
the steamer. We hailed it, and got a reply, and as the Bishop
went up the sides of the ship three hearty cheers were given by
the passengers and the crew; and we returned to the shore,
which we had some difficulty in regaining. Those whom we
had left on shore were truly thankful to hear that the Bishop
was safe on board, for they had fully expected that he and his

U

party would, in all probability, be tossing in the Channel the whole night in an open boat!"

The Bishop was so much struck with the captain's courage in keeping the appointment he had made, that he presented him with a silver snuff-box as a token of his appreciation of his services, with this inscription : " Presented by the Bishop of Winchester to Captain Goodridge, of the steamer *Lady de Saumarez*, in remembrance of a fog off the island of Alderney, August, 1843."

The Bishop, writing shortly after on business to Mr. Ryan, says : " I beg to send my particular remembrances to the Judge, whose image is now before me, looming in the fog, and of whom I was compelled to take so unceremonious a leave, under circumstances not a little exciting. Of Mrs. Ryan, to whom also I wish to be remembered, I could take no leave at all."

The following letter, also written to Mr. Ryan, at Alderney, a few months later, shows the manner in which the Bishop entered into the minute details of each parish, and the peculiar circumstances affecting the position of his clergy. Many incumbents have made the remark that his knowledge of their parishes was such as would lead you naturally to suppose that from the earliest days of his episcopate he had taken a special interest in that particular parish. This was certainly Mr. Ryan's feeling, at any rate, in his comparatively distant and isolated post.

" Farnham Castle, April 2nd, 1844.

"My dear Sir,

"I have heard, with much satisfaction, by your letter of the 14th ult., that you have succeeded in finding a suitable schoolmistress. I trust she will answer your expectations, and, by God's blessing, will be made an instrument of usefulness to your island. Your parochial details are very interesting to me, and not less the little glimpses you give me of the outstretching of your own eye to the ' regions beyond you.' I can sympathise with you cordially in the privations of your insular situation as regards the difficulty and infrequency of communion with like-minded brethren. In this respect your lot partakes of that of the missionary. But you are also happily freed from much of the contradiction which many of your brethren are called upon to endure, and you are not so much exposed as many to the inroads of strange teachers, and you are not obliged perforce to enter into the miserable disputes and doctrinal aberrations of the present day. God has mercifully ordained compensations for the hardship of most lots, and it is very interesting to trace them.

"I shall always be glad to receive any communication from you, whether more, or less, or not at all partaking of the nature of necessary business. And you may rely on my interest in your ministerial charge and your own well-doing.

"I am, my dear Sir,

"Your very faithful servant,

"C. WINTON.

"Rev. V. RYAN."

One service in which the Bishop took part, on the 3rd of December, 1843, must have been peculiarly full of interest to him—the consecration of his old friend Lonsdale as Bishop of Lichfield. Lonsdale had begun his career in life at Lincoln's Inn, and it is said that his final determination to forsake the study of law for that of divinity, and to take Holy Orders, was in consequence of an earnest letter written to him on the subject by his college friend Sumner.* Singularly cheering, therefore, must it have been to the Bishop of Winchester that he should be allowed thus to welcome to the episcopate one who, but for him, might never have thus consecrated his talents to the service of Christ's Church.

Mrs. Sumner was called upon in the spring of 1844 to lose her only surviving sister, Mrs. McNiven. The sisters, married,

* This was stated by Bishop Abraham at the opening of the Lonsdale Quadrangle, St. Chad's School, Denstone, Aug. 1875.

and living in a land far from that of their birth, naturally clung
closely the one to the other, and her death at the early age of
forty-eight was a subject of great grief to the Bishop as well as
to Mrs. Sumner.   He thus writes to Coleridge announcing the
termination of Mrs. McNiven's illness :—

"St. James' Square, May 5th, 1844.

" MY DEAR COLERIDGE,

          " After what I told you a few days ago, you will not be
surprised to hear that all is over at Perrysfield.   She departed
in sleep on Friday evening. . . . . You who knew her, will be
able to estimate our loss.   She leaves a void which none can
fill, and I have no doubt that you who have been called to
bear the severance of many ties entwined around your heart
with closest and tenderest intimacy, can recognise with me the
mercy of God in loosening, one by one, the chains which bind
us to earth, and in bidding us thus to set our affections on things
above.   My dear friend, you have learnt the lesson better than
myself.   I would not willingly linger behind you.   Pray for me
that in the trials which may remain, I may not be found inconsistent with my profession, or unmindful of the mercies with
which I have been blessed beyond the lot of most men.

" I am ever most affectionately yours,

" C. Winton."

In the autumn of 1844, the Bishop was called upon, in his
official capacity, to consecrate new colours presented by Lady
Pakenham,* to the 49th regiment.   The action of Christian
ministers in connection with " blessing the colours," is so often
animadverted upon, that it may be well to reproduce the
Bishop's speech on the occasion, delivered with great animation
in the barrack-yard at Winchester, as it seems to put the matter
on the proper footing.   The weather was most favourable, and
in the *Times* of the day, the number of spectators present was
estimated at ten thousand.   He said :—

---

* Sir Hercules Pakenham was Lieutenant-Governor of Portsmouth at the time.

"Soldiers of the 49th! I have sought and obtained the kind permission of your gallant commanding officer to ask your attention for a few brief moments, before I invoke the blessing of Almighty God on these your honoured banners, shortly to be raised and wave among your ranks, as your own proper and distinctive standard—to be sullied never—to be abandoned only with life itself. And let it not excite surprise in anyone, that on this memorable occasion I come among you, a man of peace among men of war. I hold that there is no one more truly the man of peace, than the Christian soldier; for though warfare be your profession—though arms be your daily pastime—though your home be in camps—yet most truly and essentially, under God's blessing, you may be the peacemakers of a contentious world. What are the true rewards of your victories? Not your own glory—not national aggrandisement—least of all the humiliation of your enemies—but the safety and peace of your country. What the recompense of your toils and privations, of your pains and perils, but the tranquillity of nations? What consolation in the loss of many a brave man, pouring out his heart's blood on the field of battle, and exchanging his life for victory, but the knowledge that after the day of agony and death, come the blessings of a safe and honourable peace, won under God by your gallant deeds, and preserved from violation by the *prestige* of your determined bravery? All history, were it needful, would attest the truth of what I say. I might find examples in every page; but your own recollections will suffice, and the memories of not the oldest of those now present may be my witnesses. Who can reflect on the early events of the present century, without gratefully acknowledging the obligations which he owes to those gallant men your comrades in arms, to whom we are indebted for the defence of our homes—our possessions—and what is dearer to us than these, our national honour and religion itself, from the aggressions and enmity of an implacable foreign foe. Who can forget that to the valour of our gallant defenders by land and sea, we are indebted for the preservation of our

native soil from the footsteps of the invader, for deliverance
from those disasters which invariably accompany a successful
enemy ? Nay, I may now call yourselves as witnesses—I may
bid you to look back with thankfulness and honest exultation
to the annals of your own gallant and highly distinguished
regiment—to call your recollection to those days when you won
those glorious laurels in Holland, at Copenhagen, Quebec, and
in China. It would have been heart-stirring to the coldest and
least enthusiastic, to hear the praises of these your exploits in
China, which I heard uttered by the great captain of the age,
the illustrious commander of the British army, when, in his place
in Parliament, he asked the thanks of the House for your
gallant deeds. These praises were well worth living and dying
for. These praises were yours, men of the 49th, and will continue for ages to come : and when you unfurl these banners, and
point to those glorious names inscribed on them, and recollect
that they are records of the glories of former times, they will
act as an incentive to gallant bearing in days to come. You
may appeal to them with confidence as the seals of your
country's renown, prosperity, and peace. These are the grounds
on which I honour a Christian soldier, and consider him in the
hands of Providence as an instrument of good to the nation at
large : and as one deeply interested in its true happiness, I bid
you God speed in the name of the Lord. As a Christian Bishop,
I bid you to remember, whether in time of peace or war—at
home in the midst of your friends, or on the battle field—I bid
you to remember Him who is the God of battles, and gives
victories to kings. Be men of resolution—be men of daring—
observant of right, ready to fight to the death at the bidding of
your Queen, for her honour, the defence of your country, and for
God. And then in the language of admonition, which, at their
investiture is addressed to the knights of that most noble and
ancient order, of which I bear the badge, 'May you so over-
pass both prosperous and adverse encounters, that having van-
quished your enemies both of body and soul, you may not only

obtain the prize of this transient combat, but be crowned with the palm of eternal victory."

The summer of 1845, witnessed a strong effort made on behalf of the suburban parishes in Surrey. A meeting of laity and clergy resident or interested in Southwark, Lambeth, Bermondsey, and other parishes, was held at Winchester House on the 7th of June, and the Bishop laid before the meeting statistics which were appalling. To speak only of Lambeth and Southwark, with a population of upwards of 135,000 souls, accommodation in churches was provided for only one in eight, and educational provision in schools connected with the church, for no more than one in fifty-five of its entire population. It was accordingly resolved that a vigorous attempt should be made to grapple with the evil, and "The Southwark Fund for Schools and Churches," was at once instituted. As much as £30,000 was soon subscribed, which was the means of raising at least three times that sum, and at the expiration of two years, the committee were able to report the formation of five new districts in the parishes of Lambeth and Bermondsey, towards which (with the exception of one in which a church had been built immediately before the foundation of the society), liberal grants had been made. Sixteen schools were erected or in progress mainly through the instigation of the society, and the assistance afforded by it. Sites, too, had been obtained for three other churches (in addition to those required in the new districts mentioned above). Undoubtedly a great impulse was given to church and school extension by this movement, for in the course of the next twenty years twenty-five new churches were built, several proprietary chapels consecrated and assigned to ecclesiastical districts, and a very considerable number of schools and parsonages also erected. The Southwark School and Churches Fund continued in operation for eight years, during the whole of which time, the Rev. Jeffery Foot acted as Honorary Secretary, and he writes to me respecting it :—

"This work deserves to be remembered, especially at the present

time, for it is an example of the efforts made by the Church to
provide a sound education, secular as well as religious, for the
neglected children of the poor, at a time when neither the State
nor any religious body except the Church was making any
effort in that direction, and so the Southwark Fund, administered under the fostering care of Bishop Sumner thirty years
ago, may be considered as the pioneer of all that has since been
done for the spiritual improvement of that important section of
the metropolis. It also furnishes an answer to those enemies of
voluntary zeal and denominational education, who have of late
years, and alas, too successfully endeavoured to impede and
fetter the work of Church education, and to discredit her efforts
in the eyes of the public. I am only one of many witnesses
who can testify to the zeal and earnestness, and unsparing
devotion of time, strength, and money, which he gave to the
spiritual improvement of that part of his vast diocese."

In the Bishop's visitation charge in 1845 he thus refers to
the loss which the diocese had sustained by the promotion of
Archdeacon Wilberforce to the Deanery of Westminster.

"In winning affections, and stirring up spirits for God, few
have equalled, none ever surpassed him. You need not be reminded of his zeal for the glory of the courts of the Lord's
house—with what untiring energy and self-devotion he brought
the powers of his high intellect to bear upon the details of his
official duty—or how he stimulated the parochial clergy by his
example, while he lightened their labours by sharing them."

The Bishop's prophetic eye seems to have foreseen the
danger likely to arise from an excess of ornamentation in our
churches. After having commended the care with which the
restoration of certain specified buildings had been conducted,
he adds in words which will well bear repetition here,

"Yet let me add a word to obviate misunderstanding in this
matter. Public attention has been directed of late years with
much of earnestness to the decoration of our places of worship.
A taste for ecclesiastical architecture has been sedulously fos-

tered. The house of cedar and of costly stone has been substituted for structures of less sumptuous expenditure, and of meaner materials. The skill of the artificer and the mysteries of embellishment and ornament have been put under lavish contribution. We are often reminded by the munificence of the builders of that saying, 'What manner of stones, and what buildings are here?'

"Do I mention this in censure? God forbid. The costliest ointment in the richest of caskets is a poor oblation to God. Do I look upon the magnificence of fabric as valueless? Far from it. David said well, that he would not offer burnt offerings to the Lord of that which cost him nothing. The fairest ornaments are the most comely in God's sanctuary. But we must be on our guard. We must keep our foot when we go to the house of God, and walk warily, lest we 'give the sacrifice of fools.'* Men's minds are apt to run riot in externals, and it is an old device of Satan to corrupt the heart by the temptations of sight. We must not be forgetful of realities in the midst of the enticements of architecture. Sin and ignorance are all around us, and it will be a fearful mistake if, when men ask at our hands the bread of life, we give them a stone. Time presses, the night is at hand, judgment impends, souls are at stake, and we dare not build our house upon perishable materials, wood, hay, stubble, while that mystery of godliness into which angels desire to look is shrouded in obscurity, or nullified by corruptions and superstitions. Created beauty, and the external splendour of the most magnificent temple which the art of man can devise, are only worth our admiration as they lead the mind to the uncreated source of excellency and honour. That church is more pleasant in the sight of God, where His living word is preached, and the sacraments are rightly and duly administered, than the costliest of temples, radiant with gold and exquisite in workmanship, with a dead and formal, or sensuous ministry, and an unsanctified people. It was a wise

* Eccles. v. 1.

father who said, '*Aurum sacramenta non quærunt; neque auro placent, quæ auro non emuntur*.' * It was not gold, or purple, or richest oblations, which gave the sanctuary of old the first title of holiness. 'Holiness becometh thine house for ever,' says David. † Holy persons and holy rites in holy places. 'I will wash my hands in innocency, O Lord, and so will I go to thine altar."

The Bishop was able to express his great thankfulness that during a period of more than ordinary disquietude in some quarters, general harmony and peace had prevailed throughout his diocese. They had "escaped those oscillations in religious opinions which are fatal to charity, peril truth, and make shipwreck of men's faith." But this was not the result of apathy or indifference. Since 1829 the congregations showed a numerical increase of about one fourth. The communicants had doubled in number. The catechumens had increased from 12,639 in 1835-6 to 17,837 in 1844-5.

" I admit," the Bishop says, " that figures taken alone, afford no certain criterion of the state of parishes. There may be a coming together, as the people cometh, without profit—a readiness to hear, with a reluctance to do—a work of formality, but little of the life of the Spirit in the soul of man. But none will deny that a good attendance on the ordinances of the church is a hopeful sign—that it negatives the supposition of a careless or repulsive ministry—that it affords at least a strong presumption of diligence, zeal, and efficiency on the part of the pastor, and of edification on that of the people. A church is rarely deserted, where the ministrations are of a faithful and painstaking order."

Turning from diocesan matters, the Bishop emphatically warns the clergy as to the steady increase of Romanism.

" Not to see the perils which menace from that quarter, would be, I think, the blindness of infatuation; to see them, and not to lift up the standard against them, if not treachery,

---

* Ambrose, De Officiis, Lib. II., cap. 28.   † Taylor's Works, II., p. 358.

would be cowardice. Whether we look to the stealthy advances of Romish doctrine, or to the positive increase of Romish power, our duty is plain and twofold: first, to vindicate the anti-Romish character of our own church, and next, to guard against the aggressive pretensions of such a power as Romanism, coming in like a flood, and advancing upon the borders of our own religious territory."

Statistics follow in proof of this position, and then after referring to the bill just passed for the endowment of the College of Maynooth, against the second reading of which he recorded his vote, he gave some practical advice to the clergy as to the course they should adopt in order to guard themselves and their flocks against "the spreading contagion."

1. The character of Romanism and the important points in the controversy must be distinctly understood.

"Rome must be judged, if judged truly, as she sits on her seven hills, not as disguised for the captivation of the souls of heretics: she must be read in her councils and decrees rather than in the fervid eloquence of her Massillon, or as exhibited in the amiableness of a Fenelon and a Pascal."

2. The essential and distinctive principles of our own Church in its polity and doctrines must be fully realised and honestly developed in all pastoral teaching.

3. The Gospel must be exhibited in all its distinctness in every department of the ministerial work, not the Gospel Romanised or the Gospel Puritanised, but the holy Gospel, the Gospel of God.

4. There must be no dogmatism upon non-essentials. It may chance, however, that things, in themselves indifferent, under certain circumstances acquire another character.

"It is in itself wholly indifferent whether the Sacrament of the Lord's Supper be administered from a table of wood or stone. But when it becomes significant, as connected with an expiatory and propitiatory, though unbloody, sacrificial offering, it is taken out of the category of things immaterial.

"The use of particular vestments in ministering, is in itself wholly indifferent. But the question became of importance in the sixteenth century, when the great principles of Church authority hinged upon it, and the distinction of different dress in different parts of the service, tended to keep up in the public mind the superstitions of the mass.* It cannot be said to be of little moment now, if these matters, trifling and frivolous as they are, peril again the peace of the Church, distract its ministers from their proper business, sever the pastor from his flock, and the people from the sanctuary.

"The postures and gestures which you use in your ministrations are matters of indifference, simply considered. Yet hear one of our divines. 'It was a long and general custom in the Church, upon all occasions and motions of solemnity or greater action, to make the sign of the cross in the air, on the breast, or on the forehead; but he that in England should do so upon pretence, because it was a Catholic custom, would be ridiculous.' † He would be worse than ridiculous, he would be an object of just jealousy and suspicion, and a stumbling-block."

5. The primary claims of our own church upon our sympathy must not be forgotten in our veneration for the church Catholic and our admiration of Catholic unity.

6. Truth may be represented so that it becomes essentially false. It becomes false if distorted, by being magnified beyond its due proportions, or elevated above its own relative importance. Toleration unduly narrowed is exclusiveness; unduly extended, latitudinarianism. The unity of the Church is an abstract good, and greatly to be desired, but men may fraternise so intimately with heresy as to palliate the sin of schism.

It is impossible, even now, to read the charge without feeling that the Bishop's whole heart was poured out and his affections

* Cardwell. Preface to "The Two Liturgies of King Edward the Sixth Compared," p. xxi.
† Taylor. "Rule of Conscience," Book III., c. 4, rule 15.

deeply moved, and verily the words of warning uttered in 1845 are not out of place after a lapse of thirty years.

Shortly after he had concluded his visitation tour, he was called upon to assist at the consecration of his friend the Dean of Westminster to the bishopric of Oxford. He had watched his career from the very first, had been united to him in the closest bonds of friendship, had himself preferred him to a benefice, a canonry, and an archdeaconry, and those who were present on the occasion have stated that it was with a voice trembling with deep emotion that he presented Wilberforce to the Archbishop as "a godly and well-learned man, to be or-dained and consecrated Bishop." If the Bishop of Winchester had then been gifted with a prophetic eye, what a vision would have floated before him ! — even that of a Bishop in the Church of God for eight-and-twenty years—one foremost through life in every good word and work—whilst confessedly most able in the administration of his diocese, yet fostering, with an enlarged heart, the Church's labours in every quarter of the globe—a very Chrysostom in eloquence—destined in God's providence to take the pastoral staff from his own hands when he was laid aside from active duty by the afflicting hand of God—and at length, *felix opportunitate mortis*, translated without lingering decay or the enforced idleness of a sick-room (which, to him, would surely have been a grievous burden) into the blest abode of rest and peace, for which, at times, his weary spirit had eagerly craved, and where a crown of glory awaited him as a good and faithful servant of his Lord !

CHAPTER XVIII.

It has been before mentioned that it was the Bishop's rule,
if possible, to visit the Channel Islands triennially. Mrs. Sumner,
much to the delight of her friends there, was able to accompany
the Bishop thither in 1846. Passing on to St. Malo, the Bishop
confirmed no fewer than sixty catechumens in the chapel of St.
Servan, and opportunity was taken afterwards to present an
address to him, thanking him very heartily for "the Christian
kindness which had induced him to visit them in a foreign land,
and to impart to them a privilege of which they should otherwise
have been long deprived."

On his return to Farnham, after a few weeks spent in Switzerland, he thus writes to Coleridge :—

" . . . . Your account of your summer occupations at Ottery
brings to my mind the old man of Verona. But your recreations have taken a higher flight than his, and I should cordially
rejoice in seeing your chapel, and looking at your plans for the
restoration of your noble church, and in an afternoon's walk
after luncheon, inspecting your planting, and your prospects in

esse and *posse*. When shall this be? *Quando ego te aspiciam?*
I will still look forward in hope, and think the time not gone
by, but only deferred. My late wanderings have been of a more
ambitious character, and we have thoroughly enjoyed them. I
had enough of duty on the continent not to make me feel
uneasy in being there, and the rapid communication with
England enabled me to have my letters in six days from Farnham, so that business was not kept in arrear. And our return
was timely. Within ten days from our quitting Geneva, the
hotel in which we lodged was in a state of siege, and my own
dressing-room pierced with cannon balls. All is now quiet
there; but the revolution is complete, and the canton is in the
hands of the lowest democratical party. Since you knew Geneva
it is greatly altered, as well in external appearance (it is now
one of the finest towns of the continent), as in governmental
detail. I cannot say I think it improved in more important
respects. Its religious tone seems to me deplorably low, and
though there is much of decency and morality, I fear it has far
more reference to man than to God. Practical infidelity seems
to me to have eaten into the core of the people. France, as far
as I have had the opportunity of seeing it, is yet more altered,
but in another way. I never could have conceived that the
outward condition of a people could have so much improved in
twenty years. They have made good use of the long period of
peace. In agriculture, in facilities of communication, in the
state of their roads, they are far beyond us, but above all in the
comforts of the common people. In this respect they present a
mortifying contrast to the state of our rural districts. Of the
manufacturing towns I have seen nothing. But their country
people are at their ease at home and abroad, in their cottages
and in the fields, and they seem to value it. . . . . ."

Shortly after this, he was engaged in a painful correspondence
with a former clergyman of his diocese, who having seceded to
Rome, and afterwards having professed his desire to return into
the Communion of the Church of England, had been living in

retirement for the space of three years, and now made application to his former diocesan to be again admitted " to preach and
teach in the Church of England, on the production of the
requisite testimonials." The Bishop replied to his application :
" I can assure you that it is with deep interest, and with
emotions of thankfulness to God, that I see you applying for
permission to resume your ministerial functions in our Church.
At the same time, I am sure you will perceive that my duty to
the members of that Church imposes upon me the obligation
of requiring from you fuller satisfaction than I now possess, as
to the entire accordance of your present opinions with the
doctrines set forth in the articles and formularies. I think
myself bound to call upon you for such an explicit declaration in
this respect, and especially in regard to the principal points of
difference between our own Church and that of Rome, as can
alone justify me in my judgment in making myself a party to
your re-admission to the post of teacher. If you should think
fit to furnish me with such a document, I should then desire to
submit it, with your permission, to the judgment of His Grace
the Archbishop of Canterbury, without whose full concurrence I
should not think myself at liberty to act in so important a
matter."

In reply, the clergyman requested the Bishop to specify the
points on which he more particularly required satisfaction, and
to bring them before him in a definite form, promising to send
distinct replies.

Meanwhile, trustworthy information had reached the Bishop
that the clergyman in question had been in the habit, within
the last few months, of attending a Roman Catholic place of
worship. He accordingly wrote to him as follows :—

" I think it necessary to acquaint you, that since I last wrote,
a statement has been made to me to which I am desirous of
calling your attention in the first instance. It is asserted to me
on the authority of a Roman Catholic priest at ——, that so
recently as since the beginning of the present year, you have

attended at the celebration of the Romish service in the chapel of ——. It becomes necessary for me to put to you the explicit question, whether this allegation is true, either in respect of the chapel mentioned, or of any other place of worship of the Romish communion, since the period when you received the Sacrament of the Lord's Supper in —— church, as a declaration of your desire to return into the communion of the Church of England."

In reply, the clergyman without referring at all to the charge brought against him, begged leave to withdraw his application for permission to minister again in the Church of England.

Not much has yet been said with reference to the Bishop's manner of life in his own home, and perhaps it may be well therefore to insert here the following description of him as he appeared to one who was introduced to him first in 1847, and afterwards became most warmly attached to him as his youngest son's wife. She writes :—

"I had heard a great deal about the Bishop's handsome looks and courtly manners before seeing him, and it was with no slight interest that I was introduced to him for the first time, and made an acquaintance which ripened into the deepest affection and the most profound veneration on my part.

"It was at a large evening party at Winchester House, one of those crowded occasions so familiar to the London world. I was very young then, and the stately presence and chivalrous courtesy of his manner made the strongest impression upon me. He moved about from guest to guest speaking to each in turn, over-looking none, and finding something good and pleasant to say to everybody. His manner was singularly dignified and graceful, and he possessed the happy art of putting the shyest and most awkward of people at their ease by his thoughtful kindness and courtesy. Few could excel him in exquisite tact, and in the habit of saying and doing the right thing at the right time; his social qualities charmed and fascinated all who knew him, and he was a centre of attraction wherever he went. He was not a brilliant talker like Bishop

Wilberforce, but nevertheless, he had great conversational powers, a richly cultivated mind, and the keenest appreciation of humour and talent, but whatever he said or did, he never for an instant lost sight of the great office he held. There was a quiet dignity even in his playful moments, a sober way of viewing things, and no parenthesis in his religion. It was interesting to watch the perfect ease with which he adapted himself to whatever society he might be in. He was as much at home with the simple cottagers on the common at Hale, or with the children in the village school, as he was among his equals or in courtly places, and his manner was especially tender and gracious to the poor. His left hand never knew the countless acts of pitying love done by his right hand to the sick, the aged, and destitute; but they will be known at the last great day.

"In 1847, when I first knew him, he was but little past the prime of life, and at the zenith of his prosperity and activity. He was full of strength and spirits, brimming over with quiet humour, reverenced—not to say idolized—by his wife and children, happy in his diocese, surrounded by a circle of earnest and loving friends, and given to constant hospitalities at Winchester House and Farnham Castle, in the intervals of his busy public occupations and tours for visitations or confirmations. Both he and Mrs. Sumner united in making the home life very perfect; an atmosphere of love and union and of sunny cheerfulness pervaded the whole family; sharp or vexatious words were never uttered, and the warmest mutual affection and sympathy in daily trifles was carefully fostered. When separations came, Mrs. Sumner kept up this family love by constant journal letters addressed to all her children, giving them minute details of the Bishop's public or private movements, and any family or social concerns of interest. These journals, continued for many years, were regularly passed round, and formed an excellent welding medium, and in return no small or great event took place in any of the children's homes details of which were not fully written to head-quarters. The Bishop and Mrs. Sumner had a

perfect storehouse of sympathy ready for joy or sorrow, and it
was passed on like an electric flash from home to home, so that
if one member suffered, all the members suffered with it, or one
member was honoured, all the members rejoiced with it.

"I suppose there never was more entire union and affection,
more peace and harmony than grew up in that family, from the
pattern of that Christian father and mother. St. Paul says 'that
if a man know not how to rule his own house, how shall he take
care of the Church of God?' and that a bishop 'must be one
that ruleth well his own house, having his children in subjection with all gravity.' The Bishop acted up to the Apostolical precept, for his home-rule was almost as perfect as it
could be, and well did Mrs. Sumner work with him by her
loving, holy influence. The golden thread of principle, the
fear and love of God, was woven into the Farnham daily life,
and made it very attractive to all who shared in it."

The close of 1846 was saddened by the death of his mother
at Godalming. She had long been confined to one room in
consequence of a paralytic seizure, and on the tenth of December she succumbed to a second attack. The Bishop writes to
a friend. "I am thankful to say that she suffered very little
pain, and as her race has been run, I could not have wished
her life to be prolonged. She was waiting patiently for her
change and is now at rest." She was buried in the churchyard
of Godalming church, having attained the great age of 89
years. Her life had been throughout one spent in comparative
retirement. At the early age of 15 she lost her father, and
seems at that time to have been under unusually strong
religious impressions, and though at her mother's wish she
entered subsequently into society in London, it always appears
to have been uncongenial to her. After two and twenty years
of happy married life she was left a widow in 1802, and the
education and training of her children must have been a very
anxious and arduous task. Right nobly did she fulfil it, and
lived to see her two sons on the Episcopal Bench, honoured,

and useful in their respective spheres. Throughout life, and up to the close of it, she was a truly God-fearing woman, and it was a great comfort to the Bishop that from 1830, when she settled at Godalming, he was able to minister to her comforts, and ultimately to close her eyes in peace.

Easter, 1847, witnessed an important change in the *locus in quo* of the Training College. Hitherto the education of the students had been carried on in premises in St. Swithun's Street, Winchester, capable of accommodating nineteen pupils. The lease of these premises was about shortly to expire, and the Board of the Training College were forced therefore anxiously to consider the best course to be adopted. The funds in hand were not such as to warrant any large outlay, and yet the fact that since the commencement of the Training College in 1840, fifty-four masters had been sent out, of whom the reports, speaking generally, were most favourable, made the Board desirous of continuing and if possible enlarging the sphere of their labours.

At this juncture the Bishop made a proposal to the Board, which was thankfully accepted. He offered to them the use of Wolvesey Palace, Winchester, free of rates, taxes and repairs. The Palace would comfortably receive fifty students. The proposal thus to utilise Wolvesey Palace was sanctioned by the Education Department, and until the erection of a new Training College in 1862, the students continued to be accommodated there. The saving of expense to the Board by this act of the Bishop was estimated at about £100 a year.

In the summer of this year the Bishop, accompanied only by his second son, Charles, made a walking tour amongst the Lakes. Singularly must it have recalled the time nearly forty years before when he had traversed the same routes. How much had happened since! What reminiscences must have been awakened! The period however, which had elapsed since his previous walking tour in this district does not seem to have diminished his powers as a pedestrian, as the following

extracts from journal letters written by his son at the time will
show.

"AMBLESIDE, *August* 21, 1847.

"My father and I started from Ambleside at about ten. I
cannot say we were particularly equipped for a pedestrian
excursion, for we had a great deficiency of pockets, which was
rather inconvenient, as we had three guide books to carry.
However, I contrived to stow away two, and my father disposed
of the other. With no other provision than these books and
our walking-sticks we set forth. Our way for the first three
miles, lay along the valley by the side of a lovely trout stream
past a chapel built five years ago by Mr. Redmayne, who has
a house here, till we came to a little hamlet called Skelwith
Fold. Here we sat down for a few minutes on a rock in an
adjoining field and enjoyed a magnificent view—on the one
side, of the peaceful waters of Windermere, and on the other,
the bold ridge of mountains, the most conspicuous of which
were the Langdale Pikes. Before starting from Ambleside we
had well studied the guide book, and had pretty well learned
the road we had to pursue, but we occasionally for the sake of
variety enquired our way of persons whom we met. It invariably happened however, that the directions they gave us were,
according to our calculation, wrong. We now ascended for
some distance, and followed a path which led along the side of
a mountain for a couple of miles till it suddenly descended,
and brought us to a bridge called Colwith bridge, near which
we saw a beautiful waterfall about seventy feet high.

"The way for the next three miles assumed a wilder
character by Little Langdale and Blea Tarn ; soon after passing the latter Tarn the road descends steeply round a mountain,
giving a magnificent view of the Langdale Pikes, which rise
immediately in front. The mountains are covered with heath,
fern, and all sorts of wild flowers, which of course my father
was constantly attracted by, so that although we had not yet
walked more than ten miles, it was getting on for two o'clock,

and we were reminded by our appetites that it was high time
for luncheon.   Our eyes had several times been irresistibly
attracted by a line in one of the guide books—'here parties
usually stop to take refreshment'—and we now found that we
were approaching this spot, which is a retired farm-house. Near
this place is a fine waterfall which we determined to see before
luncheon—it is between the two Langdale Pikes, called Dungeon
Ghyll. By the time we returned from the cascade we were very
ready for our repast.   You would have been amused to see us
feasting away at a great rate on bread, cheese, and milk.

"After this luncheon we set forth again with re-invigorated
steps, it being about three o'clock.

"Our road now lay through a tolerably fertile valley for
about two miles, till we came to what the guide-books call
Thrang Crag, where the rock in a slate quarry is excavated in a
most extraordinary manner.   From this we ascended a high
hill, whence we had a beautiful view over Elterwater, Loughrigg
Tarn, to Windermere, and soon after we crossed the hill, and
had in succession the most exquisite views of Grasmere and
Rydal Water.   After a short distance further, the path descended to the bank of Rydal Water, and it was difficult to say
whether the distant view or the nearer prospect was to be preferred.   After walking about half a mile further we came to
the turnpike road, and another mile and a half concluded our
delightful excursion at Ambleside.

"We were neither of us particularly tired. We had walked
about twenty-two miles, and in the evening my father occupied
himself in writing letters.

"To-day we went in the morning to the church in the village.
Between morning service and dinner (after reading our letters)
we walked to Foxhow and called on Mrs. Arnold—dinner at
four.   In the evening we walked to Brathay chapel, Mr.
Redmayne's, which is most picturesquely situated in a wild
spot. To-morrow, if the weather is fine, we propose going to
Bowness, and thence walking to Coniston, etc.

"KESWICK, *August 24th.*

"We left Ambleside this morning at nine, my father paying, as we took our leave, a just compliment to the landlady for the well-aired sheets, the waiter for the civility and attention, and Mr. Boniface himself for the general good management and unexceptionable character of the establishment.   At the door of the hotel who should be standing but Chief Baron Pollock, and Le Fevre . . . . at last we extricated ourselves from land-ladies, Chief Barons, and landlords, and mounted our car.   We had determined to send Cox" (the Bishop's servant) "by coach to this place with the luggage, and to go ourselves in a car over Kirkstone to Patterdale (ten miles).

"The road to Patterdale lies over a very high hill, rising first 1,300 feet and then falling 900.   At the top is a house which bears an inscription, 'This is the highest inhabited house in England.'   From this point the road descended precipitously for about three miles, the car being jolted in such a way as to make my father tremble for his bones, for by some accident the spring always bumped on *his* side.

"After two hours' drive from Ambleside, through very fine, bold, lofty scenery, we came to Patterdale inn, which is situated in a tastefully laid out garden.   We intended to take a boat here, and asked for a boatman accordingly, but were told that it was very doubtful whether any was to be had, as they were greatly in demand.

"'We will walk down to the edge of the lake and wait there for the boatman,' said my father.

"'It's not the least use your going there,' quickly answered the hotel-keeper, who was annoyed at our not staying at the hotel; 'the boatman won't come any faster, you had better walk about in the garden.'

"'Thank you, I prefer going down to the lake.'

"'But suppose I can't get a boatman ?   You won't be able to have a boat, for they are all locked up !'

"'Then we shall walk on.'

"So having shown ourselves very resolute, we marched down to the lake, where we found an intelligent carpenter, who gave us some valuable hints about the best route over the mountains to Keswick. We had given the boatman a quarter of an hour's law, and having waited twenty minutes, truth and consistency demanded that we should not wait any longer. So we went on. Our path first lay up a steep valley for a long mile and a half, till we came to some lead mines. Here, as the route we had selected is a very unfrequented one, not mentioned in the guide-books, we consulted the superintendent of the mines, who gave us accurate and particular directions. From this spot we had to ascend by a most precipitous path, in some places nearly perpendicular, for about two or three miles, and having reached the summit of the pass, to descend by an equally precipitous track to the valley on the other side. This pass is a very fine one—the views on each side are magnificent ... On descending into the valley, we found ourselves very hungry, and went to a small house, which looked at a distance like a 'traveller's rest,' but proved to be a delusion. A friendly blacksmith in the neighbourhood advised us to apply at the first farmhouse we came to. Accordingly we determined to follow his recommendation, and having come to a bettermost kind of cottage, walked in, told the good woman 'we were very hungry, having walked a long way, would she give us a bit of bread and cheese?' She was not a woman of many words, but she intimated her intention of complying with our request, and began to set about supplying our wants. Slices of bread, oatcake, and bits of cheese were soon placed before us.

"'Can you give us a little bit of butter, d'ye think?'

"'Hum.'

"'Have you not got any butter in the house? Don't you make your own butter?'

"'Yes, we makes butter once a week, but we are sometimes rather short of it at the end of the week.'

"However, she produced some very decent butter, of which

we partook without hesitation, as we did not intend that she
should be a loser in a pecuniary point of view by her hospitality.
She then gave us each a cup of milk, and, being an industrious
woman, forthwith sat down by our side and began to comb
her child's hair.   Luckily we were very hungry, so we never
minded. Having concluded our humble repast, we made our
best acknowledgments, and proceeded on our way, which lay
through a deep valley called ' St. John's Vale,' and up the side
of a mountain, till we came suddenly on a very pretty chapel,
most picturesquely situated.   Here we slaked our thirst at a
well in the churchyard, and continued our pilgrimage. We
were now about three miles from Keswick, and it was not four
o'clock yet, so we determined to make a slight *détour*, and go
to see a circle of Druidical stones which lies at a little distance
from the road.

"Luckily we fell in with a man who described the way to
us, and, after a little searching about, we came upon them.
They are very curious, like all such things, and that is all
that can be said of them.   Keswick was now distant about a
mile and a half, and we could see the smoke in the distance.
Consequently we were not likely to have any very great
difficulty in finding our way ; but I (having studied the map,
and ascertained that of two roads one was rather the shorter)
ventured to observe, ' I think our best way now will be to
make for the Penrith road, and enter Keswick that way.'
' Oh, there's no difficulty,' says my Lord, ' when we see the
place before us ; we'll go straight over the fields.'   Thinks I to
myself, ' Maybe you'll be getting into mischief trespassing over
the fields so close to the town ;' but I said nothing, and we
went as the crow flies.   After some little time we came out by
what at first we took for a farmhouse, but soon discovered to
be a gentleman's residence.   The only way out was through
the private road in front of the windows.   I saw another road
about fifty yards off, but there did not appear to be any mode
of reaching that road.   ' Never mind ; what signifies ? it's a

friend of mine who lives here.' ' Ah, I suppose it's Mr. Marshall' (the Marquis of Carabbas of the Lakes). We passed a gate and another private road. On the gate was a board on which might be written ' *Trespassers beware;*' but the board was turned from us, so I went warily and opened the gate and peeped, and read ' *Please be careful to shut the gate.*'

" ' There,' said my father, ' I told you my friend was a benevolent man.' At the gate of the grounds was a cottage and a boy.

" ' Does Mr. Marshall live here, my boy ? '

" ' No, sir, Mr. Joshua Stranger.'

" ' Mr. Joshua Stranger ; dear me, I wish I had known that. I told you he was a friend of mine. Mr. Joshua Stranger has built a church at Wandsworth, and is in other respects a man well-known for piety and benevolence.'

" Moral—Never be afraid of trespassing in private grounds.

" ' We must take the first good opportunity for going up Skiddaw,' was one of the last observations made before going to bed last night. Not that we have had bad weather, on the contrary, we have been most fortunate in that respect ; having had only one day, Sunday last, on which anything which could be called rain has fallen; but when one ascends a mountain one wishes to have a good view, and, therefore, of course one is anxious to take a fine opportunity. This morning was beautifully fine ; it would never do to miss the opportunity, so immediately after breakfast Cox was summoned. Now Cox is very spirited and a great mounter of hills, and he had walked up Skiddaw yesterday, and, therefore, knew the way ; so we asked him which way we were to go.

" ' Don't you mean to take a guide, my Lord ? '

" ' No, I think we shall do very well without a guide.'

" ' But suppose a fog should come on whilst you are on the top, my Lord ? '

" ' Oh, then we shall *feel* our way.'

" At twenty minutes past nine we started. The top of

Skiddaw is 3022 feet above the level of the sea, and six miles from Keswick. You must know that in our expeditions we never take any refreshment with us, but depend entirely on the chance of finding some farmhouse or publichouse in which bodily wants may be attended to. There were a vast number of parties going up the mountain, and when we got about half way up we were overtaken by two gentlemen and a lady on ponies. 'How do you do, my Lord?' said one of the gentlemen, shaking hands with my father. He then introduced his daughter and son, and offered his pony to my father, which offer, however, was declined with thanks. We then proceeded together to the top, and it was not till after some time that my father recollected him to be Mr. Oxenham, one of the masters of Harrow. By this time a cloud had come over the top of the mountain ; but every one who has been accustomed to mountain excursions knows that the clouds go away as rapidly as they come, so we never minded. On we went, higher and higher, until we entered the cloud that was passing over the top of the mountain. As we proceeded we met a party descending.

"'What can you see?'

"'Nothing.'

"We went to the top, however, but not all our eyes put together could see more than twenty yards. After waiting at the top, I suppose, nearly half an hour, my father and I set out to descend by the other side of the mountain to Bassenthwaite. The guide of one of the parties on the top had told us we should find a track after a little time, so we went boldly on ; but the fog seemed to get thicker and thicker, and instead of finding anything like a path or track we at last scrambled down a perpendicular ravine, until at length we emerged from the cloud, and had at once a splendid view over the Solway Frith to the hills of Scotland.

"The place in which we found ourselves was as steep as the side of a house or steeper, and consisted of loose slates, so that, to say nothing of the innumerable bruises to which our ancles were constantly subject, we were every now and then in danger of falling. My father, in one of his three falls, scraped his arm a good deal.

"To cut the matter short, we at length got safely to the bottom, and, it being then (say) half-past two, we enquired if there were any house for refreshment within any reasonable distance. At last we went to a farmhouse and had a draught of milk. We then made an effort to get a boat to row to the end of Bassenthwaite; but Mr. Rooke, the owner of the boat, was out, his men were busy, and his wife a 'strong-minded woman;' so this failed, and we were forced to content ourselves with walking along the shore and admiring the view from thence. From the end of Bassenthwaite Water to Keswick it is about four miles, and, as we took short cuts across the fields (being, as my father said, afflicted with highroadphobia), we did not get to Keswick till half-past four. My father refreshed himself with letters and lemonade, and I ditto, and we then had a pleasant row on the lake for an hour, Cox being of the party. Thus closed our day—at least dinner followed, but that is all a matter of course, or rather of courses, about which we say nothing."

At Crosthwaite's museum at Keswick the Bishop found in the traveller's book, under June 14, 1810, the entry, "Mr. Sumner, Milford, Hampshire," and the following amusing incident is narrated as having occurred at Penrith.

"Between the services to-day we took a walk and dined. After evening service my father went into the vestry to speak to the rector, Mr. ———. 'Ahem, my Lord, I hope—ahem— you didn't mind—the fact was—ahem—I have been away the greater part of the week, and I did not know you were expected, or I should not—ahem—I hope you did not mind hearing what was familiar to you—but I thought I could do nothing better.' The fact was that the good man, finding himself pressed for time, had taken a great part of his sermon from a printed one of my father's."

The following description of a good parson by an old boat-man on Wast Water is inimitable :—

"Old John Ritser sat by my father answering his questions. Amongst others, 'Who is the parson?' 'One Muster ———.' 'Is he a pretty good parson?' 'Yes, he's a capital good parson, a very careful man. I saw him yesterday strupped a-shearing his wuts.' . . . At about 4 P.M. our car landed us, and we commenced the ascent of the 'Black Sail,' a steep pass of two good miles up, and half down, then a valley of say a mile, after that the pass of 'Scarfgap,' say one and a half mile from one side to the other. These passes were very steep and very rugged, and our guide had allowed us three hours for the passage, but, by making considerable exertions, we accomplished it in little more than two hours, and reached Gatesgarth at half-past six. Here we found our Keswick car, into which we gladly stepped, and made the best of our way home, the driver on the way remarking to one of our party, 'I beg your pardon, my Lord, but that's a trying excursion for a genelman of your years.'"

No sooner had the Bishop returned from this walking tour, which, though he had now numbered fifty-seven years, he thoroughly enjoyed, than he had to buckle on his armour. He was a man of peace and, therefore, it was with considerable pain that, at the close of the year, he felt himself compelled to join publicly in the opposition to Dr. Hampden's appointment to the see of Hereford. Eleven years before, on Dr. Hampden's appointment by Lord Melbourne to the Regius Professorship of Divinity at Oxford, one of his works had been censured by a formal vote of the majority of the convocation of the University. And when, in 1847, Lord John Russell nominated him to the vacant see at Hereford, the storm broke out afresh. Thirteen bishops protested against the appointment : the Bishops of London, Winchester, Lincoln, Bangor, Carlisle, Rochester, Bath and Wells, Gloucester and Bristol, Exeter, Salisbury, Chichester, Ely, and Oxford. The protest was very temperately worded, representing to the Premier "the apprehension and alarm which have been excited in the minds of the clergy by the rumoured nomination to the see of Hereford of Dr. Hampden in the soundness of whose doctrine the University of Oxford has affirmed by a solemn decree its want of confidence," and their conviction that "if this appointment be completed, there is the greatest danger both of the interruption of the peace of the Church, and of the disturbance of the confidence which it is most desirable that the clergy and laity of the Church should feel in every exercise of the royal supremacy, especially as regards that very delicate and important particular the nomination to vacant sees."

Lord John Russell replied very vigorously to the protest, as it appeared to him that if he should withdraw his recommendation of Dr. Hampden which had been sanctioned by the Queen he should "virtually assent to the doctrine that a decree of the University of Oxford is a perpetual ban of exclusion against a clergyman of eminent learning and irreproachable life; and that, in fact, the supremacy now by law vested in the crown" would be "transferred to a majority of the members of one of our universities."

Notwithstanding the protest the nomination was persisted in and, after an unsuccessful appeal to the Court of Queen's Bench on the part of some of the protesters, Dr. Hampden was duly consecrated Bishop.*

An interesting event occurred in connection with the Hants confirmation in the autumn. For the first time a confirmation was held specially for the lads at the Reformatory at Parkhurst in the Isle of Wight. It is thus described in a letter written at the time by an eye-witness.

"Nothing can have been more interesting than the whole scene of the confirmation at Parkhurst. The Governor and Chaplain have long been anxious to obtain the Home Secre-

* See "Memorials of Bishop Hampden," pp. 143-164. Also Martin's "Life of the Prince Consort," vol. i., 469-471.

tary's permission to request the Bishop to hold one in the prison, but which had hitherto been withheld. Sir Richard Simeon (local visitor of the prison) immediately upon hearing of the Bishop's intention to confirm in the island, wrote on the subject to Sir George Grey, who after consultation with the officers of the prison, &c., gave the long withheld permission. Great care has been taken by the chaplains to admit none to confirmation whose penitence and sincerity there was any ground to doubt, and it is a good sign of the general state of the prison that out of nearly 400 lads 290 were admitted to be confirmed. Many were refused, not from deficiency of knowledge, but from the absence of moral qualifications. Several withdrew after being addressed on the subject, one on the very day in conse-quence of having been betrayed into anger. In the building used as a chapel all the members of the establishment were assembled, and nothing can have been more proper and serious, naturally, not forced, than the appearance and demeanour of the poor boys. There was an intelligent expression of impressed feelings on the face of each as they came up to the rails in military order, which shewed they were perfectly alive to the solemn nature of the voluntary profession of faith they had just made, and gave one good hope that they really desired the blessing which was about to be pronounced over them as they knelt one after another to receive imposition of hands. Of the Bishop's address it would be impossible to speak too highly. It was entirely to the point, earnest and deeply impressive, going back to the causes which had brought them to that prison, dwelling on God's goodness in receiving again into favour those who had forfeited their title, referring to the advantages they had at Parkhurst, and warning them against falling back into sin when in a foreign land, let loose from restraint and possibly without the public means of grace. He concluded with address-ing a solemn warning to those who had not been confirmed through presumed unfitness."

It was not often that the Bishop took any part in the

debates in the House of Lords, but in the early session of the
House in 1848 he felt it his duty to come forward somewhat
prominently on the Protestant side in the debates on the bill
introduced by Lord Lansdowne to enable Her Majesty to
establish diplomatic relations with the Court of Rome. He
strongly opposed the bill, thinking it might be fraught with
dangerous consequences in the future, and he pointed out that
the words "Sovereign Pontiff" were for the first time applied
in any bill brought before Parliament to the Pope of Rome. In
the Roman Catholic Relief bill he had been called the Pope of
Rome. The Bishop's first appeal for the substitution of some
other phrase for that of Sovereign Pontiff was not successful,
but on his renewal of the subject at a subsequent stage of the
bill, the obnoxious words were changed to "Sovereign of the
Roman States."

In February, 1848, Archbishop Howley died. It was supposed
at the time that Lord John Russell hesitated whether to
recommend for the vacant Archbishopric the Bishop of Lichfield (Lonsdale) or the Bishop of Chester (Sumner). The
appointment, however, was offered to the Bishop of Chester,
and he was accordingly translated to the See of Canterbury.
The Bishop writes respecting the appointment on February
19th.

"It is quite remarkable how universal a consent has been
given to my brother's appointment. Of course I am not well
placed to judge of this, and I do not speak from what is said to
me, but I hear of the satisfaction in all quarters, high and low,
in so many indirect ways that it is impossible to doubt it. This
is a most important augury for good, because it is plain that it
will greatly increase the power for usefulness which his position
will in itself give him, up to a certain point, but which would
be greatly diminished if public opinion were not generally with
him. I cannot say how thankfully I look forward to closer and
nearer intercourse with him."

In another letter of the same date, he speaks of what he

hears in connection with the appointment as being "in a strain which makes sweet music in the ears of a brother."

Referring to his confirmation at Bow Church the Bishop writes :

"March 10, 1848.—I have just returned from London, where the confirmation has gone off very well, Arthur Perceval[*] having discovered that he could not scripturally proceed in the teeth of 1 Tim. v. 19.[†] The church and vestibule were quite full, and as he passed through the latter there was a cry of 'God bless the Archbishop of Canterbury,' and on getting out into the street the people gave three cheers."

It was the Bishop's painful duty at the close of the year to suspend one of the clergy of his diocese for three years, in consequence of his having been publicly baptised by immersion by the minister of a Baptist congregation. I only refer to the case now because it affords the opportunity of showing the exceeding delicacy and tenderness with which the Bishop treated the offender, even when, as in the present case, he felt that he must act with firmness. Writing to a clerical friend of the suspended clergyman, he says:—

"I forward a copy of the sentence in ———'s case, and shall be much obliged by your calling on him from me in the course of to-morrow, and communicating it to him as a private intimation from me of what Wooldridge" (the acting registrar) "will deliver to him the next day officially. I think this will be more delicate and more satisfactory to him than allowing him to receive it first at the hands of the deputy-registrar. Be so good also as to state to him that while I have executed my duty in this respect under a strong sense of the obligation which my office has imposed upon me, it has not been without a very

---

[*] Mr. Perceval was disposed to object to the confirmation of the Archbishop on the ground that he had been in favour of the bill which diminished the number of Bishops in the Irish Church.

[†] "Against an elder receive not an accusation, but before two or three witnesses."

deep feeling of concern for himself personally. If anything prevents you from calling upon him to-morrow, be so good as to communicate with Wooldridge, to whom I write by this post and desire him to delay on Saturday until you have first exe cuted your message."

In January, 1849, the Bishop held a meeting at Farnham o the archdeacons and rural deans of his diocese to consider the subject of school inspection. It had been his habit from the time of his first entering upon the See of Winchester to hold meetings of this character at irregular intervals as occasion seemed to demand. And very pleasant gatherings they were The Bishop always seemed to be specially in his element when presiding at such assemblies. He was an excellent chairman— his attention never flagging. For keeping speakers to the point in dispute, for summing up at the conclusion the points of those who had taken part in the debate, for harmonising dis cordant views, and smoothing over difficulties, few were his equal. The meetings extended over two or three days, during which time the archdeacons and rural deans were, of course, his guests; and as the courteous host on such occasions, none ever surpassed him. When the dispenser of hospitality thoroughly enjoys entertaining those who receive it, it would be strange indeed if the feeling were not reciprocal; and none, I am sure can look back on those gatherings without recalling many plea sant hours spent in friendly discussion of general topics of inte rest, and in the enjoyment of social intercourse of no common order.

It was shortly after this meeting that the shadow of an impending trial fell upon the Bishop's family life. In the spring, during his residence in London, Mrs. Sumner began to show evident signs of failing health—so much so, that in May she was obliged to leave London and take up her abode for a time at Brighton, accompanied by some of her children. She did not return to Farnham until after the ordination in July, and it was evident that her state was such as to cause the

gravest anxiety. The least excitement or over-fatigue brought
on violent palpitations of the heart. The Bishop was fully
aware of her critical state. He writes to Archdeacon Hoare on
August 20th:—

"You will be grieved to hear that I am under much anxiety
about Mrs. Sumner. She has a return of the palpitations of the
heart, with considerable aggravation, and we greatly need your
prayers. I have been obliged to postpone the consecrations in
Hampshire, fixed for next week, for I could not possibly leave
her under present circumstances."

The months of July and August were passed in most painful
anxiety. Hopes for Mrs. Sumner's ultimate recovery were
raised one day, only to be dashed to the ground the next. Her
children were in constant attendance upon her, and all was
done that the most tender and careful nursing could suggest
Mrs. Sumner's unselfish character came out strongly in her
illness. She was always thinking of others, never of herself.
The least attention shown was gratefully acknowledged, and
there was nothing so painful to her as the necessity which was
forced upon her of giving trouble to those around her. Towards
the close of August the Bishop could no longer conceal from
himself that there was but little hope of the illness terminating
otherwise than fatally. Coleridge, on hearing from him to this
effect, writes :—

"I heartily pray, and will pray, that God may be as gracious
to you and to her in this matter as He undoubtedly has been
in bringing you together, blessing your union and showering
happiness on you within and without for so many years. . . . I
beg you will give her my kind love, and tell her how grateful I
am to her for unwearied kindness towards me now from 1814—
five and thirty years—and how earnestly I pray for her happiness
in time and eternity. . . . I do not speak of coming to you,
but pray remember that I will at any time, with the greatest
pleasure, if I can be of any comfort to you."

The forebodings, which the Bishop had expressed in writing

to his old friend, were only too soon fulfilled, for on Sunday, the 2nd of September, he was called upon to stand by the bedside of his dying wife. For the last twenty-four hours of her life the whole family were gathered together in her room, almost momentarily expecting her last breath. During all this time Mrs. Sumner, in her wakeful moments, repeated texts of Scripture or broke forth in expressions of joyful hope and expectation. Not a word was spoken to her for fear of arousing her from this happy state of semi-entrancement. Her only source of distress was that her loving husband, and children, and faithful servants gathered round her bed should be kept in such a prolonged state of suspense on her account. For the last six hours of her life she calmly slept, and at half-past two o'clock on Monday morning, September 3rd, her spirit took its flight.

She was buried in the churchyard of Hale, where a stone, with the following inscription, marks the place where her body lies awaiting the great Easter morn—when, clothed in incorruption and glory, it will be raised by Him who is the Resurrection and the Life: "Jennie Fanny Barnabino, the beloved wife of Charles Richard Sumner, D.D., Bishop of Winchester; born Feb. 23, 1794, died Sept. 3rd, 1849. 'She loved much.' 'Them which sleep in Jesus will God bring with Him.' 'Surely I come quickly. Amen. Even so come Lord Jesus.'"

It is not for me to say much of one so near and dear to me, but I must be permitted to bear my testimony to the fact that Mrs. Sumner's character was a very beautiful one. Her loss was proportionately felt. With mental qualities of the highest order, and social powers which greatly attracted all those with whom she came in contact, she consecrated all to the service of her heavenly Master. Retaining to the last the warmth and fervour which she imported from her foreign home, she had made herself the friend and counsellor of many a troubled soul. She was a true mother in Israel, and throughout her married life a help meet both in domestic and public life to the husband whom she dearly loved. The Bishop was greatly touched by the expressions of sympathy which poured in upon him from all sides. The inhabitants of Farnham, in the course of an address transmitted to the Bishop, said :—

" In assuring your Lordship that we can never feel indifferent or unconcerned at the happening of any event—whether of sorrow or of joy—which to us appears to affect your Lordship's happiness ; we cannot on the present occasion conceal from ourselves that she who has been called to her rest had, during her sojourn among us, laboured abundantly in behalf of our local charities and industrial institutions—was the ever tender sympathiser in our afflictions, and the ready friend of the poor and needy."

The Clergy of the diocese addressed the Bishop in these words :—

" We, the undersigned clergy of your Lordship's diocese, affectionately desire to present the united expression of our deep condolence upon the recent affliction, which, in the providence of the all-wise Disposer of life and death, has deprived your Lordship of the most exemplary companion, your family of a most affectionate parent, and the diocese at large of a most faithful promoter of peace and charity, and of all which is lovely and of good report. With very many of us the expression of personal kindnesses is not wanting to enhance the sympathy which we feel in your Lordship's present grief. But our thoughts are arrested by the remembrance of higher services on the part of her, who was truly an help-meet amidst your ministerial anxieties and cares, as well as in the conduct of that courteous and liberal hospitality unceasingly exercised under your Lordship's roof : and whether we reflect on our incidental occasions of intercourse with you on matters of professional duty, or on the more formal assembling of your clergy for conference on sacred things, or on the statedly recurring ordination of fresh candidates for the work of the Ministry, we are reminded throughout of manifold instances of her labour in the Lord, whose loss we deplore, and of the Christian influence which she deemed it her privilege and joy to exercise towards all alike.

"These virtues, and the end of such a conversation, will long, we trust, be remembered by us all; and we fervently pray that He, by whose sovereign will this grievous trial has reached your Lordship's house, may sanctify it to the highest Christian ends ; that the light of your example may shine with augmented lustre before the Church to the furtherance of the Gospel of His Grace, and to the increase of your joy, in the presence of the Lord Jesus Christ at His coming.

"Our hearts' desire and prayer for you and your family is, that grace may be with you, mercy and peace from God the Father, and from the Lord Jesus Christ in truth and love, both now and for ever."

This address was signed by 684 clergy.

The Bishop replied through the Archdeacons of Winchester and Surrey, and after acknowledging the address with feelings of real thankfulness, adds :—

"This touching proof of brotherly feeling, shared in common by so large a body of men with whom I am connected in the most sacred bonds of duty, has deeply affected me. I hope I am not wrong in recognising in it an observance of the Apostolic rule, 'that there should be no schism in the body, but that the members should have the same care one for another, and whether one member suffer, all the members suffer with it.' I shall never cease to be grateful for the manifestation of this spirit.

"My family will derive consolation in their bereavement from the knowledge that the character of her who has been removed from them was truly appreciated by those who had opportunities of forming a judgment, and will recognise in the affecting language of the address the best memorial to a beloved and revered mother. For my own part, I shall ever regard this kindness shown so seasonably in the hour of the heaviest personal visitation which I could be called upon to suffer, as a remembrancer of the relations existing mutually between the clergy and myself, a new bond of union and friendly regard, and a powerful incentive to a more entire devotion of time and thoughts to the duties of my diocese.

"That your own homes, and those of our brethren in the ministry, may be long spared, if it be God's gracious will, from afflicting dispensations, that you may be succoured in the hour of trial and sorrow by the consolations of the Holy Ghost the Comforter, and that the Divine blessing may be vouchsafed abundantly to your pastoral labours in your several parishes is my earnest prayer."

Coleridge writes most affectionately :—

. . . . . "I have heard of you from time to time, and most thankfully, that you have been graciously supported under your great affliction. And so I trusted you would be; all the circumstances of your misfortune I had full confidence would be consoling, and tend, upon reflection, to soothe and strengthen you. It is a delightful consideration, that many things which increase our sense of the value of what we lose, at the same time suggest topics of consolation for the loss, and supply strength to bear it. Humanly speaking, your loss is irreparable ; it is great now, as much as you can bear, more than you could bear unaided ; and yet, humanly speaking, it must go on increasing—as your own strength and health decline, as your children become more and more absorbed in their own circles and pursuits, you will need more of that perpetual comfort and help which the κουριδίη ἄλοχος, the dear love of early manhood, the fond and faithful companion of all your toilsome years, the sharer of all cares, the sympathiser in all sorrows alone might be expected to afford as the lights were declining towards your setting. But fear not. I do not fear for you ; you have nothing painful to look back upon, and as the time for your own departure approaches, you will be more intent, and more cheerfully intent on the prospect of a blessed re-union, than mindful for the little intervening circumstances which attend on your stay here. And above all other things your prayers, and the prayers of many for you will, I cannot doubt, avail for your support and comfort. You are specially blest in your children, numerous, kind, united and good: your excellent brother, your many faithful and affectionate early friends. You are blest in your occupation, heavy as it is, yet with its tendencies the right way. And you will seek for comfort, I doubt not, trying for the sake of your children, and friends, and the Church, to be comforted, and enabled to do your duty peacefully, and with an equal mind." . . . . .

The Bishop of Oxford writes :—

"ROMSEY, *Sept.* 4, 1849.

"MY DEAREST LORD,

"The sad intelligence conveyed to me by Robert's letter (for which may I heartily thank him through you) could not be unexpected. Yet, as always, it comes at last with a startling reality when the blow does fall. May the God in whom you trust be very nigh unto you in this hour of sorrow. I rejoiced to hear that the last hours of her who has now passed from us to the gathered company of those who sleep in Him, were gilded by the light of His presence. Such remembrances are so eminently soothing, and yet quickening. I was for some time on Monday at Brighstone, where, through your kindness, so large a part of my own happy married life had been spent, and where therefore I was specially prepared to enter into your present feelings with full sympathy. Many times did my heart turn to you, and many times have you and yours been named in my prayers. It would be a painful pleasure to me, if it were any way soothing to you, my dearest Lord, to be present with you at the last sad scene of respect and love to her remains. You stood by *me* at such an hour, and this and relationship may perhaps admit me where, from the impossibility of admitting all who I know would wish to come, it is difficult to admit any. . . . . .   "Your very affectionate,

"S. OXON."

Writing a few days later to condole with a friend on the loss of a father-in-law, Bishop Wilberforce says:—

"How does God deal with us! One by one brought into that net; and taught by that Cross. Your dear Bishop, who always rose to my thoughts with his purity, and goodness, and success, when I read 'Now Joseph was a very prosperous man;' he too smitten. Well! it is for a little while, and it is well."

Mrs. Opie, whose acquaintance the Bishop had made through the Gurney family, and who had corresponded in most affectionate terms with Mrs. Sumner, writes:—

"Castle Meadow, *9th Month*, 1849.

"I cannot refrain from expressing to thee, my dear and respected friend, my deep sympathy with thy heartfelt sorrow on this affecting occasion. I know thou hast every possible consolation under such a trial, and art sure that the beloved and lamented one has entered into 'the pearl gates,' and that another voice is now heard in the blessed choir above. Still, thou canst not help regretting the removal of the endeared companion of so many happy years, and the void she has left in that home which she blessed, and those scenes which she adorned. But thou knowest where to seek the help required, and believing that as 'thy need will be thy strength,' I earnestly, respectfully, and affectionately commend thee, dear Lord Bishop, to Him who can alone raise up again those whom he hath bowed down!

"Amelia Opie."

The following letter, written by the Bishop to the wife of one of his sons who, in consequence of illness, was unable to be at Farnham at the time of Mrs. Sumner's death, will show the spirit in which he received the blow:—

"Farnham Castle, *Sept.* 3, 1849.

"Dearest M.,

"I send you back G., the messenger of heavy tidings to you. And yet we must pray to be enabled to forget our

selfishness which would have kept her here. For the loss is to
us—to her what gain! G. will give you details of the whole.
Indeed, I could not write them were it necessary, which it is
not. This is the only line I have yet written to anyone, but I
could not let him go without carrying with him some little
token of my tender affection for you, now to be doubled if
possible, as you must look in future to me alone for the concentrated love of your two lately acquired new parents.

> "Ever, my dearest M.,
>
> "Your most affectionate father,
>
> "C. WINTON."

The Bishop left Farnham for a couple of months' change of
scene, accompanied by some of his children, and at the beginning of November returned to the Castle. In the following
letter to Mr. Dallas, he refers to the arrangements which had
been made, by which he would for a time at any rate have a
son resident with him. The letter is dated from Farnham,
Nov. 14, 1849.

. . . . . "I returned hither on Friday last, for the first time
to my home, now void. My children (George and Mary are
with me, and will remain to the great comfort of Emily and
myself) are to me everything that children can be, and more
than this; but they neither can, nor expect to be able, to
make me forget that in every room there is one wanting who
is associated with every thought in all places, and here
especially. It is quite wonderful to myself how strong is the
undercurrent of this association, and how unconsciously it is
connected in my mind with every subject on which I talk or
think."

CHAPTER XIX.

The Gorham Case.—Bishop of Exeter's Pamphlet.—The Archbishop's reception
of it.—Conciliatory Message from Bishop Philpotts to the Archbishop in his
last illness reciprocated by him.—Agitation in the Diocese respecting the
Baptismal question.—The Bishop's views on the subject.—Doubts the wis-
dom of a Synodical declaration.—Letter to Mr. Keble.—Extract from the
Bishop's Charge.—Opinion as to the Canterbury Settlement in New Zealand.
—Papal Aggression.—Bishop's Reply to Address.—Interview with the
Bishop of Coutances.

THE year 1850 opened very gloomily. The ecclesiastical
atmosphere had been disturbed by several severe storms, the
reverberation of which still echoed through the heavens. Men
were longing for peace but it came not.

The Bishop was not wont to take other than a cheerful view
of events, but at this time his mind was full of anxiety for the
future. He writes to his eldest daughter at the time in France:—

" January 22, 1850.

" I cannot say that I look cheerfully upon public affairs.
They seem to me to wear a very grave aspect. But happily they
are not ruled by us, and I pray they may be ordered for good."

The Gorham case was then in its last stage. In 1847 the
living of Brampford Speke, in the diocese of Exeter, was offered
by Lord Chancellor Cottenham to the Rev. G. C. Gorham. It
was necessary that Mr. Gorham should send a testimonial to
the Lord Chancellor, signed by three beneficed clergymen, and
countersigned by the Bishop. The countersignature of the
Bishop is merely to testify to the fact that the three clergy are

beneficed in his diocese, and are worthy of credit. The Bishop however declined to countersign the testimonial and wrote in the margin :—

"The clergymen who have subscribed this testimonial are highly respectable ; but as I consider the Bishop's counter-signature of such a document, if it be unaccompanied by any remark, as implying his own belief that the party to whom it relates, 'has not held, written, or taught anything contrary to the doctrine or discipline of the United Church of England and Ireland,' and as my own experience unfortunately attests that the Rev. George Cornelius Gorham did in the course of last year, in correspondence with myself, hold, write and maintain what is contrary to the discipline of the said Church, and as what he further wrote makes me apprehend that he holds also what is contrary to its doctrine, I cannot conscientiously coun-tersign this testimonial."

Mr. Gorham remonstrated, but in vain; but on the circum-stances being explained to the Lord Chancellor, he waived the absence of the Bishop's countersignature and presented Mr. Gorham to the living. But on Mr. Gorham's applying to the Bishop for institution, the Bishop stated that he should feel it his duty to ascertain by examination whether Mr. Gorham was sound in the faith before he instituted him. Accordingly Mr. Gorham was submitted to an examination, which lasted for nine days, at the close of which, in March, 1848, the Bishop declined to institute him on account of alleged unsoundness of doctrine. Mr. Gorham appealed to the law to put him into possession of what he deemed to be his just rights, and a suit was instituted in the Court of Arches. In February, 1849, the case was fully argued, and in August the Dean of Arches, Sir Herbert Jenner Fust, pronounced judgment against Mr. Gorham. Appeal was at once made to the Privy Council, and on March 8th, 1850, the judgment of the Judicial Committee was read by Lord Langdale, reversing the sentence pronounced by the Judge of the Arches Court, and declaring that the Bishop of Exeter had not shown sufficient cause why he should not institute Mr. Gorham to Brampford Speke. Motions were made in the Courts of Exchequer, Common Pleas and Queen's Bench, calling in question the validity of this decision, but they were ineffectual, and on the sixth of August Mr. Gorham was instituted to the vicarage of Brampford Speke by Sir Herbert Jenner Fust, acting as official Principal of the Archbishop of Canterbury.

Immediately after the delivery of the judgment of the Judicial Committee, and previous to the motions made in the Law Courts, the Bishop of Exeter had published his celebrated letter to the Archbishop. Never probably had any ephemeral production so rapid a sale. On the title page of the copy that now lies before me are the significant words " Twenty-first edition." In this pamphlet the Bishop enters into an elaborate defence of his own position in the whole matter, and concludes with the following trenchant words: "Meanwhile I have one most painful duty to perform. I have to protest not only against the judgment pronounced in the recent cause, but also against the regular consequences of that judgment. I have to protest against your Grace's doing what you will be speedily called to do, either in person or by some other exercising your authority. I have to protest and I do hereby solemnly protest, before the Church of England, before the Holy Catholic Church, before Him who is its Divine Head, against your giving mission to exercise cure of souls within my diocese to a clergyman who proclaims himself to hold the heresies which Mr. Gorham holds. I protest that anyone who gives mission to him, till he retract, is a favourer and supporter of those heresies. I protest in conclusion, that I cannot, without sin—and by God's Grace, I will not—hold communion with him, be he who he may, who shall so abuse the high commission which he bears.

" I am, my Lord Archbishop, with that 'due reverence and obedience' which I have pledged to you, and with earnest prayer that such reverence and obedience to you may never be forbidden by my duty to our common Master, your Grace's affectionate friend for nearly thirty years, and your now afflicted servant,

"H. Exeter."

I believe that the only notice which the Archbishop took of the Bishop of Exeter's letter was to send him a note written in his usual quiet, gentle way, explaining some circumstance of no great importance, which the Bishop had misapprehended in his pamphlet. This note contained no complaint whatever of the language of the Bishop, and on reading it the Bishop is reported to have said, " I have had a letter from the Archbishop, which is the letter of an angel, and not of a man." The Archbishop nevertheless felt that an amende was due to him from the Bishop of Exeter, and could not feel so affectionately towards him as he had done in years gone by. It is gratifying, however, to know that in 1862, when the Archbishop was seized with his last illness, a conciliatory message was borne to him from the Bishop of Exeter by the Bishop of Winchester, and that a message of a similar character was returned to Bishop Philpotts.

I have thought it well thus to give a résumé of the principal events connected with the Gorham case, because the minds of the clergy throughout all England were, no doubt, at that time much agitated by it. The diocese of Winchester was no exception to the rule. It required all the tact and judgment of the Bishop to restrain the excessive zeal of some ardent spirits. The following extracts from letters written at this time will sufficiently show the tone of the Bishop's mind with respect to the subject generally.

To Archdeacon Wigram, who was just about to hold his visitation in Hants, he thus writes :—

"Perrysfield, Godstone, April 7, 1850.

"My dear Archdeacon,

"I think it very probable that in the course of your ensuing visitation you will be pressed in some quarters with a

requisition to call the Clergy together, either in reference specifically to the late decision of the Judicial Committee, or to the
Baptismal question arising out of it.

"I should deprecate most earnestly any such movement. It
would be dangerous, in my judgment, at any time, but at the
present moment I think it would be fraught with inevitable
and very serious evils.

"The great bulk of the Clergy of the diocese, with the exception of a few extremes at either end, are probably in essential
agreement on the subject of Baptism, taking the doctrine as a
whole, and in all its bearings, although differing from each
other imperceptibly, and often unconsciously, in shades of
opinion, and in the steps by which they arrive at their conclusions. But if you call on them to frame a normal rule, or
attempt to bind them by a definition, these differences will
become so patent, and too probably in the heat and exaggera-
tion of argument so material, that agreement will become impossible. And I should expect no other termination of such a
discussion than that all would range themselves under the
banners of one or other of the two extremes, however really differing from both in their own separate and individual opinions.

"I can conceive no greater misfortune for the parishes of the
diocese, with all their Clergy and laity, than a house so divided
and such an array of parties.

"And then, if you begin to define, where are you to stop?
Why limit yourself to Baptism? The seventeenth article of the
Church has been held diversely by different persons ever since
it was framed. Why not attempt to procure a quasi synodical
recognition of a particular view of the doctrine of election?
It can scarcely be doubted that if you once begin the work of
stringent limitation and authoritative interpretation, you will
have as many apples of discord as you have articles.

"The peace of the Church often threatened, and sometimes
even partially disturbed, has hitherto been preserved by God's
blessing on its moderation. It can only now be maintained, if

maintained at all, by mutual forbearance and abstinence on either side from pressing extreme opinions on the consciences of others.

"I know not how far these views will meet your own ; but I think it right you should be acquainted with them previously to setting out on your visitation. And though I do not wish to obtrude them unnecessarily on any, I leave it to your own dis-cretion to make what use you please of them, if occasion should require.   "I am,

"Your very faithful friend and brother,

"C. WINTON."

Again, to a friend, he writes on the same day :—

"If —— means that I should advise the Archbishop to be a party consenting to a quasi-synodical exposition of doctrine on the part of the Episcopate, I must entirely differ from him as to the expediency of such a step—and did I agree with him, the advice would be altogether nugatory, as no such unanimous document would be signed by the Bench. I very much doubt whether it would obtain the signatures of a majority. And do you not see, that no such interpretation of doctrine as would satisfy those whom —— appears to think ought to be satisfied, would be signed by the Archbishop consistently with his con-currence with the late judgment."

Again, with reference to another proposal he writes three days later :—

"I return ——'s letter. Of all the panaceas proposed I think his is the most wonderful. That he should see any 'safety' in a declaration by the Bench of Bishops of their unaltered adherence to the article 'one baptism for the remission of sins'! Why he has only to attend Divine Service with us on any Sunday morning and he will hear everyone make our declaration orally. Does he not see that the whole gist is in the interpretation ; and unanimous interpretation is a very different thing from unanimous declaration of adherence to the

Church's formulary. I have never yet met with anyone who has 'taken up Gorham,' in the sense of assenting to his doctrine; and certainly I, for one, disclaim all sympathy with *it*, though not all sympathy with him as believing him to be within the pale of the Church's tolerance."

To Mr. Keble he writes on April 24th:

"In acknowledging the receipt of the petition inclosed in your letter, signed by a very large proportion of the communicants in Hursley parish, I request you will assure them that although I am unable to see any adequate grounds for the perplexity and alarm which they represent themselves as experiencing, I cannot but entertain a deep respect for their conscientious scruples, and desire, as far as may be consistent with my own duty to the Church at large, to sympathize with them in their trials.

"I am constrained, however, to remark that the petitioners seem to misunderstand the nature of the recent judgment, and the question which the Judicial Committee had to decide. It was no part of their duty to define doctrine, or to construct a formula by which every shade of difference respecting a given point of faith was to be tested, but to determine whether by the specific wording of any of our existing articles and formularies, taken in connexion, a person holding certain stated opinions ought to be excluded from the ministry of the Church. Accordingly they left the doctrine of the Church what they found it,—they have expressly disclaimed the right or the intention of making alterations,—they have not required you to change your faith and teaching,—they have only pronounced that the view of another is not so irreconcilable with honest subscription to formularies that it may not be held and taught concurrently with your own, without exposing the holder to the penalty of forfeiture.

"I cannot see that any inferences can be fairly drawn from such a decision, which ought reasonably to cause disturbance in the minds of well-informed and dispassionate inquirers.

z

"Your parishioners ask me, in the conclusion of the petition, to aid them in removing any doubt which may have arisen on this point, namely, whether or no the Church holds it needful to be believed that original sin is remitted to all infants in Holy Baptism, by the only merits of our Lord and Saviour Jesus Christ.

"But I demur to the question.

"I find in one of her creeds an acknowledgment of belief in one Baptism for the remission of sins, and I heartily assent to such acknowledgment. But I do not find in any of our formularies or articles, or in Holy Scripture, the express terms of the proposition which you submit, and I hesitate to go beyond what is written. I think it safer and wiser and more consistent with the uniformly moderate spirit displayed in our Liturgy and Articles, and specially more in accordance with the express teaching of the sixth article, not to define more stringently than the Church herself, or to lay down as authoritative a single and precise formula as needful to be believed on a point not so plainly and certainly declared in Holy Scripture as to preclude the possibility of admitting in respect of it any shade of difference. This would be a private interpretation which I do not consider myself authorized to give. In declining to narrow the limits which the Church has not limited, or by the force of a particular form of expression to exclude from the Church those who, for the last three hundred years, have not been adjudged to be without her pale, I hope I am in harmony with the whole of her charitable spirit, and following the example of the first Council at Jerusalem who refused to put a yoke upon the necks of the disciples which neither their fathers nor themselves were able to bear.

"I heartily pray that both yourself and those over whom you have been called to exercise pastoral care, may be strengthened to hold the faith in unity of spirit and in the bond of peace ; and may the grace of the Lord Jesus Christ, and the love of God, and the Communion of the Holy Ghost be with you all. Amen."

The following, written a month later, refers to a proposition that Convocation should issue a synodical declaration on the point at issue.

"ST. JAMES' SQUARE, *May 23rd*, 1850.

"DEAR SIR,

"I have received your letter of the 19th inst. transmitting a petition from certain priests and deacons resident in the county of Hants.

"Such an address would deservedly command my serious respect and attention under any circumstances, and is especially entitled to my most careful consideration, if, after viewing the question at issue in all its bearings, I still find myself unable to arrive at the same conclusion as the petitioners.

"You ask me to take steps for obtaining licence for the clergy to meet in Convocation, with a view to settling the Church's doctrine on the spiritual grace of Holy Baptism, so far as that doctrine may have been disturbed by recent events.

"But I cannot admit the fact which appears to be assumed. I cannot see that the decision of the Judicial Committee affords any legitimate ground for the alleged disturbance of doctrine. It is notorious that ever since the reformation of our Church men have been recognized as within her pale who have held opinions more or less widely different respecting the effects of infant Baptism. And the late judgment seems to go no further than to abstain from narrowing that liberty which has hitherto been enjoyed by members of the Church, without reproach or imputation of heresy. And in maintaining this principle, the judges have been studiously careful to disclaim any authority or jurisdiction to settle matters of faith, or to interfere in any way with the belief and teaching of the petitioners or others.

"But I cannot refrain from adding that, if the fact were otherwise, the annals of Convocation seem to warn us, with no uncertain voice, that such assemblies, especially in days of controversial heat and excitement, have tended rather to widen

z 2

the breaches in our Zion, and to quench the spirit of charity
among us, than to promote the desirable end of establishing
unity of doctrine in the bond of peace. Rather, as it seems to
me, do the times invite us to study more carefully the tone of
moderation which characterizes the teaching of our Church on
subjects of an abstruse and difficult nature—when Holy Scripture does not define dogmatically and in express terms—
earnestly exhorting one another to love and mutual forbearance,
and remembering always the Apostolic counsel, 'Whereto we
have already attained, let us walk by the same rule, let us mind
the same thing.'

"I am, dear Sir,

"Your very faithful friend and brother,

"C. Winton."

The advisability of a declaration by the bishops on the subject, was much mooted at the time, the Bishop of London
favouring such a step. The following notes, found amongst the
Bishop of Winchester's papers, refer apparently to the line taken
by him in the consultations which took place with reference to
this matter amongst the members of the Episcopal Bench.

"1. Declaration would impinge on the consciences of those
who hold the Calvinistic interpretation of the seventeenth
article. They would maintain that only those who are finally
saved are the subjects of a change, wrought by God, whereby
the child of wrath is made a child of grace.

"2. Also of that much larger class, who, without actually
embracing the Calvinistic doctrine, contend for the hypothe-
tical construction of the baptismal service and catechism,
because it is only, as they conceive, by such construction,
that the expressions of the Prayer-book can be reconciled with
the word of God. The necessity for such a supposition would
be removed if it could be proved from Scripture that all infants
do undergo the change, wrought by God, whereby the child of
wrath is made a child of grace.

"3. Also of all those who look with jealousy on the claim made for the Church to decide dogmatically points not evidently concluded in God's word—who approve the forbearance of the Church in leaving so much margin wherever Scripture has not accurately marked the line of definition. Word it as you may, it must be definitive on a subject on which there has hitherto been much latitude allowed. Definition must be either constructed with ambiguous and double meanings, or it must be so stringent as to exclude many who for three hundred years have been within the pale of the Church.

"Observe absence in the latter part of the Catechism of all question as to the benefits of Baptism. There are questions common to both sacraments: 1. What the outward sign. 2. What the inward grace. 3. What is required of persons baptized or communicating. But there is nothing to correspond as to Baptism with the question as to the Lord's Supper. What are the benefits whereof we are partakers thereby? Is not this a speaking silence?

"Putting forth a declaration a hazardous experiment.

"Signal for a war, into which worst passions on both sides would be brought into collision.

"Incalculably injurious to Church.

"Most prejudicial to true religion.

"Disturbing effect on consciences of a large number of clergy of various classes.

"A combined agreement on a theological point, cannot be issued by bishops, without its assuming a character of authority which would be deficient for good on account of its informality, and nevertheless would be abundantly powerful for evil in disturbing men's minds. It would be the shadow without the substance of power—a specious effort for peace, with only a spurious influence of sanction.

"Declaration of Her Majesty in the Convocation of 1562:

"'That for the present, though some differences have been ill-raised—yet we take comfort in this, that all clergymen within our realm have always most willingly subscribed to the articles established, which is an argument to us that they all agree in the true, usual, literal meaning of the said articles; and that even in those curious points in which the present differences lie, men of all sorts take the Articles of the Church of England to be for them, which is an argument again, that none of them intend any desertion of the articles established.

"'That therefore in these both curious and unhappy differences, which have for many hundred years, in different times and places, exercised the Church of Christ, We will therefore that all further curious research be laid aside, and these disputes shut up in God's promises, as they be generally set forth to us in the Holy Scriptures and the general meaning of the Articles of the Church of England,'" &c. &c. &c.

In the charge which the Bishop delivered in the autumn of this year, and which, as usual, bristled with diocesan statistics, he referred at considerable length to the Gorham case, and (rather contrary to his usual wont) expressed very fully his own views respecting infant Baptism. It may be well to give the passage in full:

"For myself, I can bless God with a thankful and a trusting heart, after the Baptism of the child, that it hath pleased God to regenerate him with His Holy Spirit, and receive him for His own child by adoption. I can believe in such a change of condition as must imply a participation in saving grace, and the remission of the guilt and penalty of original sin, though without freedom from remaining infection. I do not define too curiously the nature of that grace of which he is said to be made a child; nor would I insist on describing that regeneration of the Holy Spirit for which I am taught to yield hearty thanks to my most merciful Father as a germ or a spark. I would avoid, if possible, the use of material figures, not employed in this connexion by Holy Scripture, or grafted into the language of our Church, in the illustration of what is spiritual. It is sufficient for me, that I can believe with all my heart, that if it please God to deliver the infant out of the miseries of this sinful world, before he commit actual sin, he certainly will be saved ; and that if he come to age, on performance of the promises of repentance and faith made by his sureties, our Lord Jesus Christ will most surely keep and perform the promise of the blessings which on His part He has covenanted to grant. And it is quite consistent with this faith, that I also believe with the same steadfastness, that, notwithstanding this assurance, the child may be 'removed from Him who called him to grace' and fall from it ; he may 'make shipwreck of faith,' and that he assuredly will do so unless he 'work out his own salvation with fear and trembling' and 'give diligence to make his calling and election sure.' Nay, further, if he come to age, I must look, notwithstanding his Baptism, for the scriptural evidence of his being God's child, ere I can then believe him such—for 'we know that whosoever is born of God sinneth not ; but that he that is begotten of God, keepeth himself, and that wicked one toucheth him not.' I see no inconsistency in this, and I can acquiesce in it, without mistrust or doubting, as agreeable to the teaching of Holy Scripture and the Church."

The charge, from which the above extract is given, was delivered not only in Hants and Surrey, but (with additions of a local character) also in Jersey and Guernsey. The following letter from the Rev. T. Brock, Commissary of Guernsey, shows that the Bishop's frequent visits to the Channel Islands only endeared him more and more to their inhabitants.

" September 3rd, 1850.

" Well, the Episcopal visit is at an end, and I do not find myself the worse for it : whether it was the very great pleasure I experienced in the Bishop's company, or the many additional occupations it brought along with it, which left me no time to think of my *ailments,* it is certain that I felt comparatively well during the whole time of his sojourn at St. Peter's.

Nothing could exceed his kindness; it is impossible not to love him; he draws all hearts to himself. I believe he feels peculiarly at home in Guernsey, and not without reason, for here he is much beloved, and received with singular respect and deference. His ministrations were all that could be wished. I heard one of his sermons on Psalm xc. 12. It was most effective, and I hear the same report of the three other discourses which he delivered.

"The charge was everything you said of it, and gave every satisfaction to right-thinking minds. Nothing could exceed the *clearness* and *fairness* of what he said of our view of the baptismal question. I thanked God for it. The charge was heard with breathless attention, and particularly the part relative to the baptismal controversy. It was purely Protestant in its tone, and Christian in its spirit. We ought to praise God unceasingly for such a Bishop. May our Heavenly Father long preserve him to the Church. It has need of such men. The charge is to be published. I long to have it in my hands."—"Memoirs of Rev. T. Brock," p. 102.

During the whole spring of 1850 the Bishop kept himself, as much as a Bishop can do, in retirement. He attended no public meetings. With reference to one which was about to be held in favour of the Canterbury Settlement in New Zealand, he writes:—

"My name is attached to the Canterbury scheme, and I wish it more success than I anticipate for it. I do not see how the eclectic character of such a settlement can be preserved, as the world is constituted. You can send out none but members of our Church; but who shall say they shall remain such? What fetters are provided which shall restrain the located settlers' feet from straying beyond the boundaries into Popery towards the north or dissent on the south? And then, what writ of ejectment will cast him out of his cleared lands and prairie meadows? I fear the wheat and the tares must be content to grow together until the harvest."

But however much the Bishop may have longed for quiet, such a thing was impossible, for the year 1850 seems unfortunately to have been unusually prolific in ecclesiastical agitations. It was in the autumn of this year that what was commonly called the Papal aggression took place. For upwards of 200 years, the Roman Catholics in England had been ecclesiastically subject to Vicars Apostolic, *i.e.* Bishops with foreign titles named by the Pope. In 1840 the number of the Vicars Apostolic was increased from four to eight, and in 1847 these Vicars Apostolic sent two of their number as their representatives to Rome, in order to petition the Pope to change this form of government for that of Episcopacy with local titles. In consequence of this mission the necessary steps were taken by the Pope, and three years later he promulgated a Bull, by which England was parcelled out into dioceses, to be presided over by Roman Catholic bishops with territorial titles and jurisdiction. All England rose in just indignation at this aggressive act on the Pope's part. Addresses poured in upon the several bishops, couched in strong language, deprecating the Pope's action, and earnestly asking for counsel, and advice how to act under the circumstances. One of the Bishop of Winchester's replies is subjoined, as showing the strong view which he took of the matter, while at the same time he endeavoured to turn Rome's action to practical good, by urging upon the clergy the additional duty which devolved upon them, in consequence, of holding fast and pure their own reformed faith:

"FARNHAM CASTLE, *Nov. 13th*, 1850.

"REV. AND DEAR BRETHREN,

"It is with no ordinary feelings of satisfaction that I have received, through the medium of the Rural Dean, an address signed by more than 100 clergy in the deanery of Southwark, on the subject of the recent establishment of a Roman Catholic hierarchy in England.

"For the assurance of your continued respect and veneration for my office I desire to tender you my cordial thanks. On all occasions of emergency and difficulty, such an assurance on the part of the clergy of the diocese cannot fail to support and encourage their Bishop under the weighty responsibility devolving on him.

"I entirely concur in your view of the grave character of the measure lately taken by the Pope to extend his influence and authority in England. It appears to me equally to call for immediate remonstrance on our part, whether we regard it as an invasion of the Queen's supremacy, and an interference with the spiritual authority of the lawfully constituted bishops of our own branch of the Catholic Church; or whether we reflect on the lamentable consequences, which have not escaped your own observation, as likely to ensue—the disturbance of the peace of the Church—the revival of painful superstitions—and the substitution of unscriptural corruptions in the place of the pure Gospel.

"However little prepared the country may have been for such an assumption of unauthorised power, it is placed now beyond a doubt, that whereas the claims of the Roman Pontiff to universal jurisdiction continue unabated, so they will be advanced from the present moment with unwonted vigour. No other course, therefore, remains for us, but to enter our uncompromising protest both against the errors of Romish doctrine and the claims of the Papal See to pre-eminence and authority within this realm—pretensions at once opposed to the spirit of our Constitution, to Church and State, and dangerous to the purity of our faith.

"With this persuasion, I gladly undertake to convey to Her Majesty the address you have entrusted to me for that purpose. As regards the course most proper to be taken to arrest the evil we are agreed in deprecating, we have been informed, on high authority, that this will form the subject of immediate and grave deliberation. For my own part, I cannot doubt that the chief ministers of a Sovereign, who holds it as one of her most glorious attributes that she is 'Defender of the Faith,' will be forward,

not only in vindicating the rights of our Church and State—
inseparably interwoven—but in maintaining also, so far as in
them lies, the integrity of our Protestant faith.

"And if from them, the lay servants of the Crown, we expect
no less, the country will justly expect of you, the ordained
ministers of the Church, that you, for your part, should be unceasing in ' your labour, your care, and diligence, until you have
done all that lieth in you, according to your bounden duty, to
bring all such as are or shall be committed to your charge unto
that agreement in the faith and knowledge of God, and to that
ripeness and perfectness of age in Christ, that there be no place
left among you either for error in religion or viciousness in life.'

" In truth, I should be wanting to my own sense of duty if I
did not seize the present moment affectionately to press this
exhortation upon your consciences, and to beseech you not to
leave any room for suspicion that there are any among us who
desire to return, or to approximate, however remotely, to the
corruptions of Rome, once solemnly renounced by our ancestors
at the Reformation.

"I may repeat to you what I have already addressed to
another influential body of the clergy of my diocese, that the
duty of separation from her communion, as well in external ·
forms as in vital doctrine, which made the Reformation necessary,
still presses on us as forcibly as ever.　And if, in times like the
present, this duty be neglected, or imperfectly discharged, we
must not be surprised if the true character of our ministers is
called in question, and the soundness of our faith exposed to
natural, if not to just suspicion.

" Suffer this word of exhortation with which I commend you
heartily to the grace and blessing of our Lord and Saviour, Jesus
Christ.

" I am, &c.

" C. R. WINTON."

After his episcopal ministrations in the Channel Islands, in
the autumn, the Bishop paid a very interesting visit to the

Bishop of Coutances.   Crossing, with his eldest son as chaplain, to Granville, they drove thence to Coutances.   The Curé of Granville, a very handsome and courteous man, met them as they got out of the carriage, and said that the Bishop of Coutances would be ready to receive his English brother at three o'clock.   At the time appointed the Bishop and his chaplain repaired to the episcopal palace, and were ushered into an oak-panelled library.   They found the Bishop of Coutances evidently prepared to receive them, dressed in his purple cassock.   One of the canons of the cathedral was by his side as chaplain.   The French Prelate came forward and greeted the Bishop of Winchester most courteously, and an hour's conversation followed.   He reminded him that Jersey was at one time in the diocese over which he presided, and asked a great many questions respecting the Church of England.   The whole interview was of a very pleasant character, and at the close the two Bishops shook hands cordially, the Bishop of Coutances saying: "Nous sommes frères, Milord;" to which the Bishop of Winchester responded heartily, "frères en Jésus Christ, j'espère."

This interview with the Bishop of Coutances was an episode in an unusually lengthened period of incessant engagements. He seems to have felt the strain upon him more than he usually did, probably owing to his previous domestic trial, and on his return home he thus writes to Coleridge :—

"FARNHAM CASTLE, *Nov. 5th*, 1850.

"MY DEAR COLERIDGE,

". . . . Your account of yourself does not satisfy me. I am unwilling to think or say of either you or Patteson—*tempus abire*—and yet, when I look at myself and feel my years, I cannot but be conscious that *non sumus quales*, as regards any of us. But I earnestly hope God will yet lend you strength of body and mind.   I returned home on Saturday after an uninterrupted work of three months and one week *de die in diem* with at least two public duties per day during the whole time, not excepting Sundays. There is too much wear and tear in this for any age, and far too much for mine; but it was a matter of necessity, and I am thankful to say that, although I have felt it, I am not otherwise than well.

"Your most affectionate friend,

"C. WINTON."

CHAPTER XX.

THE commencement of the year 1851 brings us back from
Rome and the Papal Aggression to dangers even still nearer
home. The ritual question began to assume a prominence
which it had not hitherto occupied. The disputes in connection with St. Paul's, Knightsbridge, had much inflamed the
public mind, and Lord John Russell's celebrated Durham letter
had roused Protestant enthusiasm throughout the country.
After long and anxious deliberation on the part of the bishops,
they resolved to issue a pastoral to the clergy in hopes of
allaying the prevalent excitement. This pastoral was signed
by all the bishops on the bench, with the exception of those
of Bath and Wells, Exeter, Hereford, and Manchester. The
pastoral was as follows :—

"We, the undersigned Archbishops and Bishops of the Pro-
vinces of Canterbury and York, do most earnestly and affectionately commend the following address to the serious consideration
of the clergy of our respective dioceses :—

[Here follow the signatures.]

"BELOVED BRETHREN,
      "We have viewed with the deepest anxiety, the

troubles, suspicions, and discontents which have of late, in some parishes, accompanied the introduction of ritual observances exceeding those in common use amongst us.

"We long indulged the hope that under the influence of charity, forbearance, and a calm estimate of the small importance of such external forms, compared with the blessing of united action in the great spiritual work which is before our Church, these heats and jealousies might, by mutual concessions, be allayed. But since the evil still exists, and in one most important feature, has assumed a new and more dangerous character, we feel that it is our duty to try, whether an earnest and united address on our part may tend, under the blessing of God, to promote the restoration of peace and harmony in the Church.

"The principal point in dispute is this :—whether, when the letter of the rubric seems to warrant a measure of ritual observance, which yet by long, and possibly by unbroken practice, has not been carried out, the clergy are either in conscience required, or absolutely at liberty, to act each upon his own view of the letter of the precept, rather than by the rule of common practice. Now, as to this question, we would urge upon you the following considerations :—first, that any change of usages with which the religious feelings of a congregation have become associated is in itself so likely to do harm, that it is not to be introduced without the greatest caution. Secondly, that beyond this, any change which makes it difficult for the congregation at large to join in the service is still more to be avoided. Thirdly, that any change which suggests the fear of still further alterations is most injurious: and fourthly, that according to the rule laid down in the Book of Common Prayer, when anything is doubtful or diversely taken, 'concerning the manner how to understand, do, and execute the things contained in that Book, the parties that so doubt or diversely take anything, shall always resort to the Bishop of the diocese, who by his discretion shall take order for the quieting and

appeasing of the same, so that the same order be not contrary
to anything contained in that book.'

"The fair application of these principles would, we believe,
solve most of the difficulties which have arisen. It would
prevent all sudden and startling alterations; and it would
facilitate the reception of any change which was really lawful
and desirable. We would therefore, first, urge upon our
Reverend Brethren, with affectionate earnestness, the adoption
of such a rule of conduct. We would beseech all who, whether
by excess or defect, have broken in upon the uniformity and
contributed to relax the authority of our ritual observances, to
consider the importance of unity and order, and by common
consent to avoid whatever might tend to violate them. In
recommending this course as the best under present circumstances, we do not shut our eyes to the evil of even the appearance of any discrepancy existing between the written law and
the practice of the Church. But there are many cases where
the law may be variously interpreted; and we believe that
we are best carrying out her own principles, in urging you to
have recourse, in all such cases, to the advice of her chief
Pastors.

"But beyond mere attempts to restore an unusual strictness
of ritual observance, we have to deal with a distinct and
serious evil. A principle has of late been avowed and acted
on, which, if admitted, would justify far greater and more
uncertain changes. It is this: That, as the Church of England is the ancient Catholic Church settled in this land before
the Reformation, and was then reformed only by the casting
away of certain strictly defined corruptions; therefore, whatever form, or usage, existed in the Church before its Reformation, may now be freely introduced and observed, unless there
can be alleged against it the distinct letter of some formal
prohibition.

"Now, against any such inference from the undoubted
identity of the Church before and after the Reformation, we

feel bound to enter our clear and unhesitating protest. We believe that at the Reformation, the English Church not only rejected certain corruptions, but also, without in any degree severing her connexion with the ancient Catholic Church, intended to establish one uniform ritual, according to which her public services should be conducted. But it is manifest that a licence, such as is contended for, is wholly incompatible with any uniformity of worship whatsoever, and at variance with the universal practice of the Catholic Church, which has never given to the officiating ministers of separate congregations any such large discretion in the selection of ritual observances.

"We therefore beseech any who may have proposed to themselves the restoration of what, under sanction of this principle, they deemed a lawful system, to consider the dangers which it involves; to see it in its true light, and to take a more just and sober view of the real position of our Church; whilst, with equal earnestness, we beseech others who, either by intentional omission, or by neglect and laxity, may have disturbed the uniformity and weakened the authority of our prescribed ritual, to strengthen the side of order by avoiding all unnecessary deviations from the Church's rule.

"Such harmony of action, we are persuaded, would under God's blessing go far towards restoring the peace of the Church. This happy result would more clearly exhibit her spiritual character. The mutual relations of her various members would be more distinctly perceived: and our Lay brethren would more readily acknowledge the special trust committed to us, as stewards of the mysteries of God, 'for the edifying of the body of Christ.' They would join with us in asserting, and, if need be, defending for themselves, as much as for us, the true spiritual freedom of the Church. They would unite with us in a more trustful spirit, and therefore with a more ready will, in enlarging her means, and strengthening her powers for the great work she has to do amongst the swarming multitudes of our great towns at home, and of our vast dominions abroad ; and that Church which has so long received from the hands of God such unequalled blessings, might continue to be, yea and become more and more, 'a praise in the earth.' "

In sending this Pastoral to each clergyman in his diocese, the Bishop added a few earnest words of his own, endorsing its sentiments, and expressing his thankfulness at the comparative freedom from divisions which the diocese of Winchester had been permitted to enjoy.

The Bishop's usual time of residence in London this year was saddened by the death of his daughter-in-law, the wife of the Rev. Robert Sumner. She was laid prostrate by fever, caught in nursing her husband who had been seized with illness whilst on a visit at Winchester House, and when he returned to consciousness, after lying for a considerable time hovering between life and death, he awoke to the sad knowledge that he was a widower ! His wife was the second daughter of Sir Richard Simeon, Bart., of Swainston in the Isle of Wight. Their union had been one of much happiness for the five short years of their married life. She was a person of an angelic temper, eminently calculated to bring sunshine to her husband's home, and when on the 23rd of April it pleased God to take her to Himself, leaving three infant children, her loss was deeply felt, not only by her bereaved husband, but by every member of the family.

It must have been rather trying for the Bishop to be called upon to pay so much attention, as from time to time he was obliged to do, to the business of the Colleges of which he was ex-officio visitor. No doubt it brought him into communication with some of the *élite* of the University, but still, when diocesan business was so incessant and so urgent, he must have found it hard to be forced to devote himself for a time to a wholly alien subject. Such was the case at the very beginning of the year 1853, when he went to pass a few days

with the President of Trinity, in order to confer face to face
with the authorities of some of the Colleges on various matters
respecting which he was called upon to advise.   With reference
to his visit, he writes :—

"All has passed satisfactorily,—and I am not without real
hope that good will be done both at ——— and at ———. At
the latter College a committee sits three times a week, engaged
in drawing up a scheme to be submitted to me, and they have
invited communications from all the non-residents, which looks
like meaning work. . . . On Monday I met at dinner at the
President's house the officers of the College—on Tuesday dined
in Hall—on Wednesday again in the President's lodgings with
Vice-Chancellor, Heads of Oriel, Wadham, All Souls, Thompson
and McBride (very amusing), Claughton (come up for a select
preacher's sermon, &c., &c. Gladstone is in Oxford to-day
(Jacobson's guest)."

Shortly after this visit to the University, it appears that some
complaints were made to the Bishop of Oxford, to the effect
that those who had been ordained by him on their titles as
Fellows of Colleges, were refused admittance into the diocese of
Winchester as curates. The Bishop of Oxford was naturally
anxious to know from the best authority whether such statements were correct, and, in reply the Bishop thus laid down his
course of action.

"I have no peculiar rule applicable to College titles. The
regulation of my diocese, not a new one, but that on which I
have acted ever since I have had its administration, is to admit
no clergy ordained in other dioceses until after the expiration
of two years, unless in exceptional cases, such as the death of
the incumbent and the like. You will remember a case which
happened some time ago, about which I spoke to you. Two
more have recently occurred, in the instances of deacons said to
have been ordained at your last Christmas ordination, who,
within a month or little more, were nominated to curacies in
Surrey. I should not have received persons from other dioceses

A A 2

under similar circumstances, and I cannot make an exception in favour of yours, and especially of College titles, which I consider to be only legitimate for persons intending to reside in College, or at least not intending at present to enter upon a parochial cure. I have had no direct communication from either of the two deacons to whom I have referred. Of one, nominated by ——, I do not remember the name. But he was stated to me to have been staying since his ordination with a clerical friend, I think in the north of England, and assisting him, and therefore obviously not engaged in College life. The other was Mr. ——, represented as having been ordained last Christmas. It would seem from your letter that this was incorrect; and if he was ordained on a College title two years ago, no objection applies to him."

It was in the summer of this year that the camp at the Chobham ridges was formed. This was called at the time "a grand military picnic," but it has turned out to have been much more than this, for though the encampment was temporary in 1853, it originated the idea of the establishment of the permanent camp at Aldershot. Chobham is within easy reach of Farnham, and the Bishop took much interest in the movement. He writes to his friend Dallas, who had served in the Peninsular war :—

"Farnham Castle, July 12th, 1853.

"My dear Dallas,

        "Will you come to us on Monday next, with Mrs. Dallas, your daughters and their respective husbands, and stay on as far in the week as you can? You will then be able to go over to the camp very conveniently from hence, and can act as my A.D.C. instead of A.C.D., and in the place of Colonel le Couteur, Q.A.D.C. on my last (and first) occasion of campaigning. It is impossible to exaggerate the interest of the field to a layman. What it must be to a veteran with clasps I can scarcely conceive . . . . Bishop McIlvaine is a man of a thousand; he unites a force and unction which are rarely found

together. And she is worthy of him . . . . as decided as
gentle. She is very like Mrs. Francis Cunningham, and it is
difficult to believe she has not Gurney blood in her veins.

" Very affectionately yours,

" C. WINTON.

"Rev. A. C. DALLAS,

   "A.D.C., etc."

An interesting event occurred in the summer of this year, by
which the Bishop was once more brought into connection with
the congregation of the British residents in Geneva. In 1846
a Committee had been appointed for the purpose of raising
funds for the building of a church in that town. The Bishop of
Winchester had laid the first stone of it on October 1, 1851 ;
and when, in the year 1853, it was declared to be ready for
consecration, a petition was presented to the Bishop of London,
requesting that his Lordship would allow his Brother of Winchester to officiate at the opening ceremony.

The Committee wrote to the Bishop of London—

" Grateful for the patronage and liberal support which your
Lordship has bestowed on the undertaking, we should feel
highly gratified by your Lordship's presiding at that sacred ceremony, but at the same time we deem it due to your Lordship
to state, that the circumstance of the Lord Bishop of Winchester
having been instrumental in re-establishing the Church in 1814
and being its first officiating Chaplain, together with his
uniform support and solicitude for its well-being, which has
marked its progress from that period to the present day—the
close family connexion and other associations that render
Geneva an object of interest to his Lordship, and the fact of his
having laid the first stone of the edifice, all combine to create a
general desire among the British residents at Geneva, that your
Lordship should be solicited under these peculiar claims on their
gratitude and esteem, to waive your right on this occasion, and
depute to the Lord Bishop of Winchester the privilege of

officiating at the consecration of the church. The Committee, aware that your Lordship can appreciate from experience the associations that connect and the esteem and regard that unite a grateful congregation to an estimable pastor, and a long-tried friend, trust that the feelings resulting therefrom will plead their excuse for thus making known to your Lordship the generally expressed sentiment of the English residents at Geneva."

The church, dedicated to the Holy Trinity, was consecrated on the thirtieth of August, and we can well conceive that the Bishop's feelings must have been stirred to their very depths by the revival of old associations. Ever since the days of his chaplaincy in 1815, the services had been carried on in the same building as that in which he had ministered. But now the ark was no longer to dwell in tabernacles, and the services at the Hospital chapel would be classed with the memories of by-gone days. Unfortunately, in connection with the service of consecration, disputes arose, which at the time caused a good deal of acrimonious feeling. The Genevese Committee were placed in circumstances of considerable difficulty. The National Church was more or less tinged with Arianism. Many of the pastors of the National Church distinctly repudiated Arianism, but the *litera scripta* of their catechism was clearly opposed to the doctrine of the Blessed Trinity as held by the Church Catholic. From this Church a body of men had seceded in 1830, represented by Merle D'Aubigné, Gaussen, and others, who had carried on their worship apart from the National Church, holding views on the subject of the Blessed Trinity in accordance with our own. The Committee felt bound by ties of gratitude to the Genevese Government. For eight and thirty years the chapel of the Hospital had been freely lent to the English congregation for the purposes of worship by the Government—the site for the new church had been presented, and every aid afforded by them from the commencement to the completion of the work. The Bishop therefore felt, with the Committee, that after having been thus assisted by the Government in the day of their need, it would be wrong to ignore their existence altogether on the day of consecration. The Committee, therefore, were unanimous in agreeing as to the necessity of inviting the Councils of State of the town and canton of Geneva and the National Church—and they were equally unanimous in inviting the Pastors of the Oratoire or Free Evangelical Church. Unhappily, the latter declined to be present at the service. Had they been there, they would have seen no "identification of the Church of England with local Protestantism," as was alleged in one of the newspapers of the day. It is hardly necessary to say that not one iota of the usual ritual of the Church of England at such a service was altered, and the pastors of the National Church heard the doctrines in dispute faithfully and uncompromisingly treated in the Bishop's consecration sermon. It is too long for insertion here, but it may be advisable to give a few extracts from it. He chose for his text 2 Thess. iii. 1.

"Finally, brethren, pray for us, that the word of the Lord may have free course, and be glorified, even as it is with you."

After referring to the peculiarity of the circumstances under which they had met together, and the building of the house of the Lord in a strange though friendly land, the Bishop proceeded to point out that from time to time false prophets had arisen, professing to speak the word of the Lord, but which was, in truth, " another Gospel."

"But if all this be not the word, where shall we find it, where hear it, how recognize it ?   That word, the true word, might have been caught by a listening ear when the heavens opened of old, and a Voice was heard testifying to Him who was Himself the Word from the beginning, with God, and God, very God, God over all, blessed for ever: 'This is my beloved Son, in whom I am well pleased, hear ye Him.' His was the word of the Lord—*the* word, the Gospel. And it might have been heard again in that, the latest commission bequeathed to the Apostles : ' Go ye therefore, and teach all nations, baptizing them in the name of the Father, and of the Son, and of the Holy Ghost.' And this is the very warrant for our churches. They are for the promulgation of the word of the Lord. This very church is to be a remembrancer for Him. It is to proclaim that His word is truth, and to pray that that word may edify the worshipper. 'Sanctify them through Thy Word.' And the successive ministers who henceforth, in God's providence, are to serve here, will be sent with a special injunction as to their delivery of this only message: 'Take thou authority to preach the word of God.' Not their own word—no word of omission, no word of supererogation, no word of adulteration or mystification, but the word of God, which is able to make men wise unto salvation, through faith which is in Christ Jesus. For other preaching they have no license. If they lay other foundation it is in contravention of their credentials. Our Church's commission is explicit and exclusive : take thou authority to preach the word of God. .

" And this, be it observed, in passing, is exactly in accordance, as it should be, with the Apostolic injunction to Timothy ;. ' I charge thee before God, and the Lord Jesus Christ, who shall judge the quick and the dead at His appearing and His kingdom ; Preach the Word.' And if any ask, 'What is the word?' I answer in the Apostle's own definition—which none can safely gainsay—'The word is nigh thee, even in thy mouth and in thine heart, that is, the word of faith which we preach, that if thou shalt confess with thy mouth the Lord Jesus, and shalt believe in thine heart that God hath raised Him from the dead thou shalt be saved ;' or yet more specifically : 'This is the record, that God hath given to us eternal life, and this life is in His Son. He that hath the Son hath life ; and he that hath not the Son of God hath not life.'"

After having enlarged on the fact that the word must have free course and be glorified, the Bishop concluded by a close personal appeal to the individual members of the congregation The word must be productive of holiness of life ; and yet the work within—the work of the Spirit who sanctifies—must be clearly distinguished from the work without, which is perfect in itself—Christ our righteousness. Finally, they were to strive to attain to that unity of spirit which shall one day pervade the whole heavenly temple. "All nations and kindreds shall be before the throne, and yet all one body. The same spirit, the same zeal, the same confession of ·faith, the same ascription of glory, the same loud voice 'saying Amen: Blessing, and glory, and wisdom, and thanksgiving, and honour, and power, and might, be unto our God for ever and ever.' Strive to breathe on earth something of heaven's atmosphere, and to realise more of the unity of the spirit in the bond of peace— that so you may henceforth be all of one heart and of one soul, united in one holy bond of truth and peace, of faith and charity, and may with one mind and one mouth glorify God through Jesus Christ our Lord."

A meeting was held after the conclusion of the service at the English Club, when a congratulatory address was presented to the Bishop on behalf of the English residents in Geneva, expressing the sense of their great satisfaction that he had been permitted to consecrate the church that day. His speech in reply is thus epitomised in the *Revue de Genève*, of September 2, 1853 :—

"Sa Grâce l'Evêque de Winchester répondit à l'adresse qu'on lui avait faite avec des paroles qui laissaient voir son émotion. Il fit allusion à son ministère à Genève, aux souvenirs chéris que la vue de cette ville réveillait en lui, après l'expiration de tant d'années, et au plaisir qu'il éprouvait de revoir des lieux qui ont pour lui un intérêt si profond, et il dit qu'il espérait pouvoir considérer cet augure heureux et propice, que, sur ce jour, comme sur celui qu'avait eu lieu la cérémonie de poser la première pierre de l'église, le Mont-Blanc était sorti du milieu des nuages et de l'obscurité dont il était auparavant enveloppé et s'était montré dans toute sa brillante beauté, emblème juste et frappant de la pureté de notre foi. Il exprima aussi le

profond intérêt que Sa Grâce l'Evêque de Londres prend au
bien-être de l'Eglise de Genève et son désir de l'avancer de tout
son pouvoir présent et dans l'avenir.   Il applaudit beaucoup à
la conduite du Comité et du Chapelain."

In the summer of 1854 the experience of the military
authorities at the Horseguards of the good effected by the
encampment at Chobham, led them to establish at Aldershot a
permanent military camp.   Those who only know Aldershot,
the Long valley, and Cocked Hat wood, in connection with
reviews, will find it difficult to realise the fact that, before the
establishment of the camp, Aldershot was nothing but a small
rural village, in the neighbourhood of which grouse and
occasionally black game were found.   But with the camp all
was changed ; rows of houses were quickly built, and a town
seemed to spring up full-grown at once.   The Bishop was not
slack in showing hospitality to the officers quartered at Aldershot.   The staff-officers, those in command, and any who
brought letters of introduction, were always welcome at the
Castle, and doubtless many, even now, of those who were then
partakers of the Bishop's hospitality, will not altogether have
forgotten the pleasant parties, when some forty guests would sit
down in the old Castle Hall, military and civilians mingled
together.   It was the wish of the general in command, that on
these occasions the officers should appear in uniform, and few
prettier sights could be seen than that afforded by the brilliant
colours of the military dresses mingling with those of the fairer
sex, and interspersed with the more sombre hues of clerical
attire.   Perhaps some who read these words may yet recall the
central figure, as of one who was exceeded by none as a host
of most winning manners, and, by his courtesy, charming all
invited to partake of the hospitalities of his table.

Hitherto, since Mrs. Sumner's death, the Bishop's youngest
daughter, Emily, had taken her place as the head of his household.   There was some fear lest this arrangement should ere
long come to an end, for, in the summer of 1854, she was

engaged to the Rev. Robert Milford.   Happily, however, he was enabled subsequently to reside at Farnham Castle as domestic Chaplain, and thus enable the Bishop for a short time longer to enjoy the comfort of his daughter's presence with him.   The Bishop thus alludes to the engagement :—

"You will readily imagine how full my heart is of various conflicting feelings, and how, at such times as these, and in such circumstances, I feel at every moment of the day and night what it is to be 'alone.'   But I desire to be trustful for the future, as I have reason to be thankful for the past."

This event gave rise to some graceful lines of poetry written by Dr. Hawtrey, who happened to be staying at the Castle shortly after the engagement was announced.

AUGUST, 1854.

On a Tree in the Garden of Farnham Castle, which is saved from falling by the strong Stem of the Ivy, which wholly covers the Trunk with its Foliage.

Ἤνιδε πῶς φύλλοις ταννήκεσιν ἠρέμα κίσσος
ἑρπύζει, δένδρον—παῖς ἅπερ—ἄγκας ἔχων,
στηρίξας δ' εὖ ῥίζαν ἐνὶ χθονὶ τοῦ προκλιθέντος—
οἷον ἔρεισμ'—ἔχεται, τόν τε τρέφοντα τρέφει,
ἀλλὰ σὺ—δισσὸν ἔρεισμα σὺν ἀνέρι—τὸν φίλον οὕτως
οὐ προλιποῦσ', Ἐρατοῖ, στέρξον ἀεὶ πατέρα.

Non vedi come l' edera
   Nel freddo e nel calor
   Coi fogli suoi quell' albero
   Circonda verde ancor !
Egli già crolla invalido,
   Ma la radice tien
   Ella ognor ferma, e al languido
   Tronco in ajuto vien.

Lo vedi—e allora, Emilia,
   L' avviso ch' ei ti da,—
   S'io'l dico, ben m' imaggino,
   Che 'l cor telo dirà.
"Fa collo sposo un doppio
   "Sostegno al patrio amor,
   "Ferma—e non meno amabile
   "Nel frutto che nel fior."

Vois-tu cet arbre avec ce lierre,
  Qui, toujours vert, toujours le tient
  Dans son feuillage, et de la terre
  Le tronc, qui chancele, soutient !

Émilie, ce que tu dois faire
  Tu l'y vois bien—et ton ami.
  Avec lui cheris ton père ;
  Fais qu'il en trouve un double appui.

Seest thou yon Tree with Ivy bound
  Through Summer's Heat and Winter's Rain,
Whose Stems fast rooted in the Ground
  The falling Trunk alone sustain ?

Full well I know whose gentle Mind
  Will read a Moral in the Tree ;
And two Supports thy Sire will find
  Still bound to married Emily.

In the autumn of the year, for the seventh time, the Bishop addressed his clergy in Visitation assembled. He pre-fixed as a heading to his charge, "The Home Work of the Parochial Ministry," and this title sufficiently describes its main features. There was the less reason why he should, as on former occasions, give many diocesan statistics, because at the same time he printed for private circulation amongst the clergy a "Conspectus of the Diocese of Winchester," which showed in a tabular form the existing provision in the diocese, as regarded external machinery, for carrying on the work of the ministry of the Church. The Conspectus showed the wonderful knowledge which the Bishop undoubtedly possessed of the minutest details connected with the parochial work of each parish in the diocese. Tables were prepared by himself, showing at a glance, in every instance, when and at what cost the church, school, and parsonage were built, re-built, or enlarged, as the case might be, and with regard to the churches, with what amount of accommodation.

From the Conspectus it appeared that at the beginning of the present century the population of Hampshire was 219,290, which in 1851 had increased to 401,377. Surrey showed a still greater increase. In 1801 the population was 268,233, and in 1851, 681,244.

The following extract from the Conspectus gives the details both as to churches and schools :—

" The tabular statement now printed, exhibits a list of sixty-one additional churches in Hampshire, and of seventy-one in Surrey, total, 132, of which 114 have been erected since 1830. In Hampshire fifty-two ancient churches have been re-built, and twenty-seven in Surrey, total, 79; of which sixty-three since 1830. In the two counties 254 other churches (Hants 147, Surrey 107) have been enlarged.

" The expenditure on churches in Hants has been £435,844, of which £365,929, since 1830; and in Surrey, £739,502, of which £517,148 since 1830—or in the two counties, since the same period, £883,077.

" In Hants forty-six additional churchyards, and in Surrey twenty-eight, total 74, have been consecrated.

" In Hampshire 217 schools have been built, and thirty-nine enlarged; in Surrey 169 built, and forty-one enlarged since 1830.

" In Hampshire 101 new parsonages have been built, and eighty-three improved, at a cost of £212,934; and in Surrey fifty-six parsonages have been built, and fifty-five improved, for the sum of £150,315. . . .

" Within the last twenty-three years, therefore, not less than a million and a half have been expended on churches, schools, and parsonages, being at the rate of more than £65,000 per annum."

Details follow respecting work in progress, both as regarded churches and schools, and the Bishop concludes thus :—

" We look with thankfulness on these signs of life. There is in them much of hopefulness and of encouragement, and in contemplating them, we thank God and take courage. But whether in our retrospect or prospect, we desire to remember that something more than the sound of the axe and the hammer is wanted. This is external. There must be the inner man. This is the spreading of the fleece; there must be the dew from heaven to moisten it. This is but the sending of Apollos to plant and Cephas to water; but God must be with them to give the increase. This is but the machinery; we want the motive power. Our buildings and re-buildings—our numerical array of workmen on the city's walls—our multiplication of schools and training of teachers, and all the accessories of our educational apparatus are as vain as the ancient defences of Jewry against the Persian invaders, if, as then, there be only a numbering of the houses of Jerusalem, and a breaking down of the houses to fortify the wall, without any looking unto the Maker thereof, or any respect unto Him that fashioned it long ago, without faith in the grace given in the Divine ordinances, and without subordinating all our learning, of whatever kind, to that fear of the Lord which is the beginning of knowledge. 'Except the Lord keep the House, they labour in vain that build it. Prosper thou the work of our hands upon us! O prosper thou our handywork!'"

CHAPTER XXI.

In the autumn of 1855 the Bishop (after spending some
weeks in the Channel Islands, where, as usual, he was enthu-
siastically received, but almost overdone with work*) much
enjoyed three weeks' holiday on the Continent. Crossing over
from Jersey to St. Malo, accompanied by one of his sons and
his daughter-in-law, he confirmed both at St. Servan and
Dinant, and thence proceeded to Nantes. Here he was joined
by his old friend Mr. Dallas, who, having served as an officer
in the British army during the Peninsular war, had promised
to act as cicerone to his Bishop during a short tour in Spain.

Passing through Bordeaux, the Bishop tarried for a day at
Bayonne, and greatly enjoyed the exquisite scenery there.
The views on the Adour with the lovely background of the
Pyrenees, formed a striking contrast to the sandy desert of the

---

* On his return home he writes : "I have been laid up with a very severe
sore throat, which *more suo* prostrated me. . . . I am now all right again, but
only allowed to use my throat in public for necessary purposes. The truth is, it
did half a year's honest work in my five weeks in the Channel Islands, and
might fairly have stopped payment before without giving just cause of complaint."

Landes district. When, however, the party had crossed the
Bidassoa, they found that the cholera was raging throughout the
North of Spain. At St. Jean de Luz the horses of the carriage
were changed outside the town, which was then traversed at
full gallop, the bell of the principal church tolling dismally all
the time. It appeared that out of a population of 700 souls, no
fewer than 152 had died in twenty-one days. At the next
village there were two huge piles of lime burning for the purposes of fumigation. The Bishop passed a Sunday at St. Sebastian. He was told that the authorities would not allow any
but a Roman Catholic service to be held in the town, but,
notwithstanding this warning, the Bishop invited a few English
who were there to meet in his sitting-room, and join with
him in the accustomed services of our Church. It was discovered afterwards that during the whole time, an Alguazil had
been keeping watch outside the door, with what object it would
be difficult to say ! The Bishop had intended to have gone on
to Madrid, but finding that the cholera was raging as violently
there as on the frontier, he reluctantly retraced his steps, and
returned home viâ Paris. He writes to Mrs. Dallas, from Farnham, on September 13, 1855 :—

"With very many thanks for the loan of your husband, I
send him back to you refreshed, I trust, in spirit, and, as I hope,
unharmed in body, by our trip. As regards this latter item, in
God's many mercies you will learn that it is not among the least,
as we have been much amongst the dead and dying. But, thanks
to His Fatherly protection, no harm has come nigh us. . . .
I need not tell you that his companionship has been delightful
to us, useful and interesting, and exciting in a thousand ways,
and especially in the recital of the scenes of his soldierly days
on the very sites themselves."

The Bishop's holidays were, in the true sense of the word,
times of recreation, for his return home was always a fresh
starting point of renewed diocesan work. He thus writes to
Coleridge shortly after his arrival from the Continent :—

"STRATTON PARK, ANDOVER ROAD, *October* 31, 1855.

" MY DEAR COLERIDGE,

"I heartily congratulate you on another grandchild.
. . . . Your grandpaternal quiver is not yet stocked with as
many arrows as mine, as I might shoot, I believe, thirty-three
times without borrowing a feather from you, or picking my own
up again for a second shot. But neither of our families have
been unpatriotic in this respect, and possibly your tortoise may
yet overtake my hare . . . I am in the midst of daily Diocesan
employments of various kinds—for they multiply like thirst for
the waters, *quo plus sunt potæ*. And the sad case of the Bishop
of London* warns me not to delay doing what I can while I can.
A few days before his seizure he wrote to me speaking of the
improvement in his general health, though not of his eyes. But
he was staying with me at Farnham just before he went abroad,
and I thought ill of him then. I cannot say how I am grieved
by this attack, which, whatever be its immediate issue, must
put an end to his usefulness. . . . .

" Ever very affectionately yours,

" C. WINTON."

At the beginning of 1856, rumours were current that the
Bishop was contemplating a second marriage. There was not
the smallest foundation for such a report, and in writing to
Coleridge he thus emphatically contradicts it :—

"FARNHAM CASTLE, *February 9th*, 1856.

" I have just learnt from Charles that Patteson has asked him
whether there is any foundation for a rumour which has reached
his ears (*mirabile*) that I am about to be married. As you
will suppose, I have authorised him to say that there is not the
shadow of a shade of a foundation for such a report. Be so
good as to tell Patteson this from me, with my love. I find

---

* On Oct. 21, the Bishop of London, after having preached in Fulham
Church, was seized with an attack of a paralytic nature.

that, not satisfied with marrying me, I am to be a polygamist, for three ladies are said to be named, two of whom I never saw n my life, and one of whose existence I was ignorant. What next, and who next ? No,

> ' I would not change my buried love
> For any heart of living mould,'

even if there were not warnings enough within me and around me to tell me that mine is not a time for marrying and giving in marriage. Within the last few days another has gone, as a remembrancer for me — the Bishop of Carlisle,[*] once my colleague at Canterbury, and afterwards beginning Episcopal life at the same time with myself. And yet he was not that member of our bench who might have been expected to go first, with London, Durham, Bangor, Gloucester, and Norwich, all *hors de combat*, to say nothing of Ely and Peterborough."

At the close of the year, the diocese was considerably disturbed by the controversy which arose with reference to the Sacrament of the Lord's Supper. The first stage of the suit of " Ditcher *v.* Denison " came to a conclusion on October 22, 1856, when Dr. Lushington, one of the assessors of the Archbishop of Canterbury, pronounced judgment to the effect, "that the doctrines maintained in the passages contained in the sermons of the Venerable Archdeacon . . . . . are directly contrary and repugnant to the 28th and 29th of the articles of religion. . . . . ."[†]

Some of the clergy of the diocese were much disturbed at

---

[*] Percy.

[†] From this sentence Archdeacon Denison appealed to the Arches Court of Canterbury, and on April 23, 1857, Sir J. Dodson pronounced judgment in favour of the Archdeacon, on the ground that the suit had not been instituted against him until more than two years had elapsed since the alleged offence. Mr. Ditcher appealed to the Judicial Committee, and on Feb. 6, 1858, that Court confirmed the decision of the Arches upon the legal objection taken to the prosecution, without reaching, and therefore without giving any opinion on, the merits of the case. This objection had been taken before, and had been over-ruled by Dr. Lushington.

this. To one who had sent to the Bishop a printed protest against the judgment, he writes :—

"FARNHAM CASTLE, *October 28th*, 1856.

"DEAR SIR,

"I have received the paper, to which your name is appended, referred to in your letter of the 23rd inst. I am at all times willing to receive communications from any of the clergy of my diocese tending to the relief of their minds and the removal of perplexities. But I must confess myself at a loss to conceive how sending me the printed statement in question can tend to reconcile you to your present position, if you feel your teaching condemned by the recent judgment. I am not sure that I comprehend your purpose ; but I must state distinctly, that I consider it no part of my office to receive protests against authorised sentences of the Church's courts; and therefore, if such is the intention of your declaration, that I cannot receive it in this sense. I must just remark that it does not seem to me to be a fair statement of the late decision to describe it as 'the only allowable interpretation of the Thirty-nine Articles on the Sacrament of the Lord's Supper.' The decision simply amounts to this, that a particular state-ment of doctrine is not allowable.

"I am, your very faithful servant,

"C. WINTON."

To another clergyman the Bishop writes on the same subject :—

"FARNHAM CASTLE, *December 16th*, 1856.

". . . . . I observe you state it to be declared by the most solemn tribunal of the Church of England, her spiritual head sitting in deliberate judgment, assisted by ecclesiastics as his assessors, that the 'Church of England does not hold the doctrine [of the Real Presence], and that the teaching of it subjects a priest to deprivation.' I cannot pass by this state-

ment in silence, lest I should seem to acquiesce in it. The
late judgment simply amounts to this, that a particular statement of the doctrine of the Real Presence is not allowable.   In
common with yourself, 'I do not hold the particulars of that
doctrine as asserted by Archdeacon Denison,' any more than
I hold them as asserted by the Church of Rome. And in
common with yourself, 'I do hold the doctrine of the Real
Presence,' and as I believe and hope in the sense in which the
great Fathers of our Church have always held and taught it.
What I conceive that sense to be—a sense in no way repudiated, but confirmed and strengthened by the late decision,
you will see distinctly, if you will take the trouble of reading
a few pages in the latter part of the last Charge addressed to
the clergy of my diocese, a copy of which I send by this post,
and especially pages 65 and 66.

"I am, your very faithful servant,

"C. WINTON."

In the summer of this year the Queen, who was staying at
Aldershot, paid a visit to Farnham Castle. The Bishop was
much pleased to act as guide to Her Majesty, and point out
to her the various objects of interest. In a letter written at
the time, he thus refers to the royal visit:

"The Queen paid me a visit last evening, with a large
cortége—entering the park on horseback at the London gate,
dismounting at the garden gate, and going over the gardens,
keep, and house, and returning to the camp through the town.
She was here an hour, and seemed interested. I showed her
her Bible, but stupidly omitted to get her to inscribe her
name!" The Bible here referred to was that on which the
Queen took the Coronation oath, which was carried on that
occasion by the Bishop of Winchester, and afterwards remained
in his possession. This oversight on the part of the Bishop
was afterwards repaired, for in one of the later years of his life
the Bible was forwarded to Her Majesty, with a request that

she would be pleased to write her name in it, and the Queen graciously acceded to the request.

The Bishop sincerely lamented Bishop Blomfield's death in August, 1857. He had always been on terms of great intimacy with him, and there was no one on the episcopal Bench whose manly and consistent character he more respected. He thus refers to it :—

"I have deeply felt Bishop Blomfield's removal. With all his faults, and he was not without them, he was a man of whom it was impossible to see as much as I saw without loving him much. And I, who knew all the difficulties with which he had to contend, constitutional from within, and from pressure without, can wonder less, perhaps, than others, that he was what he was, rather than that he was not what he was not. In him a great light has been extinguished."

The Bishop, just at this time, was considerably pained by an inquiry which he was forced to institute into certain charges of injudicious zeal brought against the chaplain of a metropolitan company. I append some portions of the Bishop's definitive judgment on the case, as showing his opinion respecting some of the revival meetings then held.

"And here I must state explicitly, that it is unquestionably desirable that an entire change should take place in one department of the religious services as now conducted at the factory. It is not without the deepest concern that I come to this conclusion. I have watched with intense interest, in common with many others who have at heart the religious and social life of the working classes, the active intelligence and the high sense of moral responsibility which have so honourably distinguished the management of your large establishment. I know well, and I respect proportionably, the unfeigned zeal and self-denying piety of the principal agent in this remarkable movement. I grieve to be compelled to give utterance to an opinion which I cannot but be conscious will come into collision with his deeply-rooted convictions. Nor am I insensible to the fact that good—perhaps in more cases than is known—may have been done under the methods adopted. Good, however, be it remembered, which has not yet stood the test of time, and the reality of which time alone can prove. Good, too, may have been done, but good unquestionably not without its alloy of mischief. The present inquiry itself, to go no further, is fraught in various ways with much serious mischief. Prejudice created without—passions excited—the wreck of hopeful projects threatened—this is all mischief in direct consequence —the good, if good it be, is but by occasion. And then, as has been said, ' God may do good notwithstanding; but are we to do evil that good may come ? '

" The evil to which I specially allude lies in the prayer meetings, which for some time have taken place habitually after the ordinary religious service. These meetings exhibit all those characteristic features which existed in the corresponding services conducted by Wesley and Whitfield, and still prevail in the so-called Revival Meetings on both sides of the Atlantic. The intermingling of both the sexes in the same room, though in different parts of it—densely crowded assemblies, prolonged to a late hour of the night—noisy praying in groups simultaneous and separate, prayer on the part of some for themselves, pleadings on the part of others for careless persons whom they are seeking to lead to earnestness, interrupted by vociferations and ejaculations, and at intervals by sudden bursts of music, and hymns poured forth at the full strain of the voice—caressings and implorings of either sex, the male converts with the unconverted males, and the females among each other—screamings and outcries, and loud weepings, often accompanied by strong convulsive movements and agonies of body described as fearful to behold ;—these, and similar tumultuous agitations, which are not the occasional outbreaks of over-wrought emotion, but the habitual and encouraged accompaniments of such meetings, seem to be altogether at variance with the Apostolic injunction of order and decency in the churches, inconsistent with the truer manifestations of His grace which He has taught us to expect, and little calculated to promote repentance towards God, and faith in our Lord Jesus Christ.

"It is difficult to anticipate the enduring effects of real conversion, or the solid fruits of the Spirit, from such over-stimulated excesses of passionate feeling, or to imagine that the Hand of God is manifested in extravagancies which by their very violence seem incompatible with the workings of true conviction on hearts enlightened by the Holy Scriptures. The strongest external influences are brought to bear upon the senses, forgetting that there is much danger in so exciting the nervous system as to give the body power over the mind. In proportion as you rouse the feelings to morbid action, you derange that calmness which is essential to the exercise of mental strength and sound judgment. Religion cannot be resolved into physical impulses, or measured by the possession of a greater or less degree of animal susceptibility. And if I am asked whether meetings in which all these elements of irregular action are found to exist, not as accidents incidental to human infirmity, but as the constituent and essential peculiarities, are in accordance with the proper administration of the discipline and regulations of the Church of England, I should be unfaithful to my duty as a minister and ruler in that Church if I failed to return an answer in the negative.

". . . In addition to the discontinuance of the prayer meetings, which do not appear to me to be susceptible of any safe modification, my attention has been turned to Mr. ——'s mode of preaching. All the evidence concurs in representing it as very striking and effective. It attracts and retains the hearer. There is no slumbering under it. Its boldness and roughness give it character and produce impression. . . . Setting aside offences against good taste which may well be forgiven, objection must be taken to the strong denunciatory language, not unmixed with harsh and irritating epithets, in which he habitually addresses those who, in his view, are the unconverted. Predominance is systematically given to the awful and terrific displays of God's justice, without exhibiting in close alliance those views of His mercy and love, which, while they lead to conviction of sin, heap coals of fire upon the head of the sinner, and melt his soul into contrition. I appreciate his zealous and fearless preaching— the fervency and even the impetuosity of a man in earnest, penetrated with a sense of the responsibility of announcing his Master's message and delivering his own soul from the sin of blood-guiltiness ; but if I have read the Gospel aright, and the mode of teaching it, adopted by its first promulgators, it is not by a ministry of terror, but of love, that the heart of stone is to be turned into a heart of flesh." *

Certainly no sign of old age is apparent in the preceding letter, but the Bishop seems to have felt, as years rolled on, that his life was now approaching the allotted span of man's days on earth. He thus writes to Mr. Dallas on his birthday :

"*November 22nd*, 1857.

"MY DEAR DALLAS,

"Very many thanks for your friendly greetings— always prized, and increasingly so as years through God's mercy are multiplied. I know not whether it is with you as with me, but I find, as age creeps on, that old friends seem more and more valuable—I miss them more when taken away—I enjoy them more when still granted to me. . . .

"Your most affectionate,

"C. W."

Another old friend at the close of the year wrote to him with a request on behalf of Eton College, that he would present the College with a portrait of himself. Hawtrey thus prefers the request.

'* Writing on March 7, 1860, the Bishop says : "I adhere to the adverse views I have always held to mixed Prayer Meetings. But I am not unaware of the difficult circumstances in which the clergy are now placed in regard to them ; less so, however, at Winchester than elsewhere."

"THE LODGE, *December 15th,* 1857.

"MY DEAR BISHOP,

"We were very sorry not to have been able to secure you on Founder's Day; but we shall live in hopes of better fortune next year. I have good reason to believe that our hall may be then in such a condition as to make it possible for us to meet there without fear of cold. You have probably heard how worthy of the Chapel and the new buildings this hall has been made by Wilder's munificence. It will bear now an advantageous comparison with any hall of equal size at Cambridge or at Oxford. The sight of this improvement naturally suggested to us a wish to see it decorated as other such places of meeting in the Universities with the pictures of College worthies. Our wish has been cordially met by Patteson and Coleridge, who have both promised their portraits. Three others we already possess, which seem to find a fitter place there than in my Lodge. . . . But we have a large list still on the Episcopal Bench, a distinguished ambassador, and the author of "Latin Christianity." We are getting unreasonable from the success with which we have begun, and try to hope that these also may be added to our living titles of honour. I cannot say how much pleasure it would give me if my request, made in the name of the College, could obtain a portrait of yourself.

"I am, my dear Bishop,
"Most faithfully yours,
"E. C. HAWTREY."

It is to be regretted that circumstances prevented the Bishop from acceding to Dr. Hawtrey's request until a year or two before his death. In spite of his weakness, he then sat for his portrait, and a full-length oil picture of the Bishop now hangs in the College Hall at Eton.

At the opening of the year 1858, the Bishop was called upon to mourn the loss of an old friend, with whom he had occasionally throughout life corresponded — Daniel Wilson, Bishop of Calcutta. He was asked by the family to preach a funeral sermon in Islington church on the morning of Sunday, Feb. 14, and this, notwithstanding the fact that he was even more than usually pressed with engagements at the time, he consented to do. The sermon was afterwards published, together with a preface written by himself, with a few particulars of the Bishop's death, which, at the time of the delivery of his sermon, had only been communicated by telegram. In his sermon the Bishop, after a short account of the life of Bishop Wilson, singles out the following salient points in his ministerial character. I mention them as characteristically showing the particular qualities which attracted the Bishop of Winchester :—

His clear and comprehensive acceptance of the great fundamental doctrines of the Christian scheme.

His settled determination of purpose, illustrated in his character by many acts, personal, ministerial, episcopal.

Caution, in a very unusual degree, blended with this determination of purpose.

As a writer, seizing hold of the prominent and essential points, and thrusting aside inferior matter to bring his mind to bear with concentrated force on what was really important.

As a Parish Priest, feeding his flock with the doctrine of the Holy Gospel—taking oversight of it in a ministry eminently catholic.

From the pulpit, as from a fulcrum, he moved men's hearts with a force of attraction peculiarly his own.

As a Missionary Bishop, uncompromising in his boldness in reproving the prevalent vices of India.

A disciplinarian, without caprice or vexatious punctiliousness, expecting and exacting deference, but only such as he was ever forward himself to pay to others where he deemed it due.

He never forgot a friendship once formed.

He was fond of power, yet full of real humility.

His disinterestedness in money matters was notorious.

One of the penalties paid by those who are spared to live to a good old age, is undoubtedly the oft-recurring pain of separation from those with whom they have consorted in life. Thus in the Charge which the Bishop delivered in the autumn of this year, he stated that fewer than fifty clergymen were then officiating in the diocese, whom he had found there at his first visitation. The Charge is entitled " Church Progress," and abounds with statistics and suggestions with reference to Church work. Two points of doctrine are specially dealt with towards the close, which show the way in which, at that time, men's minds were drifting. He says :—

" It is with pain I see a tendency in the minds of many to give a meaning to particular passages at variance with the whole tenor of the doctrine of our Reformed Church, and to cull out from the writings of individual divines of high name opinions sometimes difficult to reconcile, sometimes in direct antagonism to expressions in our liturgical forms and articles. But as nothing is more easy than to exhibit these discrepancies, so is nothing more fallacious. You may prop up any diversity of doctrine by a catena of isolated passages from our soundest theologians, the general tenor of whose writings is notoriously opposed to the particular view they are quoted to support. Words loosely employed, forms of expression which have ac-quired in lapse of time a certain controversial meaning not ori-ginally belonging to them, phrases capable of being interpreted in more than one sense, are often pressed into a service very different from that designed by their authors. There is no such fixity of meaning in the language used in different treatises, and at different times of life, by the same divine, as can make a super-ficial reader certain that the author is always strictly consistent with himself. But, whether consistent or inconsistent, whether uniformly orthodox with a logical precision, or otherwise, it is not on individual divines, of whatever weight or wisdom, that we are at liberty to pin our faith. To the definitions and explanations of the framers of our formularies, gathered

collectively and expressed authoritatively—not to the detached
dogmas of any one of them in particular—we have given our
assent, as to the recognised standard of appeal for all the
members of our communion. We are pledged, not to the
private judgment of the profoundest and the holiest
amongst them, but 'always so to minister the doctrines and
sacraments, and the discipline of Christ, as the Lord hath
commanded, and as this Church and realm have received the
same.' "

The other point referred to is Private Confession. The
Bishop first considers the " doctrine of our formularies on this
subject "—the homily on Common Prayer and Sacraments, our
liturgical services the two Books of Common Prayer of
1549 and 1552, compared with that of 1661, and concludes
thus :—

"The system of the confessional is as foreign to the spirit of
the Gospel as to the manly common sense and independent
mind of the great mass of the members of the English Church.
The spirit of the Gospel is 'repentance towards God, and faith
towards our Lord Jesus Christ.' The mind of our congregations
will not tolerate an empty formalism in the place of these life-
giving truths, or the substitution of an unscriptural confession
to sinful man, of like passions with themselves, in the stead of
sorrow for sin before God, 'with groanings that cannot be
uttered,' true conversion of heart, and holiness of life. They
will never endure to see the weaker members of their families
subjected to an authority which, if it does not taint and con-
fuse the moral sense, subdues the mind to the extinction of all
independent volition, and chains it captive with passive submission to the will of a spiritual director.

"And then, mark the consequences, too much to be dreaded
as probable, if not inevitable. There will be a jealousy attaching itself to those domiciliary visits which form so important a
part of your pastoral duty. The cottage door will be closed
against you, or averted faces will meet you, and suspicion cloud

the brow of your parishioners as you enter. That familiar intercourse which has so often cleared a doubt, or solved a difficulty,
or thrown a light upon your public teaching, will be restrained or rejected altogether, and you will find yourselves
paralysed in one of the best arms of your ministry. For such
a loss, the setting up of a confessional will be a sorry compensation."

At the close of the year death again laid his hand on one
dear to the Bishop. His third son, Robert, had never recovered
the loss of his wife under the peculiarly sad circumstances
which have been before narrated. His home had lost its sunshine, and he had carried on his pastoral work diligently as
before, but with a sad and aching heart. He struggled long
against despondency, but it told upon his general health, and
in December of this year he succumbed to an illness which,
probably, under happier external circumstances, would not have
proved fatal. The Bishop writes to one who had, not long
before, mourned the loss of a son :—

"Although I needed no letter to assure me of your deep
sympathy, it is very grateful to my feelings to have received it.
And the more so, because no one has more of a father's heart
than yourself, and no father has had his heart more exercised
by similar trials. And I know that this event in my family
has reopened again the recent wound which has stricken so
severely you and yours. But you have your comforts, and so have
I. Grievous as is this affliction, how much heavier would it
have been if I had not been permitted to see the unmistakable
marks—evident to others as well as to myself—that God had
been ripening and preparing dearest Robert for his departure
before He saw fit to take him to Himself. This is my—is our
—consolation, and with it He enables us to say thankfully
'It is the Lord,' and to recognise His love in thus mingling
mercies with His judgments. Yesterday was a trying day—
rendered yet more affecting by the marks of respect and love

on the part of brethren and parishioners. We are all—I thank God—fairly well."*

To his brother-in-law, Dr. Wilson, he writes :—

"FARNHAM CASTLE, *December 24th.* 1858.

"One line I must send in acknowledgment of your letter. I have present with me, in the midst of our bereavements, the inexpressibly comforting thought, 'To depart and be with Christ is far better.' And O, how far better than all the care and turmoil of this sin-worn world. And I see in his whole course how God was preparing him for this early removal; and though He took him soon, yet He took him not till there was a ripeness and readiness to which so many are now bearing a testimony, very precious to a father's heart. You have gone through these trials, and know them; but we will both say, 'Blessed be the name of the Lord' for what he takes as for what he leaves us."

To one who was at the time mourning over the loss of a son's wife, he writes :—

"None can enter more feelingly or, I am persuaded, with

---

* It may, perhaps, be permitted to a brother to make the following extract from a letter written to him at the time by the present Lord Coleridge :—

"For some years past our paths had diverged, and I saw little of your brother Robert, but when I was at Oxford, and especially when I first went up there, I saw a great deal of him, and owed a great deal to him, which I can never forget. He acknowledged the claims of an hereditary friendship, and though he knew nothing of me but that I was the son of his father's friend, he gave me countenance and notice when it was very kind in him to give it, and very valuable to me to have it. And I am sure no one could be near Robert Sumner, as he was in those days, without the opportunity at least of being the better for it. He was certainly as good and pure a man as ever I knew, and amongst the many happy and good thoughts which the recollection of those days revives, not a few belong to walks with him, and evenings spent in his company. And I remember well, that even differences of opinion only increased my respect for him ; he was so thoroughly religious, and so manifestly true and simple in all his thoughts and words. And nothing even in later years, though I saw him less, disturbed the grateful recollections of those Balliol days."

truer sympathy than yourself, into the trial we are called upon
to bear under our present bereavement. You and yours have
so recently experienced a like affliction—I might say are still in
the midst of it—that you can judge better than most, of the
void in our hearts, and of our saddened feelings, when we look
at these three young children, now doubly orphaned. But, like
yourselves, we too have our best consolation in the assurance
that to those that are gone to die was gain. And here indeed
God has vouchsafed us in one sense greater mercies than to you ;
for dearest Robert's life, since the early removal of his wife, has
been one of deep suffering, body and mind, and he is taken to a
happy reunion, and to a rest which he knew not here, and seemed
not likely to know again. And in this view our affliction is
lighter than yours. May God give to all of us, especially to
your dear son, the strength sufficient for our need."

CHAPTER XXII.

IT will be remembered that the Rev. Robert Milford, since his marriage with the Bishop's youngest daughter, had lived as domestic Chaplain at Farnham Castle, serving from thence a curacy in the neighbourhood. In the beginning of 1859, this arrangement was terminated by his appointment to the Rectory of Brightwell, Berkshire, and consequently his necessary removal thither with his wife and family. From this time, until the Bishop's paralytic stroke in 1868, his six surviving children with their respective families were in the habit of coming to him in succession for two months at a time, and relieving him from the cares necessarily falling upon the head of a large establishment. The Bishop, therefore, was able still to enjoy—what he so dearly loved—domestic society. Few public men ever retained so entirely the love of home and family life as he did up to the very last.

A question, which had been for some time troubling the Bishop's mind, became ripe for settlement in the early part of the year. Complaints had been very frequently made as to the unhealthiness of Wolvesey Palace as a Training Establishment for Masters. No expense was spared by the Bishop to make the premises more healthy; but, in the autumn of 1858, notwithstanding all that had been done, no fewer than ten out of thirty-eight students were temporarily invalided, seven of whom were unable to attend the Government examination at Christmas; and, in the case of one, the illness terminated fatally. A temporary arrangement was made by which the students, while taking their meals and receiving instruction at Wolvesey, slept at a house in the town specially engaged for the purpose, with the sanction of the Committee of Council on Education. It was evident, however, that this could not be a permanent arrangement; and, at the close of 1858, a meeting of the Diocesan Board of Education was held at Winchester, over which the Bishop presided, when the various questions opened out by the new aspect of affairs were thoroughly discussed. Some of those present were in favour of discontinuing the institution altogether; some were in favour of uniting with the diocese of Chichester in the formation of a joint College for the two dioceses; but the Bishop never wavered in his opinion, expressed strongly but temperately, that it was most desirable that the diocese should have a distinct Training College of its own at Winchester, and that it was advisable at once to endeavour to raise the necessary funds for the purpose.

Before a final decision was arrived at, it was determined that a Committee should be formed to inquire as to the results already obtained, and the reasonable probability of there being a sufficient supply of pupil teachers from the diocese to fill the vacancies annually occurring in the institution. This committee made searching inquiries into the questions submitted to them; and the result of their inquiries was so satisfactory, and so overwhelming as to the beneficial influence of the Training College, that the Board resolved unanimously to appeal to the diocese for funds for the erection of a building suitable for the purpose. The Dean and Chapter offered a site in a most eligible situation and £500, and the Bishop intimated his intention of contributing a similar sum towards the £10,000, which it was estimated would be required. Ere three years had elapsed the requisite amount had been raised, and the building erected and opened for the purposes for which it was designed.*

The Rev. J. Smith, who for many years was a most efficient Principal of the institution, writes to me in the following words respecting the hearty co-operation of the Bishop :—

" His interest in everything connected with schools was unmistakable. At the first Whit Monday gathering of 1,000 children at Wolvesey, a heavy rain compelled us to shelter them for tea. As this was followed by almost a raid of the mixed multitude into every room of the house, I wrote to the Bishop apologetically, but he answered that no use to which the premises could have been applied, would have gratified him more. . . . . Among the many and great works originated or expanded by Bishop Sumner, I can only speak of the Training College. The small institution which was placed under my charge in St. Swithun Street, would hardly be taken for the germ of the noble college which now graces your city and your diocese. How far the progress of that institution was promoted by Bishop Sumner, I will not attempt to define ; but this I know that I can recall to mind his own hope and cheerful encouragement when many despaired, his conciliatory influence amidst differences of opinion, and his resolve to stand by the institution when its late premises were condemned for unhealthiness, and when the Training College itself would have disappeared, but for the noble efforts of many friends, all of whom acknowledged Bishop Sumner as their head."

In the autumn of this year, after a month spent as usual in incessant work in the Channel Islands—the only single half-

* See page 406.

holiday which the Bishop had in anticipation allowed himself in Jersey being unexpectedly occupied with receiving Her Majesty, who was cruising about the Channel Islands—the Bishop paid a most interesting visit to Ireland. His party consisted of one of his sons, a daughter-in-law, Mr. Jacob, and Mr. Dallas. The latter had throughout life taken the deepest interest in the success of the Society for Irish Church Missions to Roman Catholics. He was the general supervisor of all the work done at the various stations organized by the society, and the Bishop anticipated much pleasure in being accompanied through some of the missionary districts by one so well able to act as his guide. Nor were his anticipations disappointed. A few weeks spent in Dublin, the Connemara district, and the North of Ireland, were sufficient to show the Bishop that a real and very important work was being carried out by the society. The following extracts from letters written at the time, show the impression left on his mind :—

"KILMORE, *Sept.* 6, 1859.

"We left Dublin at seven this morning for Maynooth, which we had the good fortune to see most satisfactorily, although had the brethren known that one of the strangers was Dallas, we might have chanced to have been stoned."

"CLIFDEN, *Sept.* 12.

"We dine to-night at 5.30, in order to be ready for tea at 7, at the Orphan's Home, when the forty girls give a kind of entertainment to welcome Dallas. This is a capital institution, for which the funds were raised principally by Mrs. Dallas, for orphan girls after the famine. We went there on arriving on Saturday evening, and the greeting and demonstrations were very amusing. It is conducted by a Miss Gore, a gentlewoman who gives herself up to the work. The girls had prepared a room with floral decorations, &c., &c. Yesterday we went in the morning to one of the Mission Churches, seven miles from here, where Dallas preached,—a wild spot, where about 200 were collected, almost all converts. In the evening at the church here, about 400 were present, nearly all converts. The sermons are all more or less controversial, and the whole air here is impregnated with controversy. I am thankful not to have my lot cast where this is necessary. It is as bad as being in the —————— diocese. The first thing I saw, on looking out of my window at 7.30 yesterday, was Mr. Rudd, one of the missionaries, talking with two boys who were listening very attentively. They were soon joined by a man, and the colloquy lasted some time. All three were Roman Catholics."

"Dublin, *Sept.* 16, 1859.

"Coming to Dublin, after Connemara, is much like Robinson Crusoe's first setting foot on an inhabited country after his desert island. It is a country to have seen—but for living ! It is no one but a missionary who could exist there. You have only to conceive the valley of Rocks magnified into a district of 50 miles by 40."

"Cushendall, *Sept.* 20, 1859.

"I do not know that I have ever seen more beautiful scenery of water and land, even in Scotland or the Lakes—or even in Italy, of which we were reminded more than once. The contrast with the bleak Connemara was most striking."

Before leaving Ireland, he addressed the following letter to the Bishop of Tuam :—

"My dear Lord,
        "I am on the eve of returning to England, but I cannot leave Ireland without sending you a word of the heartiest congratulation on the vast work which I have seen in your diocese since I called on you at Salt-hill. If envy was permitted, I could feel the passion very strongly. It is a glorious thing to be connected, as you have been, with such mighty

operations. I know not which to admire most—the devoted-
ness, ability, and patience of the agents, or the faithfulness and
constancy of those on whom they have acted. Your missionaries are men whom any Bishop would thankfully see planted
in every parish of his diocese, if he could get them. And it is
wonderful to me how you could have been enabled to procure
the services of so many combining the rarely united qualifications of mental acuteness, discretion, and self-devotion.

"It will be a gratification to you to know that I have seen
the churches crowded, meetings thronged to overflowing, and
late-comers, who could find no room, swarming like bees all
round the buildings; and schools which I have never seen
equalled for knowledge of Scripture and readiness of application
in any part of England. It has been a wonderful sight to me
to observe the lads coming in from 'saving their oats' at a
sudden summons, sitting down in their shirt-sleeves, with a
Bible in their hands, and turning to passages as familiarly as if
they had nothing to do in life but to study them.

"The testimony borne, throughout all the parts I have
visited, to the effect of the missionaries' work upon those who
are not converts, has been uniformly the same. Many are
inquirers. The influence of the priests has been remarkably
diminished, and all admit the irreproachable conduct and the
patient endurance and forbearance of both missionaries and
converts.

"I am, my dear Lord, very faithfully yours,

"C. WINTON."

"Dublin, Sept. 29, 1859."

There was another movement inaugurated about this time
in which the Bishop took very considerable interest, and which
he aided very materially both by his pecuniary contributions
and his never-failing counsel. Nearly a year previously it
had been proposed by Mr. (now Canon) Gregory to form an
"Association for augmenting poor benefices in the deanery of
Southwark." It was wished to raise an annual sum of £400,

" to be apportioned year by year to one of the many benefices having a less income than £150, with the understanding that the incumbent should raise an equal sum, and by obtaining from the Ecclesiastical Commissioners a further benefaction of equal amount to meet the £800 thus obtained, each incumbency in the deanery would, in course of years, be raised to an income of at least £150." It was not until the close of 1859 that the preliminaries were finally arranged; but so effectually were the foundations of the association laid that in 1863 the Committee were able to report that the object of their efforts was attained by the better endowment of every poor benefice in the deanery, and the Association was therefore merged in the Surrey Church Association after midsummer 1863, having succeeded during the term of its existence in raising (with the sums which were collected to meet its grants) no less than £20,000.

It will be seen, from one of the extracts given above from a letter written by the Bishop when in Ireland, that he was constitutionally a man of peace and averse to controversy. But, unfortunately, on his return to Farnham he was constrained at once to enter into the consideration of a most unhappy theological conflict. It appeared that in 1858 the Rev. D. J. Heath, vicar of Brading, in the Isle of Wight, had published a volume of sermons entitled "Sermons on Important Subjects." This volume of sermons was brought under the notice of a clerical meeting in the Isle of Wight, and a Committee, consisting of some of the members of the Society, was appointed to confer with Mr. Heath on certain passages selected from the published volume. This Committee reported unfavourably to Mr. Heath; and accordingly, on August 16, 1859, a resolution was passed at a meeting of the Clerical Society, protesting against the system of theology advocated by him, and earnestly beseeching him to abstain from propagating his opinions, and to withdraw the volume from circulation. It may be sufficient to state here that the doctrines complained of, and ultimately condemned as unsound, referred

to the cardinal points of justification by faith—the atonement
made by Christ for man—and the forgiveness of sins.

A further resolution was passed requesting Mr. Heath
voluntarily to withdraw from the Clerical Meeting. Mr. Heath
declined to withdraw unless a resolution was adopted to the
effect that no imputation was thereby cast upon his professional
character; and, the meeting being unwilling to pass such a
resolution, it was agreed that in future no invitation should be
sent to Mr. Heath to attend the Clerical meetings. In consequence of this resolution, Mr. Heath commenced a system of
preaching and lecturing on theological subjects in Ryde; and
complaint with reference to this was formally made to the
Bishop by the incumbent of the parish in which he thus
preached. Upon this, the Bishop wrote to Mr. Heath expressing his earnest desire that he should in future abstain from the
delivery of lectures on religious subjects in a parish of which he
was not the incumbent. Such conduct was an interference
with the parochial system entirely at variance with the principles of our Church, and gave great and natural offence to the
clergy. Mr. Heath replied that the clergy of the island, by
"turning him out" of their Society, had grossly attacked his
professional character, and that if they would withdraw the
resolution complained of, and re-admit him to their Society, and
make a public apology in the Isle of Wight for their conduct,
he would leave off defending himself by lectures. In reply, the
Bishop stated that the Clerical Society of the Isle of Wight
was a purely voluntary association, entitled to admit or exclude
members without any official interference on his part; and that
therefore he could not enter into any question between the
Society and Mr. Heath. The Bishop requested Mr. Heath to
reply distinctly as to whether he refused to comply with his injunction to abstain from the lecturing complained of, reminding
him of the promise made at his ordination reverently to obey
his ordinary, and also of the oath taken by him at his institution.
Mr. Heath declined to act in the manner pointed out by the

Bishop, maintaining that the clergy had invaded episcopal functions by adjudicating upon his book, and that whenever the clergy chose to behave professionally towards him he would behave professionally to them.   After one or two more ineffectual attempts to prevent Mr. Heath acting as he had done, the Bishop, after much and anxious consideration, announced his intention of instituting proceedings against him; and, accordingly, in the beginning of the year 1860, Articles were exhibited against him in the Court of Arches.   Objection was taken that the articles were insufficient, which was ultimately allowed; and the articles were twice reformed, and the case came for consideration before the Court in June 1861.   In November of the same year, Dr. Lushington pronounced judgment against Mr Heath, and appeal was made by him to the Judicial Committee. On June 6th, 1862, Lord Cranworth delivered the judgment of the Committee confirming the previous judgment of the Arches Court, and stating that, unless Mr. Heath revoked the errors of which he had been convicted, their Lordships would have no course left but to advise Her Majesty to confirm the sentence of deprivation under the Act.   Mr. Heath stated that he had nothing to revoke, and he was accordingly deprived of his incumbency.

I have thus detailed the steps of this unhappy suit, *seriatim*, because at the time misrepresentations were current respecting the matter.   The Bishop acted with great pain, and after most serious deliberation.   But he felt, after reading the sermons and the defence which Mr. Heath had made to the Clerical Society of the passages objected to by them, that, when appealed to by one of the clergy of his diocese to defend his parishioners from such teaching, he had no option in the matter.   The issue of the suit shows that the opinion which the Bishop had formed of the unsoundness of Mr. Heath's views when tested by the formularies of the Church of England was correct.   I cannot refrain from giving the subjoined letter which the Bishop received on the subject.   It shows the bitter animus which was felt by the Bishop's opponents.   I withhold the name and address, which were correctly given by the writer, who has since died. He was a country doctor in one of the Midland counties,. who, for the last few years of his life, after reading the newspaper, was in the habit of writing letters to any public man whose conduct was either pleasing or displeasing to him. It is to be hoped that not many of them were as scurrilous as the subjoined :—

"MY LORD,

"Your Lordship having done your utmost to prevent Mr. Heath providing bread for his family, must now necessarily want some excitement previous to the delivery of the sentence of the Judicial Committee. The King of Dahomey (may God bless his memory) is going to have a great occasion, *i.e.,* sacrificing two thousand Fantees on the grave of his father. Now, my Lord, would not this be a very glorious opportunity for your Lordship to enjoy your appetite 'e'en to satiety,' that the appetite may sicken and so die? The atrocities practised on these occasions are, according to Mr. Hutchinson, so revolting to ordinary individuals that they would no doubt be exquisitely enjoyable by your Lordship, who seems to have an enjoyable relish in proportion to the distress you occasion others. May the Almighty turn your stubborn heart, and grant you what you deny your fellow Christian, is the fervent prayer of your Lordship's obedient and very humble servant,

"A. B."

"I need not tell your Lordship that, if I can in any way forward your views by using any influence I may possess with the African Steam Navigation Company to ensure your passage to Lagos, I would be really delighted to do so. It would be a great relief to the peaceably disposed portion of the community if your Lordship would find room among your suite for that troublesome pest, Sir ———"

On the other hand, soon after the conclusion of the suit, the

Bishop received the following address, signed by all the clergy
.of the Isle of Wight, thanking him warmly for the part which
he had taken in the Heath case.

TO THE RIGHT REVEREND THE LORD BISHOP OF WINCHESTER.

"My Lord,

"We, the Clergy of the rural Deaneries of the East
and West Medina, in the Isle of Wight, earnestly desire to
express to your Lordship, our sense of the deep and lasting
gratitude which we owe to you, for the firmness and faithfulness
with which you have laboured to vindicate the pure doctrines of
the Church of England from novel and erroneous interpretations.

"That debt, indeed, belongs to the whole Church : but the
acknowledgment of it seems especially to devolve upon us, inasmuch as we can best estimate the danger which threatened
our flocks, and the injurious effects which such teaching,
coming with the authority of the Church, but totally opposed
to its doctrines, was working amongst the people of this Island.

"We deeply appreciate the conscientious motives which led
your Lordship to encounter so many difficulties and to incur so
much of serious cost and anxiety, in the discharge of a duty,
personally most painful, but eminently needful 'for the defence
and confirmation of the Gospel,' and we desire most heartily to
assure you both of our sympathy and gratitude."

The Bishop replied very cordially.

"I have to acknowledge the receipt of an address unanimously signed by all the clergy of the West Medina, in the Isle
of Wight, and by all the clergy in the East Medina to whom
there has been an opportunity of presenting it. This address
expresses the approval of the clergy of the course I recently
felt it my duty to take in instituting proceedings against a
member of your own body, and connected with myself by
diocesan ties, whose teaching has been authoritatively pronounced by the highest judicial tribunal to be at variance with

the doctrines and articles of our Church. I undertook this painful task, in the first instance, on the representation of a large number of the clergy of the Island, that the purity of the faith of their flocks was seriously endangered by the promulgation of the views in question, not only in the parish in which they originated, but, in spite of earnest and repeated remonstrances, among their own parishioners in populous parts of the neighbourhood. During the whole course of my long episcopate I have never been called upon to discharge any duty so repugnant to my personal feelings, and necessarily attended with so much difficulty, and consequent anxiety, in the conduct of proceedings, happily so unusual, if not altogether unprecedented, in our Church.

"But I am bound to remember that, on my consecration to the sacred office I hold, I was invited to profess my readiness, the Lord being my helper, with all faithful diligence to banish and drive away all erroneous and strange doctrine contrary to God's word, and I could not conscientiously bring my mind to any other conclusion than that the time had arrived when, at whatever cost, the sincerity of my solemn promise must be tested by action. Under circumstances so full of perplexity in their progress, and so painful in the necessarily penal result of the proceedings, it is in the highest degree consolatory and encouraging to me to receive this hearty assurance of the sympathy and gratitude of so important a body of my reverend brethren."

The spring of 1860 was an unusually busy time, for in addition to confirmations in Surrey,* the Bishop was much occupied in organising and setting on foot "The Surrey Church Association." Hitherto Hampshire and Surrey had been united for purposes of Church work in the Education and Church-Building

---

* The Bishop writes with reference to his confirmation tour :—

"MORDEN, *March* 31, 1860.

"Thus far in my work—I thank God—without let or hindrance, and with unexampled satisfaction in the catechumens. It has been quite cheering to me, notwithstanding the pressure of business which sometimes threatens to weigh me down and keeps me in perpetual activity of mind if not of body."

Societies. But it had been felt for some time that Surrey did not take its proper part in the work, and that it was difficult to keep up the interest of the county in societies for which the central place of meeting was so distant as Winchester. True it was, that, since the Bishop had come to the See, the number of churches in Surrey had been more than doubled; but population had increased immensely at the same time, and " it was felt that yet greater results might be obtained from efforts specifically local." Accordingly, after much consideration, it was resolved to organise a society for the county of Surrey alone, with the following objects in view :—the improvement or providing of additional Church accommodation—the erection of school buildings, and the furtherance of the general purposes of education in the principles of the Church of England within the Archdeaconry—the augmentation of endowments—and the erection and improvement of parsonage houses. Meetings were held at the principal towns in Surrey, at many of which the Bishop presided ; and the result was that, whilst in 1858 the subscriptions from Surrey to the Diocesan Church Building Society amounted to only £93, and in 1859 to £65, while to the Diocesan Education Society they were still less, the balance-sheet issued by the Surrey Church Association in June 1861, showed a total in donations and subscriptions of £2360, the Bishop heading the list with an annual subscription of £100.* The Society gradually rooted itself firmly in the county; and, up to the time of the Bishop's retirement, the subscriptions were maintained with more or less fluctuation at about £2000 a year. He retained his interest in it to the last, and invariably presided at the quarterly meetings of the council.

Once more, in the spring of 1860, the Bishop was called upon to part with one of his Archdeacons. Wigram, whom he had appointed Archdeacon of Winchester in 1847, was promoted to the See of Rochester, and on Ascension Day was consecrated

---

* For the various statistics connected with the Surrey Church Association, I am indebted to the Rev. Joseph Wallis, the indefatigable secretary of that society.

in the parish church of St. Mary Lambeth, the Bishop of Winchester being one of the consecrating bishops.*

For the thirteen years during which he had acted as "oculus episcopi" there had been the most intimate relations between Bishop and Archdeacon. In every movement carried on for the welfare of the diocese he cordially co-operated with his chief, and the Bishop was heartily sorry for himself to lose the benefit of his services in the diocese, though rejoicing in the larger sphere of usefulness opening out before him in the See of Rochester. The Archdeaconry thus vacated was conferred by Lord Palmerston, without any solicitation on the Bishop's part, on his old and faithful friend, Rev. Philip Jacob.

The Bishop, in writing to Coleridge, thus refers to the appointment of Archdeacon Wigram :—

"April 5th, 1860.

" . . . . . It is more complimentary than convenient that the Crown can make no high appointment in the Church at home or abroad without a foray into my diocese.† In the present instance my right arm is cut off to furnish Rochester with its chief ruler. But it is a consolation to have a confident belief that Wigram's episcopate will be of a most useful character. He is a very stirring man—full of energy and devotion to his work—and himself the foremost in setting an example of labour and self-denial in promoting it. I know few men more untiring in the discharge of *their proper duties* (a rare acquirement), or more efficient in performing them. I cannot doubt that he will carry a blessing with him. Your

---

* Writing on April 15, 1867, the Bishop thus refers to Bishop Wigram : " I have greatly felt the sudden death of the Bishop of Rochester. He was one of the most single-minded, straightforward men I have ever known, somewhat cold in manner, but full of energy and devotion to his work. The diocese will never have a more disinterested and unselfish head."

† The Bishops of Oxford, St. Asaph, Gloucester and Bristol, Newcastle, the Mauritius and Sierra Leone, and the Deans of Hereford, Windsor, and Westminster had in the course of a few years, been preferred to the posts which they then held, after having been beneficed in the Winchester diocese.

account of dear old Patteson is the best I have heard for a long time.   Give him my cordial love."

In the autumn the Bishop's services were again called into requisition in connection with the Church's work in Switzer-land; for, on September 6, he consecrated the English Church erected at Chamounix.   No one more thoroughly enjoyed the change of scene and relaxation afforded by a few weeks' run in the "play-ground of Europe" than the Bishop did; and he took the opportunity to go on (accompanied as usual by one of his sons) to Zermatt, which was then coming into notoriety as the rival of Chamounix.   He thus writes from Geneva :—

"Our progress hitherto has been very much favoured.   We have met with no *contretemps* notwithstanding an encounter with the Emperor and Empress at Lyons.   It was interesting to be able to judge personally of his reception.   There can be no mistake as to his popularity there.   The whole town was *en fête*, and all the neighbourhood collected into it in holiday clothes and the best of humours.   The illuminations were mag-nificent, far superior to anything of the kind I have seen in England, and not confined to the Governmental displays, which were very many, but universal throughout the private houses. The town sparkled everywhere with small tricolor flags, and the whole scene was very gay.   There are very many English here. Yesterday the church was full to suffocation.   I preached for the Hospital funds. . . . To-morrow I confirm—about twenty are expected, including some from Lausanne and Vevay.   . . ."

From Zermatt the Bishop (now, be it remembered, in his seventieth year) writes :—

"ZERMATT, *Sept.* 9, 1860.   4,300 feet above the Sea.

"You will see by my date that we have attained our object. On Friday morning Charles and I started at five o'clock by char to Argentieres, whither we had sent on our mules before. We passed the *Tête noire*, which I had never before thought so beautiful, and reached Martigny in time for the train to Sion, which however set us down two leagues short, in consequence of the inundations, which have broken up the railroad. . . . . We were fortunate enough to find places in the diligence for Italy, which landed us at Visp about ten o'clock. Mr. Mesac Thomas,* Secretary to the Home and Colonial Society, accompanied us from Chamounix, and at Martigny we fraternised with Mr. Miller, member for Colchester, who lives at Tooting, and his daughter ; so that on Saturday morning we set off at six o'clock a tolerable cavalcade for Zermatt. Think of my taking a ride of eleven hours, and feeling to-day as little fatigued as if I had not been on horseback ! We reached Zermatt a little after five, and are not disappointed. To-day has been most favourable for a full view of the mountains, which, being nearer than Chamounix, are more effective."

His appreciation of the scenery gave rise to the following lines, composed by him after the day's excursion. His old Eton habit of writing verses clung to him through life :

> " Grata sub Autumni radiis peregrantibus umbra,
> Gratus et aspectus desilientis aquæ ;
> Gratus et afflatus venti, Zephyri ve noti ve
> Si quis sole calens dixerit, Aura veni !
> Gratus odorque cibi generosaque pocula vini,
> Grata quies noctis, gratior ipse sopor.
> Summa viator ama montis—Sic itur ad astra—
> It melius Christi qui bene novit iter."

The services of the English Church at the time of the Bishop's visit to Zermatt were held in one of the hotels ; but it was a great satisfaction to him to find that steps had already been taken for promoting the erection of a church, and during his stay he selected a site for the building, and, as many of those who read these lines will doubtless know from personal experience, a church has since been built on the spot, and consecrated.

---

* Subsequently Bishop of Goulburn. The acquaintance thus made ripened into a warm and lasting friendship.

Although the Bishop was constitutionally cautious in starting untried methods of action, yet, if no principle was involved, he was always ready, as far as he could, to co-operate in any movement started by the zeal of those with whom perhaps on many points he might differ. He was liberal and large-hearted, and tried to view questions of difference as they arose in a broad and comprehensive spirit, and was ready to confess that a line of conduct adopted at one period of the Church's history, need not be necessarily stereotyped for all time.

An occasion arose in 1861 with respect to which this disposition was clearly shown. That year was remarkable in the annals of the Church, for the practical revival of the functions of Convocation. The Bishop had in past years expressed an opinion adverse to the awakening of its dormant powers, but the Church's opinion was gradually expressed in an unmistakable manner in favour of Convocation sitting, at any rate, as a deliberative body. Men felt that on subjects affecting the vital welfare of the Church, it was only fair that those whose expressed opinions might be supposed to carry with them considerable weight, should have the opportunity of making their views known in a constitutional manner. Ten years before, petitions had been presented both in the Upper and Lower House, and the thin end of the wedge thus inserted had been gradually driven home. In 1860, debates of some length had taken place respecting the twenty-ninth canon, and certain suggested occasional services; but in 1861 both Houses were for a considerable length of time occupied with the consideration of the volume which at that time attained such unhappy notoriety, entitled "Essays and Reviews." Acting with reference to Convocation as he had previously done with reference to the Ecclesiastical Commission, the Bishop frankly accepted the existing state of things, and notwithstanding his previous utterances adverse to Convocation, now did all in his power to make it an engine of usefulness in the Church of England. No one was more punctual in his attendance at the

Sessions of Convocation than he was, and no debate of importance took place in which he did not take considerable part. I believe I am correct in saying that few if any carried greater weight in the Upper House than he did. His words were always well weighed, and his views cautiously expressed, and backed as they were by the experience of an episcopate extending over so many years, they could not fail to have much influence with his brother bishops.

This volume of "Essays and Reviews" called forth fresh addresses to the Bishop on the part of the clergy both of Surrey and of Hampshire. In the Bishop's replies, he speaks of his thankfulness "that our diocese is free from the taint of opinions subversive of the very foundations of our faith;" and adds :— "I prize, in common with the Memorialists, the liberty our Church has ever allowed in the fair interpretation of the Holy Scriptures, and her own formularies as grounded upon them ; and while I deplore the abuse of this latitude of which they so justly complain, I join in the prayer that, by the blessing of God, we and the people committed to our spiritual charge may be stimulated to more earnest watchfulness and preserved in the reverent acceptance of that 'Gospel of Christ which is the power of God unto salvation to every one that believeth.'"

In the course of the next few months death was busy amongst the Bishop's contemporaries and friends. First of all, in July, 1861, he was called upon to perform the last sad offices by the open grave of his old friend Patteson. The funeral came in the very midst of his ordination examination, but he could not refrain from absenting himself from the midst of the candidates for four-and-twenty hours, in order thus to show sympathy with the mourners and his respect and affection for the friend whom he had lost. Then again, in February, 1862, he truly mourned over the death of Edward Craven Hawtrey. Once more he read the touching words of our Funeral Service over the remains of an old and tried friend, and committed his body

D D

to the ground in the sure and certain hope of the resurrection
to eternal life through our Lord Jesus Christ.

He thus writes to Coleridge :—

"LAMBETH, *February* 6, 1862.

" MY DEAR FRIEND,

" Very many thanks for your kind letter, of which I
reciprocate the feelings most heartily. Many circumstances
conspired to make Tuesday last a trying day to me—and it
must have not been less so to you with a bodily ailment then
pressing upon you. The thought was very present to me that
sixty years had passed since I first entered that Chapel, and
that I was then committing to the grave a friend of as many
years, with two others standing by—and the only two survivors—
of equal standing—Lonsdale and yourself. But I was thankful
to have been able to be there, and to be a participator in a
solemn scene, the memory of which few of those present will
ever forget. It is a singular coincidence that I should have
officiated on the same occasion within a year for the wardens of
two of the greatest public schools in England.* Perhaps you
are not aware that I ordained Hawtrey and the present Provost
of King's.

" Your most affectionate friend,

" C. WINTON."

But ere long a deeper sorrow fell upon him, for in May, 1862,
his brother, the Archbishop, was seized with congestion of the
brain, which, though it was subdued in twenty-four hours, left
him weak and prostrate. The Archbishop had now reached the
great age of eighty-two, and it was impossible but that his
family should be in considerable anxiety respecting the issue of
the attack. The Bishop writes to one of his daughters :—

"ST. JAMES' SQUARE, *May* 5, 1862.

" You will be greatly concerned to hear that the Archbishop

---

* Rev. R. S. Barter, Warden of Winchester College, who died in 1861, and
Dr. Hawtrey, Provost of Eton.

has had another attack—not exactly of the same character as the last, though I look upon it as more serious. We dined at Lambeth on Saturday with a large party, and he seemed well and cheerful as usual. Yesterday morning he read the lessons at the morning service in his own chapel, and walked in the garden afterwards ; but at the early dinner which they always have on Sundays he talked incoherently, and it was soon plain that there was considerable congestion of the brain. Ferguson and Columbell were sent for, and such remedies used as could be ; but he was in a very doubtful state all the evening, with a little amendment about ten or eleven, when I left him with a prospect of a quiet night, which was happily realised, and this morning I found him improved in various respects. Still it is impossible not to see that at his age the issue is very doubtful, and my fears preponderate. I am going again presently."

The Archbishop, however, contrary to expectation, rallied, and was able to go down to Addington ; but, in August, he was again laid prostrate by illness. The Bishop was at once summoned to his side, and found him in a very critical state. He writes :—

"FARNHAM CASTLE, *Aug.* 21, 1862.

"I returned from Addington yesterday evening. The Archbishop's state is very critical. . . . His mind is perfectly clear, and he is as calm and composed as ever. The sight is most edifying, and when I think of his fulness of years, even cheerful. His days are but too surely numbered, unless some great and unexpected change takes place in the symptoms—and my personal loss cannot be estimated, but for himself I have nothing to desire."

The Bishop was right in his anticipations as to the Archbishop's speedy death ; for, on the sixth of September, he passed away in the midst of his sorrowing family. The Bishop thus writes to Coleridge :—

"Farnham Castle, *Sept.* 10, 1862.

" My very dear Friend,

" Many, many thanks for your sympathising letter. I was on the eve of writing to you, and I should have written days ago, but for the pressure of necessary business, which, as you will readily understand, devolves upon me at the present moment very heavily. You rightly appreciate my personal loss. It is very great; for he has been to me, for more than half a century, father, brother, counsellor and friend. And of late years the similarity of our employments, and during a part of the year at least, our daily meetings in public and private have thrown us so much together that a greater void is created by his removal than can well be imagined. And then the agreement of our ways of thinking on many things, and in many modes of action, gives an additional poignancy to the severing of a tie which bound us together by more than ordinary brotherly feeling. Yet I should be unthankful if I were to feel myself alone in the world, while so many children and grandchildren and dear friends are left me ; and though you and I both feel that the latter drop off year by year—*anni prædantur euntes*—we have still a goodly number, and will be grateful. You will be glad to know that my brother's last days were as calm and peaceful as the whole of his life. He was mercifully spared from suffering, and died rather from exhaustion of life than from the effects of disease.

" Very affectionately yours,

" C. Winton."

It was a great pleasure to the Bishop to receive the following letter from his old pupil Oakeley, expressing his sympathy with him at his loss.

"39, Duncan Terrace, Islington, N., 19*th Sept.*, 1862.

" My dear Friend,

" I know that in times of affliction it is not unwelcome to you, to feel that you have the sympathy of an old friend necessarily separated from you in body, though not in spirit, and I may as well tell you that I have thought of you in your recent loss, which I am sure you must have felt severely. Your dear brother was always very kind to me, and since I was here, gave me at my request an order for a poor man's admission to a Hospital of which he was Governor. I had also learned to respect him in my early youth through knowing you so well. It is forty-five years this very day since I came to Highclere. The memory of those happy years and of all I learned from you is ever fresh, and I feel it to have been the foundation of much that has followed. . . . I sometimes hear of you through my old friend the Bishop of London, (Tait), and was very glad to be told that you are well and strong.

"I am, my dear Lord,

"Ever yours affectionately

"FREDERICK OAKELEY."

One event which happened in the spring of this year must not be entirely passed over in silence, in consequence of the touching record of it presented by the Queen to the Bishop. He was called upon as Bishop of the diocese in which Osborne is situated to confirm the Princess Helena; and shortly afterwards Her Majesty presented him with a handsomely bound Prayer Book, in remembrance of the event, with the following autograph inscription :—

"TO

THE BISHOP OF WINCHESTER,

IN RECOLLECTION

OF THE CONFIRMATION OF

PRINCESS HELENA.

FROM

HER SORROWING WIDOWED MOTHER,

VICTORIA R.

"OSBORNE, *April* 17, 1862."

One of the misfortunes of occupying a public position, is that private feelings must give way to public duties. The Bishop, whilst the still recent death of his last surviving brother was fresh in his memory, was called upon as Bishop to take a prominent part in the opening of the new Training College for Students at Winchester. It will be remembered, that in 1858 it had been determined to erect at Winchester a new Training College. The matter had been carried out after considerable difficulties had been successfully encountered, and the building being now ready for use, was, with much ceremony, dedicated on October 13th to the purposes for which it had been built. In the Bishop's opening speech in the Training College, after having expressed his regret that circumstances had arisen which prevented the students from occupying Wolvesey as he had always hoped they would do for the term of his episcopate, he thus defined what he conceived to be the requisite qualifications for a country schoolmaster.

"We want to have rural men for rural parishes. Their training must be of a somewhat peculiar kind. It must not embrace—it need not at least embrace—so many of the higher classes, even of elementary education, as for those masters who are intended to cope with intellects in the manufacturing districts, or with the artizans of our greater towns. True it is, that we must improve the mental power of our students, but we must not make them above their work. We think it our duty to provide a class of men, who, elevated to a certain extent above the immediate population around them, should yet be of themselves, so to speak, able to teach them the common things of life to which their daily work calls them, and not be, from the degree of education which they have received, above teaching the most rudimental and most elementary parts of education to the youth committed to their charge."

There was a special service in the Cathedral in the afternoon, at which the Bishop of Oxford preached, and a banquet was held in St. John's rooms in the city in the evening, to celebrate the opening of the College. Lord Palmerston presided at the dinner, and was supported by the magnates of the county, lay and clerical. The Bishop was singularly happy in his remarks in proposing Lord Palmerston's health. One extract from his speech must be given.

"I happen to have been educated at the same University with the noble Lord. I further had the advantage of belonging to an association, of which, in his day, the noble Lord was also a member. I had the misfortune to be the last secretary of that association, and its records fell into my possession. A smaller society (the Speculative) was merged into a larger association which afterwards took the name of the Union. The Speculative society had no more distinguished and no more conspicuous member than the noble Lord; and of this I cannot give a better proof than what I find recorded in the minutes. I have looked over the books and I find these three propositions submitted by Lord Palmerston, on each of which he contributed an essay. I will take the liberty of reading these three propositions, and I trust the noble Lord will excuse me. The first proposition was, whether it would be politic for the Portuguese government to transfer itself to the Brazils, which was supported by the noble Lord. The second is no less remarkable—whether it is right or likely that Russia will acquire such a degree of power as will endanger the rest of Europe. The third proposition was, whether the American colonies were justified in asserting their independence. Now, I put it to the meeting, whether the noble Lord could have had a better training for the position he now holds," (that of Prime Minister) "than the discussion of such subjects so many years ago. He came to the contest prepared: he had all his arguments ready; they were his own then—they are his own now; and I need not say that, if they were effective then, they are effective now. I trust the noble Lord will excuse these references to his youthful indiscretions. I will not further put his character to the proof than by reading one other extract from those minutes—it is not a proposition by the noble Lord, but a resolution on the part of the Society itself. The resolution is, 'that the thanks of the meeting be given to Lord Palmerston for the dignity and ability with which he had supported the honour of the chair, and that the secretary be requested to convey to Lord Palmerston the regret of the members at his resignation.' I will make one little alteration in the text, and venture to say that that resolution will express the unanimous feeling of the present meeting:— 'That their thanks be conveyed to Lord Palmerston for the dignity and ability he had displayed in the chair.' We have not yet to express our regret for his resignation, and I hope it will be many years to come before the country will experience the loss of his valuable services."

It is needless to say that Lord Palmerston received these reminiscences of Cambridge days in the most genial and good-natured manner, and responded to the Bishop's words very heartily and cordially.

Almost immediately after the opening of the Training College, the Bishop entered upon his ninth visitation of the diocese. His opinions upon some subjects of controversy at the time are thus given in his charge. After referring to church accommodation and the additional buildings provided, he says:—

"In this additional provision, the poor have largely participated. Open sittings, which, in new churches at least, are commonly now admitted without prejudice, have done much for their accommodation; and, in the opinion of many, unappropriated sittings generally throughout the church, would do more. To continue the appropriation of sittings to non-attendants is clearly an abuse, and an abuse which ought to be remedied as often as it occurs. The exclusive right should be in abeyance for the absent, and be transferred to the present. But for my own part, I cannot think the appropriation of particular places to habitual church-goers a wrong doing. It is

agreeable to statute and ecclesiastical law, as well as consistent
with our English habits, and congenial to our domestic usages,
that members of the same family should worship together—
husband and wife, parents and children, kneeling side by side,
and in each other's sight ; the younger looking up to, and pro-
fiting by, the example of the elder, and the elder unravelling,
if needs be, the little intricacies of our liturgical arrangement
for the young, or controlling by a look or quiet word their
wandering attention."

With regard to preaching, he makes the following remarks:—

"And, further, it is to be remembered that, although the
culture of the intellect is essential for mental power and clearness of expression, yet to reduce preaching to a mere intellectual exercise is to degrade it. The Apostle characterizes the
preaching the unsearchable riches of Christ as a 'grace given.'*
It is a gift—a gift to be stirred up, indeed, that the fire may
burn more vividly, but deriving its efficacy in proportion as it
is possessed in demonstration of the Spirit and of power. It is
the meditative habit, rather than intellectual fertility, which
produces a clear and permanent impression of divine truth, and
makes the food and nourishment of efficient teaching.

"I have used advisedly the expression, 'efficient teaching.'
Preaching and teaching are not synonymes. A sermon may be
effective, without being efficient. It may be vigorous, without
being operative. It may please the ear, or tickle the fancy,
without reaching the heart, or affecting the conscience. Many
preachers, popular in their congregations, are not teachers—

> 'Such as Paul
> Were he on earth, would hear, approve, and own.'

They have to address a company of educated hearers, often
uninterested in the solid truths of the Gospel, and requiring to
be fed with a pabulum for the understanding. There is a
demand for something striking and startling, something new,

---

* Eph. iii. 8.

something which gratifies the imagination, which savours of
research, or is suggestive of discussion and argumentation; and
the temptation is strong to seek for topics which admit of
display, and minister questions rather than godly edifying.
This was not our Lord's method; it was not St. Peter's, after
the descent at Pentecost; it was not thus that, by his sermon
in Solomon's porch, he converted five thousand. It was not the
way of St. Paul at Areopagus, even in the presence of the
polite and learned Athenians, or when he filled all countries
from Jerusalem to Illyricum with the Gospel. His preaching
was not with enticing words of man's wisdom, but the wisdom
of God in a mystery, 'rude in speech, yet not in knowledge.'"

"There is no lack in modern sermons of impressiveness or
rousing power. The preaching is, for the most part, Christ and
Him crucified; the arrow which is launched at the hardened
heart is chosen from no other quiver than the Lord's armoury
has furnished; the pool is troubled, as by an angel, for the
disordered soul; the foundation is well and truly laid. But
where is the superstructure? Where is the building up? Who
supplies the strong meat after the milk? Who disciplines and
guides the awakened conscience? Who enters into the details
of Christian duty? Who teaches to 'observe all things whatsoever' the Lord 'has commanded?' The result is a meagre
and shallow Christianity, very little insight into the life of God
in the soul of man,—a very low standard of personal holiness
and saintliness of character. Congregations listen to a dogmatic theology, irreproachable, except in excess,—they detect
nothing in the orthodoxy of the language to disturb their
traditional belief,—they recognise the old doctrinal truths,
supported by the usual texts, but go away unaffected by the
hearing, as full of worldliness as before, without a curb on their
anger, malice, and uncharitableness, habits of life uncorrected,
tempers unrestrained, affections unsanctified, passions unmorti-
fied, without growth in grace or spiritual mindedness. If we
have erred in these things, it is well we should be reminded of

our duty; and should the hand which smites be somewhat rough and the pain inflicted somewhat sharper than the wounds of a friend, we may be content to accept it as wholesome discipline administered for our good by the love of our Divine Master."

The following hint is not unimportant : —

"In one of my early Charges I asked whether there was the habit of counting the absent as well as the present in our churches and at our sacraments. Such a counter-book, if honestly kept, would be an useful remembrancer for aggressive movements against the absentee or the indifferent. Suppose, for instance, every member of every family tabulated within your parochial register, with a memorandum severally annexed as to what each ought to be in respect of outward observances, regard being had to time of life and opportunities of means of grace. Place side by side, in parallel columns, the facts as they concern each, showing, in other words, not what they ought to be but what they are. It should be the aim of the pastor to make the second column tally exactly with the first as to every soul under charge. In as far as it differs from this identity his mission to that particular soul has to that extent failed. It is probable that such a counter-book, if the standard be properly elevated, would make strange revelations in many a parish. And in proportion as it discloses a fearful state of things, it supplies the most powerful imaginable incentive to make him who is to give account of all, and to answer for his dealings, not with the few, but with the many, 'forget the things that are behind, and reach forward to the things that are before.' Statistics drawn from such a book—figures, of course, or facts, not names, or descriptive particulars equivalent to names in a small neighbourhood—if judiciously put forth on proper occasions, would have an awakening effect. They would lead to thought, possibly they might excite opposition, but they would promote life and make the conscience wince, of which opposition, so arising, is an unmistakable sign."

Touching the endowments of the clergy, the offertory is thus referred to:—

"Is there no mine yet unfathomed, which may be profitably worked, if only we can hit the vein? Can the Offertory be made available for this purpose? There are not a few who think so, and some who have made trial of it, and, as it is asserted, with success. Can their example be safely imitated? To this inquiry there could have been but one answer a few years ago from any prudent observer of the signs of the times. Weekly collections had long fallen into desuetude in our Church. Their reintroduction was a novelty, and attempted at a time when other novelties, of a more questionable nature, attracted public attention and incurred general dislike. Rightly or wrongly, the subject became a party question, and he who favoured it was regarded with so much suspicion that the introduction of the practice proved a signal for strife and alienation among the members of the Church. These feelings had their origin in an honest jealousy for the truth, and a dread of imbibing insensibly a dangerous sympathy with Romanizing views at variance with the essential and distinctive teaching of our own Reformed Church; and it would have been most unwise, not to say criminal, to have tampered with them. Wherever, if anywhere, they still exist in connexion with the Offertory, I should earnestly deprecate its introduction. But if, as I think, the lapse of time has been sufficient to show, in most instances, that the practice, apostolic in its origin, and coeval with the earliest ages of the Church, has nothing in itself which need alarm the conscience of the most sensitive adherent to the simplicity of evangelical truth, then I know not why that leaf of our Prayer-book should be closed to us; or why we should refuse to invite our parishioners to lay by in store for the wants of the Church, as well as of the poor, on the first day of the week, after the example of the early Christians in Galatia and at Corinth. The power of the pence is yet to be developed; and where it can be tested, without exciting dissensions and dividing the flock, it may not only be the means of giving exercise for the performance of a great Christian duty, but of realizing results which might supersede, to a considerable extent, the necessity of having recourse to precarious and insufficient aid from external sources."

It will be thus seen that at any rate the Bishop was no party man in the usual acceptation of the term, but was ready to adopt what approved itself to his judgment, from whatever quarter of the Church the suggestion might arise. Mr. Keble, in writing to Sir John Coleridge, thus speaks of this Charge :—

"I have only just got our Bishop's Charge, and it is really admirable to my mind, better even than the newspapers led me to expect; better, I think, as a composition. There was often a sort of strain in what he wrote and preached, which in this he seems to have quite got rid of; and then, as to the matter, it is *very* instructive ; and the tone is so firm yet so candid. I am very thankful, and hope to be the better for it, though it is rather late to mend; but no more of that."—*

* Coleridge's "Memoir of the Rev. John Keble," p. 476.

CHAPTER XXIII.

THE year 1863 once more shows the diocese in a state of distress. The publication of the Bishop of Natal's works inflamed men's minds to a pitch of excitement rarely witnessed. Addresses from all quarters poured in upon the Bishop, signed with wonderful unanimity by the clergy, deprecating the views which Bishop Colenso took with regard to the interpretation of Holy Scripture, and especially that, holding such views, he should still retain the office of a bishop in the Church of England. The Bishop replied to the memorialists with much earnestness and warmth.

In answer to one address he writes :—

"The quotations from this work" (on the Pentateuch) "which you have embodied in your address, amply justify, in my judgment, your solemn remonstrance against the retention of the office of a bishop in the Church by one who holds such opinions. It seems to me to be an outrage alike against religion, and moral feeling."

To another he replies :—

"In common with the whole of the diocese, you appear to have felt deeply the dishonour done to the Holy Scriptures, and even to our blessed Lord Himself by that publication, enhanced as the scandal has been from the quarter whence it has proceeded. It is consolatory to observe the general and emphatic protest of the Clergy against views so pernicious ; and the Laity will not fail to remark with satisfaction that they incur no risk of witnessing in their parishes the inculcation of sentiments alike subversive of the Truth, and, in the mouth of ordained ministers of our Church, repugnant to moral honesty."

The Bishop was very thankful to be able to make arrangements at the beginning of this year, by which his daughter, Mrs. Gibson, who had just been left a widow,* was enabled with her family to rent a house about a mile and a half from the Castle. This added very much to the Bishop's comfort and happiness. "Culverlands" was always an object for a walk or drive as the case might be, and the intercourse between the two houses was kept up constantly and uninterruptedly until the Bishop's death.

He was present, on the 10th of March, at the marriage of the Prince of Wales. On his return from Windsor he writes :—

"The scene there (I will not call it the sight or the spectacle —though in a sense it was such) was really most touching, partly owing to the large number of the members of both the families who were present, and partly to the admirable demeanour of the bride and bridegroom. The first by her manner is found to win all hearts, and I doubt not she has secured that of her husband. The arrangements were all excellent, and very well carried out—pomp without parade, and everything becoming the station, yet with entire simplicity."

In the autumn, after three or four weeks spent in the Channel Islands, where he was assisted in his work by his friend the Bishop of Mauritius, who had formerly served the parish

---

* The Rev. William Gibson, Rector of Fawley, had died at the close of 1862. He was a most earnest clergyman, devoted to his work, and much beloved by all who knew him.

church at Alderney, the Bishop crossed over to France, and, after confirming on his way at St. Servan and Dinant, spent a fortnight very pleasantly in Spain. It will be remembered that a few years previously the cholera had prevented his carrying out his intention of seeing some of the principal places of interest in that country. This year he happily was able to accomplish his purpose, accompanied by one of his sons, his daughter-in-law, and as his Spanish guide, Mr. Dallas.

The following letter shows how keenly the Bishop entered into the interests of the tour.

"SARAGOZA, Oct. 11, 1863.*

" My date will shew you that we have left Madrid, and are setting our faces homeward. We hope to sleep at Barcelona to-morrow—at Perpignan on Tuesday—on Wednesday at Tarascon or Avignon—on Thursday at Lyons—on Friday at Paris, and on the following Monday either in London or Farnham, at the latter place if possible. Madrid is disappointing in everything except the magnificent collection of pictures, worth in itself the journey, and not to be effaced from the memory. Two days' visits were all we could give, and we scarcely looked at anything but the Velasquez', the Murillos, and the Raphaels. Perhaps I ought to add the Spagnolettis, which are in very great number, and highly excellent in their way, but his subjects are so repulsive as to take off greatly from the pleasure of looking at them. He is truly a sensation painter of the first order, but his style is not poetry. We had intended to go to the Escurial on Friday, which is an hour and a half by railway, but the morning was rainy, and we altered our plan, the more readily as its principal attractions have been removed to Madrid. We saw in the afternoon, what is perhaps more unique, the royal stables, a most wonderful exhibition of useless luxury, nearly 500 horses and mules, (200 mules, 300

* At Saragoza the Bishop was much interested to find that, at the hotel at which they stayed, sixteen persons met every Sunday evening, for prayer and study of the Scriptures.

horses) all of extreme beauty except one unfortunate English
horse.   There were only two of ours—one very good, the other
greatly inferior to all its neighbours.   There were 190 carriages
of all sorts and ages, state and ordinary, large and small, some
of them extremely handsome in their fittings of embroidery and
various furniture.   While we were there the preparations were
made for the day's drive,—five carriages and six, drawn either
by horses or mules, the Queen's carriage drawn, as we had seen
it before, by the latter.   Behind the cavalcade came an open
break with two mules, coachman and two footmen, containing
two perambulators for the younger children, for it seems they
all go out driving *en famille*.   The whole was escorted by
about twenty cavalry, two or three equerries, and as many out-
riders.   We afterwards met the whole party again in one of the
streets, and had a good view of the King and Queen.   The
harness department is most curious.   The long room may be
300 feet, fittted up in all parts with cases holding every sort of
horse furniture, suits for coachmen and postilions of every
degree of state, housings, saddles, bits, all in the most polished
state, many of them of the oldest times of the Philips and
Ferdinands, with their histories attached to them.   The country
is far from what I had anticipated—as far as Madrid, extremely
uninteresting, all desert and sand.   Between Madrid and Saragoza it is much more interesting—high rocky elevations, and
most picturesque passages between them, running out of the
extreme of savageness into a happy valley of small extent, fertile with olive trees, occasional orchards, and other produce.
But the houses or rather huts exceed in discomfort all that can
be imagined.   The best are nothing more than hardened mud—
the generality, caverns scooped out of the sand or rock.   The
people, too, seem degraded beyond any that I have seen.   To-
day is a great fête day here.   There is to be a procession with
some gigantic Gog and Magog's carriage in it—why, I know
not—and it collects from all quarters an innumerable multitude
This gives an opportunity for seeing men and manners, but we.

would rather have their room than their company, for we are
considerably inconvenienced in consequence ; and the noises by
day and night—I know not which are the worst or loudest—
are incessant.   We are at a great distance from news, and have
learned very little : at Madrid we saw a *Times* and a *Galignani*.
It is surprising how easily we reconcile ourselves to ignorance
as to what is passing around us.   After all, we probably know
much more than those through whose country we passed yesterday.   I much question whether the majority of them could tell
whether Louis Philippe or Napoleon is on the throne of France.
The changes of temperature are considerable with us.   At
Madrid we were quite cold, and great coats and flannels were
in requisition.   It is now fairly warm again.   The grapes are not
yet picked here—wheat sowing—the Indian corn all gathered."

In the course of the summer of this year, the Bishop was
enabled to set apart a considerable sum of money for the purpose
of augmenting ill-endowed benefices in the diocese ; regard being
had first to the wants of Southwark.   The See was possessed of
a valuable estate in Southwark, let out on lease of lives, two of
which had dropped.   The Bishop, instead of renewing the lives,
made overtures to the Ecclesiastical Commissioners, and they
agreed to purchase the Bishop's rights in the property for a
capital sum of £13,270 and an annuity of £3,200 during the
term of his Episcopate.*   The whole of this sum—both capital
and future income, which ultimately amounted to £34,900—

---

* Archdeacon Jacob, in a sermon preached on the Sunday after the Bishop's
death, says with reference to this :—"The spirit of Bishop Sumner was, beyond
a doubt, that of unselfishness and genuine humility.   Whenever he spoke of
himself—and how seldom was it ever done—he never spoke without an evident
shrinking, and when others did so he looked unhappy.   I remember when he
constituted me one of the trustees of the Fund for Diocesan Objects, consisting
of the capital sum of £13,270 and an annuity of £3,200, instead of appropriating
it—as he had an undoubted right to do—to personal or family objects, his only
remark to my look of surprise was, ' I hope you do not think I have done
wrong.'   I remember his once saying to me, years ago, when I told him some
one complained that he had not paid his subscription to a local charity, ' Has it
been asked for ?   How *can* I recollect the times of payment of four hundred
subscriptions ?' "

was placed by the Bishop in the hands of the two Archdeacons
and the Chancellor of the diocese of Winchester, as trustees for
the purposes above mentioned.   Fifteen of the poorest benefices
in the deanery of Southwark were at once largely benefited by
the Bishop's liberality.   It may not be out of place here, in
connection with this donation, to say one word as to the
Bishop's generosity in money matters.   For many years he was
in receipt of a splendid income from the See of Winchester, but
his gifts were equally splendid.   In the early days of his Episcopate, he devoted £400 per annum of permanent income for
the purpose of augmenting the endowments of some of the
poorer livings in his gift.   He was a liberal subscriber throughout life to the various metropolitan and diocesan charities ;—
helped many a poor clergyman to take a trip to the seaside,
when, otherwise, it might have been impossible for him to do
so ; paid a large proportion of the stipend of many a curate in
poor incumbencies ; and was never appealed to in vain for any
charitable object in the diocese which commended itself to his
judgment.   To a confidential friend who wrote to him respecting a donation to a particular church, he thus replies :—

"I have no thoughts of subscribing more than £25 to the
rebuilding of ——— church.   My ordinary rule is to give £50
to an additional church, and £25 to a rebuilding.   There is no
reason why I should depart from it in this case.   The See has
no property in ———.   In A—— it has much.   But there
were many reasons why I gave largely there, and the last £100
was given to extricate the parish from the difficulty in which
they were placed by the absence of the incumbent, which
rendered the loan to which they had agreed for £800, on credit
of the rates, impossible.   The farmers came forward in a most
praiseworthy manner to raise the sum, and I thought it became
me to respond to their exertions.   But the line must be drawn
somewhere, and I go to the extreme length of my tether.
——— has an interest in one church, I in 750."

None know better than those who have been engaged in the

work of church-building how difficult in ordinary cases it is to
raise the required sum; and doubtless many an incumbent or
layman in the diocese of Winchester can recall the encouragement given to him by the Bishop when, perhaps, his zeal and
enthusiasm threatened to give way to chilling opposition. I
subjoin a letter of this cheering character, by means of which
the incumbent to whom it was addressed was induced to persevere in the good work which he had undertaken, and ultimately
raise the sum of £3000, by which the work was completed.

"FARNHAM CASTLE, *Jan.* 10, 1846.

"MY DEAR SIR GEORGE,

"Mr. Ferrey's report is quite in accordance with what
I had anticipated from his intelligence and honest principle.

"I shall be sorry if you give up the case as lost withou.
another attempt. As you have now got the confirmation of
Mr. Clutton's view, why not revert to your original plan and
endeavour to raise the sum required for carrying it into effect.
If you fail, you cannot help it, but I do not see why you should
despair without a trial. True it is, you may not succeed, but
let it at least be said of you, *magnis tamen excidit ausis.*

"I am, my dear Sir George,

"Your faithful servant,

"C. WINTON.

"The Rev. Sir George Glyn, Bart."

As an instance of his desire to follow the Scriptural rule of
not letting his left hand know what his right hand did, it may
be mentioned, that after his paralytic stroke in 1868, it was only
with the greatest possible difficulty that he could sign his name.
His bankers, therefore, were instructed to honour all cheques
drawn by his eldest son, who was residing with him. On opening his letters one morning, his son was surprised to find a
communication from his bankers to the effect that if the
Bishop authorised another person to sign for him, he must
not draw cheques himself; and on inquiry it turned out

that the Bishop, wishing to make a donation of £50 unknown even to his son, had written and signed a cheque to that amount himself.

At the beginning of the year 1864, the Bishop was placed on a Royal Commission appointed to consider and revise the various forms of subscription and declaration required to be made by the clergy of the Church of England. He had always been of opinion that, whilst it was absolutely necessary that some security should be given by the clergy of an Established Church that their utterances from the pulpit should be in accordance with certain definite and known doctrines, yet that some relaxation from the extremely stringent words hitherto used in the declarations of conformity might be allowed. And this was the view taken by the Commission, and subsequently adopted by Parliament in 28 & 29 Vict. cap. 122, which amends the law as to the subscriptions of the Clergy.

At the same time that the Bishop was nominated a member of this Subscription Commission, he made up his mind to retire from the Church Estates Committee. For eight years he had served most diligently on this Committee, not only during his residence in London, but going up weekly from Farnham for the purpose. Almost every question which comes before the Ecclesiastical Commissioners is first sifted and reported upon by the Estates Committee, and the consequence is that the work arising from the responsible consideration of multitudinous details, which devolves upon the members of the Committee, is enormous. The Bishop had been anxious for some time to retire ; but the Ecclesiastical Commissioners had been subjected to a good deal of censure from various quarters, and the Bishop did not wish to shirk responsibility in connection with that body. In 1864, however, they were able to put out a report of a very favourable character. The country, moreover, was beginning to see that in matters of considerable difficulty, though no doubt mistakes had occurred, yet that on the whole the course adopted by them had been of immense benefit to the Church; and the Bishop, therefore, felt that the time had now arrived when, without impropriety, he might retire and leave the work in younger hands; and, accordingly, he resigned his post at the beginning of February.

With reference to his labours in this branch of Ecclesiastical work, Lord Eversley, one of his co-commissioners, has written to me in the following terms:—

"His good deeds in our extensive diocese, in which he laboured so assiduously, will long live after him. But few people were aware of another work to which he devoted himself with unremitting zeal; and those only who, like myself, had the good fortune to be associated with him for several years on the Estates Committee of the Ecclesiastical Commission, can testify to the admirable manner in which he discharged the varied and complicated duties which it entailed upon him. His familiarity with a very difficult branch of Church law was remarkable; and the pains he took to arrive at a just and equitable solution of the intricate questions which were so frequently brought under the consideration of that Committee insured him the respect and regard of all his colleagues."

Mr. Pringle, the Secretary of the Commission, thus writes to me:—

"My memory is still quite fresh with regard to Bishop Sumner's active connection with this office over a period of some fourteen years. During the last eight years of that term, the part taken by the Bishop, as Episcopal member of the Estates Committee, in the consideration and direction of the business, was very prominent. Neither bad weather, nor absence in distant parts of his diocese, ever stood in the way of his attendance, during the eight or nine months of the Commissioners' session, at the weekly meetings of the Committee. And the Bishop was to be found likewise in his place at the less frequent general meetings of the Board, ready to furnish, in his own lucid and forcible, yet always temperate method, any additional explanations then required as to the grounds of reports made by him and his colleagues on the Committee.

"Apart from Bishop Sumner being always ready to advise or concur in a decision based on principle and merits, irrespective of personal considerations, and without being influenced by apprehension of odium, he brought, in 1856, to the aid of his colleagues on the Estates Committee, and to this official establishment, a peculiar knowledge of the statutes relating to, and the practice adopted by, the late Board of the Church Building Commissioners; and, but for the assistance rendered by Bishop Sumner in that respect, this office must have encountered an unknown and possibly an overwhelming increase of the difficulty which was experienced in carrying on the business of the defunct Church Building Commission, which was then transferred to it.

"The onus of that transfer had been seriously augmented by the simultaneous passing of the important Statute known as 'Lord Blandford's Act,' which contained provisions affecting substantively, and otherwise, those of the Church Building Acts. Bishop Sumner had taken a great interest in the business transacted by the late Board, and he continued to render the most invaluable aid in its management by the Ecclesiastical Commissioners from 1856 to 1864, when he declined to be re-elected a member of the Estates Committee, but left his colleagues fully sensible of the services he had, in these matters, rendered to themselves and to the public.

"It is almost superfluous to add my assurance that Bishop Sumner's manner of receiving and making communications, whether important in themselves, or so only to individuals, was so peculiarly kind and felicitous as to have become proverbial with everybody here with whom he came in contact."

It has been before mentioned that the Bishop's extensive correspondence did not prevent his occasionally occupying his time in composing pleasant *jeux d'esprit*. While staying at the house of one of his sons for three or four days' rest at

Easter, 1864, he received the following lines from Sir John Coleridge, and, as will be seen, was incited to return English for Latin verses.

SENECTUTE LŒTUS.

Obrepens tacito levique grassu
Non ingrata nec invenusta prorsus,
Pulchritudine sed tuâ decora
Succedis domui senecta nostræ.
Salve sanctior hospes et mearum
Posthac quotquot erunt comes dierum,
Quid quod me renuit chorœa dulcis,
Et cœtus juvenum procaciorum ;
Quod sit mens hebeti retusa sensu,
Sublatisque sodalibus relictus
Stem mecum meditans, ut alta rupe
Quæ circumspiciens maris tumultus
Noctu, sola silens, videtur almum
Expectare novæ jubar diei—
At non omnia perdidi, nec omnes.
Me cœli facies, novoque vere
Tellus innumero implicata flore—
Me mulcet volucrum, cadente sole,
Submissum arboreâ melos sub umbrâ.
Mulcent me unus et alter, eriguntque
Quos mecum pueros, senesque mecum
Dulci firmus amor ligat catenâ.
Atque O si potero, Pater Benigne
Pro tantis meritas referre grates,
Conjux optima restat, et propago
Vitâ carior, et corona vitæ.
Nec me certa latet comes senectæ
Humano metuenda mors timore.
At sperare licet, licet—decetque—
Fidentesque Deo ibimus per umbras
Ibimus per iter tenebricosum—
Quo tu Christe Redemptor anteisti,
Mortem morte domans, tuoque amore
In cœlos homini viam recludens.

March, 1864.

The Bishop replied as follows :—

"OLD ALRESFORD RECTORY, *March* 26, 1864.

"MY DEAR COLERIDGE,

"Your hendecasyllables are my delight. A thousand thanks for them. . . . They gave me a sleepless night in trying to recollect and repeat them by heart, and in return I inflict on you the consequences. . . . . . In my view, the mischief of the judgment" (that in the case of Williams v. Bishop of Salisbury, and Wilson v. Fendall) "is not in the sentence itself—for the articles exhibited were so loosely and carelessly drawn, that they would hardly have warranted any other decision—but in the very inconsistent, and extra-judicial comments which accompanied it. The lawyers are in the habit of advising official visitors, to give their judgments and abstain from reasons; why will they not practise their precepts. I am here for three days, then for as many at Brightwell, then working my way through the east of Surrey to London, where I purpose being early in the week after next, and where I hope to meet you ere long.

"Always most affectionately yours,

"C. WINTON.

"Sir John T. Coleridge."

The following lines were enclosed with the foregoing letter :—

TO SIR JOHN T. COLERIDGE, IN RETURN FOR LATIN HENDECASYLLABLES.

χάλκεια χρυσέων.

Friend of my youth, whose early promise gave
    The presage true of civic crowns in store,
Soft sounds thy lyre, as lull of ocean wave,
    Or echo sweet of strains long loved before.

Friend of my manhood'! ne'er forgot and dear,
    Though each in different paths life's labour plies ;
Thy classic muse recalls our schoolboy year,
    Youth's joyous smile, and springtide's cloudless skies.

Friend of my latest age, though blanched my head,
    And slow the life-blood in the lazy vein,
Still clings my heart to thee, nor cold nor dead
    The thoughts that bring me to thy side again.

Time was, when haply Father Thames might see
    Four stalwart youths in fair Etona's grove,*
Arm link'd in arm, in closest amity,
    Emblem of hearts in unison and love.

---

* Coleridge, Patteson, James, and himself.

That fourfold tie is broken.   Time's cold hand
   Has severed hearts which nought besides could sever :
Twice has the tyrant loos'd the golden band,
   And two are gone though still remembered ever.

They beckon us to follow—soon we must—
   We wait God's time—content to go or stay,
So please Him, earth to earth, and dust to dust,
   Or if He wills, to work the live-long day.

May'st thou, dear Friend, in ev'ning's closing hours
   Still richly blest, enjoy thy happy home,
Own the sweet influence of a Saviour's power,
   And cry with latest breath, " Lord Jesus, come."

The Bishop did not resign his post as a member of the
Estates Committee a day too soon, for very heavy extra work
devolved upon him in connection with the preparation of a new
Conspectus of his diocese, and the inauguration of a fresh effort
to grapple with the spiritual deficiencies of South London.   The
Conspectus once more gave very interesting diocesan statistics ;
showing that, between 1851 and 1861, the population of the
diocese had increased by 96,643 ; and that, since 1829, 176 new
churches had been built, and 100 rebuilt, in the two counties ;—
the total expenditure on churches, as far as could be ascertained,
being £1,704,914; on parsonages, £525,229; on schools, £522,039;
—making a grand total of £2,752,182.*

But, notwithstanding the fact that so much had been done,
much still remained which called loudly for a special effort to
be made.   Accordingly, on July 20, a meeting of the Council of
the Surrey Church Association was by special invitation held
at Farnham Castle ; at which, after much consideration, a
Committee was appointed to inquire once more into the spiritual
wants of the suburban parishes of the diocese, and report
thereon to the Council.   In due time this Sub-Committee
reported, and though able to state that, since 1845, twenty-five

* During the Bishop's episcopate, he consecrated about three hundred churches
(new and rebuilt); very nearly four hundred, in addition, being enlarged during
the same time.

new churches, several proprietary chapels, and many schools and parsonages had been built, yet that there was still a great need for further church accommodation; and that, although the incomes of all the livings in the deanery of Southwark had been raised to a minimum of £200 a year, whilst the value of some had been further increased by the munificent liberality of the Bishop of Winchester, yet there were still twenty-six benefices in that part of the diocese unprovided with parsonage houses. Some seventy or eighty additional clergy were urgently required, and it was shown that provision ought at once to be made for sixty-one new schools.

This report of the Sub-Committee was taken into consideration on March 7, 1865, at a meeting held in the library of Lambeth Palace under the presidency of the Bishop; and it was consequently determined that strenuous efforts should be made to raise a special fund to be entitled "The South London Church Extension Fund;" which title was, in 1866, three years before the Bishop's resignation, changed to "The Bishop of Winchester's South London Fund." Upwards of £20,000 was raised on behalf of this fund under the presidency of Bishop Sumner, and the money expended in the various objects for which it was instituted.

In connection with these efforts which the Bishop thus made for the increase of Church machinery, Church services, and Church work generally in the diocese, it is curiously interesting to read the following letter, which, in the autumn of 1864, the Bishop received from one of the most influential laymen in the whole of the diocese.

    " My dear Lord,
        " I have for some time thought that the Church services at ——* are more frequent than is usual in country parishes, and take up too much of the time and exhaust too much of the strength of the vicar and curates, and prevent

---

* A parish with a population of between five and six thousand.

them from doing more good by visiting the poor of the parish.
The church is very large, and cold, and reading and preaching
in it involve a great exertion of voice, which, often repeated,
sensibly strains the organs concerned in the effort. I asked
Mr. —— the other day to send me the statements contained
in the enclosed letter, and I now submit them to you, in order
to have your opinion as to whether some of these services might
not be dispensed with, and with a view of asking you by what
authority such a diminution in the services could be effected.
It seems to me that the services in —— church on Fridays
and on Saints' days might well be discontinued ; the Wednesday
evening services, which Mr. —— says are well attended, being
retained ; and it might be a matter for consideration whether,
in a town of limited population, it would not be enough to
administer the sacrament once instead of twice a month. I
am persuaded that any arrangement which could lighten the
church duties of the vicar and curates, would tend to the real
interests of religion. I believe that the services on Fridays
and Saints' days are very ill attended. The vicar and his
curates display great zeal in the performance of their duties,
but I am convinced that a somewhat different distribution of
their time and application of their physical strength would be
advantageous to the real interests of the parish.

"I am,

"My dear Lord,

"Your obedient servant,

"——."

At the close of the summer of 1865, the Bishop was called
upon to mourn the loss of a dear grandchild, aged only fifteen
years. Sophy, the youngest daughter of the Rev. Robert Sumner
(who had died in 1858), was taken ill at Farnham Castle,
where, with her two sisters and guardian Aunt, she was staying
on a visit ; and while everything was done that the most tender
nursing or skilful medical attendance could devise, no remedies

availed to arrest the fever, and on the 20th of August she passed away.

The Bishop writes the next day to Coleridge :—

"FARNHAM CASTLE, *Aug.* 21, 1865.

"MY DEAR FRIEND,

"... . For the last fortnight we have been under great anxiety about one of my grandchildren, the youngest orphan daughter of Robert. She came here with her Aunt and her sisters, and was seized with fever the day after her arrival, and never left her bed afterwards. Yesterday, Sunday, she entered into the rest of an eternal Sabbath a short hour after prayer had been offered for her in the parish church. Doubtless that prayer was best and most mercifully answered in her removal. She was a good and very amiable child, and we shall greatly miss her in the family circle. The last six months have lessened that circle considerably. Emily has lost her mother-in-law; and George, very recently, the uncle of his wife, Sir Benjamin Heywood, a very remarkable man, and one of the most devotionally-minded and kind-hearted I have ever known. He was quite reverenced in his family, and deservedly so. I remember, years ago, soon after I was made a Bishop, going with Archbishop Howley, then Bishop of London, to the Duke of York, just before the death of the latter, and the Archbishop's remarking that he had arrived at the age when, year by year, he was left more and more alone, friends dropping off, one by one, and ties loosening, and all giving unmistakable warning that his own hour could not be far distant. The same feelings have come to me, and doubtless to you also. *Singula de nobis,* &c. And I have been specially reminded of this lately in looking at the recently published volume of ' Eton Annals,' which show how very few of our contemporaries, and even of those below us, are still surviving. May God bless you and yours, my dear friend, now and always.

     " Your most affectionate,

       " C. WINTON."

The following letter from Queen Emma of Hawaii, in connection with this subject, will be read with interest :—

"HURSLEY, WINCHESTER, *Aug.* 21, 1865.
    "MY LORD,
        "I cannot allow this evening to pass away without
expressing to you the very great sorrow with which I heard of
the affliction which has befallen you and yours. I grieve much
to think that your kind exertions on that Sunday for the
Hawaiian Church should have been the means of separating
you from the last moments of your dear Grandchild.*   Under
the circumstances, the event must always remain impressed
upon my memory; and I sincerely hope, that you, who have so
often told others in what direction to look in the hour of
bereavement, may find your solace only, where only it can be
found.
                    "I am, my Lord,
                        "Your very faithful friend,
                            "EMMA."

Immediately after the funeral of his grandchild at Hale
church, where she was laid by the side of her grandmother,
the Bishop left Farnham for a month, in order that all proper
precautions might be taken for the purification of the castle.
He bent his steps towards the extreme west of England, accompanied as usual by two of his children, and on this occasion
by three grandchildren also.   The party went viâ Totness, Dart-
mouth, Torquay, Plymouth, Falmouth, and Truro, as far as Pen-
zance, where a stay of a week was made, in order to explore the
surrounding country, including The Land's End, and the Botallock Mine.   Great was the surprise of those in charge of the
mine, to find the Bishop determined to be one of the party to
descend into its depths.   This is no trifling undertaking.   In
the first place, the boring at that time extended half a mile

---

* The Bishop was preaching on Sunday, August 20th, in Farnham Church, in
behalf of the Hawaiian Mission, and on his return to the Castle found that his
grandchild had breathed her last.

under the sea, at a depth of about 200 fathoms; and, besides this, the descent was made in a little truck which ran at considerable speed on rails down the shaft in total darkness. The party were specially equipped for the expedition in flannel suits provided for the purpose by the proprietors. The Bishop was honoured by being dressed in one shortly before worn for the same purpose by the Prince of Wales; and, like his companions, he carried a tallow-candle stuck into a piece of clay by way of a candlestick. The captain of the mine, who took the party down, expressed himself as amazed at the pluck and spirit of the Bishop. By Bude, Ilfracombe, and Lynton, the Bishop gradually worked his way home again.

Almost immediately after his return to Farnham, he was requested to preach at the opening of the Surrey County School at Cranleigh. He had taken very great interest in the gradual growth of this school, which had been built at a cost of about £10,000, and throughout he had been one of the most zealous promoters of the undertaking. He heartily rejoiced at the successful inauguration of the school; and, in after years, at its signal success.

The Christmas of 1865 was marked by one of many family gatherings which took place at the old castle. The Bishop in his family relations was quite patriarchal.* He was never happier than when he had assembled under the castle's hospitable roof as many of his children and grandchildren as could be collected together. The house at Farnham was singularly well-adapted for such occasions; for there were numerous rooms in out-of-the-way places, where children could be packed away, and the reception-rooms were large enough to hold any number. Thoroughly enjoyable these periodical meetings were: family union was kept up by them, and the remembrance of them will long live in the minds of those who were privileged to be

---

* The Bishop's family at this time consisted of six children, all married :— John Maunoir, Louisanna, and Charles, born at Highclere ; Sophia Albertina, and George Henry, born at Windsor ; and Emily, born at Farnham. At the time of his death he had seventy-eight lineal descendants.

present, and to be permitted (as was the custom at these times)
to join in the public thanksgiving at church for special mercies
vouchsafed to the family. The following letter, written to the
wife of one of his sons when, in consequence of recent fever in
the family, she and her husband and children were necessarily
absent at one of these seasons, is given as a sample of the
graceful, loving way in which he penned his family notes : "Your
affectionate note of this morning acted beneficially to thaw the
frozen current stagnating about the region of the heart owing
to the inclemency of the weather, which everyone so provokingly
calls seasonable. My fingers will scarcely hold the pen, but I
must force them into action so far as to say, that you have been
greatly in our thoughts, though absent; and that our gathering,
though complete in other respects, has been spoken of daily as
incomplete without you. I am happy to say that, notwithstanding
the snow, which delayed her arrival till a late hour, and her
advanced age, which renders her somewhat tardy in her movements, Mrs. Judith Bird was able again to make her annual
visit.*

"She did not forget to bring with her a little souvenir for the
members of the rising generation, or the juveniles, as in her
patronizing way she calls them ; and she kindly left with me a
token of grand-maternal love—to use her own words—for the
three absentees. The enclosed Post-office Order will acquit me
of my commission, and fulfil the affectionate intentions of the
good old lady."

The following account of the Bishop in his domestic relations,
and of these family gatherings, is written by the same pen as that
to which I am indebted for the reminiscences in chapter xviii.,
page 305.

---

* The Bishop was in the habit, on these occasions, of—in schoolboy phrase—
"tipping" all his grandchildren. On the occasion referred to, one of the party
dressed up as an ancient dame, and was introduced as Mrs. Judith Bird (an
ancestress), and produced from her old-fashioned pocket sundry coins wrapped
up in paper and duly labelled, in the Bishop's own handwriting, for each one of
the grandchildren.

"In 1849 the great sorrow of the Bishop's life came upon him in the death of Mrs. Sumner; he was shut up in such loneliness of heart as only those can know who have suffered a like affliction; he seemed absolutely unable to talk of his grief, or to receive words of comfort, and we could only soothe his sorrow and show our sympathy by watchful attentions. Our little baby (the only grandchild then under his roof), was a great pleasure to him. Every evening we brought her down and put her in his arms; he used to carry her about for an hour at a time, fondling her, and apparently finding some sort of relief to his spirit in the act of amusing her.

"We could never get him to speak of Mrs. Sumner, but after her death he became more tender and loving in manner, and more intent on living for others; he grew more dependent on his children, and they never left him alone from that time, one or other always being his guest: the reverence and devotion of his sons and daughters was unvarying and absolute, and it cannot be a matter of surprise that he delighted in being surrounded by them and his grandchildren. They looked to him for advice in the smallest concerns as in the greatest; they watched every opportunity of helping or serving him, and he seemed to be the very centre of their thoughts. Later on, at Christmas' times, it was his delight to get some of his many descendants in large numbers to the castle, and it was a goodly sight to be at a 'family gathering,' when the walls and corridors rang with merry voices, and fathers, mothers, and children, were revisiting the dear old home, making holiday in the most exuberant manner. Suddenly a whisper from the elders 'my father,' from the juniors 'grandfather,' and there was a general calming down, respectful not depressing; for who delighted in the fun and merriment of his grandchildren more than he did! Enjoyment was doubled whenever he shared in it, but always in his presence the merriment took a quieter and more subdued tone, and something of reverence mixed with it. What a memory those meetings have left in the hearts of his children! The

Great Hall at Farnham, with its old oak fire-place, where the Christmas fire blazed brightly, the pictures gaily dressed with holly, the long table stretched from end to end, round which were seated a joyous company of some forty children and grandchildren with the Bishop in their midst, glancing eagerly to that part of the table where for the time being the merriment seemed greatest, or watching with an amused look the little ones of various ages and sizes who were leaning over, or peeping through the balustrades of the galleries overlooking the hall, to observe what was going on below, and longing for a summons to dessert.

" Then the bursts of glee-singing, or rounds and catches from these vivacious and impatient spirits—the rush and clatter down stairs and clustering round Grandfather's chair, till by parental signs each little individual became absorbed, and almost lost sight of, between the elders for a time.

" Then the entrance of a strange figure, an ancestral Aunt Maria, or Aunt Judith, tall and solemn, carrying a huge basket full of various parcels of different shapes. She was greeted with shouts and laughter, and a crowd instantly surged round her. The strongly marked features, very handsome but slightly masculine, which appeared from under her curls and mediæval headdress, occasioned a few whispered suggestions of 'Papa,' but these were instantly quelled, and Aunt Judith presented a parcel to each of her descendants with a solemn and appropriate remark, which was usually a cause for fresh bursts of fun.

" The gifts were extremely handsome, and the next move was a universal stampede to the Bishop's side, and a chorus of 'Thank you, father,' 'Thank you, grandfather.' He was almost overwhelmed with gratitude and caresses, and looked as glad as the chorus.

" Then the games, and the pleasant interchange of mutual interests in the drawing-room till the bell rang, and the party streamed into chapel for evening prayer.

"Such days can never come again, but they live in the memory, and it is good to have known them.

"But to pass from this home life where the Bishop shone so prëeminently ; we were with him twice in the Channel Islands, once in Spain, twice at Geneva and among the Oberland Alps, once in Ireland and also at the Paris Exhibition. My husband was his chaplain, and I had no office but that of 'lady in waiting.' The Bishop had always seemed so consistent and equable in his home life that I was constantly expecting to find him less perfect when off his guard. I used to observe him very narrowly, wondering if he would fail in 'little things of daily life' abroad. I wondered and watched the more because, as it was said, he had been irritable and autocratic in earlier days, but when we travelled with him, in highways and by-ways, by steam, rail, diligence, outside car, voiturier, mule, or whatever it might be, or were lodged in hotels, miserable country hostelries, second-rate inns, mountain chalets, or ship berths, and experienced both the pleasures and annoyances of travelling, never once was he perturbed or irritated even for a moment. The hot sun, the dust, the Spanish insects and viands, the vexatious waitings, long fastings and blunderings which must come to the best travellers, the rainy days and disappointments, everything was met with the most unruffled cheerfulness and apparent enjoyment. This perfect serenity of temper, this patience and good-humour, was a lesson to every member of the party, and made a profound impression on me. He was a very interesting person to travel with, owing to his appreciation of scenery, architecture and art, and he saw everything that was worth seeing with the enthusiasm of a young man. It was good to be with him at all times, and especially in travelling, for his conversation, information, and enjoyment were a perpetual feast. He admired intensely a tremendous thunderstorm in the Val Moutiers, through which we drove in an open calèche in pelting rain, which I thought not only extremely disagreeable, but really alarming. He was the first to propose our going down the Botallock tin mine in Cornwall, and, clothed in a white flannel dress, and with a tallow candle stuck in the wide-awake which completed the costume, he led the way to the car on rails, down which we were propelled half-a-mile below the sea, into a depth where the heat of the atmosphere was, to say the least, very uncomfortable. 'The first Bishop who had ever ventured down,' said Captain Johns, the guide, with some exultation. He was exceedingly at home on a vessel, and enjoyed steaming about among the Channel Islands, even on the Swinge—a horrible experience—where you roll about over rapids till Alderney is reached. He gave life and courage to our party in Spain, when we had to gallop through Fuentarabia because the cholera was raging, and when, at St. Sebastian, the death-bell was tolling every hour, and people were dying by hundreds. His interest in every place of historic association, in people, their manners and customs, and language, in botany (always one of his favourite pursuits), and above all, in everything beautiful in nature and art, awakened a sort of enthusiasm in his fellow-travellers, and made it impossible for them to be spiritless or dull. Such tours at home and abroad live in the memory, like the family gatherings at Farnham, as red-letter days—amongst the bright and pleasant holidays of our lives."

CHAPTER XXIV.

The Bishop's Opinion on the Division of the Diocese.—Addresses on the subject of Ritualism.—Suit in the Court of Arches.—Pan Anglican Synod.—Decided Stand made by the Bishop.—His Motion carried.—Tenth Visitation of the Diocese.—Last Visit to the Channel Islands.—The Love and Respect in which he was held there.—Letter from Mrs. Carey Brock.

It is hardly necessary to say that the division of the diocese of Winchester was a subject which, from time to time, occupied much of the Bishop's attention. He felt very strongly that the work of the diocese was more than any man—however Herculean in constitution, or unsparing of labour—could successfully grapple with. Much must—so the Bishop felt—be left undone, which he would fain have done. But still the matter was not one which could be settled off-hand. It could not be made a question of territorial dimensions or of arithmetical calculation of population. Consideration must be paid to the metropolitical character of the diocese—the third in point of dignity —as well as to the position of the Cathedral, with the canonical body clustered around it in the centre of Hampshire.

The question was much mooted in 1865 and 1866.

In the former year the Bishop thus expressed himself with reference to this point in the Upper House of Convocation :—" I have to present a petition from 335 noblemen, gentlemen, and clergy in the county of Surrey, praying for an increase of the Episcopate. They say that it has been recommended by the suggestions, although not by direct resolutions, of this house; and they desire to express in emphatic terms their entire concurrence, in a general sense, in those suggestions. They say

truly that the diocese of Winchester, since I have been called
upon to superintend it as its Bishop, has more than doubled in
population; that in the county of Surrey the churches have
been more than doubled in number; that 200 churches have
been added to the number there were when I took office; that
the population of the county has doubled, having risen from
600,000 to nearly 1,300,000; that the diocese extends from
Rotherhithe to the Cathedral of Coutances in France; that it
includes the whole of Surrey (except those parishes in the
diocese of London), Hampshire, the Isle of Wight, and the
Channel Islands; and I do not know whether I might not say
that as Jersey was once in the diocese of Coutances, so now
Coutances is in mine. But the petitioners object strongly to the
suggestion that Surrey, or any portion of it in the metropolitan
district, should be annexed to the diocese of Rochester. They
consider that it would be inconvenient that the bishop, both as
regards his cathedral and his residence, should be removed to a
distance from a large portion of the metropolitan district; they
also consider it would be exceedingly desirable to have a bishop
who should reside within the metropolitan district, not necessarily in one of the important suburban parishes, but at a short
distance, in the midst of the opulent merchants who reside out
of town owing to the facilities of communication. For all these
reasons they pray that in any plans which may be devised for
the increase of the Episcopate, Surrey should have a bishop of
its own, and not be annexed in part or wholly to the diocese of
Rochester. The petitioners comprise the High Sheriff of
Surrey, the Lord-Lieutenant, eleven members of Parliament,
including three of the county members and four members for
boroughs within the county, five chairmen of quarter sessions,
many magistrates, and from 100 to 200 beneficed clergy. I
entirely concur in the prayer of the petition. I have had communication with many who have signed the petition, and with
others living in the county, and my decided opinion is it would
be a most unfortunate step if any portion of the county of

Surrey were attached to the diocese of Rochester. Surrey deserves a bishop of its own; and if it does not have one it should remain as it is rather than be attached to Rochester. As regards the Channel Islands, my own opinion is that they should be erected into a separate see."

It will be seen by the following letter, written by the Bishop in 1866, that he had changed his mind with respect to the best mode of dealing with the Channel Islands :—

"I have often expressed my opinion as well in public as privately, that the see of Winchester requires alteration. The plan, as far as I can collect it from the report;" (*i.e.*, the report of certain proceedings in Convocation at which the Bishop was unable to be present) " now proposed, has two recommendations which are likely to give it a favourable reception with all but Surrey men. It gives a better area and boundary to the Rochester diocese, and it relieves the Archbishop from a portion of his diocesan duties. But that it will be carried into execution, at least within any time that can be calculated, appears to me wholly improbable. The object of the resolution is to move the Archbishop to ask Lord Russell to bring in a Permissive Bill for the erection of three new sees, provided adequate endowments are forthcoming. Will he consent? I greatly doubt it, especially under the present circumstances of his Government. If he does, will the House of Commons pass it ? I think this also is very questionable, looking to the experience of former propositions. But suppose the act passed, from what source is the endowment to be derived? Not from the Ecclesiastical Commissioners, for the funds derived from the Episcopal estates are merged by Act of Parliament in the Common Fund. Local offers have been made to some extent for Cornwall, but I have not heard of any in other quarters.

" Since I began this letter—interrupted two days ago—I have seen the Archbishop, and find on inquiry that he has taken no step at present. I acquainted him with the strong objection taken to the scheme in Surrey, and as I believe by both Laity

and Clergy, and that it would not be in my power to support it
against the strong opposition with which it was sure to be met.
Winchester ought to be relieved—it is difficult to say how.
There would be serious obstacles, even if funds were provided,
in founding a see for the Channel Islands, and that relief, if
given, would not be material. I do not myself see the way to
any ;movement at present, but you may be assured that no
movement will be considered by me as hostile or in any degree
whatever as personally offensive."

It may be remembered that in 1851 when the pastoral of the
united body of bishops was published, the Bishop of Winchester
was able to say that his own diocese was comparatively free
from the ultra-ritualism complained of. Of course in so large a
diocese there must always be considerable differences of opinion
amongst the clergy, and consequently differing practices. No
one was more tolerant than the Bishop, or more large-hearted
in the view which he took of the subject generally, provided
only that the practices of his clergy were restrained within what
he believed to be the limits marked out by the Church of
England. And as years passed on the Bishop became more
and more tolerant of views not altogether coinciding with
his own. Under date Oct. 1, 1866, he writes to a friend,
referring to a speech made by one of the public men of the
day:—

"I think it may be doubted whether one great religious
danger of the day is 'the tendency to fetter unduly Christian
liberty,' &c. I am not sure whether the tendency—for the most
part—is not in an opposite direction. I feel myself, and I think
very many feel similarly, a disposition to enlarge the legitimate
boundaries of Church comprehensiveness far beyond what I
should have done twenty years ago, and I act upon this
principle."

But towards the close of 1866 matters connected with one
church in the Isle of Wight pained him exceedingly. I only
mention them now because they were the means of eliciting

from the Bishop a somewhat elaborate statement on the subject
of ritualism. The clergy of the Island memorialised him with
reference to the particular practices complained of, earnestly
disclaiming any participation in them or the teaching which
they were supposed to subserve, and requesting the Bishop to
take such measures in the exercise of his " Episcopal authority
as might seem best calculated to check such practices referred
to as extravagant, and to stop those which openly contravene
the law."

In his reply, dated Jan. 10, 1867, the Bishop says:—

" . . . . . . I entirely participate in your objections to
the practices in question ; I have observed them with deep
concern, and although I have reason to believe that, at present,
these excesses are confined to a very few churches, as far as my
own diocese is concerned, I am fully aware of the discredit they
bring upon the Church generally, and of the evil consequences
which must result from their continuance without effective
check and control.

" You will not be slow to believe that I am painfully alive to
the responsibility which rests upon myself as Diocesan, in regard
to the treatment of this excessive ritualism. There are only
two modes, as it appears to me, by which it can be met—either
first, by resort to legal coercion, or secondly, by appeal to moral
obligation.

" The opinions recently given on several of the questions at
issue, by some of the most eminent legal authorities, as well at
the Common Law Bar, as in the Ecclesiastical Courts, afford
some data for judging the probable result of proceedings in the
Courts of Law, and if I am correctly informed, steps have been
already taken for trying this issue. At the same time it cannot
be dissembled that very serious difficulties must necessarily
arise at arriving at a decision on matters out of the common
range of litigated questions.

" The bearing of rubrics upon canons, and of canons upon
rubrics, the ambiguities of statutes sometimes at apparent

variance with each other, the effect of the disuse of centuries
upon ancient usages, the conflicting evidence of the ancient
usages themselves, are all considerations which greatly complicate
the case, and render resort to legal measures, except in the last
instance, extremely undesirable. Add to this the technicalities
of the law, and the mischief which would arise from possible
failure, an issue which cannot be lightly appreciated, or too
strongly deprecated.

"Appeal to moral obligations has not been withheld, and had
it been more successful, the memorial which you have presented
would have been superfluous.   There are, however, some recent
indications which may lead to a hope that, aided by the light
which the opinions of Counsel have thrown upon some of the
questionable practices, deference may be paid, if not to modern
episcopal injunctions—to directions such as were issued by Ridley
in his Visitation Articles, that the ministers 'do use only the
ceremonies and gestures appointed by the Book of Common
Prayer, and none other.'   I must frankly confess, however, that
I should entertain more sanguine expectations of this result, if
the ceremonies introduced were no more than ceremonial.   But,
as you have yourselves pointed out, their real importance lies
in their teaching of doctrine, and this is so far from being concealed that it is openly alleged as the main reason for contending for them.   They are called 'the very language of dogma'—
and again, 'Ritual is valuable only as the expression of doctrine,
and as a most important means of teaching it, especially to the
uneducated and to the poor.'

"If this be so, and if the doctrine taught be not the doctrine
of the Church of which we are members and accredited
ministers, as interpreted by the plain meaning of our Articles
and Liturgy, the deviation from her teaching, by whatever
means, and at whatever cost, must be effectually corrected.
The principle of forbearance has its limits.   If exhortation
and godly counsel fail of effect, and the promise of reverent
obedience be set at nought, the solemn engagement to banish

and drive away all erroneous and strange doctrines must be observed, and the truth of God's Word vindicated by all lawful means and earnest contention for the faith, as this Church and Realm have received the same.

"It is sometimes alleged in support of ritualism that it compensates for defects, that it supplements the short-comings of others, to whom disregard of the Church's rules in essentials is, I believe, often erroneously imputed. It might be answered that the faults of one extreme, if there be such, do not extenuate the faults of another, and that re-action must not be carried into extravagancies. But the best answer will be by carefully removing all plausible pretence for it. Fair allowance must be made for the ordinary customs in general use for three centuries, for the difference of times and the circumstances and usages of the age in which we live. But apart from these considerations, should there be want of due solemnity in the conduct of Divine Service, mutilation of its offices, scant observance of times and seasons, exaltation of part of the ministers' duties, to the detriment or neglect of others, violation of the Church's regulations in their true spirit and meaning, if found to exist in any of the Churches, which I am far from believing to be the case—these are faults which should be remedied with scrupulous attention . . . . . . Fervently commending you to the Grace of God with prayer for the Divine blessing on your ministries,

"I am your very faithful friend and brother,

"C. WINTON."

Again—replying to an address very numerously signed by the clergy of the Archdeaconry of Winchester on the same subject, under date March 30, 1867, he says :—

"You state your conviction that, for the satisfaction of our lay brethren, and for the vindication of the true character of our Church, some authoritative check upon the observances of which complaint is made is now imperatively demanded. I concur entirely in this view. There is no doubt that these external observances are exercising a very serious and growing influence upon the public mind. It will be a great mistake to suppose that they are an offence only to a section of the clergy. They have become a prominent object of attention among all classes, and are acting to a very dangerous extent on the attachment of the intelligent laity to the Church. They cause, not division only, but alienation. Irritation and angry feelings are excited, and end in secession. Measures, however, are in progress, which, it is hoped, will have the effect of procuring a settlement of the questions at issue, to which all parties must pay obedience.

"As regards the vestment question, I have reason to believe that an application is about to be made to the Sovereign for a Royal Commission, to inquire into and report upon the true meaning of the rubric prescribing the ornaments of the Church and of the ministers. The law once defined, the main difficulties would be removed. I should gladly see the conclusions on this subject of the Committee on Ritual of the Lower House of Convocation established authoritatively. Those conclusions are, that the clerical vesture should be in accordance, as far as relates to parish churches, with the Advertisements of Queen Elizabeth, which, while ordering the use of the cope in cathedrals and collegiate churches, enjoined the use of the surplice in all the ministrations of the parish churches ; and this was subsequently embodied in the canons of 1603.

" Meanwhile, and awaiting the issue of these proceedings, I earnestly deprecate all personal bitterness and angry contention in your intercourse with those that differ, even upon the most important articles of our Faith. By a more diligent study of the Divine Word, by a closer adherence to the full meaning of the articles and formularies of our Church, by a careful attention to clear and explicit statements on points of doctrinal truth, our duty is to strive to imbue our flocks with a due appreciation of the blessing enjoyed by the members of the

Church in her scriptural Liturgy, and to guard them sedulously from the contagion of pernicious error. Above all, let not prayer be wanting that God, at His own time, and by methods of His own, may be pleased to banish and drive away all erroneous and strange doctrines, and to bring all into 'the unity of the Faith, and of the knowledge of the Son of God.' "

Once more; to an address presented to him at Winchester House with clerical and lay signatures, of members of the Church of England, in the three metropolitan deaneries of Southwark, Lambeth, and Streatham, the Bishop replied as follows:—

"Before I make any formal answer to the address which you have forwarded me, I desire to say that I value very highly the opinions of the laity. Ever since I have had the duty of superintending the diocese, I have always considered it to be one of my first obligations to confer with the laity, and to receive suggestions from them. I am very happy, therefore, to see so large a body of the laity of the three deaneries, and to have the opportunity of learning from them their opinions on the subject. I will now make a formal reply to your address. It is with extreme regret that I feel myself compelled to acknowledge that the introduction of an excessive ritual into some of our churches gives but too much reason for the expression of opinion contained in your address, and amply justifies the alarm felt by a numerous body of the laity resident in the three deaneries of Southwark, Lambeth, and Streatham. If the practices to which reference is made were purely novel and indicative of nothing more than an increasing love of ornamentation, there might be grounds for tolerating them, however objectionable in point of taste. But the gravity of the question really consists in the return to forms and modes of worship once rejected from our churches as inconsistent with the principles of our reformed faith. They confessedly involve doctrines at variance, as we believe, with the plain meaning of our Articles and Liturgy, and once, and, as it was hoped, for ever, solemnly repudiated by the Church, of which, clergy and laity alike, we are members. On some of those practices you have animadverted, and as I think justly, connecting them with the declaration recently presented to the Archbishop of Canterbury, and you give as your opinion, that the time has arrived when prompt measures must be adopted to restrain and correct the grievance of which you complain. But those measures, as it appears, can only be effected through the authority of the courts of law. You refer to the resolution on ritualism passed unanimously at a very numerous meeting of the bishops in the Upper House of Convocation of the province of Canterbury, and you express your hope that I shall not be content with it. That resolution, in addition to pointing out minor evils, set forth the dangers of favouring errors deliberately rejected by the Church of England, and fostering a tendency to desert her communion. This was an attempt to guide by the force of opinion, proceeding from a quarter entitled by position to respect and deference; but where persuasion and remonstrance fail, the Episcopal bench have no summary mode of action. They can only act authoritatively through the medium of the law; and you are not ignorant of the uncertainties attending the prosecution of intricate and difficult questions, whether of doctrine or discipline, in the Ecclesiastical Courts. Since, however, that resolution was passed, a suit now in progress has been commenced in the Court of Arches, with the view of testing the legality of some of the most objectionable practices of the ritualists. Whatever be the result in the first instance, there can be no doubt that ultimately the case will be carried to the highest court of appeal, and a decision obtained on the questions at issue, which will be at once final and binding on the practice as well as on the conscience of the clergy. The law, on which high legal authorities deliver conflicting opinions, being thus defined and settled, the main difficulties will be removed, and private judgment could not countervail the decision of the court.

Meanwhile, a Royal Commission has been issued, which has already commenced a wide field of inquiry. In the constitution of the commission you, in common with others who, rightly or wrongly, have freely expressed their distrust elsewhere, appear to have little confidence. At the same time, whatever be the conclusions at which its members arrive collectively, good cannot but result from the full ventilation of the subjects under discussion by men of different minds and various phases of thought, acting under a sense of the deep responsibility of the duty assigned to them. It would be worse than useless during the actual pendency of the suit at law, on the one hand, and the simultaneous action of a commission on the other, to institute further proceedings to be carried on *pari passu* in an additional prosecution. I am painfully sensible of the truth of your remark, that the circumstances which have given rise to your address are destroying the confidence and exercising a very prejudicial and growing influence upon the attachment of the laity to the Church. They cause, not division only, but alienation. They paralyse, as I have myself had reason to experience, to a great extent, the progress of Church extension ; they threaten the very existence of our polity as the Church of the nation. But pending the issue of proceedings already in progress, I earnestly deprecate all hasty movements which may increase the difficulties and weaken the hands of those who are labouring to protect the purity of some of the most important articles of our faith. For my own part, while holding no sympathy with an excessive ceremonial, which I deem inconsistent with the simplicity of the Church of the Reformation, and pained at the jeopardy in which some of her distinctive doctrines appear to be placed, I cannot see my way to do more at present than promise consistent discouragement, and assure you of my determination to repress error of doctrine and excessive ritualism by every lawful means within my power. And I earnestly ask your prayers that God will be pleased, at His own time and by whatever instrumentality, to banish and drive away all erroneous and strange doctrine, and to bring us all into the unity of the faith and of the knowledge of the Son of God. I wish to add a few words. A suggestion is made as to the withholding of the license of the curate. That is not altogether so easy and summary as some might think. The bishop has not the power to remove him absolutely at his own will. The curate has the right of appeal to the archbishop, and the latter is bound by Act of Parliament, and has to decide according to law. In all cases of difficulty he has the assistance of his legal assessors. No bishop of any degree of prudence would subject himself to a reversal of the dismission. He would not act unless he was quite satisfied that he had just grounds for such action. I am free to say, in the present state of things, it would be very difficult to deal with incumbents, and I think that it would scarcely be right and fair to deal with the weaker one, and let the really great offender go scot-free. Besides, the curate is not always a free agent. He acts under the direction of the incumbent, and it would be hard to deal with him and not the incumbent. It has been my misfortune to be concerned in more than one suit in the Ecclesiastical Courts, and I can speak of the delays which occur and of the difficulties attendant on a suit. I can assure you that the matter has long had my earnest consideration, and I thank you for the expressions of confidence in me. It really gives me intense anxiety."

In consequence of the representations thus made to him by the great majority of the clergy of the Isle of Wight, and the reports which reached him from many quarters of the excessive ritual persistently carried on at Swanmore near Ryde, the Bishop thought it his duty at the beginning of 1867 to institute proceedings against the incumbent of that church for certain practices, which, as was alleged, were contrary to the formularies of the Church of England. This matter was not entered upon without much previous and anxious deliberation. Consultation was held with several of his episcopal brethren, the opinion of two eminent lawyers was taken as to the probable issue of a suit, and at length the Bishop deemed it his bounden duty to do what in him lay to banish and drive away practices, in his opinion, tending to the inculcation of superstitious errors. The case was heard before Sir R. Phillimore, and in February, 1870, judgment was given in the Bishop's favour on all the points argued. "The defendant was charged with the ecclesiastical offences of adding to the ceremonies and rites prescribed by the law to be used in church, by the burning of lights, and the use of incense, and in addition he was charged with causing or permitting two lighted candles to be held, one on each side of the priest, when reading the Gospel, such lighted candles not being required for the purposes of giving light." The use of incense and the lighting and burning of the candles, according to the facts proved, were pronounced to be illegal acts, and the defendant was admonished to abstain from such practices for the future, and was condemned in the costs of the suit. There was no appeal from this judgment, and though much pained at being thus forced to enter into the law courts as the prosecutor of one of his own clergy, yet the Bishop was deeply thankful that the issue of the suit proved that he had taken no narrow view of the case, but that which was pronounced, after many and able arguments on both sides, to be in accordance with the authorised formularies of our Church.

Besides the subject of ritualism, there was another matter, which, during 1867 much occupied the attention of the bench of Bishops—I allude to the Pan-Anglican synod. In February, 1866, an address from the bishops, clergy, and laity of the Canadian branch of the United Church of England and Ireland was presented to the Lower House of Convocation of the province of Canterbury. In this address the members of the synod, after having detailed some of the peculiar difficulties affecting the colonial Church, expressed an earnest desire that "the members of the Anglican Communion, in all quarters of the world, should have a share in the deliberations for her welfare, and be permitted to have a representation in one General Council of her members, gathered from every land." In consequence of this address, his Grace the Archbishop of Canterbury (Longley) was requested by the Lower House to direct the appointment of a committee, to consider and report upon the subject. The Archbishop appointed a committee, which, in June, 1866, reported strongly in favour of the movement. This report was considered in the Lower House in February, 1867, but at the suggestion of Archdeacon Wordsworth (now Bishop of Lincoln), the House, instead of adopting it, carried the following motion :—

"That this House tenders its sincere thanks to the committee on the address of the Canadian church, for the labour which they have bestowed on the subject, and for the report which they have framed and presented to this House, and desires to convey to his Grace the Archbishop of Canterbury, a respectful expression of an earnest desire that he would be pleased to issue an invitation to all the bishops in communion with the Church of England, to assemble at such time and place, and accompanied by such persons as may be deemed fit, for the purpose of Christian sympathy, and united counsels on matters affecting the welfare of the Church, at home and abroad : that this resolution be forwarded to the Upper House."

There was undoubtedly a very general feeling in the Lower House of the Convocation of Canterbury that such a conference as that which was prayed for would be calculated to be very beneficial to the highest interests of the Church. Such too was the opinion of the Archbishop of Canterbury, for it appears from a statement in the Upper House of Convocation, as well as from the letter subjoined, that the Archbishop had already made up his mind to assent to the request preferred by the Metropolitan of Canada. He thus writes to the Bishop of Winchester :—

"LAMBETH PALACE, *Feb.* 8, 1867.

"MY DEAR LORD,

"I am extremely sorry that you could not be present at our meeting to-day, for it was one of the most interesting and important at which I have ever been present. There was a debate of four hours, and the result was the unanimous adoption of the resolution of which I enclose a copy. [The resolution was—'Agreed to unanimously at the meeting of the Archbishops and Bishops at Lambeth, February 8th, 1867. We, the archbishops and bishops of English, Irish, Colonial, and American Sees, here assembled, pray your Grace to invite a meeting of all the bishops of the various churches holding full communion with the united Church of England and Ireland.'] The Bishop of Illinois spoke in a most earnest and effective manner in behalf of the resolution. He said that he could not possibly carry back tidings more gratifying to the whole American Episcopate than those which were embodied in the resolution. He could answer for all his brethren—and they are forty-four.

"Then the two Irish archbishops were present, besides some of their suffragans, and the Archbishop of Armagh said he could answer for them all. The Metropolitan of Canada was also present, speaking in behalf of all his suffragans. Then, besides the seven colonial bishops who were present, I have received tidings by letter from ten others, of their willingness to attend an invitation to the effect of the resolution, should it be made, and New Zealand also concurs. So that the resolution having really the approval of between ninety and a hundred bishops of churches holding full communion with the United Church of England and Ireland, I felt it impossible to resist the appeal, and I hope you will feel with me, that when there is an evident yearning after such a meeting as this in all the various churches so situated, it would be wrong to frustrate their earnest wishes.

" Believe me,

" My dear Lord,

" Yours very truly,

" C. T. CANTUAR."

Accordingly on the 15th of February, the Archbishop, speaking in the Upper House in reply to some objections urged by the Bishop of St. David's, gave a short and simple explanation of the object of the gathering. No declaration of faith was to be made, and no decisions come to which should affect generally the interests of the Church. The bishops would meet together for brotherly counsel and encouragement, in the hope that the bonds already existing between the colonial and the mother Church might be strengthened. There would be no attempt made to enact any canons or to make any decisions binding on the Church.*

The Archbishop accordingly issued his invitations; and, on the 24th of September, the Conference assembled for three days' discussion in the Hall at Lambeth, under the presidency of the Archbishop. Seventy-eight bishops were present, and never perhaps, in the annals of the English Church, was a more important conference held. There were rocks ahead, and shoals on every side; and there were not wanting some who doubted whether the good ship would be safely steered through the stormy waters. Most unfortunately, in my opinion, the details of each day's discussion have not as yet been allowed to be made public. But I believe that the following account of the part taken in the Conference by the Bishop of Winchester is absolutely correct; and I know that many of those who were then gathered together were of opinion, at that time, that the firm stand taken from the very outset by the Bishop of Winchester, in which he was nobly backed by his intimate and dear friend Bishop McIlvaine of Ohio, amongst others, preserved the Conference from falling into inextricable confusion. Parties were at that time in a complicated state. The discussions which had arisen in connection, first with the "Essays and Reviews," and then in connection with Bishop Colenso, had greatly strengthened the hands of the High Church Party. Men found it difficult to take a dispassionate and legal view of the matters in dispute; and there were some who, availing themselves of the unpopu-

---

* "Chronicle of Convocation," Feb. 15, 1867, p. 807.

larity of Colenso, endeavoured to gather recruits to their side,—
who, disgusted with the teaching of "Essays and Reviews," forgot
that opposition to one special form of error, however grave, does
not involve soundness on all other points of doctrine, and that
although in this particular instance they might be glad to join
their forces with those of the High Church party, yet still that
in many and very important matters they were far from being
united. It is not, therefore, surprising to find, that difficulties
arose at the very outset of the Conference.

The first sentence of the introduction to the resolutions submitted to the assembly, was couched in the following words :—

"We (the) Bishops of Christ's Holy Catholick Church, professing the faith of the primitive and undivided Church as based
on Scripture, defined by the first four general councils."

The apple of discord was at once thrown down by the Bishop
of Vermont, who objected to the terms "first four general
councils," maintaining that they did not offer a full exposition
of the faith of the Church, and raising the question whether the
number six should not be substituted for the number four.

The Bishop of Illinois wished to omit all reference to numbers.

The Bishop of Winchester then rose and pointed out the
different designation of the members forming the conference in
the words proposed to that by which they had been summoned.
They had been summoned as "Bishops of Christ's Holy Catholic
Church in visible communion with the United Church of England
and Ireland." He thought it most desirable that this phraseology
should be adhered to. He further took objection to the sentence
"professing the faith of the primitive and undivided Church,"
for these words seemed to him to represent two things. By the
primitive Church he understood the Church of the first three
centuries, but by the undivided Church he understood the
Church up to the eighth or ninth century. If his view was
correct, it seemed to him that to speak of the English Church
as professing the faith of the primitive and undivided Church,
would involve the speaker in a difficulty in conducting an

argument with a Roman Catholic. He therefore suggested
that the words should run thus : " We, the Bishops of Christ's
Holy Catholic Church, in visible communion with the United
Church of England and Ireland, professing the faith delivered
to us in Holy Scriptures, maintained by the primitive Church,
and re-affirmed by the Fathers of the English Reformation, now
assembled, &c." The Bishop's speech of which the above is
an outline, was very loudly applauded, but a doubt arose
whether the word " re-affirmed " could be correctly used in the
manner proposed.

The Bishop of Ely (Harold Browne), thought it expressed
very accurately what did take place at the Reformation, but
the Bishop of Winchester ultimately suggested that the word
should be entirely omitted, so making the word "maintained"
to govern the whole sentence.

The Bishop of Ohio very strongly supported the Bishop of
Winchester, and ultimately, after two or three amendments,
including the Bishop of Vermont's, had been put and lost, the
Bishop's was carried by 38 to 21. I have been assured by
one who was present that the feeling of thankfulness and satisfaction at the result was very strong amongst the majority of
those in conference assembled. They had felt deeply anxious
during the progress of the discussion, which was a protracted
one ; and it seemed that, humanly speaking, nothing but the
wisdom, prudence, and conciliatory bearing of the Bishop of
Winchester, whilst united with great firmness, averted what
was at one time much dreaded—open disruption amongst the
assembled Bishops. There is little doubt but that at that time
the English Church was passing through a most perilous crisis ;
the danger was imminent, and at one time it appeared as though
the Conference would rather promote disunion than tend to
peace. I believe that, under God, nothing but the consistent
course taken throughout by the President of the Conference,
backed as it was by the majority of the bishops present, prevented a catastrophe of the gravest character.

The Archbishop of Canterbury (Tait), writing in 1873 to Bishop Sumner, thus refers to the part which he had taken in the Conference :—

"ADDINGTON PARK, CROYDON, *April* 18, 1873.

"MY DEAR LORD,

"Let me thank you very heartily for sending to me the two interesting letters, which I return, respecting the last days of our dear brother, the Bishop of Ohio.

"It is satisfactory to know that due honour will be paid to the dear remains in Westminster Abbey.* This seems to be very soothing to the whole family. . . . . Much will the Bishop's loss be felt in England and America. He was a true bond of union, not only between the two Churches, but also between the two countries, and this union was cemented by his genuine Christian character. How well I remember the important position taken by you and him at the Lambeth Conference, which so much tended to the happy issue of that meeting. I trust you are keeping pretty well. All the accounts I hear from time to time speak of your quiet enjoyment of your family life. . . . .

"Ever yours sincerely,

"A. C. CANTUAR.

"The Rt. Rev. BISHOP SUMNER."

Almost immediately after the Bishop returned to Farnham from the Lambeth Conference, he set out on his tenth visitation of the diocese.† It was impossible but that the Bishop should feel how unlikely it was that he should ever be permitted again to meet his clergy at visitation, and there is a

---

* The allusion is to Bishop M'Ilvaine, of Ohio, who had died on the 10th of March, at Florence, and whose remains, through the kindness of the Dean of Westminster, were placed for four days in Westminster Abbey in the course of their removal from Italy. A special service was held in the Abbey before they were taken to Liverpool for transmission to America.

† At this time only twenty-one incumbents in the nearly 400 cures of Hampshire, and no more than three in the 250 parishes of Surrey, were ministering in the same places as they were at the Bishop's entrance upon the see. Not a single member of the cathedral body remained who had welcomed him on his first coming to Winchester.

gravity and seriousness about his utterances which show the deep responsibility which he felt.*

I subjoin the passage in which the Bishop referred to the Lambeth gathering. After speaking of the establishment of a Diocesan Conference as a matter to which his attention had been turned, and the possibility of which he was seriously considering, he adds, "I am the more encouraged to indulge in these hopeful feelings from my recent experience of the Conference of bishops of the Anglican Communion, in which it has been my privilege to participate. I hear the question raised, What are the results? What decisions? What settlement of faith and discipline? And if none of these conclusions can be promulgated, they who looked without warrant for the exercise of the functions of a general synod are disappointed, and inquire why this concurrence of bishops of the Reformed Church from distant quarters of the globe? Churlish would it have been, and unbrotherly, if the application for united counsel under difficulties, proceeding from the Metropolitan and Bishops of the Canadian Church, supported by the unanimous assent of a numerous meeting of archbishops and bishops of the Home and Colonial Church, had been met with a stern refusal. But independently of this constraining motive, I count it gain if men of various shades of theological opinion, but all acknowledging One Common Head, and bound by the same sacred obligations to promote the glory of God and the salvation of souls to the best of their power, should have met together, face to face, in mutual conference, and discussed the most spirit-stirring subjects with perfect openness of speech, but with no interruption of friendly feeling, and in the confiding

---

* A letter from Charles Kingsley, received immediately after the delivery of the Charge, says: "Allow me to express the deep gratification—and I trust edification—which I received from your charge. Had I not been compelled to return by the 3 P.M. train, I should have joined my voice to those which—I doubt not—have already urged your Lordship to publish it. May you be long spared in the same wonderful vigour of body and mind to speak to us the words of peace and wisdom, and Gospel truth."

freedom of brotherly love.   I count it gain if hearts have been warmed to sympathy with brethren, separate by accident of position, but one in the bonds of the Gospel; if information has been imparted, from this or that quarter, which local knowledge alone could supply; if the ties of fraternal affection and Christian Communion have been more closely drawn in union with our common Lord.   Above all, I count it gain if we have been permitted to kneel together in united worship, and 'with one mouth to make our supplications to God, even the Father, that by the power of the Holy Ghost, He would strengthen us with His might, to amend amongst us the things which are amiss, to supply the things which are lacking, and to reach forth unto higher measures of love and zeal in worshipping Him, and in making known His name.' "

In the autumn of this year, the Bishop paid what turned out to be his last visit to the Channel Islands; and in connection with this, it may be well to insert the following extract from a letter written by Mrs. Carey Brock, wife of the Dean of Guernsey, showing that, as at first, so up to the last, there was no portion of his diocese in which the Bishop was more respected and beloved than in the Channel Islands:—

"The general remembrance is the same everywhere, as of one whose very presence was a delight to us all, so universally beloved did he make himself amongst us by his genial kindness, his wonderful consideration for everyone's feelings, and his sympathy with all.   I think this was what made him so much beloved.   He had a kind word for everybody, and never seemed to forget anyone, rich or poor—all were treated with equal thoughtfulness by him.   We used often to admire the way in which he would always, no matter how busy or tired he was, *make* time to go and visit those who, since he had last been amongst us, had lost their husbands.   The widows of our clergy seemed specially to call forth his tender sympathy; but no doubt this was the case everywhere.   I have thought that it must be not *only* because he had such a dear tender heart for all, but because he knew so well what that special desolation was, that he longed to pour in his share of balm wherever he felt this wound still was. I don't think he can have been loved more truly in any part of his large diocese than he was here. The sympathy and liberality of his character seem the features best remembered here. A lady here once said to me that she always thought of him in connection with that verse, ' All these things did Araunah, *as a king*, give unto the king.' What he did was always done in such a kingly way. I am sure no servant of God ever more fully carried out the Apostolic injunction to ' do good, and be rich in good works, and ready to distribute and willing to communicate.' The delight of *having* always seemed with him to consist in the delight of *giving*. It seemed such a pleasure to him to be able to give pleasure to others. I remember so well when I wrote my book on the Collects, and my husband wished it to meet with a few words of approbation from our Bishop, I thought it such presumption to trouble him on the subject, when I knew how much engaged he was with so many important matters, that I mentioned it to him most tremblingly one day, asking his advice about it. I recollect so well the very place where we stood in the dear old breakfast gallery, and his kind look as he took my hand and said, ' My dear, always look upon me as an old friend.' So the proofs of the book were sent to him, and to my surprise, when he returned them, it was with the preface which is now attached to them, and which of his own free kindness he had taken the trouble to write. Back, through a long course of thirty years, my mind recalls him always the same, and it is one of the truest subjects of thankfulness of my life that I was allowed, I may say by God's good providence, that last visit to Farnham just before his death, and how he kissed my children when we parted with a tender blessing sort of way that touched my very heart."

CHAPTER XXV.

THE BISHOP'S ILLNESS, RESIGNATION, AND DEATH.
1868—1874.

The Bishop seized with a stroke of Paralysis.—Partially recovers from the attack.
—Letters from the Archbishop of Canterbury and Bishop of Oxford.—
Arrangements made for his Eldest Son to live with him.—Bishops' Resigna-
tion Act passed.—Thereupon he at once resigns his See.—Letters from the
Archbishop and Mr. Gladstone.—Addresses and Letters on his Resignation.
—Bishop of Oxford appointed as his Successor.—Gathering at Farnham to
meet the new Bishop.—Lines by Dr. Monsell.—The Bishop in his Retire-
ment.—Gradual Failure of Health.—Reminiscences by the Wife of one of his
Sons.—His Death.—Is buried in Hale Churchyard.—Lines by Dr. Monsell.

AND now, in God's good Providence, the end of the Bishop's
life of incessant activity drew near. The shadows were deepen-
ing around him, and soon he would be called to enter upon that
lengthened time of waiting which was appointed for him ere
weariness and weakness gave place to rest and peace in his
eternal Home.

At the beginning of the year he issued the usual notices with
respect to a circuit for confirmations in Hampshire. He was
intending to set out from Farnham Castle on the 7th of March,
but on the afternoon of the 4th the hand of God arrested him
in the very midst of his work, and he was struck down by
paralysis.

There had been no very apparent failing of strength previously, except that, on the morning of the day on which he was
seized, his voice, whilst he was reading prayers in chapel, trem-
bled so, that one of his daughters who was present looked up,
fearing that he was taken ill. The Bishop himself must have
felt that he was not in his usual state of vigour, for at breakfast

that morning a riddle* was asked, and on his quickly guessing it he said, " Oh, come ! I have not lost that power at any rate." That afternoon it was his intention to go to the school on the Common (which he entirely supported) to witness the distribution of some prizes, but just as he was entering his carriage he was seized with a paralytic stroke. It was at once seen that he had lost his power of speech, but he was able with the help of the servants to go to his accustomed seat in his study. Here he remained until the evening, unable to speak, but with his mind still active, for he made signs to one of his daughters to hold up before him all the letters which he had written that day to see that the addresses were correct.

Mr. Sloman, the local medical man, was soon in attendance, his children were summoned from their various homes, and Dr. Gull came down from London in the course of the evening.

The Bishop was carried up to his bedroom,† where for three weeks he lay with life trembling in the balance. The greatest sympathy was shown by all classes in the town, and the diocese was moved to its very centre. Three times a day the church at Farnham was opened for special prayers for the Bishop's recovery, and many availed themselves of the opportunity thus afforded them of praying for their friend and Bishop. In all the churches throughout the diocese the prayers of the congregation were fervently offered for one who had so long ministered amongst them.

And so it went on for three weary weeks.

Who does not know by experience those painful hours when

---

* The Bishop was, throughout life, very fond of guessing riddles. On one occasion, when Archdeacon Wilberforce was staying at the Castle, one had been asked, to which, after a considerable time, the Bishop gave the right answer. Wilberforce was still puzzled by it, but not liking to be beaten, refused to be told what the solution was. They retired for the night, and after a short time the Bishop heard a knock at his door, which was gently opened, and the Archdeacon's voice was heard, giving the correct answer !

† To show the exceeding simplicity of the Bishop's tastes, it may be mentioned that, as was the case with Bishop Lonsdale (" Lonsdale's Memoirs," p. 140), so with Bishop Sumner, ever since his wife's death in 1849 he had occupied a small servants' room, without any change in the furniture of the apartment.

the life of one most dear hangs upon a thread—when but little can be done for the sufferer, and when the words of the medical attendants are drunk in by the eager listeners as though life and death were well-nigh in their hands ! All that skilful attendance and the most tender nursing could do was little more than to watch the battle between death and a giant's constitution. In the end it was so ordained by God that, as in 1832, so again in 1868, his vital energy should gain the mastery, and slowly but surely his powers of motion and, to a certain extent, of utterance returned.

One of his sons, who was obliged to leave Farnham on account of his own duties, writes on March 29 :—

"I came back after my week's absence yesterday, and find that my father has really made good progress in omnibus—quite as much as I expected. His powers of speech are gradually returning. He can say a vast deal more than he could when I left—and better—and with much stronger voice. Sometimes he cannot make us understand what he wants, which is of course distressing to both parties. But when he can say what he wishes to say, and sees we act upon it, he dismisses the subject from his mind, and troubles himself no more about it."

Not only throughout the diocese—where, as was natural, the most intense anxiety existed amongst the clergy when they heard of their Bishop's seizure—but from all parts of England much sympathy was shown with the Bishop's family in their time of trouble. The Archbishop of Canterbury writes :—

"It was with very deep concern that I received the sad intelligence of your good father's serious illness, and I am much indebted to you for giving me such early intimation of it. His loss, should it please God to take him from us, will profoundly affect me, for his matured wisdom and wide experience have been of essential benefit to us in our episcopal counsels, and it will be very long before we look upon his like. May it please God to restore him to his former health and his former usefulness. Protracted helplessness I should not wish for myself, and therefore could not wish for him. But whatever be the issue, may he enjoy that peace of God which passeth all understanding. Be assured that my thoughts and prayers will be with you all in your very heavy trial."

The following is from the Bishop of Oxford :—

"Culverton, *March* 7.

"I have been almost incessantly in thought at Farnham since I heard of the attack. I love him dearly. Yours is a much better account than I had heard elsewhere, and gives some hope of *real* restoration. Otherwise it would seem so happy and glorious for one so ready to be taken at once with no pale gradations of delay and interrupted work for his Lord."

Again, to Mrs. Ridley,* one of the Bishop's daughters, he writes :—

"Lathbury, Newport Pagnell, *March* 8.

"I have not liked to write to any of you during these sad days, not knowing what anyone would announce. Archdeacon Jacobs this morning seems to me to report real improvement, which, it if might lead to a restoration of at all his old life, how blessed it would be.

"I am really continually with you all in thought and prayer, and have lost almost two whole nights through the vividness of the whole Farnham scene being so before me. Yet, with all, I could not help feeling a sort of triumph for him if he should be taken thus : with the fulness of his work in his hands, with no lagging interval of uselessness and trying weakness. But however it is, God will be with him.

"It is a special pleasure to me that my work at our last meeting was to join with him in drawing up that resolution of Convocation on Ritual which all but one of us agreed to." †

---

* Sophia, the Bishop's second daughter, married in 1841 the Rev. William-Henry Ridley, Honorary Canon of Christchurch, Oxford, and Rector of Hambleden, Bucks.

† The resolution referred to was as follows :—

"Resolved—That having taken into consideration the report made to this house by the Lower House concerning certain ritual observances, we have concluded that having regard to the dangers (1) of favouring errors deliberately

Once more, on April 2nd, the Bishop of Oxford writes :—

"Many thanks for your letter.   It is indeed cheering, and it is full of hope.   It would be a delight to receive him back from the grave to take his old leading place amongst us.   You must have been one of us to know fully the value of that pre-sence,—the wisdom, gentleness, consideration for others, highly gentlemanlike tone, scholarly bearing and fairness he has brought into our discussions.   Will you give him, if it may be, and certainly all around him, my hearty love."

Meanwhile of course arrangements had to be at once made for the carrying on of the work of the diocese.   Through the kind co-operation of the Bishop of Sodor and Man and of Bishops Ryan and Hobhouse, the confirmations in Hampshire were held according to the plan previously laid down, without the alteration or delay of a single day ; and ultimately, whilst commissions were issued to the Archdeacons of Surrey * and

rejected by the Church of England, and fostering a tendency to desert her com-munion ; (2) of offending even in things indifferent devout worshippers in our churches, who have been long used to other modes of service, and thus of estranging many of the faithful laity ; (3) of unnecessarily departing from uni-formity ; (4) of increasing the difficulties which prevent the return of separatists to our communion—we convey to the Lower House our unanimous decision that, having respect to the considerations here recorded, and to the rubric concerning the service of the Church in our Book of Common Prayer, to wit—

"'Forasmuch as nothing can be so plainly set forth but doubts may arise in the use and practice of the same, to appease all such diversity (if any arise), and for the resolution of all doubts concerning the manner how to understand, do, and execute the things contained in this book, the parties that so doubt or diversely take anything shall alway resort to the Bishop of the diocese, who, by his discretion, shall take order for the quieting and appeasing of the same, so that the same order be not contrary to anything contained in this book ; and if the Bishop of the diocese be in doubt, then he may send for the resolution thereof to the Archbishop ;'—

our judgment is that no alterations from long-sanctioned and usual ritual ought to be made in our Churches, until the sanction of the Bishop of the diocese has been obtained thereto."—*Chron. Conv.* 1867, pp. 710, 711.

* The Bishop had, in 1859, appointed the Rev. J. S. Utterton, Vicar of Farnham, to the Archdeaconry of Surrey, and a Canonry in Winchester Cathe-dral, in the room of Archdeacon Hoare, whom in 1847 he had transferred from the Archdeaconry of Winchester to that of Surrey, which he resigned in 1859.

Winchester, whereby such portions of diocesan work as could be
carried out by presbyters were committed to them, Bishop
Ryan, in accordance with Bishop Sumner's earnest request,
undertook to act as a quasi-suffragan Bishop for the whole
diocese.   Both the Archdeacons and Bishop Ryan executed the
duties committed to them most ably, and it was a great comfort
to the Bishop that he could thus place the work of the diocese
in such competent hands.   No general Act had as yet been
passed enabling bishops to retire, and great exception had been
taken at the time by many to the special Act by which Bishops
Blomfield and Maltby had been enabled, in 1856, to resign their
sees.   The Bishop accordingly determined to wait a short time
to see whether the anticipations of the medical men with
respect to his speech would be fulfilled, and then to act as
might seem most conducive to the best interests of the Church.
Arrangements were made by which his eldest son, the Rev. John
Sumner, with his wife and family, should permanently reside at
the Castle, and thus be able, under the Bishop's directions, to
carry on all correspondence in connection with the diocese.

But, contrary to the expectations of his medical attendants, the
Bishop's speech did not return as they had hoped; and whilst
he could make himself understood by those immediately about
him, yet it soon became clear that it was not likely that he
would ever be able to officiate in public again; and accordingly,
when in 1869 an Act was passed enabling bishops to resign
their sees, the Bishop at once announced his intention of acting
upon it.   There was no hesitation or delay on his part, and
although some considerable time necessarily elapsed before the
various preliminaries were definitely arranged, yet the Bishop's
intention was made known immediately upon the passing of
the Act.   On the 12th of August, a letter was written at his
dictation to the Archbishop of Canterbury, intimating his desire
to resign his bishoprick, and declaring his willingness to accept
as retiring pension a considerably smaller sum than that to
which he might lay claim, and also expressing a hope that he

might be allowed to retain Farnham Castle and park for his residence during the remainder of his life.

The Archbishop replied as follows :—

"ADDINGTON PARK, CROYDON, *Aug.* 14, 1869.

\   "MY DEAR LORD,

"I have this morning received your letter of the 12th in which you express your intention of resigning your bishoprick. I will not fail at once to communicate the substance of your letter to the Prime Minister, and feel no doubt that such arrangements as are indicated by you will be carried into effect, so as to enable you to complete your resignation. I cannot, write on such an occasion, my dear Lord, without telling you of the love and respect in which you have ever been held, both by myself, and I think I may say, by all our brethren. We have felt it a great loss for the last year to miss your counsel, and your kindly presence amongst us ; and I am sure there is not one of us who will not feel the further severing of the ties which unite us to you, if you complete your intention of resigning. The Church of England in these anxious days, can ill spare that long experience, and that gentle but far extending influence which you have exercised, and to which all your juniors on the Bench have so long been accustomed to look up. Writing in this room, I feel my personal affection to yourself enhanced by thoughts of your dear brother, and his great kindness to me when I came to the See of London. I am sure that the work done by him and you will long live in the grateful remembrance of all good Christians.

"Believe me, my dear Lord,
"Affectionately yours,
"A. C. CANTUAR.

"The LORD BISHOP OF WINCHESTER."

The Archbishop at once put himself into communication with Mr. Gladstone, and acquainted him with the Bishop's intention of resigning his see. He also in his letter referred to the desirability of the Bishop being allowed to reside at Farnham Castle. The following was Mr. Gladstone's reply :—

"WALMER, *Aug.* 15, 1869.

" MY DEAR LORD ARCHBISHOP,

"I return the Bishop of Winchester's letter of which I keep a copy.

"I think the course most satisfactory in itself, and to the Bishop, would be that I should refer his letter with the Act to the Law Officers, the Attorney General, Solicitor General, and Queen's Advocate, and should request them to advise me what are the steps necessary to be taken by the Bishop, in order to enable the Crown to act, and what will then be the formal manner of the Crown's proceeding. But I have no difficulty meantime, in answering the implied queries of the Bishop.

" 1. The Crown will be advised to grant, when the preliminaries have been fulfilled, the full pension desired by the Bishop within the terms of the Act.

" 2. Farnham Castle can only be granted on special grounds. It appears to me that two such may be alleged: (*a*) The great comfort and importance of that residence to the Bishop as an invalid (I should like to have your Grace's formal assurance of this); (*b*) that that residence is in no way necessary for the incoming Bishop. And I should advise accordingly in ready compliance with the Bishop's desire, which appears to me to be very just. If your Grace approves the method of proceeding I propose, I shall upon being so informed at once adopt it.

" There is an inconvenience in the length of interval caused by this early announcement, which led me to ask myself whether the Bishop's intention could remain private for the present. But I think it would be unjust to him and to the Church, if secresy were to be observed.

"I remain with much respect,
" Your Grace's very sincere and faithful,
" W. GLADSTONE.

"His GRACE THE ARCHBISHOP OF CANTERBURY."

The Archbishop of Canterbury replied :—

"Addington Park, Croydon, Aug. 17, 1869.

" My dear Mr. Gladstone,

"I beg to acknowledge your letter of the 15th to-day received. Your proposal to consult the Law Officers of the Crown as to the steps necessary to be taken, in order to enable the Bishop of Winchester's intended resignation to be carried through according to his wishes, seems to me to indicate the natural and proper course. I can have no doubt that looking to the circumstances of the case—the Bishop's long and valuable services, and his present state of health—it is right that his request to retain possession of Farnham should be acceded to. The Bishop points out that his successor would have two other residences belonging to the see.

"Believe me to be,
" My dear Mr. Gladstone,
" Yours sincerely,
" A. C. Cantuar.

"It seems to me to be only due to the Bishop that his intentions should be made public."

A month after, the Bishop of Winchester received the subjoined letter from Mr. Gladstone :—

"Balmoral Castle, Sept. 18, 1869.

" My dear Lord Bishop,

" Thus far I have not been in direct communication with your Lordship on the subject of your meditated resignation, and have only had to assure the Archbishop how gladly I associated myself with your most reasonable request for the retention of the palace at Farnham.

" I now write to state that in order to ensure regularity, I referred your Lordship's letter, together with the Act, to the Law Officers of the Crown, and that I have received their opinion. The course of proceeding now appears pretty clear, though no papers remain in the Treasury or Home Office to illustrate the precedents of 1856; and, as I thought it might be for your Lordship's comfort and satisfaction, I have desired an official letter with a sketch of the necessary steps to be prepared and addressed to you.

"I have only further to say that if any point should arise, on which it may appear to be in my power to facilitate your Lordship's proceedings, I trust you will not scruple to inform me, and to assure you how fully I share the sentiments of respect, regard, and regret, with which the Church and the public view the approaching termination of your long tenure of the See of Winchester.

"I remain, my dear Lord Bishop,

"Most faithfully yours,

"W. E. GLADSTONE.

"The LORD BISHOP OF WINCHESTER."

As soon as the Bishop's retirement was carried into effect, addresses poured in from all sides, signed both by Laity and Clergy, expressive of the deep regret with which they viewed the severance of the bond which, for so many years, had united them. High Church and Low Church alike recognised with thankfulness his wise, loving, and impartial rule. The various Colleges of which he had been the visitor were quick in acknowledging the "unvarying kindness, courtesy and attention" which had marked all his intercourse with them. The council of the Surrey Church Association, at their first meeting held after the Bishop's resignation, came to the following resolution :—

"That the Council of the Surrey Church Association cannot meet for the last time under the Presidency of their revered Bishop, without placing on record some expression of their personal love, and filial respect for that Good Father in God who will be taken away from their head so soon. To his wise and temperate rule over their deliberations, his watchful and unwearied interest in every minute detail of their work, his generous and ready help whenever it was needed, they owe under God much of that measure of success which their Association has been permitted to enjoy. And, whatever may be the record of its future, this must ever be the bright memorial of its past, that it was born and grew into its present vigorous existence, under the fostering care of one who will long be remembered in this diocese as its good and gentle Bishop.

"Of his unceasing sympathy with them in their work, they have no more doubts than they trust he has of the tender interest with which their best wishes follow him into that evening of rest which now succeeds to his long and toilsome days, and whilst they assure him of their constant prayers for his welfare, they ask his abiding benediction."

Private friends too swelled the chorus, expressive of the regret and prayerful sympathy with which they viewed his retirement, and the Bishop, though unable to answer them except through an amanuensis, was deeply touched by the loving feelings so unmistakably shown towards him. His old friend Coleridge writes :—

"*Sept.* 28, 1869.

". . . . . . I sympathise with you in the feelings which must, I suppose, be in your mind in retiring from what may well have seemed to you life-long duties, since you have discharged them so actively for so many years. Notwithstanding this, however, I do not think your regret will be so lasting as will be your comfort in retirement ; and it will be entirely without any bitter thought while it lasts. Few men will be more happily surrounded by a domestic circle. You have a numerous, united, affectionate, dutiful, and satisfactory family—and yet you will have time, and know how to use it for your own quiet thoughts.

> ' 'Tis meet that we should pause awhile,
> Ere we put off this mortal coil,
> And in the stillness of old age
> Muse on our earthly pilgrimage.'

"I understand you retain Farnham, and I am glad of it—and even more glad that you have the heart to limit so considerably the amount of your retirement allowance. It is the most dignified answer to aspersions, and it is a parting gift to the Church, which I hope will be wisely used, and accepted in a grateful spirit . . . . God grant you, my dear friend, quiet happiness in your retirement for so long as He may see to be good for you."

The Bishop of Salisbury (Moberly), at whose elevation to the Bench the Bishop had truly rejoiced, writes :—

"Ever since the time when I was appointed to discharge duties such as those which have been yours for so many years ; and still more since your intention of relinquishing them has been made known, my heart has yearned for an opportunity of expressing my deep and heartfelt sympathy with you, and my gratitude for many years of considerate kindness culminating in the confidence which sent me to dear Brighstone. May the best blessings of Heaven rest upon your Lordship's age and repose. And—I can ask no greater blessing for myself—may some portion of the same love and reverence that follow you into retirement go with me when I shall be called to give up the work which, with great anxiety and trembling, I am entering upon."

Lord Chichester writes in a letter marked "private," but which he has given me permission to publish :—

"I always look back with a sad pleasure to the time when we so frequently met,* and shall never forget your helpfulness to us in business, and your uniform kindness and good humour which won all our hearts. There is but one feeling amongst all the good men that I meet, upon the occasion of your retirement. All feel that the Church has sustained a great loss, and many, especially your own clergy, that they are losing their best friend and a wise and kind father. It must surely be a comfort that your life's evening 'should be thus honoured, for all this

---

* On the Church Estates Committee.

sympathy and affection has been earned in our Master's service, to whom I know you will ascribe all the merit and the glory. May He continue, my dear Bishop, to be your stay and support during the remainder of your earthly journey, and your portion for ever."

At a general Court of the Governors of Queen Anne's Bounty held shortly after, the following resolution was passed and forwarded to the Bishop :—

"The Governors being desirous of recording their sense of the services rendered by the Right Reverend Charles Richard Sumner, D.D., late Lord Bishop of Winchester as a Governor of this Corporation, during the long period of forty-four years, and their high estimate of the unfailing liberality with which he has ever seconded their efforts to improve the small Livings within the Diocese of Winchester,

"Resolve unanimously, that, in conformity with the directions and under the powers contained in the first charter, 3rd Anne, the said Bishop Sumner, as a Benefactor, be retained and recognised a Life Governor of this Corporation."

It was in October 1869, that Bishop Wilberforce was appointed to succeed to the See of Winchester. He was cordially welcomed by his old patron, and Bishop Sumner did all in his power to smooth the way for him in his new diocese, by handing over to him all necessary papers, and by giving him such detailed information as he alone could afford with reference to the multifarious affairs of the diocese. Bishop Wilberforce thus writes to one of Bishop Sumner's sons, under date Oct. 6, 1869 :—

"I thank you with all my heart for the affectionate welcome of your letter. I feel how painful any change must be to you all, and I feel almost to hate myself for being his successor. I thank you for your promise of prayers. I never felt so much to need them. When I was first Bishop I did not know all the difficulties before me. Now I know them, and know how they will be aggravated by following Him. Your prayers then and your help I welcome with an intense thankfulness. In the wonderfully painful separation from my diocese, it is not a little palliation of the pain to know that in the new diocese I have some as old and affectionate friends as you and your dear wife. . . . God knows how inadequate I feel to take up your father's work."

It will be seen that the relations existing between Bishops Sumner and Wilberforce, were of the most affectionate character, and no one could be more ready than the latter to acknowledge the invaluable help which he received from his predecessor in the See of Winchester. The *Guardian* of Dec. 29th, thus records a very graceful act on the part of Bishop Sumner in introducing to his successor as many of the Clergy of the diocese as could be conveniently invited to Farnham Castle. The initials appended to the extract disclose the writer to have been Dr. Monsell :—

"On the 20th of December the late Bishop of Winchester gathered together, by wide-spread invitations, some hundred of his Clergy to meet their new Bishop at Farnham Castle. The idea was gracefully conceived, and admirably executed. The fine old Castle was thronged once more with its accustomed guests. The eldest son of the late introduced the present Bishop wherever he was before personally unknown. The venerable host, though much recovered, was not visible save to a very few, but his presence was felt and owned in the magnificent hospitalities of his home ; and at the close of the *levée* about 120 sat down to luncheon in that fine old baronial hall which is such a remarkable feature of the Castle. It was a touching and memorable day, conveying as it did the kindly good will of the last of our Prince Bishops to him, who without the external insignia of so great an office attaching any longer to him and his successors in that once princely see, will bring as much of personal dignity and grace to sustain its position unsullied as could be desired or found. Long may good old Bishop Sumner enjoy his beautiful home and the rest which is now within its walls secured him ; and long may his successor be spared health and strength to administer the affairs of (take it all in all) the widest and almost most important diocese in the English Church.

"LAST OF OUR OLD PRINCE BISHOPS! FARE THEE WELL!

" 'Twas a fair day, in fairer Advent-tide,
That gracious season when the wintry world
Brightening before the rising sun of Christ
In blessings bourgeons.   At his courteous call
From thorpe and hamlet many a mile around
Thronging to do him honour, and receive
His parting benediction, came a host
Of Winton's clergy to the Castle-gates
Of him who had been long their Lord and Friend.

Years, and the whelming weight of sacred cares,
(For love of God and man too long sustained),
Had well nigh crush'd him : and for months upborne
By loving prayer, that on his people's hearts
Lifted him Godward, he entrancèd lay
Midway 'twixt earth and heaven.   Until the Hand
That hurts to heal, and saddens but to save,
Gently to earth restoring ; the full heart,
Its first thank-off'ring on God's altar laid,
Self-sacrifice for Christ and for his Church.

And now his pow'r passed on to other hands,
He, with that life-long gracefulness of thought
Which never failed him, by a twofold act
Of farewell and of welcome, into one
Welded together the two Episcopates,
The Old in parting ushering in the New.

Last of our Grand Prince Bishops !   In whom met,
In perfect harmony the functions rare
Of Prelate, Pastor, Noble, Father, Friend !
Lord of the Castle, and its broad domains,
Its old seigneurial rights, and dignities,
Within whose hall, and at whose board he made
His humblest brother welcome as his peer.
Lord of the Castle !   By the cottage hearth
Familiar found in sickness, want, or care,
Lord of the poor man's heart—a prouder home !

Last of our Old Prince Bishops !   Fare thee well !
Tho' Throne and Crosier to another pass,
Enthronèd still art thou in every heart
That once obeyed thee.   And in future years,
(Which may God lengthen long as He see good,)

Oft will men pause before thy Castle-gates
And thinking of thy long day-work for God,
And thinking of thine evening calm and clear,
And thinking of thy coming endless rest,
Will talk as if we ne'er shall see again
Such days in England, as the days of old,
In which the good Old Lord of Winton reign'd.
But one in England could thy Crosier wield,
And he with thy good will thy work prolongs.

"J. S. B. M.

"FARNHAM CASTLE, *December* 20, 1869."

Four days previously Bishop Wilberforce had been solemnly enthroned in Winchester Cathedral, following the precedent set by Bishop Sumner. The beautiful lines subjoined were composed with reference to this event by Dr. Monsell:—

" 'SILENCE IN THE GREAT CATHEDRAL.'

" There was silence deep and earnest
    By the wond'ring people made,
Silence in the Great Cathedral
    As those thousands knelt and pray'd ;
Pray'd, while he—in God their Father—
    Rapt in adoration there,
Low before the holy altar
    Made his off'ring and his prayer.

" Years had pass'd since at that altar
    He, with youth's best joys replete,
All his life's most precious ointment
    Pour'd out at his Saviour's feet : [*]
Pour'd out of the broken vessel
    Of a heart, bow'd down but brave,
That thenceforth its whole devotion
    To a Life of Duty gave.

" How that Life hath kept the Promise
    Made in secret suff'ring there,
Witness now those kneeling thousands
    In that fellowship of Prayer :
Witness years of ceaseless toiling,
    Weary ways unwearied trod,
Never resting—never tiring
    In the endless work of God.

---

[*] Mrs. Wilberforce died in the Close of the Cathedral.

"Silence in the great Cathedral :
  Not a breath of whisper stirr'd,
  Yet in heaven the loud heart-voices
  Of those worshippers were heard :
  'Will to work, and strength to labour,'
  'Souls to save'—and 'Christ their plea ;'
  Giver of good gifts and perfect !
  Say Amen ! and it shall be."

To one of the family writing to Dr. Monsell respecting the lines which he wrote on the two Bishops meeting at Farnham Castle, he sent the following letter in reply.

"EGHAM VICARAGE, SURREY, *3rd January,* 1870.

"Your letter so full of heart and good feeling gave my dear wife and me the truest purest pleasure, for we both love your dear father very sincerely, and through all his illness our personal love and prayers have followed and endeavoured to sustain him so far as prayer could do so. When by the solemn silence in the Cathedral on the day of the enthronement, I was moved as I was on the spot (for the first verse of that little poem was composed in the Cathedral) to endeavour to commemorate it, I felt a secret jealousy in my heart that the first offering of my muse should be to the rising, instead of the dear setting sun of our diocese; and, therefore, when that wondrously graceful act of your dear father's on the 20th of December offered as it did so many points of interest to one's mind and heart, I resolved that the next Guardian should contain such tribute to him as I could render, and so those lines appeared.

"I felt as if blank verse was more suited to the dignity of the occasion; besides my ear was attuned to the rhythm of the Holy Grail which I had been reading aloud over and over again to all my friends. . . . I have always loved your dear father with a very admiring love, and if I admired him in the glow and vigour of his health and power, how much more when I saw him the other day looking so grand and gentle, like some beautiful column, a little shaken and disturbed and no longer

able to sustain a superincumbent weight, but even more
graceful and beautiful than it ever looked before.

"I think he loved me, and one line in your letter strengthens
that thought, and is most pleasant to me.

"Certain it is he has no heart, in the vast crowd of those who
love him, more true or more tender than mine."

And now the task of the biographer of the Bishop of Winchester is completed. We have reached the time when the
diocese over which he had presided for forty-two years passed
under the hands of another, and he who had for so long a
period of his life been its guiding spirit lived on from day to
day in quiet retirement, apart from theological strife, alone
with his God—Yes—Alone with his God. Although he was
surrounded throughout the next five years by a loving and
united family, the members of which vied with one another in
paying all honour, deference and marks of love to their revered
head, the Bishop nevertheless lived alone for hour after hour;
up to the very last taking an interest in books and entering with
affectionate sympathy into all that concerned his children;
but the free interchange of thought with those around him was
still denied him, for the same stroke which deprived him of
speech, also prevented his making his thoughts known in
writing. But notwithstanding his affliction the Bishop always
made an effort to be cheerful, ready with a kindly smile to
greet his children, though the relapse into quiet sadness showed
that it *was* an effort. He preached daily, as was often
remarked, in his silence, as eloquent a sermon as he had ever
done in days gone by. On bright afternoons it was his habit to
take a drive through the lovely scenery with which the neighbourhood of Farnham abounds, and his garden was a never-
ceasing source of pleasure to him. Everything that love could
prompt was done for the Bishop, not only by the members of his
family, but by his faithful and attached servants; and few have
passed the later years of life with more love, affection, and

respect, shown on all sides, than did Bishop Sumner. Whenever diocesan duties called Bishop Wilberforce into the neighbourhood of Farnham he was always a welcome guest at the
Castle. After one of these visits at the close of 1871, he writes:—

"FARNHAM CASTLE, SURREY, *Dec.* 27, 1871.

"The dear Patriarch was at church this morning and communicated as usual. I felt it very strange to administer to him
in that church. An inversion of 'the less is blessed of the
greater' I could hardly stand; yet his silver hair and placid
God-trusting face witnessed to me afresh that He never forsakes
his people. All old life came back; my visit with my father
and my mother and my darling just given to me; with all as it
then was and as it is now both with him and with me! Well—
the time is short—the night far spent—the day at hand."

It will readily be conceived how great was the shock which
the Bishop felt when told in July 1873 of his successor's sudden
death. Nothing so much tried him during the whole course of
his illness. Mysterious indeed are the ways of God. Strange
certainly it was that Bishop Sumner should have thus been
permitted to linger on in weakness, whilst his successor, in the
zenith of his power and influence, was translated almost like
Enoch of old from earth to heaven. But so God ordered events,
for not until a year after Bishop Wilberforce had been gathered
to his fathers, was Bishop Sumner called to his rest. The
tenth of July was the last day on which he was able to dine
with the members of his family, and from that day until the
end came he grew gradually weaker and weaker. Sir William
Gull was called in on the fourteenth, but he could say or do but
little for the patient sufferer. On the seventeenth the Holy
Communion was administered to him, and to all his children
and grandchildren present, and some of the servants; for it
seemed as though he could not linger on for many more days,
and all were anxious once more to be associated with him in
that holy ordinance. But the lamp flickered on for some time

longer in the socket, and it was not until the fifteenth of
August at midday that God called him home, and his weary
spirit was at rest.

The following account of his illness and death is written
by the hand which furnished previous reminiscences of the
Bishop:—

" I used to think his character was a very perfect one, perhaps
because he had been so richly prospered in a variety of ways ;
and that he was more consistent than other men, because it is
comparatively easy to keep right when nothing goes wrong
about you ; and I wondered if this self-control and patience
could bear rough weather, and stand steadfast in the crucible of
pain and weakness.

" The Bishop had a great dislike to all illness, even in others,
or invalid habits. Sickness in any shape was very abhorrent to
him, and so the cross came in that way ; for six years he was
paralysed in speech, stricken down by weakness and brought,
in various ways, into a painful experience of bodily tribulation.
He lost his power of writing, and could only sign his name by
copying it from a piece of paper in front of him. His whole
work was taken from him, the See was resigned, and the chief
object of his life passed into other hands. It was like a man
living after his own death, and all the while his mind was left
untouched by the stroke. He could realise to the fullest extent
the deprivation, the blank, the loss, and the pain. It was
pathetic to see him eagerly reading the Hampshire and Surrey
papers, with accounts of functions and ecclesiastical proceedings,
or watch as of old for the post, and finding one letter, or none,
turn away with a sigh, remembering that there used to be
twenty-five or thirty letters on his plate daily. He saw his old
friends and tried to speak to them, but the words would not
come—only one here and one there ; it was difficult to make
out what he said, and by degrees he became almost absolutely
silent, scarcely ever speaking, except to those accustomed to him.
His tall figure grew bent, and his face sadder, and not all

the devoted love and affection of those around him aroused the
old cheerful joyous look, beyond a mere passing gleam. It was
during these six last years, when the burden of life grew heavier
till the end came, that he proved, by God's grace, the true
metal of his religion. He took the trial with the same patience
and calm endurance, the same submission and sweetness which
he had shown in small vexations in happier days, and if he was
loved and admired in the earlier time, when he was in the
swing of life and work, he was infinitely more to be admired
during those last six years, when he was cast into the refiner's
fire till the image of his Master was reflected in him.

"Shortly before his death he received the Holy Communion,
with all his children, many of his grandchildren, and several old
and valued servants. The Bishop of Guildford and his grand-
son, Henry Sumner, officiated at the Holy Service, and those
who were present at it will not forget the scene. The aged
patriarch with his beautiful, calm old face and the silky white
hair, grown long during his illness, brushed back over the
pillows—his children, grandchildren, and servants kneeling
round the bed and about in the room, which could not hold all
the numbers ; and so the corridor outside his sick room was
also filled with the younger members of his family—the full
volume of sound which came from the worshippers, and the
voice of the dying Bishop rising distinctly throughout the
service amid all the other voices—his clear consciousness, and
visible emotion in receiving the Sacred Elements.—And then,
when the service was ended, he expressed a wish that we should
kiss him. One by one, from the eldest to the youngest, we
gave him, as we then thought, a last loving kiss on his dear
forehead and long thin hand. He put his arm round the neck
of those dearest to him, and drew them close to him in a very
tender and touching manner. He could not speak distinctly,
but this loving act said eloquently all he meant to say of gratitude for devoted ministrations, and affectionate farewell. His
faithful servants reverently followed the example of his own

family and approached the bed, bending down to kiss his hand,
but he leant forward his head, and gave them too the sweet
privilege of children. It was hard to be calm, and the sobs
and tears would break forth from many and many an aching
heart. When the last farewell was over, and the room was left
in quiet and stillness, it seemed as if his spirit must be singing,
'Lord, now lettest thou thy servant depart in peace.' All of
earth seemed to be settled and over, and yet he lingered in the
border lands a time longer, growing feebler and feebler till the
expression on his face was that of a little child ; and on August
the 15th, after long hours of painless sinking, during which
time he was surrounded by all his family, and prayer was being
offered up continually for him—he suddenly gave a start, his
whole face lighted up with a look of wonder, awe, and astonishment, and, one moment after, he had entered the Rest which
remaineth for the people of God, and had joined that goodly
company who have washed their robes and made them white in
the Blood of the Lamb. The fight had been fought—the battle
won,

> 'And he may smile at troubles gone
> Who sets the victor-garland on.'

The good God grant us grace to follow him as he followed
Christ. Amen."

On the 21st of August his remains were laid in a vault in
Hale Church-yard by the side of those of his wife. Crowds
from the neighbouring town flocked to pay their last testimony
of respect to one whom in life they loved. Clergy and laity
from all parts of that diocese over which he had so long presided were there. Friends who had stood side by side with
him in life, rejoiced with him in his joys, sorrowed with him in
his sorrows, stood round the open grave with children and
grandchildren—a loving band of mourners. There were many
present who called to mind the time when he whose remains
they followed to the grave was in the forefront of the Church's
battle, doing his Master's work with holy zeal and energy.

actively employing all his powers in the service of Christ. The simple inscription on the coffin was :—

"CHARLES RICHARD SUMNER, D.D.,

Born Nov. 22, 1790.

BISHOP OF LLANDAFF, 1826 ; BISHOP OF WINCHESTER, 1827 ;
RESIGNED, 1869.

Entered into his rest, August 15, 1874."

And so the grave closes over good Bishop Sumner. Respected by all who came in contact with him, heartily loved by those who were admitted to close intimacy with him, his memory will ever be fresh and dear to those who truly mourned his loss. It was touching to hear one after another recounting the history of former days, in which the Bishop's kindly heart had been specially drawn out towards them. Each seemed to look upon it as something special in his own individual case, and knew not that it was part of the Bishop's nature. Withdrawn as he had been from duties of active life for five years, he was gradually maturing for the Master's call, and none could look upon his gentle, loving, calm face, without feeling that it told of inward peace, as of one ready and waiting for the great change. His sorrowing family and friends, though tempted to say

Quis desiderio sit pudor aut modus
Tam cari capitis,

yet find comfort in the Christian hope, " If we believe that Jesus died and rose again, even so them also which sleep in Jesus will God bring with Him." And surely at that great Easter morn, he who faithfully served his Lord, laboured in His vineyard, and patiently abided His call, will not be found wanting !

I cannot conclude this attempt to perpetuate the memory of a revered Father better than by the following lines written by Dr. Monsell :—

"LAST OF OUR OLD PRINCE BISHOPS! FARE THEE WELL!

" We laid him in his quiet grave
With solemn pomp and heart-felt woe,
With tears gave back the gifts God gave,
We all had learnt to love him so.

I I

" And yet an under current stole
    Of hidden joy thro' every breast,
Joy for a freed and happy soul
    Gone to its everlasting rest.

" A life-long battle fought and won !
    Jordan with all its swellings past !
The victor crown'd with God's 'well done ! '
    The absent child gone home at last !

" Fruit richly ripe—whose sweetness here
    Full many a fainting soul had found,
Gather'd where angel-reapers cheer,
    Into God's garner, safe and sound.

" A goodlie tree—the grateful shade
    Of whose out-spreading boughs of love
Shelter for many a heart had made ;
    Cut down to build God's house above.

" A Father—by his children borne
    On hearts and shoulders, honour'd, home ;
Who, tho' their own deep loss they mourn,
    Joy that his gain at length has come.

" The memory of bygone years
    The Hope of Christian Faith recalls,
Across the blinding mist of tears
    The rainbow gleam of Promise falls.

" We look into the happy land
    And, thro' its ever-radiant air,
See him beside his Saviour stand,
    And wish that we were with him there :

" Or rather wish that thro' the days
    That yet remain unnumbered, we
May so walk in his holy ways
    That our last end like his may be.

" For all, who knew and loved him, know
    Amid the sinful sons of men,
How hard 'twill be, where e'er they go,
    To find his like on earth again."

THE END.

BRADBURY, AGNEW, & CO., PRINTERS, WHITEFRIARS.

www.ingramcontent.com/pod-product-compliance
Lightning Source LLC
Chambersburg PA
CBHW032010110726
47901CB00004B/1035